*Books by John Hopkins*

*Tangier Buzzless Flies* 1972
*The Attempt* 1967

*TANGIER*
*BUZZLESS FLIES*

# *TANGIER BUZZLESS FLIES*

*John Hopkins*

1972 *ATHENEUM* NEW YORK

The title chapter, in slightly different form,
originally appeared in *The New Yorker.*


*Library of Congress catalog card number* 75-167891
*Published simultaneously in Canada by McClelland and Stewart Ltd.*
*Manufactured in the United States of America by*
*Halliday Lithograph Corporation,*
*Hanover, Massachusetts*
*Designed by Kathleen Carey*
*First Edition*

*For my father and mother and Gurdon*

# *TANGIER BUZZLESS FLIES*

# *Tangier Buzzless Flies*

HERE IN TANGIER I have discovered a variety of fly that has no buzz. Right now there are about a dozen of them hovering noiselessly in the middle of the room, darting here and there, chasing each other as they play their games. They are serene and pay no attention to me, and I like to watch them. They are not like those angry giants who roar in through the door and hurl themselves against the window and mirror. Nor are they in any way similar to the persistent Saharan flies. Those flies stick to you. Brush one away and it returns to the same spot. Swat at it and it comes immediately back. If you go into the southern oases during the date season, you will see them swarming over the faces of children, who do not bother to brush them away. You see them on bare arms and legs, on open sores, on fruit and meat in the markets, on excrement and dead animals. Unless you are careful, they will drink at the corners of the eyes and mouth without your knowing it. You see the resulting trachoma

—cloudy, opaque eyeballs and sightless eyes that have shrunk to slits. People blind in one eye pay no attention to the flies sucking at the other.

Although Tarfaya is not an oasis—there is hardly a tree of any kind in the region—the flies are just as thick. Tarfaya was formerly a Spanish outpost on the western Saharan coast at Cape Juby—a ghost town now that the Spanish have contracted the northern border of their Saharan territory, leaving Tarfaya to Morocco. Sand dunes as high as your head impede passage in the streets. Crumbling Spanish façades with the paint peeling off, broken windows, and doors sagging and slamming in the wind mark the exterior appearance of this town. Almost all the buildings are unoccupied. The rather elegant esplanade along the beach front, where the Spanish took their evening strolls not so long ago, is submerged in sand. The quay has been partially destroyed by the sea. A few hundred meters offshore stands a strange empty castle built by the British when Tarfaya was a fortified trading post in the nineteenth century.

Driss and I had arrived in Tarfaya by truck from Rio de Oro in order to meet a convoy coming down from the north that would take us as far as Tan-Tan, where the hard road to Marrakech begins. I had been nearly three years in the western Sahara, prospecting for oil in the employ of the Spanish government. Last year I moved from El Aaiun to La Guera in order to commence operations in the southern extremity of the territory. La Guera is another tiny Saharan port town off the main shipping lines, situated about eight hundred miles south of El Aaiun, below the Tropic of Cancer near the Mauritanian frontier. The town itself consists of nothing more than a low haphazard grouping of structures, with a red and yellow flag whipping in the wind, signifying Spanish military presence. The country inland is practically impenetrable, a limitless waste of marching crescent dunes and shimmering salt flats. Sand storms are frequent. These abrasive winds, which generate tremendous charges of static electricity, may blow for days.

One day not long after my arrival in La Guera I was down on the beach supervising the unloading of some drilling equipment. A launch was plying back and forth between the beach and a coastal steamer, which lay offshore in the milky green water. Black stevedores, standing knee-deep in the waves, were taking crates and barrels on their shoulders and wading ashore and piling them on the beach. I noticed a young fellow giving orders, and when the launch went off for another trip, we got to talking. He told me that his name was Driss and that he was a Moroccan from Tangier working in the lighthouse at Cape Blanco, about twenty miles south of La Guera. The launch was also unloading supplies for the lighthouse. I told him that I knew Tangier quite well myself, being in the habit of spending my summers there, when the heat of the Sahara brought my work to a halt. I learned that his father was the keeper of the Cape Spartel light near Tangier. The father was close to retirement age now, and Driss, the eldest son, was being trained as his replacement. He had already passed some years in the lighthouses of Spain and France, and was now doing a final tour in Africa before returning to Tangier to take over from his father. Lighthouse tradition has it, as Driss told me, that the care of the light should remain in the same family if possible, for the son is familiar with the light and is accustomed to the life. I told Driss my name, Joseph Cabell, and explained what I was doing in La Guera. He said he'd heard about an American looking for oil in the desert.

Driss invited me to come out and visit the light if I liked. I said I would, and a few days later I found myself driving my Land Rover out along the sandy spit of land called Cape Blanco. There was no real road to speak of, and what with the sandy dunes and wiry dune bushes it took me a long time to get there. It certainly was one of the wildest and most isolated spots I'd ever visited. Driss came out to meet me and showed me around. The actual keeper was a Spaniard, who spent most of his time in town, so Driss had assumed all responsibility for the light and the radio, which sends out signals in Morse code. I saw immediately that he was an expert. I spent the night out there talking to Driss as the waves beat on that desolate shore. Overhead the great radial light swept through the blackness. I asked him if this wasn't a lonely occupation, and he replied, not at all—God looked upon this work with favor because the light guides the ships by night and saves the lives of sailors.

Subsequently I spent many days on Cape Blanco, and when Driss had some time off he would walk the twenty miles into La Guera, where we would meet. Often I used to take him out into the desert and show him my own domain of solitude. So between the lighthouse and the desert we spent many nights together. To Driss the desert and sea were never inhospitable, or really dangerous, as I regarded them. They represented formidable forces that had to be treated with respect, but he felt at ease among them. God was everywhere. I admired this extraordinary assurance, which allowed him a security of being that I had never felt. Of course, he was homesick for Tangier, as he had been away for so long, but he was happy in the desert or wherever his travels might take him. Moroccans are famous travelers, he said. They have been all over the world. But they always return home in the end.

Certainly these past months spent in the desert with Driss have been the happiest period of my life. One day, when we had been drilling for oil, we struck fresh water. As it poured out of the ground in a great fountain, the Bedouins who had gathered to watch danced around with such joy as if we had discovered gold and silver and oil all together. But the Spanish military men who happened to be in camp at the time in anticipation of witnessing an oil discovery stood by sullenly with their arms crossed. All they wanted was the oil. Driss remarked that it was far better to find water in the desert than oil. In fact, I had already advised the Spanish government more than once that while no oil had been found in their Sahara, great reserves of fresh water were in evidence. They never listened; they wanted only the black liquid and insisted that I continue my search for it. But from that day onward I ordered my crew to commence drilling wherever I thought water was indicated, and we found that practically all of Rio de Oro floated on it. Driss and I laughed, and the normally severe Bedouins continued to dance like children under a sprinkler. Of course, I had to cap those wells to prevent the water from flowing away uselessly into the desert, but the water was there.

Those were good times for us both. Driss kept the coast safe for the passage of ships and fishing boats, and my discoveries might one day transform a part of the desert into a place of greater security and prosperity for the Bedouins and their camels. Soon we became quite well known among the local people, Spanish fishermen and Bedouins alike, who said we carried with us baraka, or the blessing of God, which means grace and good luck. Wherever we went together, among the Bedouin tents or over to the fishing harbor of Port Etienne in Mauritania, we were always greeted with smiles and hospitality. We had baraka between us.

When Driss's training period was drawing to a close, I decided to leave the desert earlier than usual in order to travel with him. Besides, summer would be coming on soon, a time when movement in the Sahara is practically impossible, so we planned to set off together by truck to the north. Driss was to take over the Spartel light, and I would accompany him and spend some time in Tangier before returning alone to the Sahara. It was better this way. If fate were to separate us, it was better to have it pull us more gently apart.

The last day in La Guera, Driss stumbled over a piece of rusty machinery half buried in the sand and opened his leg to the bone. The wound bled freely on the sand, which absorbed his blood, leaving only a dark stain. We had a long and arduous trip before us—nearly ten days by truck before we could reach Marrakech—and neither of us considered this an auspicious beginning. I was concerned about tetanus, as the injury had occurred in a place frequented by donkeys and camels. There was no vaccine to be found in La Guera, and when we reached Villa Cisneros three days later I was all for flying out to the

Canary Islands, but Morocco lay only two days' journey away and Driss was eager to cross the border after so many years away from home. By then, too, the cut seemed to be healing properly, so we went on. It had been a good trip otherwise. Like the Saharans traveling with us, we were accustomed to desert transport. After the first hours of rough riding, a stoicism sets in as the body adjusts itself to periods of prolonged hardship. There is less desire for food and drink. The bounces, the wind, the violent changes in temperature, the endless desolate landscape—the whole physical world becomes remote and abstracted. One could go on forever. With no thoughts in the head, the senses expand across the sands. My only desire was for a pipe of kif, but the sensation this trip produced in my body was similar to its effect.

Most of the time we were passing through extraordinarily flat land, following the cement pylons that the Spanish had placed every few kilometers to guide travelers across the empty spaces. It had all been under water once, and the remains of shells were everywhere. At one place where we stopped for a rest Driss found an enormous fossilized oyster shell, which he kept as a souvenir of the trip. I took some photos of him standing beside one of the pylons. He wasn't smiling, for the leg was still giving him considerable pain.

At one point we traversed a perfectly smooth white desert bounded by low white hills streaked with black where erosion had exposed the substrata. The shimmering mirages approached to within a few hundred meters from all sides except windward and sometimes obliterated the view of the next pylon. Then the terrain became rougher, as we moved through an ancient lava flow. Pieces of broken table land and rocky domes like gigantic burial mounds protruded from a plain whose surface was porous and hollow. Fragmented boulders looked like the bones of prehistoric animals. Enormous skulls with sockets and teeth, joints and pieces of vertebrae were piled together. A frightening sight. Stalagmites and stalactites, caverns and fissures, and rock formations resembling the giant carcasses of spiny fish—I've never seen anything to equal it. And from this decaying landscape the dust rose as fine as powder; it clotted in Driss's wound under the bandages, I later discovered. I wanted to wake him and tell him that we were in fact passing near a great underground reservoir some sixty miles in length, but he had finally got himself into a reasonably comfortable position among the cargo and had fallen into a fitful sleep. I didn't disturb him. Besides, he looked so miserable and helpless there curled up in his djellaba, and he would have considered this wilderness of death a bad omen. Even I felt relieved when we left the lava flow behind.

We rested for a day in El Aaiun. It was a Sunday, and we spent the afternoon in a cement park in front of the bar La Union. We looked out over the unoccupied cement benches and the cement tiles, over the tan-washed houses with the great white domes, down the dusty street. Inside the bar someone was playing a guitar, and a solitary legionnaire was seated outside a wooden chair. The wind was whipping a swirl of dust and paper along. The street ended, open, and across the dry canyon of Seguia el Hamra the peaked ridges of the sand dunes were visible, shaped by the wind off the stratified bluffs.

I had been pleading with Driss to take a plane out to Las Palmas, where the leg could receive proper medical treatment, but he refused. He wanted only to return to Morocco as soon as possible. At last I gave up arguing with him, and we spent the rest of the afternoon taking photographs of each other in that empty square.

North of El Aaiun, the night before we would reach Tarfaya, our truck bounced to a halt in the desert, and Driss and our Saharan companions climbed down and faced the east. I walked away from the truck and looked off into the darkness, thinking I saw flashes of light along the horizon. Then the moon rose round and bright as neon; the earth seemed a great flat disk surrounded by blackness. At my feet stones polished by the sand reflected the moonlight. I have always thought my presence on these plains dramatic; my solitary figure fills the empty space. Yet, as often happens, the darkness was becoming warm and seductive, and I felt myself being drawn into it, when a hand touched my shoulder. Driss stood beside me, his forehead glazed with sand from the prayer. Together we stood looking out, and I was glad to have him at my side. How vulnerable we were out there, where even the land lacked protection. This would be our last night together in the Spanish zone. Tomorrow the scene would shift, and we would be on our way north into Morocco. I loved this desert, but I wasn't especially looking forward to returning to La Guera alone one day, having left Driss far behind in Tangier. I told Driss this, and he nodded his head and looked at the ground. After a while he put his arm around me, and we turned back toward the truck, with Driss leaning on me for support. The Saharans had got a fire going and were preparing tea—it had been decided that we would spend the night there. We put on our djellabas and took our places around the fire and received the steaming glasses of tea, which we held between a thumb and finger at the rim and base of the glass, so as not to burn our fingers. I took out my toba, the small engraved metal pipe of the Sahara that I always carry in my pocket, and before dinner we all had a few smokes of the freshly cut kif I had bought in El Aaiun. Being a good cook, Driss was assisting the others prepare the meal. Our traveling companions were Mauritanian merchants, tall black men clad in indigo robes, bound from Nouakchott to the markets of Marrakech. As I watched Driss chatting with them in the firelight, I became uneasy. Often when I'm happy a fear comes over me—not fear that the joy will end, but fear that circumstances unexpected and beyond my control will arise to prevent me from ever feeling joy again. Right away I attributed this feeling to the kif; this time, however, I was unable to shake off the apprehensiveness. After the meal, when the others had rolled up in their djellabas around the dying fire, I related my fears to Driss. He frowned, but said nothing. I asked about his leg, and he replied that it felt stiff and gave him some pain, that was all. Much later that night, after the moon had set and the fire was a mound of dull coals, I woke up to find him putting on my wrist his silver bracelet from Mauritania. To my questions he answered that if anything happened, this bracelet would act as a bond to keep us from separating too far apart.

This sunlit room with its yellow table and curtains is peaceful now. I lie on my bed with my hands behind my head and listen to the wind. Outside the window canes bend and thrash, palm fronds rattle, there is sand and dust flying in the air. Something is slamming and slamming. Will the wind never stop? Glaring sun falls out of a white sky, and I'm cold. This Tangier weather is worse than in the Sahara.

A small detachment of Moroccan soldiers was stationed in Tarfaya, with a caid in charge. We were given a room in a deserted Spanish barracks, and the military came forth with fresh bandages for Driss's leg, but there was no doctor, no vaccine there, either. All those in need of a doctor are shipped out to Tan-Tan, I was told. I also learned that the truck convoy had been stopped by sand far to the north, so we were stranded. The room where we were to live and wait contained two beds, two mattresses, and two blankets. No running water. I unpacked our suitcases and spread our possessions around, making the room ours, but still it was pretty grim. Next I changed Driss's bandages. Once again the sand had penetrated the old wrappings and had entered the wound. He was complaining that the leg was stiff, and I could see that it was giving him a good deal of pain. He looked so helpless lying there on that miserable bed, and I wondered what I ought to do. I went to the window, which opens onto a large sandy courtyard that must once have been a military parade ground. Beyond, I could see the coast and desert to the north. Cape Juby is not really a cape, but just a hump of land into the ocean where the coastline changes direction. There Tarfaya is caught between the sea and the desert. Marching crescent dunes surround the town on three sides; some have even entered and covered the smaller structures on the outskirts. Flying sand comes swirling over the rounded surfaces; it enters under the door and through the cracked windowpanes. I could taste the grit between my teeth.

"Yusef," Driss was asking behind me, "do you think we ought to have flown out to the Canaries?" It was too late to think about that now, I told him. We were stuck in Tarfaya. "I'm sorry, Yusef," came his voice, as if from a distance. "Do you think everything will be all right?" I went and sat down on the edge of the bed. Darkness was falling quickly, and we had no candles to light the room. I tried to reassure him. The wind might die down tonight; by tomorrow the truck convoy would have arrived from Tan-Tan, and we'd be on our way again. As soon as we reached Tangier, we'd see a good doctor about his leg, and soon he'd be well. "Yusef," Driss said after a while, "I wish we were back in La Guera. We should never have left." That was nonsense, I said. We were in Morocco now, and everything would be all right. "I hope so," he replied and lay his head back on the rolled-up djellaba I had arranged as a pillow. He shut his eyes and didn't say anything more. The room had become quite dark, and I said I would go out and look for some candles. "All right, Yusef," came his voice.

Our first evening in Tarfaya: soldiers stand guard on top of sand dunes, a bugle blows as the sun goes down into the sea. Wind. When I came back with the candles, Driss was still complaining about the stiffness in his leg, and I massaged it as best I could without disturbing the new bandages. Later I went out to Tarfaya's only café, which had been set up in the lobby of an abandoned movie theater. M'barek, the proprietor, cooked up a camel tajine to take back to Driss. He regrets the departure of the Spanish from Tarfaya. El Aaiun, which the Spanish still hold, is where he wants to go. I told him I'd been in and out of that town over the past three years and didn't think much of it. But everybody works down there, he insisted. Men, women, little children, even the dogs work and are happy. In Tarfaya there is nothing. He showed me around the empty movie theater explaining that during the Spanish time there used to be a new film every night; the projectors were still upstairs, ready to go. In the café were two boys from Oujda, a thousand miles to the north, who had walked all the way to Tarfaya looking for work. Their names were Mohamed and Mohamed. Mohamed I is a lean, ungainly fellow, who wears an old felt hat with matches in the rim and a dirty brown shirt with a package of Casa Sports showing through the chest pocket. He has sideburns and ragged blue jeans and boots, and the pockets of his trousers are embroidered with safety pins. He's a nervous type who can't sit still for long and spends his time pacing back and forth in the café. As for Mohamed II, he wears a skullcap and a long dark overcoat and a pair of battered sneakers and no socks. They both sleep in M'barek's café and play cards all the time. Mohamed deals, Mohamed picks up the cards. They smoke too many cigarettes because they are sad. They all want to know if I'm married. M'barek asks why don't I marry an española. Mohamed I and Mohamed II naturally want to go to El Aaiun but have no pass; so they planned to stay in Tarfaya, fish a little, sell boards they find washed up by the sea, look for some special seaweed that is bought (thirty-five francs a kilo) for transport to Agadir, and wait for the tourist boom.

I took the tajine back to Driss. He was lying on the bed with the candle next to him on the floor. Suddenly the wind slammed the door behind me with a bang and blew the candle out. Driss screamed in the darkness. I put down the food and relit the candle. Driss was clutching at his leg and yelling; the muscles had gone as hard as wood. The toes had so clenched that they had turned in on themselves. I rubbed and rubbed the leg and tried to make him relax in spite of the pain. Finally the muscles began to loosen up; he moaned for a while and closed his eyes. I made him as comfortable as possible and sat down in the flickering candlelight to watch him, feeling alone and helpless, as the camel tajine went cold and untouched on the floor.

The next morning the wind was still blowing. The sky was neither clear nor overcast but so full of light that I had to squint my eyes in the glare. I banged on the caid's door, and he finally opened, clad in blue pajamas. I told him that my friend had shown the first signs of tetanus and had to be transported out immediately. A few minutes later the caid was on the radio to Tan-Tan; before noon an old Dakota flew low over the town with a great roar, made a circle, and came back. We all ran out to the edge of town, but the airstrip was hopelessly buried by the dunes. As the plane flew around and around looking for a place to land, M'barek tried to mobilize everyone to dig out the runway, but I could see it was futile. Even the oil drum markers had disappeared in the sand. The plane made one last circle and flew away.

The radio had said that the convoy had not yet left Tan-Tan, and the truck that had brought us to Tarfaya had neither oil nor fuel. I went down to the sea. A dead porpoise was being eaten by stray dogs on the beach, and the flies swarmed around. Some bright-colored fishing boats had been stranded by the low tide —too small to take us out of there. The sea tossed with white-caps; waves foamed over the broken pier. Only the castle off-shore seemed firm. Sea gulls floated above it. I turned back toward the town. In the windy streets ravens perched and fluttered along the crests of sand dunes. Arabs squatted behind mud walls. Their long blue robes and turbans protected them from the wind as they soaked up warmth from the sun. I lacked this warmth, this assurance and protection. The wind tore at me, I could not escape it. Coming off the desert, it smelled of dust and excrement.

That afternoon Driss went into a state of spastic paralysis. The pressure of the wind burst open the door with a loud noise, and by the time I had shut it his entire body had gone rigid. His back arched right off the bed, the hands and feet gripped and curled, and his jaw locked in an awful grimace—the "sardonic smile" of tetanus; although his muscles were contracting with all their strength, he could not move, because the muscles were pulling against each other with equal tension. Before long he was exhausted, with no possibility of rest, and he was in terrible agony. I could see that he would soon die, because nothing could be done to save him.

After dark M'barek and the Mohameds came to visit us in the barracks. They sat on the floor with their legs crossed. M'barek had brought along a charcoal brazier from the café and began to make tea, and Mohamed II opened his transistor and let the music of Mauritania into the room. Later the voice of the taleb reading from the Koran came on, which seemed appropriate. We didn't say much, but just drank the tea and smoked our tobas. The room was full of the broken images of death. I tried to think of the experiences Driss and I had had together in the Sahara, but the past drifted away from me; I tried to think of the future, but tomorrow meant nothing. I felt grateful for the presence of these young Moroccans, and they must have given Driss some comfort, too, for he lay flat on the bed now, although the muscles remained solid. The eyes were closed and his breath hissed between the locked teeth.

Late that night I went out to the parade ground and lay down on a sand dune. The wind had died down; it was a clear Saharan night with a sky full of stars. The sea was faintly audible; somewhere a dog barked. Except for our dimly lit window, the barracks stood black and ominous all around. I prayed to all the prophets of the desert—Moses, Christ, and Mohammed—for some miracle to save him. I asked the gods of the wind and the Sahara and of truck drivers for help. Then a satellite came along, threading its way through the stars, clicking up against some of them—an oddly irregular course. I prayed to that as well. In fact, I wished I were up there riding that satellite far above this desolate African coast, away from the flies and the wind, released from the responsibility of death. But that thought vanished in a second, and I jumped up and hurried back to the room.

Not long afterward Driss went into another—and final—spasm. His body rose from the bed like a specter, the blanket draped over him, until only the back of the head and the heels touched the mattress. The mouth was stretched into that terrible smile, and he seemed to be humming. I attempted to push him back down, but the muscles were completely rigid. I lay on top of him and put my arms around him, but he remained arched like that until dawn, when the body collapsed on the mattress, and he was dead.

"*There is no God but God and Mohammed is His Prophet!*"

The chant was repeated over and over, back and forth, as the small procession wound slowly through the sandy streets of Tarfaya. I walked in the rear with M'barek and the Mohameds and the caid, who all took turns carrying the body. Driss, wrapped in a white cloth, was borne on a simple wooden litter at shoulder height. We crossed the useless airstrip, chanting, as blue Saharan robes fluttered in the wind, and ends of long black turbans, loosely tied, trailed behind the men. Only men walked in this procession: they had come and washed the body and wrapped it in the white cloth. Now they were taking it to the grave. Chanting, we passed through the dunes and came out onto a flat space where stones stood upright in the sand. A shallow grave had been dug, which the wind was already filling. The body was put down by the grave, a prayer was said by the taleb, as I stood a little distance away on a mound of sand. Not being a Moslem I could not participate. The body was picked up and placed in the grave, the head toward the east. Sand was showered on it. This is the crucial part: communication with Driss was over. The grave was quickly filled. We all left except for the taleb, who remained at the graveside reminding Driss of his religious duties and obligations. Gabriel would soon come to lead away his soul, and the taleb asked the soul questions concerning the faith, so that Driss would not forget in the presence of Gabriel.

The truck convoy, which had finally reached Tarfaya that same afternoon, was about to depart for Tan-Tan the following day when the taleb appeared, saying that Driss had visited him during the night. The graveside advice had not been necessary, and the taleb declared that Driss was a good Moslem. I thanked the taleb and tipped him, and he stepped away, mumbling a blessing. The motors started up. M'barek and the caid shook my hand. The two Mohameds were already up on the truck; they were going to accompany me to Tangier. I told my friends I'd probably be back this way on my return trip to Rio de Oro. God willing, they replied. A bearded soldier I'd seen at the funeral came forward and shook my hand. The whole town was out to see the trucks off. I climbed aboard and waved, and the convoy headed out through the sandy streets of Tarfaya.

Soon we were out in the Sahara. Ahead lay unbelievably vast empty spaces with plateaus and headlands jutting and jutting until they fade into the haze of heat and distance. No wonder the ancient peoples thought the earth was flat. We rode all day and all night with the same Mauritanians who had been with me the whole way from La Guera. During the night we stopped every few hours and built enormous fires in the desert to make tea and warm ourselves. A convoy of seven trucks was taking me farther and farther away from that place outside Tarfaya where Driss lies. The next morning at dawn I took three oranges out of my bag, handed two to my young companions, and we began to eat them as the truck jolted into the gray light.

As I have been dozing the afternoon light has been slipping from this room, and some of the buzzless flies have disappeared. I wonder, where do flies go at night? Only two remain here with me now. I think about the possibilities that are lost and the possibilities that remain. Driss lies under the sand of Tarfaya; I find the memory of him overwhelming. Being a Moslem, he was sure that the laws and events of the universe were ordered by God's will. Sandstorms, shipwrecks, and death had already been written, so it was pointless to resist them. This was a great source of strength to him; yet he tended the lighthouse with care, and considered my discoveries of water to be both blessings of the desert and blessings to my skill. Together we were a part of the order of things in that remote region of the western desert. We dealt with the elements and turned them to man's favor; therefore we held the favor of God and received the respect of men wherever we went. But one must not spend too much time alone, either in an isolated lighthouse or out on the windy plains, and we were happy to have one another in those empty places. Together we achieved a balance between nature and ourselves not to be met with again. I never thought I'd be leaving him alone down there.

Now I see the sun is going down, and the wind has abated. As for myself, I ought to leave this room and go into the streets. This seems a great task. I'm not sure when I'll be returning to the desert, where I have my obligations to the Spanish government. My plans are indefinite. On my wrist I wear his silver bracelet. It, too, has its power to take me back to Tarfaya and to La Guera, as Driss foresaw. In the meantime, however, it is a comfort to stay a few more minutes in this bed and observe the two remaining flies. They play their harmless games oblivious of my presence. If I did not have them to watch, I do not know what I would do.

# *M'siksif's Café*

In the alcove at the rear of his narrow café, M'siksif was preparing tea; into a long-handled tin pot he emptied a heaping teaspoon of green China tea and added several spoonfuls of sugar; next he filled the pot with hot water from a large copper samovar and eased it in among the glowing coals underneath. While the tea was steeping, he took out his sebsi, expertly filled the tiny clay bowl with kif from a leather pouch, held a flaring match to it, and inhaled deeply. He then handed the pipe to a large bearded man. Returning to the samovar, M'siksif crushed several spears of fresh mint between his hands, stuffed them into a glass, and strained in the boiling tea from the pot. Holding the glass by the rim, he carried it to a young boy in a ragged djellaba, who was sitting cross-legged on a raised platform near the door, playing a flute. The boy thanked M'siksif with his eyes and went on playing. As M'siksif was collecting empty glasses from the other customers, the sound of approaching footsteps could be heard from the street. Sebsis quickly disappeared into the folds of djellabas, the sound of the flute ceased, and the boy peered out through the doorway. The footsteps came closer, slowed, and Cabell stepped into the café.

"Yusef!" exclaimed M'siksif, and he came forward and threw his arms around him. "Ah, Yusef!"

Cabell shook the hands of the other men in the café and sat down; the sebsis reappeared, and he accepted a pipe.

"Yusef, it's been a long time."

"A year."

"Usually you send postcards, but I haven't received one."

"It's true. I haven't written to anybody."

"You always tell me when you plan to come to Tangier, but this year there's been no word from you."

"I've been preoccupied, I guess, and busy."

"Have you found any oil yet?"

"No oil, just fresh water."

"Water in the desert? Then it's not a desert any more. It must be a garden."

"No, still a desert."

M'siksif was preparing another glass of mint tea. "Yusef, you look tired; you've come to Tangier for a rest."

"Yes."

"When did you arrive?"

"A few days ago."

"A few days? And it took you all that time to come to see us?"

"Tonight I went walking for the first time. I heard the music from the boy's flute and began to follow it. I was sure it came from your café."

"He plays well—he'll play for you anything you like—he's come today from Agla. Do you remember the village of Agla, Yusef?"

"Yes, of course. Agla is famous for its pears."

"That's right. Not so long ago, if you approached the bay of Agla in a small boat or canoe, the scents of the orchards came to you across the water—apples, and peaches, especially the smell of pears."

"No more?"

"Now the people don't tend to their trees as they used to, and many of the orchards are dying or growing in a wild state. The fruit isn't the same."

"What about those big toads out there? Do they still exist?"

They were speaking in Arabic, and the other customers were listening closely.

"The elephant toads of Agla. No, there aren't many of them left now, although last year I spied one that must have weighed at least five kilos."

"Ah!" The other customers exclaimed together.

M'siksif handed Cabell a glass of tea. "A Swiss lady who lives in the Marshan asked me about them once. This Nazarene told me that if I catch an elephant toad from Agla for her, she will take it to the zoo in her country, and the zoo people will pay me 500 dirhams!"

"Ah!"

"Do you believe it, M'siksif?"

"No, who would pay so much for a toad?"

"A zoo might."

"If I come upon one and can trap it, I'll give it to the Nazarene woman."

"Will you take me to Agla one day, M'siksif?"

"Any day you like. Let me tell you something, Yusef. There's a strange woman living in Agla now—lives alone in her husband's house, for the man has gone off to France to work. This woman wishes to be a man."

"Funny thing. Why?"

"We don't know, but she goes about dressed in a man's clothes. She must be a Christian or a Jew, but she's admitted into the mosque here in Tangier and prays with the men—such a thing has never happened before—she speaks Arabic like we do, and it's said that she can write it as well. I've heard that she spent many years in the Sahara."

"What's her name?"

"What is her name?" M'siksif asked his friends.

"El Hassani," one of the men replied.

"That's not her real name!" cried the man with the beard.

"Then what is her real name?"

"I don't know—she must have another name, a Christian name."

"She can't have a Christian name because she's not a Christian."

"What is she, then?"

"A Jew!"

"She can't be a Jew because she's allowed into the mosque with the men."

"Do Jews pray with Moslems these days?"

Everyone in the café began to argue.

"You know she's not a Moslem."

"She prays five times a day."

"She drinks wine."

"So do you."

"Her husband is a Moslem."

"Do you know him?"

"He comes from another part of the country."

"Nobody knows him."

"How can she have a husband when she's a man?"

"She not a man, she's a woman."

"How do you know, have you slept with her?"

"She's a Christian woman, I'm sure of that."

"Born a Jew!"

"Her husband says she's now a Moslem."

"What does her husband know?" asked M'siksif. "He's in France, and she sleeps with everyone in Tangier."

"That's true."

"They say that she lies down before her dogs as well."

"Does she sleep with you, M'siksif?"

"He never sleeps with Christian women or Jewish women."

"Or any woman, if I can help it."

Everyone laughed. The boy reached across and pulled on M'siksif's beard, and the men bent double with laughter.

"M'siksif prefers the goats of Agla."

"They are Moslems."

More laughter. The boy was holding his belly and nearly rolled off the edge of the platform.

M'siksif began to fill his sebsi, and the laughter subsided.

"Yusef, what do you think of such a woman?"

"So she's here in Tangier now, is she?"

"Do you know her?"

"I think I've heard of her before. In Smara."

"In Smara. Ah."

"Two years ago there was some talk of a woman dressed as a man who crossed the Jbel Ouarkziz on foot to Smara. She lived in the tents of the R'guibat and ate their food and slept with the men. The Spanish knew nothing about her until she left the tents and began to go into the bars at night and drink with the legionnaires. Apparently she could outdrink any of them, got drunk every night, and slept with the soldiers. This went on until it was discovered that she was not a R'guibat woman at all, but a Nazarene. The Spanish thought she was a spy and put her in jail and finally expelled her from the territory. But the Saharans spoke highly of her. She prayed five times a day; she knew something about medicine and was a kind of healer among them."

"In Agla some people say the same," put in the man with the beard.

As the conversation continued, Cabell smoke many pipes of kif, exchanging his own kif with that offered him by the other men in the café. Later, when he rose to go, everyone shook his hand once more, and M'siksif accompanied him outside.

"Yusef, is something the matter?"

"Nothing. I'll be all right."

"What has happened?"

"I'll tell you. Not now."

M'siksif looked at Cabell for a few seconds before speaking.

"The eyes are bad, Yusef."

Cabell nodded. "No sleep."

"No sleep and worse. What can I do?"

"Nothing. How's the family, M'siksif?" Cabell asked, changing the subject.

"They're all fine. No sickness this year, thanks be to God."

"And the children? Are they all in school?"

"As you advised me, I've placed Rachid in the French school and Zohra in the Spanish school."

"What about Abdelhak?"

"Abdelhak is studying in the Italian school, where he's learning about electricity."

"And Said?"

"Said's in the American school. Kinza, Abdelkebir, and Batoul are in Moroccan schools. But it's so expensive, and you know that I am poor. So many children, so much noise in the house, and so little money. It's not easy, Yusef."

Cabell reached into his pocket and pulled out a 100-dirham note. M'siksif took his hand in both of his.

"Thank you, Yusef."

"M'siksif, if you had fewer children, I'd come to your café more often, but it costs me too much money."

"If God had given me fewer children, Yusef, I wouldn't need to have a café at all."

"Then you'd have no place to invite your friends. You'd be sitting in the house all day, surrounded by women. You'd be bored."

M'siksif laughed. "Where do you sleep, Yusef? Shall I send the boy with you to my house?"

"I'm already at the Hotel Splendid."

"Like before?"

"Like always. M'siksif, you can do me a favor now. I've come from the Sahara with two boys. They're trained masons, and they're in need of work. Can you find them something?"

"Jobs are difficult to come by in Tangier. Practically all the young men are idle."

"I realize that, but you must know of something."

"You say they're masons? They know how to build houses?"

"Yes."

"This coming week I want to put up a summer café at the beach of Merkala. Send the boys to me; they can help and afterward, if they're good boys, they can look after the café during the summer."

"Good. I'll tell them."

"Yusef, are you sure you don't want to talk? I'll shut the café, and we'll go to my house. I'll bring along the boy, if you like, to play for us."

"I have many things to tell you, M'siksif, but I'm too tired to talk now, and I've smoked too much kif."

"Alright, Yusef, you know best."

It was late, long past midnight, and the little square of Fuente Nueva lay silent and deserted under the light of a single street lamp. The fountain was dripping into the grate, and cats crouching by piles of garbage banked against the walls dispersed as Cabell came out of an alley and crossed the square; when he disappeared up another narrow street, they reassembled, taking up their positions around the garbage, as the sound of his footsteps faded.

A few minutes later he came out into the Socco Grande, where the fruit and vegetable stands remain open all night. An argument before one of them suddenly developed into a fight, and two drunken Moroccans rolled in each other's arms on the pavement. They crashed against a fruit stand, and a pile of glistening oranges tumbled onto the street. At the all-night cafés the customers looked on impassively, as they puffed on sebsis and sipped the steaming tea. In the taxi rank the drivers slept in the back seats of their automobiles.

Cabell continued up Calle Libertad, past the American Library and the Hotel Minzah, to the Place de France. From there he mounted the rue de Fez to Café Marco Polo. The place was about half full—mostly Spaniards and Moroccans, talking together or reading newspapers over their coffees and beers or simply gazing sleepily off into the darkness. Cabell took a seat at a table on the sidewalk and ordered a coffee. The table next to his was piled with books and papers, and a stocky gentleman was shuffling papers and thumbing through the thick volumes. Cabell was watching him when a young Moroccan boy stopped before his table.

"Hey, look at me," the boy said in Arabic.

"I'm looking," Cabell replied.

"You know me?"

"No."

"You used to live in the Kasbah. You've been away."

"That's right."

"I know you. I know your friends."

"Oh?"

"Hey, where have you been?"

"In the Sahara."

"The Sahara? That's a bad place, huh?"

"Why do you say that?"

"I didn't say it, you say it."

"Did I?"

"Hey, you know me?"

"I don't think so. Perhaps."

"You know this man here?"

The boy was pointing at the man with the books.

"No."

"This is Mi Amigo Maxwell."

Cabell nodded to the man, who had been following the conversation; suddenly there was a shout from across the street, and the boy ran off into the darkness.

"It may be that I do . . ." Cabell mumbled to himself.

"It may be that you do what?" asked the man with the books.

"It may be that I know that boy."

"He's around here every night. Everybody knows him."

The waiter brought Cabell's coffee.

"Are you here every night, too?" Cabell asked.

"I've no choice."

"Why not?"

"Café Marco Polo wins by default. It's the only café in town where you can eat after midnight."

"Oh."

"There's no action in Tangier. The town's dead. Everyone on the streets is broke and mean. A young man like yourself shouldn't be here."

"Why not?"

"There's nothing for you here, no artistic improvement, and you become worse the longer you remain. Look at me, I've been here twenty-two years."

"I think that boy's the son of the snake charmer in the Kasbah."

"Do you see that Moroccan sitting over there," the man went on, "the one with the patch? He was the first person I saw when I got off the boat—never known him or spoken to him or ever learned his name, but I can't forget his face, which hasn't changed, except that he lost an eye somewhere along the way. I remember saying to myself as I came down the gangplank: 'There's a Moroccan; that's what they look like.' Every time I see him I'm reminded of all the time I've wasted in this town."

"I think I know who he is."

"Who?"

"A fisherman. I've seen him around. People say a fishhook got caught in his eye; that's how he lost it."

"You talk as if you knew everybody in town. Been here long?"

"I come and go."

"The longer I stay here the more mystified by human nature I become. It's incredible. You're looking upon someone who has seen better times. Well, it's the truth. By the way, Maxwell's the name. What's yours?"

"Cabell."

"Pleased to meet you, Cabell."

There was a jukebox in the Café Marco Polo, the sort with the screen above it, where the musicians dance and sing in brilliant colors when someone drops in a coin. A great noise of guitars and handclapping now erupted, while a woman in a bright orange dress went through a flamenco routine with clattering castanets. A group of ragged urchins appeared out of the darkness to watch through the window. They were barefoot and dirty and took no notice of the people seated at the tables as they pressed themselves up against the glass. A tall man with long hair wearing a suit and vest who had been standing at the bar came out and stared at the children; one by one, beginning with the smallest, the children took notice of him, until they were all looking up at him with huge glistening eyes.

"Looks like a film director," whispered Maxwell.

"He's barefoot."

"So he is. Gets dressed up like that but too damn lazy to put his shoes on. See what I mean?"

"What?"

"Tangier. A town for lazy bastards, myself included."

The man began to move back and forth, shadowboxing with the children. At first they retreated along the wall, not knowing what to make of him, then ran off across the street, where they took refuge with someone seated on the stoop of a darkened filling station. In another minute they returned, however, as if drawn by a magnet, and took up the dance and shadowboxing with the tall man.

"Looks like he's got them hypnotized."

In and out among the tables, up and down the sidewalk, out on the street they chased and fought each other in pantomime. They made no sound except for their bare feet on the pavement —all noise was coming from the jukebox.

"Looks like an imbecile ballet," commented Maxwell.

It became evident that the man was trying to isolate one older girl from the others, but she knew the game and kept the little ones clustered around her for protection. The dance continued until the music abruptly shut off; the children faded away once more into the darkness of the filling station, and the man walked off down the street.

"You see what I mean, Cabell? The town is starving; people dance in the streets like ghosts. I suppose those children sleep in that petrol station, that is, sleep during the day and prowl the streets all night like insomniacs."

"What's that you're doing there with all those books?" Cabell asked.

"These are my translations. I enjoy reading Latin and Greek in the original, and do a few translations for my own pleasure. A simple pleasure."

"I see."

"I live in the Hotel Nicaragua down by the waterfront. There I keep my few possessions. It's a Benedictine sort of life I lead, devoted to a few scholarly pursuits. Otherwise I live in the streets and come to the Marco Polo every night to study the classics, write letters, and read the newspapers in order to keep abreast of world economic and political events. But now there's too much noise and too many boys. Tangier's going downhill, and the Europeans are going to pot—they live their lives too slow and easy, like the Arabs. That film director fellow's a good example, forgets to put on his shoes; next thing you know it'll be his trousers. I've gone downhill less than the others, but I can't face the capitals now, what with all that dashing around and energy being expended."

"So you'll remain in Tangier."

"Choices become limited over the years. I suppose it's time that does it. I've become lazier and less inclined to move about. I know it's wrong, I should pack my bags and see the world, but who would I travel with? I need a comrade to take me out of here—I'll never be able to do it alone."

"So Tangier's no good?"

"Occasionally I walk out to the Sharf at dawn with a friend, and the sun coming up over Cape Malabata and the bay reconciles one to the place. I prefer the cool of the mornings and evenings, you know, it's easier on the sinuses. Hot weather irritates my sinuses. You know, Cabell, if I were an American I'd be rich. As it is, I'm just old."

"Not so old."

"As I said, I've done less backsliding than most—I've got my books—but I'm over fifty now, and the process has set in. You know, it's not a gradual process at all."

"What's that?"

"Aging. You can go for months, even years, without detecting a change—then within the period of a week or even a few days you see yourself growing old right before your eyes. I've woken up in the morning to find myself looking very much older than when I went to bed. It's no joke, and it all begins at twenty-eight or twenty-nine, when the first wrinkles appear beside your ears. You have them."

"Well, I ought to. I'm forty."

"You don't look it, Cabell. I'd say you were a youthful forty, despite those big rings beneath your eyes. You have quite a suntan, I see. That's from living in the Sahara desert, I suppose."

"How did you know I've been in the Sahara?"

"You told that boy."

"That's right, I'd forgotten."

"Is it some kind of secret?"

"No, it's not a secret."

"You seem to be worried about something, Cabell. Sorry, I don't mean to pry."

Maxwell lit another cigarette—he smoked them down to the last half inch. "Here I've spent nearly half my life in Morocco without ever having seen the desert. Everyone says it's beautiful, but what would I do in the desert? I love my days when they're full, but I find them intolerable when I have nothing to do. But then, even the simplest problem confounds me. Sometimes I can't remember if I'm human any more. But you like the desert, Cabell. What do you do down there?"

"I think I must go."

"No, please don't. Stay a while longer."

Cabell got to his feet and staggered against the table. The waiter, who had been standing nearby, caught him and guided him back to his chair.

"Say, are you all right, Cabell? You've turned as white as a sheet, look like you're about to faint. Better sit down and rest for a moment."

"What time is it?"

"Four o'clock. Early yet."

A man carrying a mandolin came along and stopped in front of the café. Placing one foot on an empty chair, he tuned his instrument and began to play. Nobody in the café paid him much attention. Maxwell had returned to his books and glanced from time to time at Cabell, who had shut his eyes. After a while the man stopped playing, received a coin from one of the customers, and moved off. The café was nearly empty, and the waiter dozed in a chair by the door. Cabell opened his eyes.

"What time did you say it was?"

"Four-thirty."

"I'm so tired. I must go."

Cabell rose unsteadily from his chair. Maxwell was rapidly stuffing his books and papers into a leather satchel.

"Mind if I accompany you?" he asked.

Cabell shrugged. Maxwell took hold of his arm, and they walked to the taxi stand.

"Where are we going, Cabell?"

"Place de la Kasbah."

"You heard him, driver."

With the quiet streets filling with gray light, the taxi was passing by the Spanish cathedral, where a group of country women in wide straw hats and red-and-white skirts padded along barefoot behind their donkeys, on their way to market.

"Do you plan to return to the desert, Cabell?"

"I don't know."

"You must like it down there."

Cabell nodded.

"I think I'd find the silence and space frightening."

"Silence can be a great thing," Cabell said.

"I wouldn't want to be stuck out there, alone and stranded."

"I'm always grateful for my traveling companions."

"I'd be grateful for the skill of whoever could get me out."

"I wish we were back in La Guera; I wish we'd never made this trip."

"What?"

The taxi reached the Marshan and was cruising by the municipal football stadium, where big eucalyptus trees grow.

"You must like your solitude, Cabell."

"I can endure solitude when I know. . . ."

"What's that, man? You're mumbling."

"I can endure sol—"

"Never mind. Solitude's all right every now and then. Don't you ever get lonely?"

"Never in the desert."

"No?"

"Too busy moving from one place to another . . . thinking about food and water and where it's going to come from . . . thinking about where I'm going to sleep."

"I guess I've spent too much time in my hotel room with too little to do—lost touch with the basics somewhere along the line."

"In the desert . . . just surviving takes up a great deal of time."

"I see what you mean. I suppose I've always taken it for granted, but now I'm beginning to wonder how much it's worth."

"What?"

"Survival."

The streets were becoming narrower, with large town houses on either side, built by wealthy Jewish families, but now abandoned and falling into ruin.

"When you've spent time in the desert . . . you realize that it will never speak to you," Cabell said.

"How could it?"

"But the desert will make you speak . . . to yourself."

"A monologue cannot last forever, except in madness."

"Many men . . . who go into the desert . . . do so . . ."

"Why?"
"In order to talk to themselves."
"What about yourself?"
"Me?"
"Yes, you. Why did you go?"
"I went to look for oil."
"Ah."

The taxi had passed through the Kasbah gate, wound along the base of the old ramparts, and entered a tunnel; at the Place de la Kasbah it pulled up before the prison and Cabell got out. The sun was rising over Cape Malabata, turning the upper half of the prison wall orange. Overhead, however, was a layer of clouds, and a light rain began to fall.

"Look here, Cabell, before we say goodbye, I have something to give you."

Maxwell handed Cabell a slip of paper.

"What's this?"
"A lottery ticket."
"Why are you giving me a lottery ticket?"
"Just take it. It might bring you luck."
"All right . . . thanks."
"You seem a bit shaky. Shall I accompany you to your hotel?"
"I'll make it."
"Are you all right, Cabell? You're practically catatonic."

Cabell turned and began to walk away.

"I don't know if we'll ever see each other again, but you can always find me at the Marco Polo."

"Good."

"In any case, don't forget to check that ticket against the winning numbers. The drawing is tomorrow. I mean today."

"I'll do that."

Maxwell shut the taxi door; the taxi turned around and drove off, with Maxwell peering through the window. Cabell was already mounting the steps of the narrow street by the mosque. In the alley across from the hotel, garbage men in their yellow slickers were having a pipe of kif. Cabell entered the hotel and went up the stairs. By the time he reached his room on the top floor, the garbage men had begun to blow on their brass horns to wake up the people, who would open their doors and bring out the garbage.

*Tangier* May 8 The Hotel Splendid still deserves its name. The owner, whoever he is, never appears, and the place is run by its staff of two. Boujma, the gardener and nightwatchman ("I work 24 hours a day"), tends the trees and flowers in the courtyard. I like to watch him from my balcony as he beds down in the garden for the night: first a mat goes down on the tiled walk, then a blanket, sheepskins, and another blanket rolled up as a pillow. The little white dog wags his tail as his master makes his bed—now his job begins. If anyone makes a move toward Boujma, the "Sultan of Dogs" growls. Boujma is a dark-brown man who wears only a faded cotton robe that falls below his knees, and a skullcap. He has a cowrie shell anklet on each ankle—he is a follower of the Gnaoua musicians—the bottoms of his feet are white. He has been the gardener at this hotel for years. He also buys and cuts kif for me.

Otherwise there is only Fatomah, a white Negress from the Dra, who cleans the rooms.

"Are you working hard today, Fatomah?" I ask her.

"Am I? Why that's the truth, Señor Cabell. Whenever you see a bucket, someone's working hard."

The only other room besides my own that she has to clean belongs to Shahid, a basketball player from Senegal. The local team has imported this ringer who they say can jump like a kangaroo. His fans call him "Congo." The walls of his room, which he keeps immaculately neat, are lined with newspaper clippings, a record of past heroics on the court, and he's very proud of his collection of Senegalese shirts. Whenever Shahid comes to my room for a visit (he's taking English lessons and I've invited him to practice with me), he straightens out the wrinkles in the bed covers, dusts around with his handkerchief, pushes the chair back into its position against the table, etc. . . . He's always scolding Fatomah for not keeping my room clean enough.

May 10 Today another visit from Omar, Driss's little brother. His friends call him Bizbouz, which means "faucet," because he talks so much. But he doesn't like that name. He comes late in the afternoon after school, carrying a satchel of books. We talk about lighthouses and about his brother. He didn't know Driss very well, as he was away most of the time, and now Omar wishes to know everything. So I am forced to speak of Driss.

The father cannot go into retirement, but must continue looking after the light until Omar is ready to assume the responsibility. Although Omar is only twelve or so, he seems to know as much about lighthouses as his brother did. I like to hear him talk, and he has become a friend of the Mohameds. My memories need no refreshing, but when the boy arrives, he deludes me into thinking that perhaps not everything has been lost. He looks so much like his brother; so many mannerisms are the same.

# *Merkala*

Leading a donkey, M'siksif and Mohamed I approached a whitewashed shack enclosed by a live cane fence. A dog started to bark from inside as Mohamed pounded on the top of an empty oil drum.

"This must be the doorbell."

There was a shout and a yelp, and the barking ceased. A gate opened and a bearded man appeared.

"Good morning, sidi," M'siksif said.

"Good morning."

"We want to buy cane."

"Good. There it is before your eyes."

M'siksif and the man began to talk about the cane and soon ·ey were arguing over the price. Meanwhile, Mohamed went and inspected the cane.

·s cane is no good!" he shouted. "It's all crooked."

do you mean, crooked?" the man replied. He took a

M'siksif and the cane man came over and sat down beside them as Omar opened his sack and took out four oranges, which they peeled with their knives and ate. Then Omar got to his feet.

"I must go now."

"Omar," M'siksif said, "you're a fisherman, aren't you?"

"Yes."

"Then take one of these canes and use it as a fishing pole this summer."

"All right."

After a lengthy inspection of the canes, Omar selected the longest and the straightest. M'siksif nodded, and the boy went off carrying the cane over one shoulder and the sack of oranges over the other. His friends watched him go, and Mohamed returned to the work, shucking the canes and looking at his hands when they received a new cut.

The site for the café was near the beach at Merkala, where the Jews' River empties into the sea. At the base of an overhanging cliff the Mohameds had cleared a level area and constructed a terrace of stones. They cut poles from the forest on the hill, and from these they fashioned a simple wooden frame on the foundation, with the cliff as the rear wall. To this frame the cane was fastened with palmetto rope to form the roof and walls, into which ferns and branches from the forest were woven. It was an uncomplicated structure: three stone steps led up to a narrow terrace, just wide enough for people to sit outside on a straw mat. Inside the doorway to the right was a small area with a raised floor for card players and musicians. To the left a longer room had a wooden bench, where the customers could sit and look out the windows at the sea. A rudimentary kitchen was located in the rear, where the cliff had been hollowed away.

As soon as the roof was up, M'siksif brought the café equipment from town. Mats were put down, the copper samovar was installed, and M'siksif hung a photograph of the Sultan and another of the Sultan's father over the door to the kitchen.

long straight cane in both hands, bent it down, and expertly snapped it off just above the ground. "Do you call this crooked? Cane doesn't come any straighter than this."

Mohamed took hold of an especially crooked cane. Bend and snap. "You call that straight, do you? About as straight as my elbow."

"My cane is straight, but each man has his own eyes. Take it if you want or look elsewhere."

M'siksif and the man went on bargaining and finally reached a price. Before long the three of them were pulling and snapping the long green canes off at the base while still debating over who was pulling the straight canes and who was purposely choosing the crooked ones. Working under a bright blue sky with the wind causing the live canes to bend and thrash above their heads, soon they had piled a large number on the ground. Mohamed took out a clasp knife and began to strip them of their leaves. M'siksif and the cane man sat down together under a tree and were chatting and exchanging sebsis, as if they had known each other all their lives. To one side stood the donkey, eating the cane shucks and awaiting its load. After a while Omar came along carrying a sack over his shoulder.

"Hey, Bizbouz, where are you going?" Mohamed called.

"Don't call me Bizbouz; my name is Omar. What are you doing? Why are you cutting cane?"

"M'siksif is building a summer café at Merkala."

"Ah, a summer café." Omar put the sack down on the ground and squatted beside it. "Good."

"My friend Mohamed is guarding a spot under the cliff," said Mohamed as he worked with the sharp knife, shucking the cane.

"Will Yusef come to your café?"

"We hope so. But we haven't seen Yusef in many days."

"He stays in his hotel room and doesn't come out very ofter Omar said.

"Ah."

"He is sad."

"Yes."
"He's sadder than my father, I think."
"Christians are strange people."
"It's true."
"They accept nothing, they think they can change the world. When a man dies, they do not know it is the will of God. Therefore they can never be happy."
"Yusef will never be happy. He gives me strange looks sometimes; I don't know what to say."
"You, Bizbouz, don't know what to say?"
"He looks and looks."
"He's looking for Driss. You resemble your brother."
"Sometimes I am afraid."
"Why?"
"He begins to tremble all over. It frightens me."
"You must help him, Omar."
"How?"
"By talking. Talk and talk to him. Don't stop."
"Talk? That's all I do."
"I thought you didn't know what to say."
"I don't know what I'm saying, but the words come out."
"Good."
Omar took out his own knife and helped Mohamed. Cane leaves have sharp edges, and they were receiving little cuts on their hands.
"Mohamed, is Tarfaya far from Tangier?"
"Yes, far. Far away in the desert."
"I'm going there."
"To Tarfaya? It's a long way to travel."
"Yusef said he would take me."
"Good. When will that be?"
"I don't know. When he returns to the desert. One member from our family must go. None of us has ever been there, and I will go with Yusef."
"Good. What do you have in that sack?"
"Oranges."

Mohamed I painted the benches and tables green; the stone foundation had already been whitewashed, twice. Glass balls from fishermen's nets, cork floats, and squid bones were hung from the rafters or fastened to the walls as decorations. As soon as the interior was completed, another terrace was constructed to one side, partly as another area for guests, partly as a plot for a small garden. M'siksif planted white gladiolas, sunflowers, melon vines, and corn; inside were potted plants whose scent wards off mosquitoes.

One day M'siksif arrived with his yellow kabyla dog, Tony, which he tied to the door and fed on bread and fish. They all lived on bread and fish. During the days it took to construct the café, both Mohameds were sleeping on the site, and by day one of them was almost always out on the rocks with a long cane pole, fishing for the pot. They caught sardines, porgies, red snappers, squids, and eels, so there was always something to eat. After a while the sun dried out the green branches and ferns, and the café became practically invisible against the sandstone cliff. M'siksif left the boys in charge of serving up glasses of tea and coffee to the fishermen who passed every day along that coast. As it was still early in the season, the beach at Merkala remained empty except for a few tourists from the camping area, and a solitary Moroccan, who came every day with donkeys to collect sand.

May 19 This afternoon M'siksif and I walked out to Agla. The weather has been ultra-terrible lately, but today was clear. The countryside is swelling and bursting with rains, which have persisted very late in the season this year. We crossed emerald meadows, where the ground is wet and spongy underfoot, with the sound of water trickling everywhere. The pastures are a mass of wild flowers, the woods are full of ferns and calla lilies, and wild irises grow so thickly together that in some places they appear as mauve carpets. Partridges and doves fly up from our path, and hoopoes flit from tree to tree in their peculiar undulating flight. Fat figs appear with fresh little leaves straight out of the trunks.

The hawks were up. Hundreds of them had risen from the woods and fields and were gliding in spirals high over the Old Mountain. And above them storks were gathering and circling and calling to each other before setting off on their annual migration to Europe. Apparently they do not like to fly over water, and they appeared indecisive at the outset, a swirl of great birds in the eddying air. As M'siksif and I watched, the storks suddenly lined out and headed across the Straits. But the wind was against them, and after an effort which took them nearly halfway to Spain, they returned in confusion, flapping desperately to regain the land.

The gate to El Hassani's house was locked, and the house itself looked boarded up and empty. It seemed like a good piece of property, with enormous eucalyptus trees at the entrance and an orchard visible on a lower level.

May 20 I desire to be with Moroccans now, I find their company soothing; they have a capacity to do away with loneliness. M'siksif and I talked about how Tangier used to be in the old days, I listened to more gossip about El Hassani, and then I found myself telling him about Driss. Walking along by his side, I felt quite safe in that spring landscape. At this point, what can I trust more than nature? Morocco has such resources of beauty, and this gives me comfort. And pain, too, because we used to take such pleasure from looking out on the world together. No more that parallel vision. They are saying that the harvests this year will be the best in the memory of the people.

# *The Late Spring Torrent*

"WHO'S THERE?" a voice called out.

"Mohamed, is that you?" Cabell replied.

"Who is it?"

"It's me, Yusef!"

A flashlight was played on him.

"Yusef, come in quickly out of the rain."

They led him back into the kitchen under the cliff, where the samovar was bubbling away and a tajine simmered over a charcoal brazier. It was a warm dry place.

"Take your clothes off, Yusef. Why are you out on a night like this?"

"I don't know."

"You Christians are all crazy."

"So this is M'siksif's summer café."

"We built it for him, and this is where we live."

Cabell stripped down and was handed a djellaba, which he

slipped over his head. The wet clothes were taken away, and a place was made for him on the mat. Mohamed I poured him a glass of hot tea; Mohamed II prepared a pipe of kif.

"Yusef, we haven't seen you in a long time."

"We were waiting for you to come to the café," Mohamed II said.

"Where have you been, Yusef?"

"At Agla."

"Ah, been looking for the great frogs, have you? M'siksif told us about them."

"No, I want to meet a woman who lives out there, a woman who dresses like a man."

"Ah. M'siksif told us about her, too. What sort of woman is that, Yusef?" Mohammed II asked.

"I don't know, I haven't seen her yet."

"But why does she dress like a man?"

"How can she pray at the mosque?"

"I don't know."

Mohamed II placed the clay pot before them and took away the lid; a cloud of steam rose from the bubbling combination of fresh sardines, tomatoes, and carrots. The brown bread was broken, and they ate until the pot was clean. Afterward they leaned back against the rock wall. A sebsi was filled and passed around; more tea was prepared.

"Why do you wish to meet this woman, Yusef?" Mohamed II asked.

"I've heard a lot about her. She crossed into Rio de Oro on foot, without a passport."

"Yes? Did she find work?"

"I don't think she was looking for work."

"Then what did she want?"

"I don't know what she wants. Something from the desert. To be a person other than herself. That's what I'd like to know."

"A woman can never be a man, even if she wants to."

"Do you ever wish you were back in the Sahara, Mohamed?"

Mohamed II shook his head.

"You, Mohamed?"

"No."

"They don't have rain like this in the Sahara."

"They could use it, though."

"That's true."

"There was nothing for us there, Yusef," Mohamed II said. "We had no work there, no friends."

"You had both, Yusef."

Cabell nodded. "I was lucky."

For a moment nobody spoke. The Mohameds were looking at Cabell.

"It was God's will, Yusef."

"Of course."

"Yusef," Mohamed I said, "be like us."

"What do you mean?"

"When a man dies, we forget; we go on about our business."

"But I loved him."

"What use has love now? Forget him."

"I can't."

"Life goes on—you can't change it."

"So you two built this café," Cabell remarked, looking around. "It's a good café."

"Yes."

"How do you like living down here by the beach?"

"We like it," put in Mohamed II, "but we want more work."

"You mean work as masons."

"Yes. Perhaps we can find work in Tangier—will you help us, Yusef?"

"Have you been to the port?"

"No."

"There's always something going on at the port."

"We don't know. You know best."

"I'll do what I can to find you something."

"Thank you, Yusef."

There was a noise outside, and Mohamed I jumped to his feet; a clasp knife fell from his pocket and clattered against the rocks.

"What was that?"

"Sit down, Tfakaz, it was only the wind," Mohamed II said.

Mohamed I retrieved his knife, went to the doorway of the café, and peered out into the darkness.

"You don't hear the dog barking, do you?" Mohamed II said. "Look at him, he's sound asleep, and you think the house is surrounded. Come back in here."

"Why do you call him Tfakaz?" Cabell asked.

"It means 'the startled one.' "

"Ah. So Mohamed I is the nervous one and Mohamed II is the calm one."

"Don't you think Tfakaz deserves his name, Yusef?"

"He's kind of itchy, isn't he?"

"He can't sit still for one minute."

"Look at him," Mohamed I broke in, pointing at Mohamed II. "He has mud in his veins."

"A slow mover, is he?"

"Slow? A regular turtle."

"So you two complement each other."

"Living with Mohamed II is like having a millstone tied to your leg."

"Hah! Listen to him talk," Mohamed II put in. "He sleeps with one eye open. He can't stop jiggling, or sharpening his knife. With him in it the whole café shakes."

"Well, don't wiggle too much. Isn't it dangerous to build a café under this cliff? Aren't you two afraid that the rain might set rocks loose on you?"

"If the rocks fall, it is the will of God," Mohamed II said.

"We are not afraid," Mohamed I added.

Rain continued to beat on the roof of the café; several leaks had developed, and pots were placed to catch the dripping water.

"Still coming down hard," Cabell commented, looking up at the ceiling.

"Yes—you must stay with us here tonight."

"Can I? Will there be enough room?"

"Do you think we would let you go on a night like this?"

"But I was already wet when I arrived."

"You're dry now, and warm, aren't you?"

"Yes."

"Then you will sleep here."

"I have my hotel room."

"But that's no good for you, Yusef. You stay inside and never see your friends."

"How do you know?"

"We know, Omar tells us everything."

"Ah, Omar. What else does he say?"

"That you need us now."

"Not only now."

"Then don't go away, Yusef, don't even think of it."

Mohamed II brought out some blankets. As they arranged their sleeping places on the mat, Mohamed I collected the empty glasses and removed the charcoal brazier to the outer room. Mohamed II leaned over and blew out the lantern, and they lay down together in the dark. Soon they were asleep and snoring.

The rain kept on through the night, by morning the Jews' River had risen, and muddy water was rushing across the beach in a gulch cut through the sand. The bay of Merkala was stained red, and muddy waves tugged sluggishly at the rocks below M'siksif's café. A mass of kelp had drifted into a cove at the end of the beach, where it was rotting on the rocks, exuding the pungent odor of iodine. Beyond the pall of rain fishing boats passed by on their way to the fishing grounds off Cape Spartel; the soft throb of their motors was audible through the mist.

The Mohameds went off to town to buy supplies, leaving Cabell behind to watch over the café. Some Moroccan boys had taken up positions on the rocks and were casting into the sea with their long cane poles. From time to time one would draw out a wriggling fish, and there was some excitement when one of them hooked a large octopus. It clung to the rocks with its suckers and would not let go; once it was ashore, one of the boys grabbed hold of it and turned it inside out with his bare hands.

Not much later the Mohameds returned, reporting that the streets of Dradeb were so flooded that automobiles could not pass. Several houses had collapsed in the rain, and the bridge looked as if it might fall into the river if the water rose any higher. For lunch the three of them dipped pieces of bread into a can of tunafish, and washed it down with glasses of tea. Afterward Cabell rolled up in a blanket and slept again. It seemed that the rain would never let up, but by late afternoon it had diminished to a fine drizzle. When Cabell woke up he said he ought to be going.

Making his way over the rocks, he came out onto a piece of the asphalt road above the beach at Merkala. At the back of the beach stood a white cement structure with the words MERKALA MILK BAR painted in large letters on one wall. Now it lay midstream in the river and seemed in danger of breaking up and being washed out to sea. So great was the force of the current that it was peeling the asphalt surface off the road and destroying the roadbed underneath. Great cakes of dark-brown earth were slipping off the bank and disappearing into the flood. A group of Moroccans had gathered to witness the fate of the milk bar. Some carried umbrellas against the rain; others held pieces of cardboard over their heads; one man was actually naked except for a pair of muddy shorts; but most wore brown djellabas, wide straw hats, and rubber boots. Standing a safe distance from the caving bank, they speculated among themeslves on the milk bar's chances for survival.

"Yusef! Yusef!" a voice called out.

Cabell turned and saw Omar approaching along the road. He was carrying a bottle of milk under his arm. They shook hands.

"What are you doing here, Omar?"

"Same as you, watching the flood. Will the house fall into the sea?"

"I don't know. What's that you've got there?"

"Goat milk."

"Do you like to drink goat milk?"

"It's for my sister; she rubs it on her face."

"Rubs it on her face?"

"I know it sounds crazy, but it works. Her face used to be covered with red spots, but now it has become clean and smooth, like a baby's. She's going to be married soon; an officer from the army camp wants her."

"So you're transporting goat milk."

"I fetch it from the goat farm at Moujehedine."

The milk bar shuddered, and a piece of wall fell away into the flood. The crowd murmured with excitement as all of a sudden three men appeared on the roof. Two were dressed in brown djellabas, while the third, a head shorter than his companions, wore a white burnoose and a white turban. They were searching for a way to escape from the milk bar.

"Smugglers," whispered Omar.

"How do you know?"

"The milk bar is where they meet and hide their contraband."

"Is it true?"

"It's quiet during the day, but at night they gamble with cards and money. Some of the games end up with fights; people have been killed in there."

"Are you sure these three are smugglers?"

"Why would anybody remain so long in a house that might be washed away any minute? They didn't want to show themselves."

Another section of the wall collapsed and was swallowed by the water; the smugglers were beginning to panic. One scaled partly down the wall and leaped onto a boulder in the middle of the stream, where he tottered for an instant, then fell into the water and disappeared. The crowd moaned; but a few seconds later he could be seen dragging himself up onto the muddy beach downstream. The second stripped off his djellaba and simply leaped into the flood and struck out for shore. Everyone was now watching the young man in the immaculate white burnoose and turban; the spectators sensed that he was proud of his clothes and didn't want to get them wet.

"Look, Yusef, that's a woman," said Omar, pointing. "It's the Nazarene from Agla!"

"How do you know?"

"I've seen her in the cafés around Dradeb. She always wears those white clothes."

Two other Moroccans standing nearby overheard Omar's words and joined the discussion. They agreed with Omar that she lived in Agla with "a great many dogs."

"What do you mean?" Yusef said. "I was in Agla yesterday. The house where she's supposed to live is deserted. I didn't see any dogs, either."

"What? You were there?"

"Yes."

"Why?"

"I wanted to meet her."

Meanwhile, the figure on the roof had pulled off the white burnoose and turban. From the bank on the far side of the flood his two wet and muddy companions were exhorting him to leap before the milk bar collapsed. Just then another large piece of the building cracked off and fell away into the water, but only partly submerged below the swirling surface. Gathering the burnoose under one arm, he jumped deftly to the exposed corner of the wall; in another instant he had leaped across to the boulder from which his friend had fallen, where he got his feet beneath him, bounded to the bank, and scrambled safely up. When the onlookers cheered, and shouted "Billygoat!" and "Pussycat!" he turned and made a little flourish of acknowledgment across the water. Then his friends joined him, and the three of them began to climb the rocky cliff to the Marshan.

"There they go. That fellow really can jump, Omar. Are you sure it's a woman?"

"Yes. Everybody knows about her."

"I must find out where she lives. You say she hangs out in the cafés of Dradeb?"

"Yes, and in the Café of the Garden of Frogs near the cow market."

"Elephant frogs?"
"No."
"Why do they call it that?"
"Because there's a swamp behind the café, where frogs sing all night. Little ones."
"Oh."
The crowd began to disperse. Omar and Cabell were walking along the muddy road toward Dradeb. Mist and fine rain enveloped the shadowy cedar trees on the hillside.
"Yusef, do you think the café will be washed out to sea?"
"I don't know."
A car came by, splashing muddy water from the puddles, and they were forced to jump aside.
"So your sister rubs goat milk on her face."
"Both my sisters will be married soon, and already they're jealous of each other. Who has the prettiest clothes? The handsomest husband? Who will have a bigger house? Aye! I told them that if they don't stop this nonsense, I won't visit them in their houses; after the weddings I'll never see them again. I think they listened to that."
"Are you a misogynist, Omar?"
"What's that?"
"A misogynist is a person who hates women."
"I don't hate women. They just do a lot of boring things."
"I know what you mean."
"Before long I must find a room of my own in another part of the city."
"You may come and stay with me anytime you like."
"Yes? In the hotel?"
"Of course. If you don't want to go home after school, come to the hotel. You can have a room of your own or you can sleep with me."
They crossed the bridge at the bottom of the Old Mountain and entered Dradeb. The street was awash with mud and water and dozens of tiny children ran wildly about. The rain had stopped at last and people were coming out of their houses.

Charcoal braziers were glowing in doorways. As darkness fell, a last-minute opening somewhere in the western sky let through a clear light which presented the chaotic sprawl of Dradeb as a precise geometric pattern of dwellings on a hillside.

May 24 Do the fishermen know what solace the sound of their throbbing marine engines bring to those on the shore?

May 29 The Moroccan fishermen who frequent M'siksif's café are quiet, kif-smoking, thoughtful (they wait on Allah), and wise in their patience. I like to be with these people now, and I'm spending many days out at Merkala. I've made friends with the blind beggar woman who sits by the side of the road with her daughter. Apparently she was raped by a farmer coming to market one day and produced this little girl who leads her around. Then there are the children who carry bread to the ovens. The other day I had a talk with Afif, the cute little hunchback boy with the beautiful eyes. He's fed up with his menial work, for which he is paid in what he carries on his head—bread. The red-haired donkey girl, who brings wood from the mimosa forests of Agla, smiles at me, and I've been watching the country women coming down the hill, carrying bundles of sticks on their backs, bound for the ovens. They chant with vehemence to drive away the pain of their loads. Driss would have been amused at my eagerness to know these people.

Morocco today is a Mediterranean civilization similar in many ways to others of the past which we admire. Days are often sunlit, opening to gentleness and tolerance, giving encouragement and meaning to life. An easy natural beauty exists here, to which I wish I could say "of course," and so be excited by the possibilities of each new day. Although I am incapable of such spontaneity, I feel that Morocco is looking after me in its own way.

June 3—the fortieth day after the burial of Driss. I was sitting on the wall of the cemetery of Bouarakia, listening to some tolba recite passages from the Koran. From my position on the wall I had a wide view of the city before me, of Tangier bay and Cape Malabata, and of Spain and Gibraltar beyond. A procession of light cumulus clouds over the Straits reminded me that good weather is here to stay, and with it the extraordinary clarity of sun and sea and air. I am looking forward to a long hot North African summer.

Then the tolba raised their voices in praise of Allah on behalf of another whom the darkness drew down. Whoever it is will not see the sun again. Down in Tarfaya there will be chanting, too; Driss's family has sent money to the local tolba to pray and eat couscous on the gravesite out in the desert. It must be hot in Tarfaya now.

# *The Spanish Consul*

SEATED IN A WOODEN CHAIR next to the hotel window, Cabell was looking down across the maze of Arab housetops to the Place de la Kasbah. A long black Mercedes with the red-and-yellow flags of Spain flying from the front fenders was pulled up on the cobble yard, and a chauffeur in a gray uniform was dashing about the vehicle, attempting to keep a band of ragged children at bay. When the chauffeur charged, the urchins retreated, while others on the opposite side ran up, tugged at the flags, and tried to open the doors. Along a rampart overlooking the sea several old, bearded Moroccan gentlemen in brown djellabas crouched down out of the wind and impassively observed the game. The day was clear and bright, and the sunlight reflected so strongly off the white walls and roofs that Cabell had to shield his eyes from the glare.

"Are you listening, Señor Cabell?"

"Yes, I'm listening. Go on."

"Your attention seems to be occupied by whatever is happening outside that window."

"I'm sorry. Please continue."

Standing in the center of the room was a tall, slender man dressed in a blue pinstripe suit. He had a handsome face and spoke Spanish with a clear Castilian accent.

"I hope you understand how important it is to my government that you return to the Sahara, Señor Cabell. You are under contract to do so."

"I know that."

"But in your letter to the Ministry of Overseas Territories you don't state clearly whether or not you plan to return. They need a more definite reply."

"Yes."

"Naturally they hope it will be a positive one."

"Of course."

"What are your intentions?"

"I've none, except I wish to remain in Tangier for the time being."

"Can you tell me how long that might be?"

"No."

"Señor Cabell, you know that you could forfeit your contract if you stay away from the job for more than three months."

"I'm not going to put any time limits on myself."

"Then you won't say when you might be returning to the desert?"

"Señor Escobar, are you familiar with your Sahara?"

"No, I'm sorry to say that I am not."

"Then let me tell you something. In the Sahara, summer conditions are such that in the interior little or no exploration is carried on from June to September."

"I realize that."

"Today is the seventh of June. So for the next three months practically all activity down there comes to a halt."

"Yes."

"I need to have at least that time here in Tangier, maybe more."

"All right."

"You can sue me for breach of contract, you can block my accounts in El Aaiun and in Madrid, you can do whatever you like, but I'm not moving out of this city until I'm ready! Do you hear?"

"You don't have to shout, Señor Cabell."

"I'm sorry."

"In that case can we expect you to return in September?"

"I don't know."

"I suppose you have your reasons."

"I do, and you must accept them."

"Can you tell me what they are?"

"Not now, just accept them. Please."

"Of course, I accept them, Señor Cabell."

"Good."

"We cannot force you against your will to return to the Sahara."

"I always spend my summers in Tangier."

Down in the square two men were standing in the shadow of the high white wall of the prison kitchen. Too far away to be overheard, they were gesticulating with their hands as they talked excitedly. One of the men was a policeman; suddenly he raised his arm as if to strike the other, and the slanting rays of the sun caught on some metallic object in his hand.

"Señor Cabell?"

"Yes."

"I've been instructed by the Ministry to have a definite reply from you."

"I just gave it to you!"

"Then you will definitely go back."

"Eventually."

"I must have a date."

Cabell got to his feet and began to pace back and forth. "In the autumn, when the weather cools off."

"Can you be more precise?"

"No!"

"Señor Cabell, please don't shout. You must be aware that your contract was made in accordance with a timetable within which the mineral wealth of Rio de Oro would be surveyed."

"Señor Escobar, listen to me."

"I'm listening, Señor Cabell."

"The Spanish Sahara covers an area almost as large as Morocco; there's an indigenous population of about twenty-five thousand, a nomadic Bedouin people practically invisible on the face of the land. You have got about the same number of soldiers down there, but you haven't got any schedule."

"That's not true."

"And you haven't got any oil!"

"I wish you wouldn't shout. Nobody knows yet."

"I've told you that already, I've told everybody over and over again, but nobody will believe it."

"But one can never be sure."

"Look, the big American oil companies sent their teams all over the territory and came up with nothing."

"Except one of the largest deposits of phosphates in the world."

"All right, so now you have enough phosphates to last you for the next hundred years, but no oil."

"My government has reason to believe there is oil in the Sahara, Señor Cabell."

"Not a drop."

"Although none has been discovered so far, there are geological indications."

"There are indications, that's correct, but the Americans found nothing and went away. Your people have found nothing."

Escobar lit a cigarette and exhaled a cloud of smoke.

"Your government just refuses to believe that there isn't any oil, that's all there is to it," Cabell added.

Escobar shrugged his shoulders.

"For the past three years I've been all over your Sahara and probably know it as well as anybody, perhaps better than anybody."

"And you've found no oil."

"I've found no oil because it doesn't exist."

"Señor Cabell, if you're so convinced that there is no oil in the Sahara, why do you even think of going back?"

"I don't know. Sometimes I think I'm off my head."

"You must have your reasons."

Cabell ceased his pacing and sat down heavily in the chair. "Yes, I do. It's because I've found something else. Something more important than oil."

"Can you tell me what it is?"

"Water."

"Yes, I'd heard that water had been discovered."

"Do you realize that beneath Rio de Oro are areas of fresh water that have never been tapped? The reserves are enormous. Now listen, does the Spanish government really want me to return?"

"They seem very anxious that you do, yes."

"Is my familiarity with the land valuable to you?"

"Apparently very much so."

"Then tell your government people to allow me to look for water, and not oil."

"I can't do that."

"Why not?"

"Madrid has asked me to contact you and to inform them of your plans. I know nothing of the details of your work."

"Don't you understand? You've got land, you've got water, and you've got phosphates to make fertilizer, all in unlimited quantities. Spain can turn the Sahara into a garden."

"That barren land?"

"That barren land can be a very rich and beautiful one."

"I suppose so."

"All the possibilities are there!"

"I see. Please don't raise your voice."

"That's the sort of enterprise to which I would be very willing to give my services."

"I agree that the prospect is an exciting one."

"Tell them that! I've already told them a dozen times, so I don't expect they will listen; but tell them anyway. Say Joseph Cabell will return to the Sahara as a ground-water geologist. No other way!"

On the roof of the prison a policeman was standing, holding a submachine gun by a leather strap. The wind was blowing with great force, and the surface of the bay was frothy with whitecaps. In the square, the conversation was becoming more animated, and shouting could be heard above the wind. Pacing back and forth, the policeman stepped into the sunlight and was followed by the other man. There was a brief exchange, and they both retreated into the blue shadow. Then another policeman appeared, with a young man handcuffed to him. Cabell, who had been watching the scene from the window, jumped to his feet.

"My God, that's Mohamed!"

"Who?"

Escobar stepped to the window and looked out.

"A young Moroccan friend of mine. He came with me from the Sahara. The police have got him!"

"What's he done?"

"I don't know, but I must find out. Excuse me, please!"

Cabell went out of the room and ran down the stairs. Escobar, after a moment's hesitation, grabbed his hat and followed him.

* * *

"Let's sit down here and have a coffee, Cabell."

"Here in public, where people can see us? Do you think we ought to?"

"Are you mad, man? What's the matter with you? Sit down."

"I'm sorry, but I've been in the police station all day."

"Are you in trouble?"

Cabell and Amigo Maxwell took seats at the table and ordered coffees.

"Not me. It's a friend of mine, a young fellow who came out of the Sahara with me."

"I thought you told me the boy died."

"This is another one."

"Oh."

"I was sitting in my hotel room, talking with the Spanish Consul General, when I looked out the window and saw the boy being led handcuffed to the Kasbah jail."

"What did he do?"

"Apparently he'd taken to robbing people at knife-point in the Medina at night."

"Nasty boy."

"He would take their money, clothes, shoes—everything—and leave them naked and penniless in the street."

"Tangier is full of hoodlums."

"No, he's not that kind."

"These days you never know."

"He's just fed up with having no work and no money."

"Who wouldn't be?"

"It's my fault, too, because I promised to find a job for him, and I hadn't done anything about it."

"What can a boy like that do?"

"He's a trained mason."

"Did you get a chance to speak to him?"

"No, they were just taking him through the prison door when Escobar and I got there. I don't even think he saw me."

"Ah."

"So I went to the police station to find out what they were going to do with him. Have you ever been there?"

"Once a year to renew my residence card, nothing more."

"Then you know those bare corridors with the wooden benches and naked light bulbs?"

"Awful place."

"All afternoon I sat in an empty room containing one wooden desk, with a chair in front and a chair behind."

"The place is always full of people just lounging around, doing nothing."

"Are they police or not?"

"Who knows?"

"Nobody wears a uniform."

"What about your friend?"

"They assure me that he'll stand trial within a month."

"And until then?"

"He remains in the Kasbah jail."

"That's bad. Apparently they sleep several hundred to a room. Squares have been marked out on the floor with each man's number."

"Oh."

"But I hear that it's become so crowded that they practically have to sleep two deep."

* * *

Cabell sprang, arched his back, and plunged into the sea. Leaving an explosion of bubbles behind, he swam down beneath the surface, passed through a tunnel formed by two massive boulders leaning against each other, glided over a field of kelp swaying in the current, causing a school of porgies to veer and dart away, and came to the surface where another huge boulder stood out of the water. A wave breaking over the rock washed him away in a swirl of white water, but he swam back, grasped at the seaweed and clusters of mussels, and lifted himself up onto the rock. Higher up, there was a warm dry spot out of reach of the waves, where the rock was flat and smooth, and Cabell stretched out on his belly.

Close to the surface of the water sunlight seems filtered through a blue lens. A fishing boat passing with a faint engine noise rose and disappeared with the swell. When the boat rounded the point and went out of sight altogether, its track did not quickly vanish, but remained like a chalkmark on the undulating surface. From high up on the limestone cliffs, distant water lanes could be seen leading to the Spanish side of the Straits, where the big ships slide in the easy water from one sea to the next. The sun was directly overhead, flaring down out of a pallid sky.

"Yusef! Yusef!"

The voice came across the water, and Cabell looked up. Omar was standing on the shore, grinning and holding up a red snapper. Perched among the chunks of rock fallen from the cliffs, Moroccan boys were fishing with long cane poles. Others were pounding and mixing bait, chatting and smoking kif, or plunging off the high rocks and splashing around in the sea.

"Yusef!"

This time Omar was pointing at the figure of a man high up on the rocks. It was M'siksif. He was waving excitedly at Cabell, beckoning him to come in. Cabell got to his feet, dove into the water, and swam to shore. M'siksif scrambled down over the rocks to meet him.

"Yusef, you've heard about Mohamed?" M'siksif was speaking breathlessly.

"Yes, I was there when they took him to prison."

"Not Tfakaz; this time it's his friend, Mohamed II."

"What has he done? Have they put him in jail, too?"

"No, but this morning the soldiers came."

"Why?"

"He's been drafted into the army."

"What?"

"He leaves tomorrow for the training camp at El Hajeb!"

# *The Blackout*

ALL AFTERNOON it had been swelling and mounting. Pedestrians along the main boulevard stopped to gape at it; down at the port cognizant fishermen squinted at it and one by one canceled the evening trip to the tuna grounds off Cape Spartel. But they did not go to their homes, choosing instead to remain in port with the boats. By sunset the cloud looked like a great red anvil towering above the Straits, and the evening Dakota from Gibraltar made a long detour over the Moroccan coast to avoid it. Sunset was spectacular: clouds scudding out of the west turned crimson as they rushed to join the vortex. Many Moroccans carried their tea things to the rooftops in order to sit and watch and speculate; later the women looked to the shutters and took the washing off the lines.

After nightfall streaks of electricity etched the darkness all the length of the Straits, and were answered mysteriously, almost rhythmically, by patterns of sheet lightning beyond the

Pillars of Hercules, somewhere out over the Mediterranean. Lights along the Spanish coast were plainly visible, with the lighthouses of Tarifa and Trafalgar flashing out their routine signals, and sometimes, when many bolts snapped together in succession, rugged hills far inland were illuminated. But no sound came from these electrical flurries: over the city the atmosphere hung, hot and heavy; there was no movement of air; and the streets were busy as usual with late shoppers and strollers. The storm seemed to be moving away.

About nine o'clock came the first rumblings, as from distant cannon fire, and sudden gusts of air lifted the awnings of sidewalk cafés, causing men to look up from their coffees and conversations. Women who had been sitting on stoops chatting with neighbors gathered their children about them and went indoors. Within a few minutes the first rain began to fall—large drops spattering on the pavement and sending little geysers of dust up from the dry places. The lights marking the Spanish coastline had disappeared. The lightning was closer now and more incessant, with thunder rattling across the skies. The streets were emptying out: Indian shopkeepers hastily slammed down steel shutters in front of window displays and hurried off; waiters cranked up awnings, moved chairs and tables inside, as customers either paid up and left or took their drinks to the bar.

When the wind began to blow, whole pages of a newspaper discarded in front of the post office raced along the pavement, then suddenly were lifted up and disappeared into the darkness. The surface of the harbor, which had been placid only a few moments before, seethed with choppy swells which poured in through the entrance of the breakwater. Fishermen who had already donned yellow slickers crouched down in the lee of the ice house, lit cigarettes and sebsis, watched their bobbing craft, and waited.

Hail fell first, rattling down everywhere in such quantities that the next day children who had never seen snow before found it stacked in windows in shady places, instinctively made hailballs of it, and threw them at each other. When the rain came down, it was in solid sheets, as if the sky were a reservoir and the bottom had dropped out. Each lightning snap became more violent than the last, with blinding, artificial light, and the intervals between light and thunder crack grew smaller. Then, with one giant burst directly over the town, followed instantly by a clap of thunder rattling away, the lights of Tangier went out. Subsequent flashes revealed the city as one vast sprawling necropolis.

Up at the Hotel Splendid one window had been neglectfully left open. Through it hail was blown, bouncing over the wooden floor, and rain, wetting the curtains and a large part of the room. Lightning flickers showed Joseph Cabell stretched out on his bed. A half-full bottle of Spanish brandy stood on the bedside table, and another empty one had rolled to the center of the room, where a cluster of hailstones banked against it, melting. A few minutes after the lights had gone out there was a sigh and the sound of bedsprings as he attempted to switch on the table lamp, knocking it to the floor in the process.

Groping his way across the room, brandy bottle in hand, he put a foot down on the empty bottle and pitched forward over the table, upsetting it, and landed in a heap by the door. The fall must have stunned him, for he lay quietly for a moment. A hand slowly felt its way up the door frame, found the light switch, and jiggled it. Nothing happened. Picking himself up, he fell backward, slamming into the wall, but kept his balance, took a step forward and tumbled over the table a second time, which, as he did so, oddly righted itself.

He was now lying beneath the open window, and as he began to move again, inadvertently swept an armful of hailstones against his face.

"Ice? . . . Where does this ice come from?" he mumbled, holding it against his face.

His head lay against the base of the bureau, and when one of his hands found a half-open drawer, he lifted himself off the floor. Feeling its way along the top of the bureau, a hand found a box of matches; with two hands working clumsily together, a match was lit and held to a candle. The candle was in its pewter holder before the mirror, beneath Cabell's chin, as he discovered his reflection before him. His face was illuminated by the upshining light, with eyes hidden in black sockets, and long shadows were cast by the chin and nose. When he attempted to smile, the image contorted; he opened his mouth, and a black hole appeared in the mask.

There was a pause for a drink, after which he slammed the bottle down on the bureau; the mirror shook slightly from the blow, causing the image to shudder. Cabell seemed to be staring through himself. Outside the window, meanwhile, clouds rushed by just a few feet overhead; when lightning flickered, dark shapes of houses were briefly illuminated. From somewhere out in the windy darkness came the sound of voices.

The mask slumped to the corner of the mirror as Cabell rested his head on the bureau and made little sucking noises with the bottle. Stuck into the frame of the mirror was a photograph of Driss, taken in the desert. In the wavering candlelight it seemed to tremble, almost to be moving on its own. As Cabell bent forward to look at it, the light caught the glistening eyes.

Cries of alarm were commingling and spreading along the street. Cabell went to the window, stuck his head outside, and looked up and down, but nothing was to be seen. The gusting wind seemed to bring the sounds from all directions at once; far away over the dark hills beyond Malabata, lightning continued to flicker. Cabell returned to the bureau, picked up a pile of photographs and began to look through them.

The first showed himself and Driss on the beach in bathing suits, leaning against each other's shoulders, with a lighthouse in the background. Driss was almost as tall as Cabell, and browner and thinner. . . . In the next, Cabell stood alone, hands on hips, feet apart, wearing a helmet, with a drilling rig behind. . . . Driss and Cabell seated incongruously among veiled, severe Bedouins before a black tent . . . together in the center of a group of smiling Spanish fishermen . . . Driss in a very serious pose on the tower of the lighthouse. . . . With Cabell and a stern Spanish and Bedouin crew, all with helmets . . . Cabell on a donkey . . . A profile of Driss squatting at the base of a mud wall, shading his eyes from the sun . . . Officers of the Legion, with tasseled caps and opened-necked shirts, in a rigid pose, all flexing their muscles. Cabell, partially concealed at the edge of the photo, is the only one smiling. . . . Driss and Cabell, down on their hands and knees, digging a Land Rover out of the sand . . . Driss astride railroad tracks, which stretch away and converge on the horizon . . . cooking over an open fire . . . drinking water from a goat skin . . . far away, kneeling in the sand . . . Cabell sitting cross-legged on the empty plain, absorbed in a book and looking very much like a scholar . . . with Driss on the back of a truck . . . In djellabas, the hoods drawn over their heads, with haggard expressions. Between them sits a toothless old woman, smiling cheerfully. . . .

Cabell dropped the photos and stared at himself. Meanwhile, the confused voices of men and women had given way to the uninterrupted wailings of women, and people were running through the street. Cabell dragged a chair to the window and sat down, resting his head on the sill; for some time he remained there, gripping the sill in both hands, until another rain squall broke over the town, and he withdrew.

The image which now heaved into sight was wet. Water dripped from the chin into the candle flame, causing it to sputter, almost to be extinguished. He picked up the remaining photographs. There was Driss asleep on the ground beneath a palm tree . . . sharpening a knife on a stone . . . breaking cone sugar with a hammer . . . pouring tea . . . offering a glass to the camera. . . . Cabell with a tame gazelle . . . Driss in a bathing suit, fishing off rocks with a long cane pole . . . holding up a fish . . . Cabell looking down at a lizard he holds in his hands . . . with an arm around a baby camel, the mother standing nearby and watching closely . . . A formal Saharan portrait of Cabell and Driss, framed by cardboard palm trees, camels, and Arabic script, staring straight into the camera, like a nineteenth-century explorer and his native guide . . .

"That square in El Aaiun, I should have said we're going to Las Palmas and that's all there is to it . . . *but I didn't!*"

His hand came forward, smashing the candle to the floor, and he was on his way across the room.

". . . seduced like a fool by the fatalism of the desert? Allah will take care of everything, you believed that, didn't you? He did, all right. . . ."

When the door came open, the curtains billowed out in the rush of air. Plunging onto the balcony, he stumbled down the stairs, making such a racket that the Sultan of Dogs set up a clamor from the other side of the garden.

The downpour had abated, but a fine rain continued to fall; there was the sound of water everywhere. The way was slippery, and Cabell hugged the walls for support as his path led him in the direction of the voices. Soon he came upon a crowd of people assembled in a narrow alley. A house had collapsed in the rain, and flashlights played over a mass of broken beams and smashed masonry as men worked furiously to clear the debris. One bright light clung steadfastly, however, to a small arm protruding from between two beams high up in the ruin, and the arm was not moving. From deep inside the house came the persistent shrieks of a woman, almost a chant, which were answered by wailings and high-pitched animal cries of her sisters in the street. The men were shouting back and forth as they dug with iron bars and shovels and pulled pieces of the wreckage away with their bare hands.

A hand was placed gently on Cabell's arm and a voice spoke his name.

"Ah, Boujma, there you are. Look at this thing that has happened. Is there anything we can do?"

"No, Señor Cabell, nothing."

"Do you know these people?"

"No, I don't. Come with me, Señor Cabell. You don't want to watch this." Cabell was wobbling on his feet, and Boujma took hold of his arm.

"Let me go!"

"It is better that you return to the hotel."

"Why?"

"You're drunk, Nazarene," said a voice.

Cabell turned to face a man in a djellaba. "Why do you speak?"

"Speak?" the man snarled. "I can smell you with my nose. We all smell you."

"Let's not stay here, Señor Cabell. There are others, friends, who will bring the people from the house. If some are dead, then they will not want strangers to see. It is the will of God."

"What has he willed for that child?" Cabell was pointing at the tiny arm.

"That it will die young."

"What if someone cares enough to make an effort?"

"What effort?"

"To save its life! What if it's not yet dead? What's God's will then?"

"Then it is written that the child shall live."

"Has its fate been altered?"

"Oh, no. Fate can never change."

"Then what's the difference between life and death?"

Boujma shrugged. "That the child has been saved. . . ."

Cabell broke away from Boujma and began to climb recklessly through the debris. At first the going was easy, and he was able to make his way with some agility through the rescue workers. Higher up, however, his clumsiness became apparent, and murmurs of alarm and disapproval rose from the women when it was seen that he was attempting to approach the child. Murmurs turned to shrieks of indignation as he was reaching up through the broken beams; it looked as if he might actually take hold of the tiny arm. All the lights centered on him at once, and one of the men who had been digging came over and roughly pushed him aside, accompanied by a curse in Arabic. Cabell, confounded by the man's action, nevertheless made another attempt to reach for the arm, and this time was knocked away by the handle of a shovel. The women were screaming at him now, and seemed as if they would enter the wreckage themselves, in order to drag him out. When he lost his balance from the blow and fell backward, landing near them, they surged forward and began to kick him and pound him with their fists. So bewildered that he made no attempt to resist, except to cover his head with his hands, he was receiving blows all over the body, as the women turned their fury against this stranger. Finally Boujma, with the help of another man, succeeded in driving them back and dragged him to his feet. His nose was bloody and his clothes were ripped, but he managed to stagger off after Boujma. The women were still shrieking at him and cursing him in their own language, while the men gave him looks of silent disapproval and returned to the rescue work.

When they reached the hotel, Boujma vainly tried to wrestle him through the doorway, but the old man hadn't the strength to handle the cursing and sobbing Cabell, who was twice his size and refused to go inside. In the end he had no choice but to let him go and sadly watch him stumble off into the darkness.

June 19 Don't know what's happening to me. I'm not myself—depressed, confused. Unable to see. This morning, more blundering—wandered out into the street and was knocked down by a taxi. Not hurt, just shaken up. The taxi driver was a nice fellow—he was more scared than I was and bought me a coffee. Still shaking, can't recognize my own handwriting. So clear today, sea clipping the sky evenly . . . I would like to walk that line.

Following orders from M'siksif, I sleep at Merkala now, not in the hotel any more. I look after the café while he's in town. The days begin early, and generally I am already awake when the sun's first rays strike these cliffs. It's so easy to go in swimming here, to splash around in cold water, to run naked on the deserted beach, to make one's own coffee, and to join in conversation with the fishermen. I feel compelled to do these things; even so, accidents like the one this morning do occur.

My schedule: About seven o'clock I walk into town, buy tea and doughnuts for Mohamed, which I deliver through the bars of the prison gate. By nine o'clock the day is beginning to stoke up, and I return to Merkala and spend the day by the sea—reading and sunning and bathing—a beachcomber type of existence. In the late afternoon I return once more to town, buy cigarettes and hot food, and again hand them through the bars. Evenings are languid; often I take one last swim before shutting the café for the night. Sometimes the water is full of phosphorus; others it's like swimming in ink. I become a fish watching the shore; often I have to repress the desire to turn my back to it and just swim out and out.

# *The Moussem at Sidi Kacem*

As THE FARMERS' BUS turned off onto the dirt road, the lights swept the darkness, briefly illuminating a field of wheat being flattened by the wind. A mud farmhouse stood by itself, and an old skinny horse stared dumbly into the lights; then both vanished into the windy blackness. The headlights swung back to the dusty road, and the ancient bus jolted on. Blasts of wind were raising great vortexes of dust before it; sometimes the wind would suddenly change direction and buffet the bus from the front or sides; then the dust would filter in through the cracked windowpanes and between the floorboards; and the passengers sneezed and coughed in the darkness.

The road was crowded with people all headed in the same direction—men in djellabas hurried along on foot, aided by the wind at their backs, country folk on donkeys and horses, city folk riding scooters and motorbikes, Moroccan ladies with their white haiks billowing out before them—they were all on their way to the moussem at Sidi Kacem. Ahead could be seen the red taillights of many more buses, trucks, and taxis; from behind, more vehicles sent their bright beams sweeping like long spokes across the hills.

Blowing its horn, the bus plowed through the pedestrians, sending them scattering, and nearly forced a motorbike into a ditch. Cabell, who was driving the bike, managed to steer it through the ruts, and it wobbled back to the main track without upsetting. Shahid was hanging on from behind. Before long they were crossing a flat plain, whose clay surface became so cracked and pitted that they were forced to dismount from the bike and walk. Ahead, hundreds of lights glimmered, and thousands of people could be seen, but as Shahid and Cabell approached from the windward direction, no sound reached them. It was only when they had arrived among the first tents and tethered animals grazing peacefully along the edge of light that other noises displaced the rush of wind in their ears—music and voices and the pounding of a great generator which supplied the electric power.

Illuminated by strings of lights which tugged and swung in the gale, a midway ran along the base of a low sandy hill. On either side a series of grass cafés had been constructed: green olive branches and palm fronds were their walls; blankets and tarpaulins served as roofs; some offered tea and coffee and soup and skewers of meat. Men sat cross-legged on straw mats playing cards, drinking tea, and smoking kif. From others came the sounds of flutes, drums, violins, and tambourines. These last were the most popular, and the grassy walls only partially concealed the faces of women and children gathered outside, peering in at the dancing boys. Interspersed among the cafés were the usual soft-drink stands, candy booths, and the stalls of merchants selling all the things the people might need in their tents.

Up and down the midway marched the crowds—gangs of youths in European dress, country men in rough djellabas, and a few tourists. Soldiers in pairs with rifles slung over their shoulders circulated in the mob. Shahid and Cabell wandered along; suddenly Shahid was surrounded by a group of his admirers. Cabell waited for a minute, but when the talk turned to basketball, he tapped his friend on the shoulder, made a sign and slipped away.

Passing through a row of tents, he entered the olive grove on the sandy hillside; the noise of the midway faded as the crowds were left behind. Here Moroccans who had traveled from Tangier or other parts of the country in order to spend the night near the tomb of Sidi Kacem had pitched their tents. These tents were of every conceivable form: some were strung from the branches of olive trees, others consisted of nothing more than a blanket draped over a crosspiece. Bushes were hollowed out and covered with a piece of material; all manner of brush shelters had been thrown up—anything that would offer protection. Even parachutes were used. All had been securely fastened down against the wind. The tops of the olive trees were thrashing wildly, but in the grove below there was comparative peace. Lamps inside the tents glowed and flickered, and shadows of the occupants were cast on the tent walls. Charcoal braziers and campfires blazed. Tethered animals with piles of fodder before them stood ruminating in the darkness. Most of the men were away in the cafés along the midway; this was the women's domain.

As he was stepping carefully among the tent ropes and stakes, Cabell came to a group of Jilala musicians seated on the ground among the roots of a massive olive tree. Beneath a swinging lamp they played on their drums and reeds as men and women swayed and slumped in hypnotic dance. The women were weaving and bobbing back and forth, spreading their arms and crossing them over their breasts; as the tempo increased they threw their heads back, their faces showing mingled pain and ecstasy, with long black hair flying. One woman suddenly threw herself forward at the feet of the musicians and rolled in the dust, moaning and screaming. The musicians, led by a wild-eyed drummer, slightly altered the tempo to control the woman;

gradually her convulsions subsided, and she rolled over on her back and lay still. It was an old woman. Someone from the circle of spectators came forward and led her away, and the music resumed its former pace. The men were bouncing from one foot to the other, bobbing their heads and slashing at the air with their arms. One was down on his knees, mindlessly dragging his hands back and forth through the soil; the movements of another, an albino, had become so violent that he had to be restrained by a long yellow turban wrapped around his waist, each end gripped tightly by a friend. Flailing his arms about and stamping up the dust with his bare feet, he was soon exhausted. When the musicians took a break, the dancers slumped to the ground, waiting for the music to begin again.

Cabell went among the animals hobbled at the edge of the encampment; it was quiet here, except for the stamping of hoofs and the wind in the high branches. At the border of the olive grove one could see the brightly lit sanctuary of Sidi Kacem; the door was open, and the pilgrims were coming and going. From here the land sloped to the beach. The moon had risen and illuminated the surface of the ocean, with the waves flowing like silver wrinkles against the shore. Moroccans wrapped in djellabas lay on the sand watching the sea. He crossed a dirt track and began to climb a low hill. The wind rushed across these naked hills, tearing at the land, and shiny palmettos vibrated and rattled in the moonlight. Cabell had difficulty making his way through.

Passing through another olive grove, where shadows of thrashing branches raced back and forth over the ground, he approached the summit of the hill where a farmhouse stood. For a moment he stopped before a large wooden door and listened: the wind was hissing through the cracks.

When he knocked a barking of dogs erupted. There must have been a whole pack of them inside; now they were just on the other side of the door, throwing themselves up against it and scratching the wood with their claws. Cabell took a step backward. A voice could be heard from inside, shouting at the dogs, a rather high-pitched voice. The scratching and howling ceased, and the voice spoke in Arabic.

"Who's there?"

"It's me."

A bolt was slid back, a small door within the big door opened, and Cabell stepped through. Before him stood a Moroccan in a white djellaba and white turban.

"Good evening."

"Good evening, sidi."

The man shut the door and slid the bolt through.

"Is Lydia here?"

"No, she's gone to Tangier."

"And her brother, Grigory?"

"Both are in Tangier."

"When do you expect them to return?"

"Sometime tonight. Lydia doesn't like to sleep away from the farm. Please come in and sit down."

Cabell was led across a courtyard as the dogs growled and muttered and lay down again. "It's peaceful here," he commented.

"Tonight, the wind seeks to purge the earth."

"Purge it of what?"

"Of the filth deposited upon it by men."

Beside a high mud wall a donkey was stamping and rattling its chain. A straw mat had been placed on the ground on the far side of the courtyard; there were pillows and straw hassocks. The man indicated with his hand for Cabell to sit down. As Cabell was slipping off his shoes, he disappeared through a doorway and came out again, carrying a brazier with charcoal glowing within it. Moving about very quickly, he placed the brazier at the edge of the mat and made other trips for the kettle and a tray with a teapot and canisters containing tea and sugar and mint. When he finally took a seat cross-legged on the mat, the glow from the brazier showed his face to be very pale. It was a young man, not more than twenty.

"So you think men are filthy?"

"What do you think?"
"How can a man be made clean?"
"Exposure to the elements might help."
"Will they purify the soul?"
"It's happened before."
"And the conscience?"
"What about it?"
"Can it be soothed by the elements?"
"Try giving yourself to the wind."
"Just a minute ago I was grateful to escape it."

The young man was snapping sprigs of mint between his fingers. "They say there will be an eclipse of the moon tonight," he said.

"Is that so?"
"It should begin soon."

"Those dogs are a menace, aren't they?" Cabell was speaking in Arabic. "Lydia has so many of them."

"You don't like dogs?"
"I don't like packs of dogs."
"Lydia loves her dogs."
"She must be collecting them."

"The farmers' children arrive on her doorstep offering puppies."

"Do they know Lydia will take care of them?"

"If their eyes are already open, she feels she must accept them."

"Why?"
"Because they have already looked upon the world."
"There must be at least a dozen of them over there."
"Nine."

Cabell took out his cigarettes, and they both smoked while the water heated up. Holding his cigarette between thumb and forefinger, the young man carried his cigarette to his lips with his right hand while his left remained on his knee.

"What's your name?" Cabell asked.
"Hamid. Yours?"

"Yusef."

"But that's a Moslem name. You're not a Moslem."

"My real name is Joseph, but my Moroccan friends translate it as Yusef."

"Have you come from Tangier to see Lydia?"

"I've been at the moussem, and I thought I'd walk up here to pay them a visit."

"It's a pity you missed them."

"They're old friends of mine, and it's been some time since I've seen them."

"You live in Tangier."

"No, I'm just in Tangier on a temporary basis."

"Where do you come from?"

"I've been in the desert, Rio de Oro."

"Ah! But you're not Spanish."

"American. I've been working for the Spanish in the Sahara."

"What sort of work is that?"

"I'm supposed to be looking for oil."

"Is there oil?"

"None."

"Good."

The kettle began to shake, and the young man poured the boiling water into the teapot, which he then placed on the coals. His turban had become partly undone, and a loop of it fell about his shoulders. The head had recently been shaved and oiled, and his naked scalp gleamed in the moonlight. While the tea was steeping, he brought out a sebsi from his djellaba, filled and lit it, and passed it across to Cabell. By the time Cabell had blown the tiny red ash onto the earth, a glass of steaming mint tea had been placed before him. The courtyard was full of moonlight; the wind seemed far away.

"So, Yusef, you come from Rio de Oro."

"Yes."

"And do you go back there?"

"I don't know yet. I must wait."

"I am waiting, too. It seems that we must both wait."

"What are you waiting for?"

"To return to the Sahara."

"Yes? To what part?"

"To any part, but I think it will be in southern Morocco. Do you know the village of Icht?"

"I've heard the name, but I've never been there."

"It's situated off the road to Tindouf, not far from Foum el Hassan."

"What will you do down there?"

"Icht will be my base."

"For what?"

"A base for exploration."

"What sort of exploration?"

"The desert."

"For what?"

"For me."

"Oh, I see."

"With Icht as my base, I'll be able to set off on long trips into the interior. I can stay away as long as I like, and always have a place to come back to."

"Moroccans are great travelers, but they always return home in the end. Isn't that right?"

"That's right."

"But what are you waiting for? Why are you sitting here in this courtyard?"

"My comrade is away in Europe."

"Oh."

"I'm only awaiting his return, so that we might set off together."

"I see."

"Look, Yusef, the eclipse is beginning!"

A reddish shadow had fallen across the edge of the moon. At that moment the wind changed direction, bringing the sound of distant shouting.

"The pilgrims must be thinking that this is a sign from Sidi Kacem himself."

"Perhaps they're right."

As Hamid was gazing up at the changing face of the moon, Cabell reached across and touched the edge of the boy's jaw with his fingers. Hamid jerked his head back.

"You shouldn't have done that."

"Why not?"

"Because you frightened me."

"I'm sorry."

"Why did you want to touch me there?"

"It was the closest part of you to touch."

"I see. Well, you know it can mean bad luck to receive a fright under the light of a full moon."

"Can it?"

"During an eclipse of the moon I imagine that it can mean worse things."

Reaching into the brazier with his bare hand, Hamid took a glowing coal between his fingers, and, juggling it expertly, quickly buried it in the earth.

"There."

"Why did you do that?"

"I have hidden another light."

"Why?"

"There's an old belief that if the moon were to be extinguished, all fires on earth would be extinguished with her."

"Ah."

"Except those hidden from her sight."

"Do you believe it?"

"Isn't there some truth in all the old symbols?"

Hamid began to prepare more tea, and Cabell brought out his own sebsi, filled it with kif from a leather pouch, lit it, and inhaled deeply. For a long time neither spoke. The moon was becoming a dull red ball in the night.

"Are the mosque and kasbah in Smara still standing, Yusef, or have the Spanish destroyed them?"

"Ah, so you've been to Smara."

"Yes."

"The mosque and kasbah are still there."

"The most beautiful architecture in the Sahara."

"When were you in Smara?"

"A few years ago."

"What were you doing there?"

"So many questions!"

"I'm sorry."

"I told you I was a traveler. I was exploring Smara."

The wind again changed direction, for the faint sound of drumming could be heard momentarily. Then it came back once more, and with it the harsh notes of the rhaita, the mountain flute.

"It must be some musicians on their way to the moussem."

They listened as the musicians passed by close to the house; the music faded away altogether and was replaced by the rush of the wind. A dog walked aimlessly across the courtyard and lay down with a groan in a hole next to the wall. The donkey was moving in the darkness, dragging its chain.

"I'm going to sleep here, Yusef. You're welcome to stay, if you like, and wait for Lydia."

"I'd like to, but I've left a friend behind at the moussem; I ought to go back."

"All right."

"Do you live here, Hamid?"

"I'm just visiting Lydia for a few days. I have a house near Tangier which I must look after."

"So that's what keeps you in Tangier?"

"Otherwise I'd be off to the desert. One day soon, though, I'll be on my way."

"To Icht."

"I want to buy a café. My friend will run it, and I'll start a little farm of vegetables not usually cultivated in the oases."

"Then you'll be free to wander in the desert."

"You don't know how much I look forward to that garden, but I'm becoming impatient. How much longer do I have to wait?"

Hamid slapped his hands loudly together. The dogs jumped up and began to bark.

"Quiet!"

When the dogs returned to their holes, Hamid began to gather up the tea things.

"I ought to return to the moussem," Cabell said.

"I'll go with you."

"Yes, come on."

As the edge of the moon reappeared from the shadow of the earth, Hamid uncovered the charcoal ember, much diminished but still glowing feebly, and held it aloft in his naked hand. Then he threw it abruptly away into the night.

The instant the door was open, the blast of wind struck and propelled them down through the olive grove. Out among the hissing bushes they stumbled along, while the moonlight glittered on the shiny leaves. The moon had sailed far to the west, leaving its track upon the water.

They came among the tents and trees and found shelter out of the wind. Most tents were dark now, as through the swaying boughs of the olive trees moonlight filtered down upon the sleeping forms of animals and people. Up on the high dunes the tomb of Sidi Kacem was as brightly lit as ever, with pilgrims continuing to pass in and out. Hamid told Cabell that he wished to pay a visit to the sanctuary and went off in that direction; the figure in the white djellaba faded away like an apparition among the twisted olive trunks. Cabell made his way down the slope and came out onto the midway. It was much less populated than before, and he wandered up and down until he found Shahid dozing in one of the cafés. Cabell shook him.

"Yusef," he exclaimed, "where have you been? I've sent my scouts everywhere looking for you. I told them to look for a tall man, a Nazarene with blue eyes, a man who walks like a king. They came back without you, saying, 'We have not seen such a man, ever.' They thought they were looking for the Sultan himself."

Shahid lay down on the mat again and began to snore, with

Cabell stretched out beside him, as the musicians played on and on, and the dancing boy would not stop dancing. With the appearance of the first gray light outside, Cabell got to his feet and woke up Shahid; without speaking a word they climbed the sandy hills by the saint's tomb, where they had a view of the wide Atlantic beach and ocean. Shahid fell asleep once more on the sand, but Cabell was sitting with his chin in his hands watching the scene below him. Moroccans were leaving their tents now and coming out of the trees and descending the sandy slopes to the beach; many had taken their clothes off and were in swimming. Meanwhile, the sun's first rays were turning the clouds orange and pink. A figure in white appeared beside Cabell—it was Hamid—together they sat looking out as horses with nearly naked men and youths astride galloped down from the sandy hills, raced across the wide beach below, and entered the sea. From the olive grove behind them came the renewed sound of drumming.

June 25 Here on the shelf is a wrought-iron pot from the Sahara—a gift from Shahid. Like all objects that come from the desert, it has that dry dusty smell of living organisms that have been reduced to powdery death. Shahid says that the pot contains baraka and will bring me good luck. Beside it lies the large fossilized oyster shell which Driss found in Rio de Oro. I don't like to be encumbered by possessions or to allow continual recollections of the past to obscure the clarity of days. But I cannot throw away these few mementos any more than I can discard memories. These objects have assumed a life of their own, and I would miss them, just as I miss him.

# *The Lighthouse at Cape Spartel*

THE HOTEL NICARAGUA, situated on the Avenida de España, a wide boulevard which runs along Tangier's front beach, used to be a hotel of style and popularity during the international days, but now the place is mostly closed down. The night watchman is seldom around, or refuses to answer the door, making entry after dark difficult; so Cabell had to come in through the kitchen and climb long flights of stairs in semi-darkness. At the third-floor landing he struck one match after another while peering at the unmarked doors, finally knocking tentatively at one. There was no response. Next he tapped softly on the door to the left and waited, but only silence followed. He was approaching another, when suddenly it was pulled open and George Maxwell stood before him, framed in a rectangle of light.

"Cabell, it's you! Come in. I'm happy to see you."

Cabell went in and Maxwell shut the door.

"Well, this is a surprise visit, although not so unexpected at that."

"Have you been waiting for me to turn up?"

"As I heard your footsteps coming up the stairs, I said to myself, now who could that be? I'm the only one who lives on this floor, so not many people come up here."

"It's kind of a spooky hotel."

"A Spanish couple used to live across the way, but they moved out some time ago, thank heaven; they did nothing but play their radio all day long. I get my sleep during the daytime, you know."

"I know."

"Anyway, when I heard you tapping at the other doors, I thought it must be somebody looking for the Spaniards. This sort of thing happens all the time in this hotel. There's never anybody behind the desk downstairs, and the doors aren't numbered."

"I had to come in the back way."

"I'm not surprised. So people wander through the hotel on tiptoe, as if they were afraid of waking the dead. They tap cautiously at all the doors, as if to see if there were anybody still living inside. You'd think the rooms were coffins. It's enough to unnerve a man—makes you wonder if you're dead or alive."

"Why do you live in a place like this?"

"Habit, I suppose—been here for years. One gets used to anything. But please sit down. Will you take a whiskey?"

"Fine."

Cabell took a seat in a leather easy chair. Maxwell's room was long and narrow, like a corridor; opposite Cabell stood a bookshelf crammed with works in Latin and Greek; an armoire and a chest of drawers made up the rest of the furniture. Beneath a large window overlooking the street lay Maxwell's bed. The room was brightly lit by several lamps.

Maxwell poured out two whiskeys. "I hope that's all right without ice. I know you Americans like ice with your whiskey, but I've no fridge."

"That's fine."

"Cheers. I'm happy you've come at last, Cabell. Look around you, and you'll see everything I own. This is it. Except for the books I've accumulated, I could pack in a minute, put all my possessions in a few boxes and be off. But I can't seem to move —been in this room for seventeen years, can you believe it?"

"Seventeen years?"

"It's not a bad room."

"Sort of shaped like a railroad car, isn't it?"

"Despite the many inconveniences of this hotel, I can live anonymously here, which is the style I prefer. You understand, Cabell, don't you?"

"What?"

"I am an exile, a voluntary exile from my own country, nothing more. As I have rejected my country, you have projected yourself out of yours."

"What do you mean?"

"You move through space and time, while I stick to one place. Am I right?"

"I don't know."

"You're free to return to the Sahara; home means nothing to you. Is that correct?"

"For the first time in my life, I'd like to have a base. I think Tangier's going to be my base."

"Yes, of course, a place to move out of and to come back to, but never to stay for long in. You're on the move, yes, you belong to the future."

"What future?"

"You dream about making a garden out of the desert—that's the future, isn't it?"

"Did I tell you that?"

"Perhaps you did, perhaps I heard it from someone else, but it's true, isn't it?"

"Yes."

"Not a secret?"

"No."

"Good. Well, this room is my base of operations. I sit here and dream of the past—you see, I have rejected the future, I don't believe in it. Instead, I spend my days contemplating what it would have been like to have lived in a conservative society."

"Which one? Aren't all societies conservative by nature?"

"Such as Homer described in the Odyssey."

"That was a rigid, tribal society."

"It had structure and definition."

"In Morocco I'm often reminded of the classical world."

"Tangier is not Athens, Cabell. Never was, never will be."

"The Mediterranean hasn't changed so much. Herd boys still stand on hilltops and pipe to their flocks."

"All barbarians did the same."

"Look at the way people dress."

"I know what you mean, Cabell. Ah! Sometimes I think that the only emotion I know is sadness; of course, I get this from my books and from making comparisons."

Maxwell smoked his cigarette down to the last half inch and ground it out. Cabell got to his feet and went to the window. The wind was shaking the palms along the Avenida de España. On the other side of the road a long row of boxcars was passing slowly; when they had all gone by, Cabell turned around.

"These messenger boys keep delivering lottery tickets to the hotel," he said.

"Don't you want them?"

"I don't understand."

"Do you remember the first evening we met?"

"Yes, at the Marco Polo."

"You seemed like you were having a hard time. Is it true?"

"Yes, it's true."

"Well, I thought the tickets might change your luck."

"But money's not my problem, not now anyhow."

"Doesn't matter. Have you been lucky?"

"Lucky? Every one has been a winner."

"Hah!"

"How do you do it?"

"I don't have a system, if that's what you mean."

"What do you have?"

"You can keep a secret, can't you?"

"Yes."

"I have a friend."

"Oh."

The wind was blowing harder now, and shook the window. Cabell finished his drink.

"I think I ought to be on my way to the lighthouse."

"To the lighthouse?"

"The lighthouse at Cape Spartel. Do you want to come?"

"Why are you going there?"

"I have a friend."

"I wish I could, but I have an appointment with Palmeta."

"Who's Palmeta?"

"A Spanish woman I've known for some time."

"Oh."

"She's a good woman, but I won't put up with her Spanish formality much longer. All that palaver and hand kissing—it's too much for me, and I can't change her now. Why, I just want her to be a 'copain,' and we could talk openly to each other, for she's an intelligent woman. If she could only behave like they do in northern England—that's where I come from. When I used to go home for a visit, I simply shook hands with my father when I arrived and again when I left."

"Your father's still living, is he?"

"Dead now."

"Oh."

"Otherwise it was just, 'Hey, how are you!' and I might have been away for five years. You didn't have to open doors or remember saint's days or any of that Spanish nonsense."

"Doesn't she supply you with plenty of tapas and drinks?"

"I've already fallen out with her over a Russian film. I wanted to leave in the middle; it was so awful, you know, another propaganda message they call cinema, but she wouldn't budge. So we had a row right there in the theater. Finally I just walked out and left her there, and she didn't speak to me for a month afterward. Can you imagine? Said gentlemen don't behave in that manner."

"Maybe she's right."

"Perhaps she is right, but I can't take any more of that bowing and scraping. She's the vainest woman I've ever known. Tonight we're supposed to have a reunion; there's a concert on at the Italian Institute. But I can't change her. I'm telling you, except for the music, I'd much rather accompany you to the lighthouse."

The taxi emerged from a pine forest onto the hills above Cape Spartel, where it was rocked by blasts of wind coming down the Straits; the driver had to grip the wheel with both hands in order to keep his vehicle on the road. It went down the flank of the hill; the Atlantic was below to the left; and the long radial beam of the lighthouse came into view. The entrance to the lighthouse compound was blocked by an iron gate; suddenly Omar appeared in the headlights and pulled the bar back.

"That's the lighthouse keeper," Cabell said.

"The lighthouse keeper—that boy?" the taxi driver was asking.

"The future lighthouse keeper. One day he will take over from his father."

"Ah, yes, the father is old and the son is very young."

"Among lighthouse keepers, the line of succession must be maintained."

"Ah. Like the sultans."

Omar was struggling with the gate in the wind; when the car passed through, he ran on ahead. The high tower was above them, fingers of light sweeping the blackness. Palms were thrashing wildly about in the wind; on the cliffs below a heavy surf could be heard crashing; salt spray flew past the feeble light above the door. Omar pulled the door open, and Cabell rushed inside.

"Thank God for this!" he exclaimed.

"It's calm in here, no?"

"What a savage night!"

They were standing in an octagonal courtyard enclosed by an arcade supported by Moorish arches. The courtyard and the arches were of the same brick; in the center a fountain splashed among potted plants and flowers. The wind seemed far away.

Crossing the courtyard they entered a room beneath the lighthouse tower where photographs of other lighthouses in the countries which maintained the Cape Spartel light in the days of the Tangier Zone hung on the walls.

"Special visitors sign the book," Omar said.

Cabell put his name in the old book.

"Let's go up now."

As they mounted the spiral stone staircase, the sounds of their footsteps echoed in the conical chamber. Windows set into the wall were rattling violently, and one broken pane let in a blast of air and the noise of the surf thudding on the cliffs. At the top of the stairs Omar opened a door, and they entered a low compartment. In the middle of the room a large metal weight was suspended by cable; the light itself could be heard turning above them.

"What's this, Omar?"

"This light has a pendulum like a clock," the boy explained. "An electric motor raises this weight automatically every two hours. Last night there was much work, as the motor broke. While it was being repaired, I had to push the light around by hand."

"The light must never go out, the light must never cease turning, Driss used to say."

"That's right."

They climbed a metal staircase and came to the big light itself; the magnifying crystal faces with their concentric lenses were revolving smoothly, sending their signals flashing out into the night. Cabell moved around the circular catwalk, passing his hands over the glass and polished brass fittings and peering at the large electric bulb which burned inside. Omar was following closely behind.

"This is a big light all right," Cabell remarked.

"The most powerful in Africa."

As the crystal faces passed, they were alternately brightly lit and cast into shadow; these moving lenses with their irregular faces were producing a subaqueous effect, as if beams of light were filtering down through great depths of clear water.

"Go on, Omar, tell me about the light."

"It has a rhythm of four flashes in each twenty-second revolution."

"The Cape Blanco light used to send out three signals each fifteen seconds. How far away can this one be seen?"

"On a clear night, sixty-two kilometers."

"And it turns on a pool of mercury?"

"Yes, and the lower reflectors are aimed at the sky as a beacon for airplanes."

"Ah. We didn't have those in La Guera." Cabell was gazing into the polished prisms, which flashed and receded and flashed again. Suddenly he stood up and took hold of a door handle.

"Where does this lead to?"

"Outside, but be careful of the wind!"

Pulling open the door, Cabell stepped out into the windy darkness; the force of the wind slammed the door against the wall with a loud noise. Omar took hold of it, hooked it to the wall, and went out after him. A narrow circular balcony ran around the top of the lighthouse tower; Cabell had walked around to the windward side. All around was an abyss of blackness stabbed by the long spokes of light. Far below the waves were hurling themselves against the rocks; out in the void not a light was visible. Cabell stood rigidly by the rail, bracing himself against the wind.

"Come inside now!" Omar shouted.

Cabell did not seem to hear.

Omar was tugging on his sleeve. "Let's go back!"

Suddenly Cabell let out a howl. Omar took a step backward

and stared at him. When he lost his breath, Cabell inhaled quickly and began again—long wordless cries into the windy darkness. After a while he ceased, seemed to relax, and released his grip on the rail. They went back inside, and Omar heaved the door shut against the wind.

The chamber was quiet and warm; the light still turned with a hum on its pool of mercury; with hypnotic regularity it continued to cast its long arm out over the dark waters.

"Let's go down now, Omar. I've seen enough."

The boy was still looking incredulously at him.

"I was competing with the wind," Cabell said, smiling.

"Why, Yusef?"

"The wind is scouring the earth."

"Why do you have to compete with it?"

"Because I must cleanse myself."

As they descended the winding stairs, Omar was telling Cabell about his old grandfather, who used to be guardian of the lighthouse. Every night he climbed the stairs to tend to the light; afterward he'd hike his djellaba up around his waist and slide all the way down the spiral banister.

They came out again into the octagonal courtyard, where the fountain splashed peacefully onto the bricks and flowers.

"Would you like to taste the water from the fountain, Yusef? It has iron in it."

Cabell tasted the water. "Too much iron for me."

"Yusef, can you stay with us tonight? I wish you would. We can sleep in this courtyard near the fountain."

A woman appeared in a doorway across the patio, and Cabell went over and greeted her. When she saw who it was, the woman began to sob and wipe her eyes with her hands, but she, too, begged him to spend the night. When he agreed, she brought out mattresses and blankets and prepared two beds by the fountain. Cabell smoked cigarettes and paced about the courtyard; when he lay down, Omar was nearly asleep and snuggled closer. Meanwhile, bands of light swept monotonously through the sky and water splashed on the bricks.

June 27 At 4:00 A.M. this morning I suddenly opened my eyes, snapping awake from a deep slumber, with the sensation of something leaping off my chest. A succubus? (I had dropped off about midnight and cannot remember ever sleeping more soundly than during those four hours.) A big dog was running down the stone path outside the lighthouse. I couldn't see him, but he must have been running as fast as he could from something that terrified him. The claws rattled on the stone. He had been a long time running; his breath sounded as if his insides were pouring out. I got up from my bed next to the fountain and let myself out of the house; the wind had stopped, and a thick mist was pouring through the trees. The old moon, barely visible in the gloom, had turned the mist green. Out in the Straits, ships were using their horns.

A terrible nightmare had awakened me at the instant the dog came running by. Driss was crying and screaming somewhere, and I was creeping through a dark house, through bedrooms where other people slept and heard nothing, trying to locate him. I found myself in a huge tunnel, with the sound of water splashing down somewhere. Suddenly I realized that this was not some gigantic sewer I was wading through, but that the lighthouse had somehow toppled over and was lying on its side. At last I came to the light. It had gone out; everything was shambles and wreckage. I found Driss in his bed—the same bed where we had slept in the lighthouse at Cape Blanco—he was thrashing and moaning under the covers. Everything was dark, but I could see that he had been crushed by whatever force it was that had uprooted the lighthouse. I sat on the edge of the bed and tried to comfort him. Not knowing what else to do, I found myself taking my clothes off and getting into bed with him. As I lay down beside him I had a moment of doubt whether this was actually Driss or someone else, possibly a woman or even myself. Then the dog ran by.

The mist felt like a cold hand on my shoulders, so I walked

up the path to warm myself and after a few moments came out onto the main road. The fog must have just have rolled in from the sea, for now the Cape Spartel horn started to pulse like a great vibrating diaphragm. As the light itself gleamed ineffectually in the swirling vapor, I had the recurring sensation that my dream had not yet ended. Continuing on down the road, I arrived at a place above Mediouna beach, where I heard voices of men and the click of hoofs on pavement. Some Moroccans leading horses came past but did not see me. I went carefully down among the rocks to the beach. From somewhere behind me came the sound of men's voices and the clank of shovels against rock. For a while I stood at the sea's edge as the waves gradually took form in the early morning light—I had come to the beach with the vague intention of bathing, but decided I didn't like the idea of my naked body floating out there beyond the breakers. The sensation of my flesh immersed in water was something I did not want to experience, as if the touch of water meant oblivion, and besides, I still was unsure that this might not be an extension of the dream.

Two summers ago I pulled a half-drowned boy out of the water off that same beach. A Jewess who knew something about artificial respiration came forward and worked on him. We all thought he was gone, but she kept pounding away in a fury, whimpering and crying as she worked to save him. Then a thick white foam began to issue from the boy's mouth and nostrils—masses of it until the boy groaned and moved on the sand. Finally an ambulance arrived and took the boy away. The girl who had saved him was sobbing and sobbing.

A tongue of wave curled around my foot; I shrank back from that wet touch and retreated to the dry sand higher up on the beach. The shovelers had kindled a fire among the rocks, and when they caught sight of me, called me over. I joined them, happy to talk and happy to feel the warmth of their fire, but it wasn't until I held a glass of tea between my hands that I could be sure that the dream had come to an end.

# *The Bottom of the Old Mountain Road*

CABELL WAS SITTING in the Café Palmeramonte at the bottom of the Old Mountain road. On a bench next to him a Moroccan in a faded blue robe lay sound asleep. The man's mouth was wide open, and flies had settled on his face and had actually entered the mouth. It was midafternoon; heat flaring down out of the sky had driven everyone off the streets. On the hillside across the road eucalyptus trees drooped in motionless silence; melting tar glistened at the edge of the pavement. From a radio inside the café came the whining voice of a taleb chanting verses from the Koran. An automobile was parked a few yards down the road, and a small gray-and-white bird was jumping at his reflection in the hubcap. Ping! the bird's beak struck the shiny metal surface. Ping! Ping! Ping! The sleeping man opened one eye and closed his mouth. The flies rose from his face; the man grunted and spat out the ones trapped in his mouth. In another minute he was asleep once more as the flies returned to their places.

A donkey carrying a man and a double pannier filled with pears was coming down the hill. As it passed by the café, Cabell hailed the rider. It was Hamid. He reined in the donkey, and the two greeted each other in Arabic.

"How do you like my camel?"

"Is that a camel?"

"A Tangier camel."

"So, Hamid, you're a farmer. You didn't tell me that."

"Not a farmer, but I have an orchard. I don't look after the trees, but why allow the fruit to rot on the ground when it can be sold in the market?"

"No reason at all."

"This is the way I live, you see, from hand to mouth."

"Where's your orchard?"

"In Agla."

"Ah. But it's not a bad life, is it? I mean filling the baskets with fruit and carrying them to town."

Hamid shrugged. "If there were something else to do, I'd do it."

"How much will they give you for all these pears?"

"Everyone is selling pears now, so the price is low, but I'm hoping for one hundred dirhams."

"That's not bad money."

"It will allow me to live for a couple of weeks."

"How often do you bring your pears to market?"

"Every couple of weeks."

"In all this heat do you still think of the Sahara?"

"You know my dreams—the hotter the better."

"I read in the newspaper that there's a Chergui over the Souss—120°."

"Good."

"How are Lydia and Grigory?"

"They're fine—sorry they missed you at the moussem."

"I'll go out there again soon."

"You must. They're anxious to see you."

"Hamid, these hot nights I'm sleeping in a café down at

Merkala. Why don't you pass by there on your way back from market? I'll fix some dinner."

"Good. First I must park this camel in the corral at Ain Hayani."

"It's M'siksif's summer café, the one at the far end of the beach."

"Yes, I know it."

Hamid let the rein out, and the donkey began to move.

"You'll come, then?"

"Yes, I'll be there by nightfall."

"Good. Do you like your food picante?"

"As hot as you can make it."

"It'll make you sweat."

"I like to sweat."

The donkey resumed its short, jerky trot; Hamid waved, and was soon out of sight. Cabell set off down the dirt track that led to Merkala. The beach was teeming with people, mostly young men from the city—running, shouting, playing football and paddleball, doing handstands and tumbling, practicing judo and karate, and splashing around like seals in the water. A few women were present—bathing with all their clothes on, or suckling babies, as they sat like sacks of laundry on mats and rugs in the shade of the rocks. Some of the ladies had constructed makeshift tents and shelters, where they were cooking and talking and shouting in strident voices after their children. One fat old Negress had actually stripped naked and was sitting completely unnoticed on the sand, contentedly raking up the warm sand around her voluminous thighs. The elongated black breasts hung to her waist and dragged in the sand.

Cabell went directly to the café, where he found M'siksif chatting with friends. He joined them and later bought a good-sized porgy from a fisherman. When the others had departed he went down to the rocks, gutted the fish, scaled it, and washed it in salt water. Next he got the charcoal brazier going. Into a clay bowl he poured sunflower oil, cut up tomatoes, onions, and a whole head of garlic. While this concoction was simmering over the charcoal, he added salt and cumin seed, fresh dill, and plenty of the hot sudani. Cutting the fish into small steaks, he laid these on top and covered the dish with the lid.

The sun was lowering now, the heat was abating, and people were beginning to leave the beach. Cabell put on his bathing suit and had a swim off the rocks. Afterward he took the tajine off the fire and shut the café with the dog inside. Walking to Dradeb, he rode the bus into the city. Up in the Kasbah, after checking on his mail at the Hotel Splendid, he delivered food to the prison. At a general store in the Socco he picked up a bottle of wine and a loaf of bread and took a taxi back to Merkala. The sun had set, the beach was deserted, and he sat down on the steps of the café to wait.

About an hour later Hamid came along.

"Did you sell your pears?"

"Yes."

"How much?"

"One hundred dirhams."

"Well, that's what you expected. Let's have a drink—you drink, don't you?"

"Yes, but I'd like to have a swim first."

"Go ahead."

Hamid went down to the rocks and bathed as Cabell watched. When he returned Cabell handed him a glass of wine. As Hamid took the glass, Cabell allowed his hand to touch his cheek.

"Why do you touch me there?"

"Your cheek is so soft."

"My beard hasn't begun to grow yet. I'm waiting."

Cabell leaned over and allowed his hand to enter the loosely buttoned shirt.

"What are you doing, Yusef?"

"What do I feel there?" Cabell was speaking French.

"A nipple—what do you think?"

"It's a big one."

"What did you expect?"

"I just had to find out for myself."

"Well, now you know what everybody knows."
"So it's Hamid el Hassani."
"Yes."
"Why do you do it?"
"I've always felt more comfortable in a man's clothes."
"And do you believe in Allah?"
"Why not?"
"They allow you to pray in the great mosque with the men?"
"Why not? I'm a Moslem."
"You're married?"
"Yes."
"To a Moroccan working in France?"
"In the mines."
"Is he the comrade you were telling me about?"
"Yes, Ali, my husband."
"And at one time you lived with the R'guibat around Smara until the Spanish caught you, accused you of being a spy, and expelled you from the territory?"
"Those bastards."
"How long have you been in Morocco?"
"Fifteen years."
"And how old are you?"
"Twenty-seven. Any more questions?"
"Always alone?"
"I came here with my mother; she's dead now."
Cabell kissed Hamid on the mouth and let his hand run once more inside the white shirt.
"Yusef, I thought I was invited here for dinner."
"You were."
"To tell you the truth I haven't had a decent meal for several days."
"For someone who complains about being poor, you wear the most beautiful clothes."
"My Moroccan friends insist that I go about well dressed."
"Like a young prince."
"No, like a student."

Cabell had his arm around Hamid and was squeezing her tightly; her turban had become untied, and the scalp was naked.

"Yusef," she whispered in his ear, "when are we going to eat?"

"Any time you like."

"I really don't have the strength for anything but eating."

"Don't you like my arms around you?"

"Yes, I do."

"Please put yours around me."

"Do you really want me to?"

"Yes, I do. I need them."

"Later, Yusef. Let's eat now."

Cabell took the tajine off the fire and set it between them. When he lifted off the lid a cloud of steam rose and the smell of the food filled the café. The bread was broken, and they began to eat. Cabell poured out more wine. With her left hand resting on one knee, Hamid dipped small pieces of bread into the tajine with her right; she ate slowly, almost languidly, but did not stop until the last drop of sauce had been soaked up from the bottom of the pot. Afterward there was mint tea.

"Yusef," Hamid said at one point, "you strike the most graceful poses I've ever seen."

"I've been watching the Bedouins for a long time."

"You're practically a Saharan yourself, aren't you?"

"No."

"Do you think we ought to travel together one day, Yusef?"

"Can you travel light? I never knew a woman who could travel light."

"Then you have something to learn about women."

"What about your husband?"

"He permits me to go off on long trips by myself."

"He must be good to you, but before we plan any joint adventures, may I send you to the desert on a mission? I want you to deliver a letter."

"What's the matter with the post?"

"This letter must be delivered by hand."

"Why not do it yourself?"
"It's a place where I shouldn't be seen."
"Why not? What place?"
"I'll tell you when the time comes."
"What's this all about, Yusef?"
"Do you remember I told you about the water in the desert?"
"Yes, fresh water and no oil, thank God."
"I have an idea how I might convince the Spanish to use the water."
"For what? Are you planning to eliminate the desert?"
"Just bring water to some parts."
"And bring in a million Spaniards to populate them."
"More like creating new oases for the Bedouins and their camels. Do you approve?"
"I'm not sure."
"When the time comes, you can decide. I'll tell you more then."
That night Hamid spent at the café, and the next morning at dawn they went swimming naked together off the rocks.

July 1 From this position up on the hill I have a good view of the beach of Merkala. Brilliant sunlight strikes the sea; shouts of bathers are muted by the surf and are dispersed over the flat surface of water; but certain voices do pierce the silence of incredibly blue air and sky. Today the air is blue. A skin diver comes out of the water and holds up a lobster. A boy is running along the shore: suddenly the sea turns black behind him, the beach glistens with heat, and for an instant the sun welds him to the sand. Groups of Moroccan boys lie with their heads together and feet spread apart, forming a star pattern.

We walked down through Dradeb to get here. I have on my blue shirt and a new pair of sandals, Shahid is sporting dark glasses, and Omar is wearing a sailor's cap. This trio wanders along until it comes upon the empty spaces; then we leap together. We have been in swimming; we have eaten a delicious squid tajine under a pine tree. Now Shahid is taking a siesta in the shade, and Omar has gone off with his fishing pole. "When the fish are biting, your head doesn't think of sleep," he says.

Tangier is so glorious now. Summer has set in at last, and I expect that I shall be reluctant to leave when that time comes. One can live here with such ease, it's a place to be free in. Interior realities come quickly to the surface and lead you on. I do not think ahead now, but no matter; there are answers to be found in the streets of this city. Tangier may be decaying; yet for me it's indestructible. Let them pull down the buildings and exchange new façades for the old, but the essence will remain. The spirit of this town does not depend on its architecture.

# *Casa Manolita*

ONE EVENING CABELL went out to Casa Manolita, the fishermen's bar on the road to Malabata. The place is all covered with vines, with concealed alcoves in the bushes where Moroccans take their girl friends and do what they want with them. Inside, a dusty collage of old bullfight notices and travel posters from the days of the International Zone covers the walls. Tiles over the door bear the inscriptions *A married man is a tame donkey* and *The animal which drinks the least is the camel: Don't be a camel!*

He was sitting at one end of the zinc bar drinking Fundador and talking to Manolita, a stocky woman with golden teeth. At the other end was a group of customers, also on familiar terms with Manolita. A tall thin Spaniard was clapping his hands as a brown-skinned girl with bleached blond hair danced. She wore nothing under her diaphanous blouse, and the large breasts were visible moving underneath.

"Algerian girl," Manolita said as she poured Cabell another cognac.

A small brown man appeared at the door; he had a face with precise peasant features and wore a hat.

"Gypsy!" someone called out from the corner.

He took out a harmonica and began to play, holding it with one hand and snapping a castanet with the other, all the while doing a little dance. Everyone clapped along with him. He finished one song, formally announced the next, and played again. Passing the hat around, he received a few coins and vanished through the door.

"Crazy," Manolita commented from behind the bar. "Crazy from eating too many beans."

The bar quieted down again until an old guitar player, guitar in hand, stepped in through the door and announced to everybody: "I'm crazy, too, and the wind makes me crazier!"

He came over and shook Manolita's hand. Cabell offered him a drink, but he refused and began to complain about his health.

"You look all right to me," Cabell said.

"Me, all right? You must be joking."

"You've got some color in your cheeks. Probably you've been out in the sun."

"No. Look closely at this cheek. It's redder than the other; they're not the same, are they?"

"It's true," put in Manolita.

"I was hit on the face this morning, hit by someone's fist."

"Goodness!"

"And my leg, my right leg hurts. Did you notice I'm limping?"

"The way you shuffle around it's difficult to tell," Manolita remarked.

"The leg was struck by a hammer. I can hardly walk."

He brought out a small leather case and placed it on the bar; sighing, he opened it and began to rummage among syringes and numerous ampoules and bottles of pills.

"What's all that?" Cabell asked.

"These are the medicines I'm forced to take."

"What's the trouble?"

"It's rheumatism of the shoulder. I can hardly play any more, and these pills cost money, so where am I?"

Manolita and Cabell looked at each other and shrugged. "We don't know."

"But I've got to take them for the pain."

After swallowing a pill, he hobbled over to the door and took a seat on a stool, where he began to untie a complicated arrangement of knots in the sack which held the guitar. Taking out the instrument, he spent a long time tuning it.

"What are you going to play?" Cabell asked.

"Whatever you want."

"What can you play?"

"Happiness songs—that's all I know."

"All right, play them."

The old man crossed his legs, pressed his chin against the sound box, and began to pluck the strings. His skin was nearly translucent, the ears were long and loose, the nose looked like a fleshy hook on the end of his face. He had long fingernails, and the fingers themselves were so loose-jointed that they bent backward when he pressed on the strings. With absolutely no expression on his face he played one tune after another.

New customers arrived and others departed, dropping coins into the tin plate before the old man as they went out. Cabell finished off another brandy and leaned back against the bar. The Algerian woman was giving him the whore's smile from across the room. Her companion, the tall man with the long blue jaw, grabbed her roughly and turned her around, but she still glanced over her shoulder. Manolita was telling someone about her daughter, who had run off to Mexico.

"I'm Mexican myself," Cabell said. "It's a fine country."

"You're not Mexican," she scoffed.

"What am I then?"

"A gringo."

Meanwhile the old man played on and on, repeating the same tunes everyone had heard before. He seemed to have gone into a trance, leaning on his guitar, until Cabell caught his attention with a signal to play something more lively. Suddenly he began to strum loudly and to tap the guitar with the long fingernails and to sing in a very high voice. Everyone looked up. The Algerian lady broke away from her boy friend and started to dance, advancing across the floor toward Cabell, with the large dark nipples bobbing up and down beneath the transparent blouse. Cabell moved out onto the middle of the floor and did a jig, and the people began to clap as they circled each other. The girl's boy friend was approaching, however; to avoid him Cabell jumped up on the table and improvised a little tap dance. The result was electrifying. Chairs and tables were upset as everyone got to his feet at once and began to dance wildly. The Algerian girl was wrestling with her boy friend on the floor; Manolita was screaming and pounding her fists on the bar, as the old man continued to play in a frenzy. When Cabell accidentally stepped on the edge of his metal plate, catapulting the coins onto the floor, the old man dropped the guitar and scrambled after the coins as the drunks at the bar rolled out into the street, somersaulting and sprawling on the pavement. Someone fell on the road and was almost run over by a passing car, which in turn swerved and went into the ditch. The driver got out and threatened the drunks who were leaping onto his car and dancing on the roof. The blond girl tried to follow Cabell outside but was tackled from behind by her lover, who straddled her body and seemed to be trying to give her a beating and rape her at the same time. Cabell had stepped to one side and was viewing the pandemonium when from behind him someone called his name.

"Who's that?"

"It's me, Yusef, Mohamed."

Mohamed I stepped out of the darkness.

"Mohamed, what are you doing here?"

"I'm out of prison."

"So I see. Are you all right?"

"Yes."

"How did you escape?"

"No, Yusef, I didn't escape."

"How did you get out, then? The lawyer said your case was to come up before the tribunal next week."

"I wrote my father in Oujda."

"And he came."

"He came and paid some money, and this morning I was released."

"Your father must be a rich man."

"Not so rich; poorer now."

Mohamed had lost so much weight that all the bones in the face were visible; the eyes had sunk far back into the sockets. He wore the same clothes as before, but now they looked as if they belonged to someone else.

"What did your father say? Was he very angry?"

"He asked me to return to Oujda with him."

"Yes?"

"But I refused."

"Why?"

"I want to find work in Tangier, Yusef—I can't return to my family in rags, a disgrace."

"Did you tell him?"

"Yes."

"What did he say to that?"

"He said I should do whatever I thought was best."

"Has he left already?"

"He went away this morning."

"Where do you sleep, Mohamed?"

"I have no place."

"Do you have any money?"

"My father gave me some, yes."

"What are you doing out here?"

"Ah, Yusef, you ask so many questions."

"But it's been such a long time since I've seen you. I don't know anything."

"I'm on my way to Villa Harris. I hear there's some construction out there; perhaps they need a mason."

"It's kind of late at night to be looking for a job."

"I want to show up early in the morning before the others."

"Before what others?"

"The others who will be asking for work."

The clients of Casa Manolita had drifted back into the bar, and Mohamed and Cabell were left by themselves.

"Mohamed, come back with me to town. You can sleep in the hotel—there are plenty of spare rooms—and tomorrow first thing in the morning, I'll take you out to Villa Harris."

"No, Yusef."

"I wish you would."

"I want to spend tonight on the beach."

"Why?"

"Mohamed and I used to collect seaweed along the coast near Cape Juby, don't you remember?"

"M'barek told me."

"There were times when we had walked so far that we would light a fire and spend the night on the shore. In prison I used to think about those times, and I said to myself the first night out of here, I'm going to spend on the beach."

"I see what you mean."

"So I'm on my way."

"Come on. I'll walk with you."

They went down the pitted road by the Coca-Cola plant and the abandoned brick factory. Behind the beach the fishermen and gypsies and smugglers used to have their lockers and shanties; it was a quarter where poor Spanish still lived, and their dogs came out to yap at the strangers. After a while they left the road and crossed the railroad tracks that run along the beach, and slid down the sandy embankment on the other side. At the bottom of the slope Mohamed took a package of Casa Sports out of his battered shirt pocket and handed one across to Cabell.

"Mohamed, what do you hear from Mohamed II?"

"I received one letter from him."

"What did he say?"

"He said he saw a house in Azrou we built together."

"Is that all?"

"He talks about life in the army."

"What's it like?"

"Here, I have the letter with me. I'll read what he says about the army."

Mohamed took the letter out of his pocket. Cabell produced a cigarette lighter and cupped his hand around the flame as Mohamed read.

". . . we get up at four o'clock in the morning. From four-thirty until six-thirty we march or run. Sometimes we have to run as much as ten kilometers without stopping. Six-thirty, breakfast. Coffee and milk and bread and marmalade. From seven to eight we make our beds and pass inspection. Afterward the work details go out. I am repairing some of the buildings in the camp, which are in such a bad condition that it is hardly worth the trouble. As I am the only one in our group who knows how to do this work, they let me alone. The sergeants do not bother me. These men are stupid and uneducated. They only know how to shout and to make trouble when there is no trouble. We all hate them; it is of no importance to us how many battles they have fought in, or how many Jews and Chinese they have killed. Twelve o'clock, lunch. Noodles, sometimes meat, bread, and tea. After the meal we have five minutes of free time to smoke a cigarette. Sometimes we are called before we have time to finish even one cigarette, and we have to throw it half-smoked to the ground or pinch out the ash with our fingers and place the butts in our pockets. In the afternoons we drill or march some more. If we practice shooting I am happy, for I enjoy learning how to shoot a rifle. We all like to shoot. Six-thirty we have dinner. A very bad soup and bread. Now we have time to smoke a whole cigarette. By seven-thirty I am in my bed; I can't keep my eyes open any more. This is the schedule six days a week. Sundays we do our washing.

"It's cold in these mountains, and I have only one blanket. But I must tell you something, brother. I do not mind this life. Except for the sergeants and the terrible weather of this place, I could become a soldier. But I will not. I think of you in Tangier. Next year I shall join you there. Is Yusef still by your side, or has he returned to El Aaiun? Tell M'siksif that I shall build the café at Merkala for him next spring. . . ."

"You miss him, don't you, Mohamed?"

Mohamed nodded.

"Sometimes one has to wait."

"I know how to wait, Yusef. We all know how to wait."

It was a warm summer night; even at this late hour, traces of the sunset remained in the sky. The thousands of lights of Tangier blinked and sparkled, illuminating the bay, the curving beach, the hulks of giant fishing barges on the sand.

"Mohamed, what was it like to be in prison?"

"Not so bad—not as bad as I had expected."

"Did you learn anything in there?"

"What do you mean?"

"I mean, do you think prison life taught you anything?"

"I learned to discipline myself."

"How?"

"I had nothing to do, so I decided to make a schedule."

"Tell me."

"I used to wake up very early in the morning, long before the others. For the next hour or so I'd do all the exercises I could think of. Each day I would devise new exercises."

"Did you have your own cell?"

"Are you joking with me? A cell means solitary confinement."

"I didn't know."

"We were all together in one big room, and I had to do my exercises on my little square."

They smoked in silence for a while. The beam from the Cape Malabata lighthouse was answered by the signal from the Sharf, as the moving water of the bay reflected a track of orange light from a big ship anchored outside the breakwater.

"Then what?"

"Sometimes we used to work on the road, digging ditches for pipes, and when they learned I was a mason, I was given a job repairing cracks in the walls."

"Like Mohamed."

"They used to leave the lights on all night. I didn't like that."

As they lay there on the sand, a noise came from a distance, louder and louder. A bright beam of light swept the beach, and above their heads the old wooden boxcars of the produce train rattled by. Suddenly there was a thump, followed by another, and a sack rolled down the embankment with a man tumbling after it. He was as startled to see Mohamed and Cabell as they were to see him; with a grunt he leaped to his feet and made off with the sack.

"Smuggler."

The wind was coming up and whistled in the wires above the tracks.

"I'll go now, Yusef."

"Don't you want to stay here? This bank will protect us from the wind."

"I need to walk."

"Go on, then. I'm going to lie here a bit longer. I drank too much Fundador, and this night air makes me drowsy."

"Yusef?"

"Yes?"

"Thank you for the food."

"That's all right."

"Without the food you brought me, I would have been sick."

"Mohamed, there's something I want to ask you."

"What is it?"

"You and Mohamed . . . were happy in Tarfaya, weren't you?"

"No, we weren't happy. You know that. We had come a long

way—walking, walking—looking for work, and there was nothing."

"But you were happy together, no? When you used to sleep on the beach . . ."

"Yes, there were some good times, Yusef."

Cabell had closed his eyes and began to snore, and for a while Mohamed watched him. Then he got to his feet and walked off into the darkness.

July 8 A prisoner has fallen off the roof of the prison kitchen and has broken his back. He lies on the cobblestones unable to move as a policeman restrains a crowd of children. There is plaster of Paris caked on the hands and wrists of the prisoner, and the rough khaki prison uniform has been splashed with whitewash—he had been painting the roof of the prison kitchen. It is a bright summer day with gusts of wind, and the wind blows dust into the prisoner's eyes. He blinks his eyes, and I can see grit in the corners and along the lids. He moves his lips as if to speak, the tongue comes out and passes over the lips where dirt has collected. The eyes are glazed and full of pain and do not seem to see us. The children are silent and respectful—they sense that his life is coming to an end. A few moments ago he was busy with his work; he was confident that he would wake up tomorrow morning and have his breakfast with the other prisoners. Even as a prisoner he shared his life with us, but now he's in a different category.

It is said that at the instant before death one's life passes before one's eyes. Certainly the approach of death must summon a crowd of broken images rushing around one—one's last unconscious effort to dispel the fear that all is coming to an end, that finally the thinking, feeling, acting man becomes a hulk under the ground. This is the painful thought—that after all the affection we have borne for this earth, it will accept only our rotten flesh. And that death is always alone, alone with the whole backlog of one's life tumbling together toward the end. I looked into the prisoner's eyes, wondering what they had seen and what visions were with him now, but they were blank, expressing nothing but pain and shock.

I, sitting in this chair in this room writing this down, must come to an end. Maxwell said that when he was still young he in fact did not believe it to be true. But the prisoner was stretched out on the cobblestones, paralyzed. Finally the ambulance arrived; the attendants attempted to lift him gently onto the stretcher; at the first movement a tremor ran through him like a current of electricity, the jaw fell open, and the prisoner was dead.

# *Lydia and Grigory*

AS SOON AS THE DRIVER cut the motor of the taxi, dogs could be heard barking and howling inside the courtyard. A bearded man carrying a flashlight stepped through the door and came forward to meet Cabell.

"My dear Joseph," he said in French, shaking Cabell's hand. "How are you?"

"I'm all right, Grigory. What about yourself?"

"Well, very weil. Come in. Lydia is waiting."

As they crossed the courtyard, Grigory kept the dogs at bay by brandishing a short leather whip. Passing through another door, they came out onto an arcaded veranda and there, waiting for them, was a tall woman wearing a pink caftan with a pink scarf wrapped around her head. She kissed Cabell on both cheeks.

"Oh, Joseph, I'm so glad to see you."

Leading the way into a large white room with a high ceiling, she introduced him to another woman.

"Joseph, this is Matilda Abramovitch. I think you know each other already, no?"

This pale young woman smiled and extended her hand; the fingers and back of the hand were tattooed with tiny blue crosses. She wore a green caftan, and her head was enveloped in a cloth expertly tied into a high turban. The eyes were heavily made up with antimony; on her fingers were silver rings, and silver bracelets clinked together on her wrists.

Cabell handed Lydia a brown paper bag. "This is for you."

"I know what it is. We'll have some right now."

The two women sat down on a sofa before the fireplace. Cabell took a seat in an easy chair and pulled a bottle of whiskey out of the bag. On the low table in front of them three glasses and another bottle with just a little whiskey remaining inside had been set out. Grigory brought a bowl of ice and went away again, and Cabell proceeded to pour the drinks.

"Joseph, you look well," Lydia said.

"Do I? Thank you. Some days I think I'm doing fine, others I feel old and tired out."

"You have such a good color. You're in good health, aren't you?"

"I'm healthy."

"But the eyes are very sad."

Matilda Abramovitch quickly finished her drink, and Cabell poured her a second. She sat on the sofa with her legs drawn up beneath her and smoked one cigarette after another; holding the cigarette between thumb and forefinger, she carried it to her lips with her right hand, while her left remained resting on her knee.

"Matilda told me of the boy who died," Lydia said.

"Do you mind if I spoke of Driss to Lydia, Yusef?"

"No, of course not."

"We will talk about it another time, if you wish," Lydia said. "I want to pay you many visits this summer."

Outside, the animals were barking and howling. Grigory entered the room with a dog on a leash, Lydia said something to him in Russian, but he paid no attention to her, and spoke to Matilda, who laughed and replied in the same language.

"Are you all Russians here?" Cabell asked.

"Matilda is Russian, too," Lydia answered. "Grigory," she addressed her brother in French, "please open the door and let Cassandra in."

Grigory mumbled something under his breath, but went to the door and opened it. A young dog burst in immediately, looked apprehensively at the guests, then quickly crossed the room and jumped up onto the sofa beside Lydia.

"This is Cassandra."

Grigory's dog growled, and Grigory gave it a tap with the whip handle. He had taken a seat in a chair next to the window on the far side of the room. He was wearing a faded denim shirt, khaki shorts, and sneakers, and all the sinewy muscles in his arms and legs were visible. His hair and beard were turning gray.

"Don't you think what I said about his figure is true, Matilda?"

"We've been admiring your physique, Grigory," Matilda said. "You have a fine shape for your age."

Grigory was lighting his pipe when suddenly a large orange tarantula appeared on the window sill beside him. Lydia screamed and Grigory leaped out of his chair as the spider dropped to the floor and with remarkable speed ran sideways across the room. Grigory bounded forward and with one blow cut the spider in two with his whip.

They examined the palpitating body of the tarantula, which had a black stripe across its back. Cabell placed his hand beside the spider, and the spider was nearly as large.

"It's the biggest one I've ever seen."

"One must be careful of them," Grigory commented as he relit his pipe. "Their bite can be more dangerous than a scorpion's."

He picked up the two pieces of the spider and threw them out the door, and they all sat down for dinner. A young Moroccan girl brought out a tureen of beet soup and placed it on the table. Lydia served up three bowls of the soup as Cabell poured the wine.

"No, dear Joseph, no wine for me," Grigory said.

"My poor brother, he cannot have this soup, either. Spicy foods give him eczema."

While the others ate and drank, Grigory stared down at his empty plate, his tough callused hands folded before him. The thick fingers had dirt under the nails. After the soup was cleared away, the girl served jellied poulet au citron. Grigory was given a piece of plain boiled chicken, which he washed down with glass after glass of water that he poured for himself from a whiskey bottle.

"You drink a great deal of water, Grigory," Cabell commented.

"Four or five bottles a day," Lydia replied.

"What other dangerous animals do you have out here, Grigory? Snakes?"

"Brother's not afraid of anything," Lydia put in. "Last summer, when I was away, he woke up in the middle of the night, turned on the flashlight, and there was a big snake coiled around his shoes in the middle of the room. Isn't it true?"

Grigory grunted.

"He went after it with a cane, but the snake slid out under the door and came in here. The generator had been turned off for the night, so there were no lights in the house, and for two hours he fought that snake in the dark. The next morning he showed it to the Moroccans, and they were afraid."

"Why?"

"It was more than two meters long."

"Was it poisonous?"

"No, just very strong and active."

Dessert was blackberries and cream, which Grigory was allowed to eat. Cabell was asking Lydia about Russia, and she told a story about her grandfather. As a young man he went to Saint Petersburg, where he fell in love with a French dancing girl. She was common and not so pretty, either, but there were very few French girls in Saint Petersburg in those days, and she had dozens of young Russian gentlemen competing for her favors. Lydia's grandfather learned that the girl desired more than anything else to be driven in a troika sledge over the snow, a romantic experience she had heard much about. Unfortunately, it was summer, but even so he promised her that she would have her sleigh and snow if she would leave Saint Petersburg and accompany him to his estate in the Ukraine. She consented, and off they went. As they traveled south the weather became warmer and warmer. Where would there be a sleigh and snow in heat like this? the girl was complaining. At last they were approaching the estate, and there, at the far end of a long allée, the chateau could be seen. And the whole of the allée itself was white and glistening in the sun. A sleigh and three matched horses awaited them. They jumped down from the carriage, mounted the sleigh and drove up and down. A sugar refinery belonged to the estate, and Lydia's grandfather had ordered a year's entire production of sugar to be laid down for the sleigh to slide smoothly over.

Grigory meanwhile had been talking in a confidential manner to his dog Olive, who lay at his feet beneath the table. Lydia had Cassandra next to her chair, and each had been feeding his dog scraps from the meal. Suddenly a row broke out—the two dogs were fighting under the table. Lydia and Grigory were shouting at each other; Matilda swiveled away from the table and stood behind her chair; Cabell pulled up his feet to keep from being bitten. Finally Grigory went down on his knees and amidst screams and yelps separated the dogs with his whip.

"I told you one dog at the table is enough!" he shouted at his sister.

"I see blood," Matilda remarked. "Whose is it?"

"Olive's ear is bleeding! Whose fault is that?"

Lydia was gently scolding Cassandra.

"One dog at a time I say! Fights every night!"

"Whose dog, then?" Lydia asked.

"Olive—she's older."

"But Cassandra would be lonely outside. You know how she barks."

"Ah! You always say the same thing."

Grigory sat down again and finished his dessert. It was his third helping. When dinner was over, they went out onto the veranda. On the high white arcade geckoes stalked moths attracted by the light. Lydia and Matilda relaxed in the cane chairs; Cabell remained on his feet staring off into the darkness.

"I can hear the sea," he said.

"The wind is out of the west tonight."

Grigory came out with the coffee. "My friends the frogs are singing tonight," he announced.

"Where are they?"

"By the well."

"Grigory has very keen ears. He's able to hear sounds that we cannot."

When they had finished their coffee, Grigory and Cabell went to have a look at the pump. The reservoir was situated in a grove of palms and eucalyptus above the house—high ground which overlooked the plain before Sidi Kacem, with the Atlantic stretching away to the west. Except for the throb of the pump filling the reservoir, no sound disturbed the silence of the African night.

They were standing beneath the palms as Grigory played his flashlight over the water gushing out of a pipe into the reservoir.

"How long does it take the tank to fill?" Cabell asked.

"About five hours. I have to get up with the alarm at one o'clock in the morning and turn off the motor. Every day there must be a full tank for irrigation.

"Is the water clean?"

"It's clean, but we always boil it before drinking. One never knows if a dog or donkey hasn't drowned in the well and polluted the water."

A smaller tank to one side held turtles. They lay on a flat rock and blinked into the beam of the flashlight.

"Lydia's very involved with her animals, isn't she?"

"Not only the animals. She worries about me and keeps me in this convent."

"Do you feel isolated out here?"

"There's plenty to keep us busy on the farm. But not many people come out this way."

"What about Matilda?"

"Oh, yes, she visits us from time to time, but one can never be sure about her."

"Sure of what?"

"Whether she's chosen to appear as a man or woman. If it's a dinner party, Lydia asks me, 'Shall I invite a gentleman or a lady to sit next to her?' "

Grigory had Olive on a leash. On the way back to the house she barked, and the other dogs answered from the courtyard.

"You see what I have to put up with, Joseph? Too many dogs with no breeding in them. Dogs with low character."

Matilda emerged from the shadows; she had changed into her white robes and turban.

"Do you want to go back with me?" Cabell asked her.

"Yes, please."

Lydia came out to see them off. The dogs were still barking. "We're happy you've come back to Tangier, Joseph. We think about you a great deal when you're away in the Sahara."

"Come and see us again soon!" Grigory shouted.

"Your room is always ready. Come to Sidi Kacem whenever you wish, and we shall talk."

Cabell woke up the driver, and he and Matilda set off in the taxi as the dogs raced along behind. The road was extremely bumpy and dusty, and the fine dust rose and entered the vehicle.

"So you're Matilda Abramovitch."

"That's my former name."

"Around Smara the Spanish still refer to you as the Red Spy."

"If I did a little spying, it was done out of my own curiosity, not for anyone else."

"The Spanish have to catch a Russian spy every now and then, you know that."

"Don't you have any reservations about working for them?"

"Yes."

"Why do you think of continuing?"

"I may give it one more try."

"After all that has happened?"

"It had nothing to do with them."

"Aren't you put off by the futility of it all?"

"I don't look at it that way."

"But you had Driss then. What do you have now?"

"A job—if I want it."

"What can that mean?"

"A profession, work . . . a place."

"Yes, I see, especially a place in the desert."

The taxi came out onto the surfaced road, and the dust was left behind.

"Hamid, do you want to go Agla or to Tangier?"

"To Agla, please."

Cabell instructed the driver to take the coast road; a few minutes later they entered the pine forest near Sidi Amar. Cabell said another word to the driver, the taxi turned off the road and went down through the trees to the belvedere overlooking the Straits of Gibraltar. It was a clear night, with the lights of Spain visible across the water.

"Will you come with me, Yusef? Would you like to see where I live?"

"All right. Let me pay the taxi."

Following a rocky trail down through the woods—in some places water was flowing, and the path was wet and slippery—Hamid nimbly led the way, and Cabell walked behind. As they passed through the village of Agla, dogs growled at them through cane fences. Beneath the looming branches of an immense eucalyptus tree was a gate; Hamid opened a padlock with a key, and they went inside.

Suddenly a large dog appeared out of the darkness and snarled at Cabell, who backed away against a tree. Hamid caught the dog and calmed him down.

"That dog there, it's vicious. You ought to tie it up."

"Blanco? He guards the house when I'm away. He's the only only one left."

"I heard you had many dogs. Where are they?"

"Someone killed them."

"Who?"

"Smugglers. They fed them ground meat mixed with iron filings."

"Why would they do such a thing?"

"They were afraid of the dogs and the dogs knew it."

Crossing a flat area beneath the big trees, they came to the house. Hamid went up the wooden steps, undid another padlock, and went inside. Cabell, left alone with the dog, waited in the darkness.

"Where have all your brothers gone, Blanco?"

Inside the house a match was lit, and Hamid emerged with a lantern. The wooden porch and façade took shape, and beyond, the tree trunks stood like massive columns. Their thick branches were festooned with long strips of bark; the night air was full of the heavy scent of eucalyptus. With Hamid holding the lantern, they wandered through the house; except for the kitchen in the rear, where some pots and pans hung over a charcoal stove, and one little room that had a rug on the floor, the house was empty of furniture.

"This is where I am forced to live."

"Why?"

"The house has been in my husband's family for years, and now he owns it. I'm the caretaker while he's away in France."

"Why don't you sell it?"

"We've been trying to for years, but nobody will buy."

"I suppose it's too far away from town, and there are no roads."

"As you can see, the house is falling to pieces. The roof leaks, and it's so damp in winter that I'm afraid to live here, for fear of catching pneumonia."

"It's kind of damp right this minute."

"It's an awful place, but I don't know what to do with it."

"The land must be worth something."

"We have pear and apple trees, but nobody looks after them."

"Isn't there any furniture?"

"Practically all stolen."

"By smugglers?"

"Sometimes they use the house as a headquarters. Either they've carried the furniture away or they burned it in the fireplace."

"I suppose they're safe here."

"If they rob this house one more time, I'm moving out."

"I'd say that you don't have anything to worry about; there's nothing more they can take."

"I hate this house."

"Perhaps next time the smugglers will set fire to it."

"That's an idea. I might do it myself."

Hamid lit another lantern and placed it next to the rug.

"Sit here, Yusef. I'll make tea."

Cabell kicked off his shoes and took a seat on the rug with his back against the wall. Blanco lay down in his place, and in the dim light the two looked at each other. From the kitchen came the sound of bellows; presently Hamid entered with a transistor radio, which she handed to Cabell. He passed her a lighted sebsi. She finished the pipe and returned to the kitchen, while Cabell found Oum Kalsoum on the radio.

"Lady Soul," came Hamid's voice from the kitchen. "Leave that on."

Cabell reached across and patted Blanco on the head. The dog raised its eyebrows and wagged its tail.

"We're going to be friends, aren't we, Blanco?"

Hamid brought a tray and with long strokes poured the smoking tea into the tiny glasses. She was sitting cross-legged before Cabell. Suddenly she frowned, jumped to her feet, left the room and returned with two brocaded cushions, which she placed behind Cabell's back. It was a warm night, and she took off her djellaba. Underneath she wore the baggy Moroccan trousers and an embroidered shirt. For a long time neither spoke. Cabell had shut his eyes. The singing of Oum Kalsoum came to an end, the Moroccan national anthem was played, and the station went off the air. Cabell opened his eyes and reached for the radio. Hamid watched his hands as he tried to find another station.

"Does that silver bracelet come from the desert?"

"Driss gave it to me."

"May I see it?"

Cabell extended his arm. "I don't like to take it off."

She examined the bracelet, then looked at his feet. "Do you always wear blue socks?"

Another long silence followed. The dog was making noises in his sleep.

"I think I've been smoking my sebsi at the wrong end," Cabell said.

Hamid laughed. "I've got you on backwards."

"What does that mean?"

"What do you think?"

They laughed together, then grew silent.

"What does it mean?"

"What does what mean?"

" 'I've got you on backwards.' "

Hamid laughed. "Don't you know?"

"No. What do you think I'm asking you for?"

"It means I had you on the wrong way around."

"What's that mean?"

"What?"

" 'The wrong way around.' "

"It means I had you figured wrong."

"How did you have me figured?"

"I had the Saharan image in my head."

"What's the 'Saharan image'?"

"You and Driss."

"What about us?"

"I thought that was the whole picture."

"It was—complete."

"But there's more to you, isn't there?"

"Yes, there is."

Cabell slipped on his shoes and got to his feet.

"What are you doing?"

"I need air. I've got to go outside."

He stepped onto the porch. The big eucalyptus trees creaked in the breeze. Dogs were barking all over the mountain.

"I'd forgotten about those dogs."

"You're not going to leave, are you?"

"I don't think I could make it up the hill."

"You can spend the night here if you want."

"Is there a place to sleep? Suddenly I feel tired. I've got to rest somewhere."

"The beds were stolen along with everything else, but I can make you comfortable on the rug."

"I'm going to stay out here for a few minutes and breathe."

Hamid cleared away the tray. From a cupboard she brought out blankets and sheepskins and arranged them on the rug. Meanwhile Cabell had relieved himself against a eucalyptus tree and was wandering around the grounds. Water was running somewhere, and the frogs were vocal. When he re-entered the house he found Hamid surveying the bed she had just made.

"That looks comfortable."

"Do you like one pillow or two?"

"Hamid, I've just had an idea how you can make yourself some money."

"How?"

"There are big frogs out here in Agla. All you have to do is catch one and send it to the Zurich zoo. They pay a hundred dollars apiece."

"Oh, Yusef."

"I'm not joking, either. One of these nights we'll go on a frog hunt."

Cabell rolled out of his pants and crawled under the covers. Blowing out the lantern, Hamid lay down beside him.

"Hamid?"

"What, Yusef?"

"Let's change places."

"Why?"

"To keep you between Blanco and me. If he's jealous, we ought not to antagonize him."

"Are you feeling all right, Yusef?"

"Just crawl over me; then there won't be any trouble."

"Blanco's not really jealous."

"Doesn't matter. I don't want any trouble."

"Why do you think he's jealous?"

"Never mind. I've got that feeling."

"He's just distrustful of strangers."

"Don't blame him, after what happened to his friends."

"Poor Blanco."

"I'm not in the mood to tangle with a xenophobic dog."

# *In Yusef's Room*

"Look at these dead flies. Fatomah has become so lazy, she does nothing but shuffle around, make the beds, and talk."

Shahid's long black hand brushed the flies from the window sill onto the floor, and he swept them along with the dust and dirt. On the shelf near the window lay Cabell's objects—the fossilized oyster shell and polished stones from the desert, one of which bore the imprint of an ancient beetle, another on which something was inscribed in Arabic. There was the black metal cook pot, an old Bavarian tea glass with a red feather in it, a small copper box, and a stone bird. Shahid carefully lifted each object, examined it and dusted under it, and replaced it in its exact position. From a peg on the wall a leather envelope hung by its braided cord. He brushed it off with a feather duster. On the bureau was a framed snapshot of Driss in his djellaba leaning against a cement pylon in the desert. The pylon was marked: E→V. Cisneros 408 kms. Beneath the mirror lay an elephant-hair bracelet, with some of the strands broken, and a silver ring. Shahid looked at these but did not touch them.

Omar was sitting at the table in the center of the room, absorbed in something he was drawing. Shahid paused from his sweeping to lean over his shoulder.

"What do you call that?" he asked, pointing with a long black finger.

A very dense, precise geometric design done in ink covered the entire paper. If one looked carefully, one could see within the lines many frightened faces peering out, and the snouts and ears and beady eyes of animals, and the shapes of fish, and human hands and feet.

"I call it Tangier."

Shahid put his finger on one of the faces and laughed. "There's Boujma and the Sultan of Dogs."

"Everyone is there."

"Where am I?"

"There."

"Ah, holding a basketball. Good. What's inside the ball?"

"That's Yusef."

"Why is he inside the ball?"

"I don't know."

"Why is he holding his knees to his chest?"

"That's just the way I drew him."

"Is he going to escape from the ball?"

"I don't know. Perhaps in another drawing. With a pen you can do anything."

Shahid opened the door, swept the little pile of dirt out onto the balcony, and shouted to Fatomah to take it away. She could be heard singing in another part of the hotel. Shahid shut the door.

"Shahid, where is Yusef?"

"I don't know, he doesn't sleep here much any more."

"I spent the night waiting for him."

"He said he was going to Sidi Kacem. Perhaps he just decided to stay out there."

"He might have gone to Merkala. Shall we go look for him?"
"Why? He'll come back."
"I think I'll walk down to Merkala and go fishing."
"Go ahead."
"Yusef might want me to do something for him."
"Like what?"
"If he wants a package of Gitanes no filter," Omar explained, "I go to the tobacco shop."
"You're his friend, why shouldn't you?"
"If he asks, 'Omar, are the watermelons I saw in the market ripe? And what about the cantaloupes?' I find out."
"Nazarenes know nothing about melons."
"If he writes a message to Amigo Maxwell, I deliver it."
"Yusef is always writing something down."
"When he wants to know what's on at the cinema, or when is the next boxing match or wrestling, I tell him."
"If he wants you to do another favor for him now, he'll find you. It's no use to go looking for him."
"I guess you're right."
Omar took up his pen once more, as Shahid went on with his dusting, all the while humming and singing to himself. At the bookshelf he paused to read the titles on the spines of the books, sighed to himself, and straightened up the bed. With that done, he went out and a few minutes later came back in one of his Senegalese shirts; this one was turquoise with typewriters and numbers and letters all over it.
"Omar, is it true that Yusef is able to find water in the desert with a stick?"
Omar shrugged his shoulders. " Idon't know."
"He says the stick is like a thirsty horse; it knows where to find water."
"A stick doesn't have legs."
"Yusef says it pulls and points at the water."
"Is it a trick?"
"He says there are many tricks in the desert."
Shahid was pacing about the table where Omar was sitting.

"We have a match against the American navy next week, so I'm on my way to practice now."

"Good."

"Will Yusef come to the game?"

"I'll tell him."

Shahid went out, and Omar stayed at the table, working with pen and ink. Later there was a knock on the door, and Boujma handed him Cabell's mail. Omar placed the letters on the bureau; for a long time he leaned against the bureau with his chin in his hands, looking at the photograph of his brother. Then he wandered around the room, examining each of Cabell's objects; a large map of Northwest Africa hung near the bed; after studying that for a while, he went back to his work.

July 17 I receive a certain pleasure from keeping this journal. A man who keeps a journal must have a good reason for doing so, and through these pages I think I begin to see an idea for order re-emerging. But finally one desires to give form to what had no form before. Form is the great thing. When did I discover that?

July 18 Cats in the Kasbah, copulating, fighting, screaming. Cats in courtyards under fig trees, in alleyways, running along walls and rooftops, silhouetted before streetlamps. Cats waiting beside mounds of garbage, cats under the tables in cafés.

# *Villa Harris*

It was a hot summer afternoon, the beach before the city was packed with sunbathers, and the water teemed with swimmers and pedal boats. Farther down the shore and away from the crowds, Moroccan fishermen sat in the shade of their black barges, repairing blue nets. The Moroccan cavalry had brought their Arab horses down to the sea for a washing; with snorts and shouts of joy the near-naked recruits were galloping the sleek animals into the waves and scrubbing them down. On the railroad tracks which run along behind the beach Cabell was doing a balancing act, emulated by two boys from the fishermen's quarter. When the tracks curved inland, Cabell went down on the beach, where he stripped down and entered the sea. A flock of country girls in their red-and-white striped skirts and wide straw hats came trotting along and giggled at his nakedness as he stood knee-deep in the water. He rushed a few steps in their direction, and they scattered like ewes before a ram. When they had gone by, he stretched out on the hard sand, exposing himself to the African sun. That afternoon he bathed several times and swam long distances out into the bay.

By the time the six o'clock whistle sounded from the port, he was out on the road, waiting by the canal, as the workers came off the construction site. Among them was Mohamed I, attired in blue overalls and sandals and wearing a straw hat. He had filled out and looked considerably browner than when he had left prison.

Hidden away among the trees and underbrush behind the beach was an old pottery kiln. Mohamed led Cabell there and introduced him to a bearded old man sitting by the door of a hut, chopping onions on a board.

"This is Kaddour."

"Good afternoon, sidi," Cabell greeted the old man in Arabic.

"He's the guardian of the kiln, and this is his hut," Mohamed explained.

"Good."

"He allows me to sleep in the hut, and we share expenses on food."

"I'm an old man," put in Kaddour. "All I'm good for is watching."

"You're working now."

"Let the young men do the hard work. I've labored enough during my lifetime."

Mohamed put down his basket and took off his clothes, and Cabell followed him down to the beach. It was still hot, and they both went in swimming. Afterward they lay on the sand and watched the sun lower over the bay.

"How do you like it out here, Mohamed?"

"The work is good, and I'm earning ten dirhams a day."

"What sort of work is it?"

"We're putting up bungalows for the tourists."

"Do you like this kind of life?"

"For the time being it's good. I'm able to save almost everything I earn."

Cabell nodded.

"I've written my father."

"Is he pleased?"

"I think so. Only one thing bothers me."

"What's that?"

"Here I am lying on this beach while Mohamed is doing his basic training up in the mountains. He must be cold and missing his friends."

Later they went back to the hut. When darkness set in, Kaddour lit a lantern. He was a small man, with compact peasant features and a Roman profile.

"He fought with Abdelkrim against the Spanish," Mohamed informed Cabell.

Kaddour grunted.

"The other night a series of propane bottles exploded over at Villa Harris, and do you know what he did?"

"What?"

"He pulled a rusty old sword out from somewhere and went charging around, hollering and waving the sword. He thought the Rif War had started again."

Kaddour chuckled when he heard Mohamed tell it.

"This boy here," he said, "he's never been in a war, he doesn't know what it's like."

"These old men," Mohamed replied, "all they have are their memories of battles. That's what they dream about, like old hounds chasing rabbits in their sleep."

Kaddour took the lid off a steaming tajine, and they began to eat. Suddenly there were noises in the bushes. Someone was out there.

"Who's that?" Kaddour called out.

"Ya Mohamed, are you there?" a voice cried out.

"Ay Mohamed, is it you?" Mohamed shouted, jumping to his feet. He rushed off into the bushes and returned with his arm around Mohamed II, who was dressed in his army uniform.

"Look who's here!" Mohamed I announced. "Look who God has brought!"

"Ah Yusef! You're here, too?" Mohamed II exclaimed.

In a minute Mohamed II was seated among them on the sand, and while Kaddour prepared tea, they ate what remained of the tajine.

"How did you know we were out here, Mohamed?" Cabell asked.

"Mohamed and I communicate with each other."

"But this hut has no address. The postman doesn't deliver letters in the bushes."

"When I arrived in Tangier, I walked around, asked a few questions, and I ran into M'siksif on the street."

"We're glad you're here."

"So am I. In the army I think about Tangier."

"Tell us about the army, Mohamed," Cabell said.

"Do you remember that first day, Yusef, when you took me to the railroad station?"

"Yes."

"All the recruits were ordered to assemble at the railroad station at six o'clock, but we had to wait all morning for the train. Nobody had any money, there was no food, and we were hungry."

"Ah."

"Finally at two o'clock in the afternoon we were told to climb into an old wooden train, and we set off. But we didn't get very far."

"What happened?"

"The train stopped in Arcila, and we waited some more. It was hot."

"You're going to tell us you did something crazy," Cabell said.

"Crazy, no, but I saw the ocean glittering in the sunlight not so far away, so I climbed down from the window of the train, and walked to the beach and had a swim."

"Fair enough."

"On the way back I spotted some watermelons in a field."

"Here comes trouble."

"Nobody was around, so I took one and carried it back to the train."

"And everyone saw you."

"It was amazing! In a minute hundreds of recruits were jumping out of the train and running across the fields."

"Oh, no."

"The farmer heard the noise and came out of his house in time to witness the invasion of his melon patch. He screamed at the recruits and chased them with his stick, but they dodged away easily and picked up the melons on the run."

"And this was all your doing?"

"Seeing where the boys came from, the farmer went off to town and came back with the police. The police couldn't take the melons back because most of them had been eaten, but they locked the train so we couldn't get out again, and we rode all the way to Meknes eating melons. We weren't hungry or thirsty any more."

"Well, Mohamed, how do you like the army? That's a good-looking uniform you're wearing."

"I like the uniform and I like to shoot, that's all."

"How long can you stay in Tangier?"

"In two days I must return."

They sat around the fire, the boys conversing and laughing and smacking their hands together over mutual points of agreement, with Cabell listening and smiling and poking at the fire with a stick. Kaddour had fallen asleep and was snoring in his place by the hut. Cabell got to his feet.

"I thought you told me he was the guardian of the kiln," he said.

"He is, but nobody is stealing bricks these days."

"Wait, Yusef," Mohamed II said. "We'll walk with you."

"All right."

They went through the bushes and in a few minutes were out on the hard-packed sand, walking along the great curve of beach. To the left the kiln was being stoked up for the night, and a red cloud of smoke and sparks issued from the chimney.

Ahead of them the lights of the city glittered and were reflected on the water; tidal pools in the sand gleamed like obsidian mirrors.

"I think I'll have one last swim," Cabell said.

"Yes, go ahead."

"Aren't you two coming in?"

"We're going to walk on together."

"I thought you liked swimming."

"We do."

"Water looks good, probably warmer than the air."

"There's much to talk about, Yusef. We'll swim later."

Cabell watched them go off with their arms around each other's shoulders, then slowly undressed himself. Instead of directly entering the water, he sat down on the sand with his legs drawn up and his chin resting on his knees. For a long time he remained in that position, unmoving, while the little waves lapped at his feet. Out at sea fishing boats were drifting, and their lights shone down into the water to attract the fish.

Finally he stirred himself, waded into the water, and swam out until he was lost from sight in the blackness of the bay. A few minutes later the Mohameds came back and found Cabell's clothes in a little pile on the sand.

"He's still swimming."

"Shall we go in?"

"No, wait," Mohamed I said. "Yusef!" he called out. "Come in and we'll swim together!"

There was no sound except that made by the little waves rushing against the shore.

"He must be too far out to hear you."

"Yusef, come in!"

"What shall we do—sit down and wait?"

The boys squatted down on the sand and lit cigarettes.

"Why would he swim so far out at night?" Mohamed II asked. "He knew we were coming back."

The two cigarette ends glowed in the dark as the boys smoked in silence. A shooting star fell across the night sky and was extinguished; the little waves continued to splash on the wet sand.

"You don't think he's drowned, do you?"

"How do I know? It's impossible to see a thing."

"What do you think we ought to do—wait here? Go for help?"

"I don't know. Yusef!" Mohamed called out once more. There was no answer.

"He's a good swimmer, isn't he?"

"Yes, but he's always doing things he shouldn't do. He doesn't look after himself."

"What things?"

"One night there was a thunderstorm and the lights went out. Next morning M'siksif found him in a ditch near Merkala. The ditch had water in it and Yusef was drunk. He nearly drowned."

"In a ditch? And now he's out in the bay in the middle of the night."

"He's not drunk."

"Still, maybe we shouldn't have left him."

"Listen," Mohamed I said, "you wait here with his clothes while I go to the fishermen's huts. I know a man there who has a boat. He's a friend of Yusef's, too. We'll come back here in the boat, and if Yusef hasn't come in, we'll row out into the bay and look for him."

"If he's under the water, we'll never find him tonight."

"Then what do you want to do, just sit and wait? Yusef hasn't drowned, he's swimming."

"Then he'll come back."

"Maybe he will, maybe he won't."

"What's he doing?"

"I know Yusef—he's just swimming."

"Why?"

"That's just the way he is, don't ask me why. He's out there somewhere, and he doesn't know where he's going."

Mohamed I went off, and Mohamed II remained with the

little pile of clothes, pacing up and down. From time to time he would stop and call out Cabell's name as the little waves flowed against the shore.

Meanwhile, Cabell had swum far out across the bay. Alternating between the crawl and side stroke, he was making his way slowly but steadily through the dark waters, leaving a wake of tiny eddies streaked with beads of phosphorus. The surface of the bay was calm, yet seemed to be flowing as it reflected the many lights of the city. The eye of the Malabata light flashed out its signal, blindly illuminating everything in its sweeping path. Suddenly a whiteness loomed up in the distance; moving forward quickly and gathering force and form in the darkness, it broke over Cabell, leaving him gasping for breath in its foamy wake. He was out at sea.

Less than a mile off Cape Malabata, open fishing boats rose and fell in the deep swell of the Atlantic as their powerful, battery-operated lamps shined down into the water. Each boat contained four or five men, who were busy with heavy lines and multiple hooks, methodically hauling in the fish attracted from the dark waters into the spheres of light. Generally there was not much talk among the boats, but occasionally a remark would ring out over the water, be answered by a shout and laughter, then silence. Among the fishermen in the boat closest to the shore was a man with a patch over one eye, and it was he who first caught sight of something moving on the surface at the edge of light. Without speaking, he nudged the fellow next to him, and in another second all four men were gazing at Cabell's naked form approaching the boat. A few feet away he stopped swimming and treaded water; in the bright light shimmering through the depths around him, he appeared like some strange aquatic beast, an albino merman.

"Hello," he said.

Gripping the edge of the boat, the fishermen leaned forward and peered at him as if he were some new fish they themselves had hooked, which had surfaced and spoken to them.

Cabell paddled closer. "Can I come on board and rest? The waves have tired me out," he said in Arabic.

Four pairs of hands reached down and hauled him out of the water; he tumbled into the bottom of the boat among the fish, which still flopped about, where he looked like some weird new addition to the catch. The leathery fishermen continued to eye him suspiciously. Cabell squirmed into a sitting position against the side of the boat and returned their stares. His attention rested on the man with the patch.

"You're Maxwell's friend, aren't you?"

The others looked at their one-eyed companion.

"No, that's not correct. He's never really met you; you just happen to be the first Moroccan he laid eyes on when he stepped off the boat."

The man said nothing.

"I see you don't even know who I'm talking about. And of course that was long before you lost your eye. It was a fishing accident, wasn't it?"

The men again shifted their attention to the man with the patch, but he said nothing.

"Can't remember who it was that told me, said a fishhook got caught in the eye and out it came, isn't that right?"

The men nodded.

"Isn't it funny, that I should have picked your boat to swim to, drawn to it like a moth to light. When you come to think of it, these fish, the ones I'm sitting on, aren't caught on hooks and lines at all, they're caught on light. Just like myself."

"Who are you? What are you doing here?"

"Swimming."

"Swimming? At night? In the ocean?"

"Why not?"

Fishermen in the other boats had begun to notice the conversation, and questions were shouted across the water.

"What's going on over there?"

"What's all the talk? Who's that doing the talking?"

"We've caught a new fish," was the reply.

"What sort of fish?"

"A loco fish. It talks."

"A talking fish? Madre mia, Stito, I told you to leave your hashish in port."

"What's it look like?"

"It sort of looks like you!"

"Like me? You belong to the race of your mother, Stito!"

"A Nazarene fish!"

"Listen to that filthy insult, everybody! He's accused me of being a Christian!"

"A Nazarene fish that talks? Por Dios!"

"Stito not only forgot to leave his hashish in port, he's got that jug of Whiskey Abdullah with him as well!"

"If God doesn't punish him, I will. With the top of my head!"

"He's gone crazy again. That fishhook not only plucked his eye, it plucked out his brains, too!"

"I swear, by God, it's a Nazarene fish!"

"If it's true, Stito, are you going to keep it or throw it back?"

"How big is it?"

"As big as you are!"

"Good Lord! Loco fisherman catches loco fish!"

"He's really gone off his head this time, hasn't he?"

Cabell had slipped down into the bottom of the boat, where he lay shivering among the fish. The four fishermen were whispering among themselves when another boat entered the circle of light. Mohamed I was in the bow, Mohamed II in the stern, another man was rowing.

"Have you seen a swimmer?" Mohamed I called out.

"Yes, he's here."

"Thanks to God. Where is he?"

"Here, in the boat, with the fish."

The two boats came together, and Cabell was lifted from one to the other. They attempted to talk to him but got no coherent reply, and Mohamed II began to put his clothes on him. Mohamed I gave an order, the man pulled on the oars once more, and in another minute the boat had disappeared into the darkness.

"Who was that?" came a voice across the water.

"The soldiers came for the fish."

"Ah! The soldiers are fishing now, are they?"

"That's right, in boats!"

"Ay, Stito! When are you going to stay off that stuff?"

July 25 Today, just before leaving Tangier, Mohamed II came to check on me and recounted this dream he had had at the army camp: In the middle of a green field was a small tree with twisted branches and a mass of tangled, intertwining roots. Somewhat like the argane tree which grows in southern Morocco, but smaller. Mohamed was sitting at the base of the tree; for some reason he allowed his hand to wander down among the roots, when all of a sudden he felt a sharp pain. A snake had bitten him. He shouted, and I came running from a long distance away, scattering herds of black goats from my path. With my knife I cut open the bite, which was between his thumb and forefinger. He was frightened and said, "Yusef, if I die my final wish is that you take care of Mohamed I." At that instant the snake appeared from the roots. I killed it and said we must take it to a doctor to see if it is poisonous. Blood was pouring out of his hand. It was a small green snake—green and white. I picked it up, and we walked down a country road. Someone was coming toward us, and I said to Mohamed, "It's Driss, I think it's Driss!" But it wasn't Driss, only somebody who resembled him. As we passed each other, I asked, "Aren't you Driss? You look so much like him." The man pointed at the dead snake I was carrying and turned his head away. Later we found a doctor who said that the snake was not poisonous.

# *Basketball*

Pepe took the ball in bounds from Ahmed, dribbled into the corner, and passed the ball to the outstretched hands of Shahid, who was standing just outside the key. Despite being double-teamed and fouled heavily across the shoulder, he arched a soft hook shot into the basket. The crowd thundered. "Congo! Congo!" they shouted. That shot tied the game with less than a minute to play, but here came the Americans breaking fast down court. One would think that this must be the African team, for with the exception of their white ensign coach, they were all black. The Tangier team included two Moroccans, a Spaniard, a Jew, and Shahid, the ringer from Senegal. Now an American took a jump shot from the outside; the ball rimmed the basket, and Shahid grabbed the rebound. Samuel and Rachid brought the ball down despite a full-court press by the frantic Americans.

"Cover number five!" they shouted. "Don't let him shoot!"

"Congo! Congo!" the fans chanted.

Shahid did get the ball, again from Pepe, but did not attempt a shot as the defenders converged on him. Instead he passed off to Samuel, who drove in for a lay-up. The ball hung spinning on the rim of the basket, Shahid leaped up and tapped it in, the whistle blew, and that was the game. Shrieking with delight, the spectators poured out of the stands and surrounded their glistening heroes. The American players came over and one by one shook Shahid's hand. His admirers gazed with awe at these muscular athletes; it was incredible that they could have been defeated.

"Nice game, Congo," said the young ensign in his white naval uniform, who had just made his way through the cluster of enthusiasts.

"Thank you," Shahid replied in his best English. "We are pleased and honored."

The crowd streamed out of the Hasnona basketball court and dispersed down the dark streets under a sky full of stars. The Americans were boarding their bus as the ensign stood by the door talking with Cabell.

"Where did that big fellow learn to play basketball?"

"He used to be on the Senegalese Olympic team."

"So that's it. He could play for anybody."

"That's just what he does, he travels around and plays for any team that will hire him."

"He can really jump, that boy. Is he a friend of yours?"

"We live in a hotel in the Kasbah."

"You're lucky."

"I suppose I am."

"Where I come from, you couldn't do that."

"Ah. Say, why don't you come have a drink with us?"

"I have to take them back to the ship. If you all come down to the harbor, you'll be welcome on board."

"All right, we might do that."

The navy bus went off; a few minutes later the Tangier players began to appear and were escorted away by their friends.

The lights above the court were shut off. Finally Shahid stepped out, dressed in a green shirt with rockets on it, and joined Cabell; across the street a group of boys caught sight of him and shouted in unison:

"Congo! Congo! Congo!"

At the Italian School a few blocks down the avenue, the Goethe Institute concert had just come to an end, and George Maxwell and Palmeta Gordillo emerged from the old Moroccan palace with the other music lovers. While Palmeta stood under the palm fronds chatting with her friends, Maxwell went out on the street to hail a taxi. One came rattling down the hill from the Marshan and pulled over to the curb; Maxwell and Palmeta got in and the taxi went off. When it reached the intersection at Calle Belgica, Maxwell caught sight of Cabell and Shahid taking a short cut across the filling station on the corner. He waved and called to them, but they did not hear.

"Who's that, Jorgito? Why are you shouting into the streets?"

"That's Joseph Cabell, the man I was telling you about, and his friend Shahid, the athlete from Senegal."

"Shahid the athlete is someone I read about in *España*, but I don't recall this Señor Cabell. Is he a friend of yours, Jorgito?"

"Joseph Cabell is the man from Rio de Oro."

"Ah, yes, now I remember. The one who finds water where nobody else can."

"That's him."

"Does he enjoy classical music, Jorgito?"

"I don't know."

"Perhaps he'd like to join us for one of our musical evenings."

"I doubt it, but I'll ask him."

The taxi was passing along the main boulevard. Sidewalks were jammed with strollers and window-shoppers who had spilled onto the street, and the automobiles honked their horns as they made their way through.

"You're so quiet, Jorgito. What are you thinking about?"

"About Cabell."

"Don't you enjoy our musical evenings any more, Jorgito?"

"I must start moving around more," Maxwell muttered to himself.

"What did you say, Jorgito?"

"I said I must start moving."

"Moving? Where are you going, Jorgito?"

"I don't know."

"May I come with you?"

"No."

The taxi drew up before Palmeta's building, and the night guardian stepped out of the shadows and opened the door. Maxwell and Palmeta rode the elevator to the fourth floor and entered her apartment; when Palmeta switched on the light, a voice from the corner said in Spanish: "Good morning."

"Good evening, Coco."

Maxwell went over to the cage. "Give me your foot," he squawked in a parrot voice.

The parrot bowed its head against the bars to have it scratched.

"You love that, don't you, Coco?"

"Ah! Ah!" muttered the parrot. "Dust the table. Sweep the floor."

Palmeta's sitting room was large and uncluttered; every object seemed to have its place. The brass standing lamp was brightly polished. Maxwell sat down in the easy chair and was glancing through some Spanish magazines while Palmeta could be heard in the kitchen, humming and talking to herself and closing the refrigerator door. In another minute she appeared bearing a tray with a bowl of ice, lemon slices, two tall glasses, two bottles of tonic water, and a half-gallon bottle of Beefeater's Gin.

"Shall I put on a record, Jorgito?"

"I've heard enough music for one evening," Maxwell said without looking up.

Palmeta was a tall, good-looking Spanish woman in her late

forties, with a very dark complexion, and she wore her hair drawn tightly back into a bun behind her head. She was dressed entirely in black; her eyes were black; she was almost gypsy-like in appearance.

Maxwell was pouring the drinks.

"It seems that the monster is almost finished," she observed, referring to the gin bottle. "Do you think we can find another?"

"The bootlegger has taken his family on vacation to Spain."

"Are you in the mood to travel, Jorgito?"

"You know I never move out of this place. One trip to Torremolinos in twenty-two years. It's disgusting."

"Is your friend Señor Cabell a well-traveled man, Jorgito?"

"He's been all over the world."

"Is he married?"

"Why do you ask?"

"I thought he might have a wife somewhere, whom he goes back to from time to time."

"I don't know; we never discussed it."

"Perhaps the poor man is a widower."

"It makes no difference. He's here, and there's no woman with him."

The parrot was whistling and climbing around the cage. Maxwell got to his feet and went to the window.

"What are you thinking about, Jorgito? Do you want something to eat? I can fry some sausage."

"I'm not hungry."

The window overlooked the lower city and the harbor, where the American warship lay alongside the quay with strings of electric lights stretching from its mast to stern and bow. Another large vessel was in the port, as well as smaller coastal steamers and the ferry boats from Spain and Gibraltar.

"I wonder where they went."

"Who, Jorgito?"

"Cabell and Congo."

"Are you still thinking about them? Please come and sit down,

Jorgito. I've never seen you like this before. Is there anything I can do?"

"Dust the table," squawked the parrot as he hung upside down from the top of his cage. "Sweep the floor."

Shahid and Cabell were approaching the entrance to the port; the policeman on guard saluted and allowed them to pass. Overhead, neon lights cast their shadows on the pavement, and the shadows grew longer as they walked away from the entrance. Rounding the corner of a warehouse, they were suddenly in darkness. Cabell was smoking a cigarette, and Shahid, a head taller, strode by his side with a long springy step. Their footsteps echoed among the empty custom sheds and looming warehouses. Entering the fishing port, with many small boats bobbing in the water, they passed rows of lockers where the fishermen store their nets, and came to the repair sheds. The big wooden hulks, supported by oil drums and planks, were just visible in the gloom; the odor of creosote was strong. Then the way before them opened up. To the right were long hangarlike buildings where cork and wheat were stored; on the left was the high sea wall. On the other side, water could be heard sucking at the rocks.

They were nearing the line of ships along the pier. The big one came from Havana—an old ship, with the rust bulging through thick layers of black paint and streaking the hull. Loading booms hung over the side, the cables and nets lay in a tangle on the pier. Except for a solitary Cuban in a fatigue hat and army clothes who lounged on the rail, nobody seemed to be on board. The sailor had an oversized head, with the eyes wide apart, and a great twisted nose. There was nothing symmetrical about him. Shahid and Cabell stopped and looked up, and he returned their stare.

"I know what you're looking at," the sailor said.

Cabell and Shahid exchanged glances.

"You think I'm a freak."

Shahid didn't speak Spanish, and Cabell translated the Cuban's words.

"I'm accustomed to people gawking; just don't overdo it, or I'll come down there and lay my hands on you," the Cuban said, holding up two powerful fists.

"We've never seen anything like you before," Cabell replied.

"That's the truth, there aren't many like me around."

"Do you come from Havana with sugar?"

"What else is there to carry?"

"How's Fidel?"

"Fidel is loco in the coco."

Shahid chuckled at this remark.

"Hey, you there. Are you Moroccan?"

Shahid shook his head. "Senegalese."

"What about your friend? He looks like a gringo to me."

"You're right," Cabell said.

"Do you belong to that gringo ship?" the Cuban asked, pointing to the brightly lit American warship moored a short distance up the pier.

"No. We're alone. We live here."

"Hey, gringo, you look sad, your face is down, but that's all right."

"Why is it all right?"

"Sad gringos I don't mind; just keep away the ones who are pleased with themselves, that's all I ask."

Cabell turned to Shahid to translate.

"Here, you look as if you could use some of this." The Cuban held up a bottle: it had a white cord attached to the neck, by which the Cuban lowered it, hand over hand, to Cabell.

"What's this?"

"Matarata they call it here. Drink it and don't ask any questions."

Cabell took a swig, and his hand went to his neck. "Ow! Matarata burns the throat!"

The Cuban laughed. "Don't be greedy, gringo. Give some to your friend."

"He's a Moslem; he doesn't drink."

The Cuban tugged on the cord. Cabell let go of the bottle and up the ship's side it went. The Cuban took a long drink.

"Ah!" He wiped his mouth with the back of the enormous hand. "All right, gringo," he said, pointing his finger at Cabell, "what makes you so sad?"

"What did he say?" Shahid was asking.

"He wants to know why I look so sad."

"He doesn't have to answer you," Shahid replied in French.

"What did your black friend say, gringo?"

"He says it's none of your business."

"Let's have another drink, then," the Cuban went on. "Matarata will loosen your tongue."

The bottle was again lowered down the ship's side. Cabell seized it and drank.

"That's it, gringo. Matarata will have the truth out of any man."

Shahid tried to take the bottle from his friend. "Don't drink so much of that, Yusef, it might be poison."

"It's all right."

"But look at the effect it's having on that lunatic on the ship."

"Let your friend drink, black man! Well, gringo?"

"I have nothing to say."

"Oh, yes, you do. Speak!"

"What do you want to know?"

"I want to know why your face is so long."

"Come on, Yusef," Shahid implored, "let's visit the American ship. This man is looking for a fight."

"Leave him alone," the Cuban commanded. "Let him speak, or he'll go for a swim under the keel of this ship."

Cabell took another drink from the bottle.

"Now, gringo, tell me your tale."

Cabell shook his head.

"Don't ask any more questions!" Shahid shouted. "We don't know who you are."

"What have you got against gringos?" Cabell asked.

"What have I got against them?" The Cuban laughed. "You mean what has the whole world got against them!"

"Well, let's hear it."

"You're a bunch of murderers, that's what! Out to slaughter the yellows and the blacks, whatever isn't white like you."

"What's he saying, Yusef?"

"Shut up, black man, I'm talking to your friend! How many Ay-rabs you killed so far, gringo? Is the list long? That's it!—you've murdered someone and you can't hide it. It's all over your face!"

"Shut up yourself!" Cabell shouted.

"Better watch out there, black man. He'll have his hands around your throat next!"

The sailor tugged on the cord, but Cabell yanked the bottle back, and hurled it at the sailor's head. He ducked, and the bottle smashed against the cabin behind him. With a scream of rage, the sailor ran down to the deck and vaulted the railing onto the pier. Cabell lunged at him and knocked him to the ground with his fist. Then Shahid pushed Cabell roughly aside and stepped in between. The Cuban jumped to his feet, but his second rush was momentarily halted, as he seemed to realize for the first time how big Shahid was. Moving in crab fashion, he tried to dodge around to get at Cabell, but Shahid caught him by the shirt and, pulling the sailor violently toward him, butted him in the nose with the top of his head. The sailor grunted and sank to his knees; there was blood on his face. He attempted to rise, and although he was a powerfully built man in the arms and shoulders, the legs appeared stunted and weak. He was struggling, but Shahid held him down; then he jerked him up and butted him in the face once more. The blood was flowing freely now; he was cut over the eye, and the large nose must have been broken. Nevertheless, he continued to howl and tried to take Shahid by the throat, but Shahid held him at arm's length, so the Cuban flailed helplessly. When he began to kick out at Shahid's crotch, Shahid dragged him to the edge of the pier, and after some difficulty in disentangling himself from the man's clutching hands, threw him over. The man floundered about in the water, his high voice reverberating against the wall of the pier. It was evident he could swim, and soon he splashed his way to the base of a stone stairway and dragged himself out of the water. Shahid took Cabell's arm and led him away; in a minute they had disappeared among the warehouses. Meanwhile, voices of alarm were rising from inside the ship. Still bawling with rage, the sailor had clambered up the stairs and was standing in a puddle of sea water. His shipmates began to appear on deck; from their remarks and laughter they apparently believed that their drunken friend had simply fallen over the rail.

When Shahid and Cabell returned to the Hotel Splendid, they found Boujma and a boy playing checkers in the garden. The boy jumped to his feet and handed Cabell a letter. Cabell's hands were still trembling as he opened the letter and read it.

Dear Comrade,

As I have nothing to eat, I want to ask you, if you can spare it, to lend me 10 DH to live on for a day or two. I'd like to buy some meat and pay back a few debts. I must admit that I've been lazy, even too lazy to pick pears off the ground and take them to market. But all that will change, I hope. Try to do this for a friend, who sends his thanks in advance. You may send the money directly by my little messenger.

Hamid

P.S. I would be happy to pay you a visit in your hotel. I have news from France and news from the Sahara, and am in need of your good counsel.

"What's the matter with Yusef?" Boujma whispered to Shahid after Cabell had gone upstairs. "His hands are shaking."

"Nothing. We had a fight with a sailor."

"Who won?"

"We did."

"Good."

# *Point of Departure*

THE FOLLOWING EVENING Boujma was cutting kif in the courtyard of the Hotel Splendid. Seated on a straw hassock before a low wooden table, he began by rubbing the dry kif branches between his hands. The tiny leaves and seeds fell onto a piece of wrapping paper spread out on the table as he discarded the empty stalks one by one. Next he shook the leaves and seeds onto a wooden cutting board, which he tilted carefully, allowing the seeds to roll down the board as he ran his hand gently over the kif. This process took some time, after which the seeds were placed in their own piece of wrapping paper and set aside. Now Boujma rested for a minute and took out his own supply of kif and had a smoke. Above his head the banana leaves stirred in the evening breeze; a few feet away the Sultan of Dogs lay in the hole it had dug for itself. The hotel was quiet, with a few noises filtering in from the street.

The pipe finished, Boujma resumed his work. Taking out a pocketknife and sharpening it carefully against a stone, he separated a portion of the cleaned kif from the main pile, pressed it firmly down on the board with his fingers and, wielding the knife like a paper cutter, commenced chopping the kif. This is a lengthy procedure, and when the kif had reached the consistency of a rough powder, he poured it into a sardine can with a perforated bottom. The sardine can contained a bright Kennedy fifty-cent piece, which he shook together with the kif. The fine kif sifted onto another piece of paper, which he folded over and placed beneath him on the hassock. The kif which had not passed through the perforations was dumped back onto the board to be recut with the next batch. And so the work went on. When all of the kif had been satisfactorily chopped and sifted, Boujma reached for a wrinkled leaf of tobacco, sprinkled water on it, and began to cut and sift it as he had done the kif. This done, he brought out the kif, which had become a warm flat cake beneath his weight, mixed it with the smaller amount of tobacco, and recut and resifted it all together. The blend had a greenish-brown color, and although Boujma had chopped it very finely, each grain of tobacco and kif was separated from every other.

Now he was stuffing the kif into a goat bladder, which with all the kif inside swelled to the size of a fist. The work completed, he smoothed out the wrapping papers and put them with the sardine can and knife and stone and board into a cupboard. During the whole process not one grain of kif or tobacco, not even one kif seed, had fallen to the ground; even the barren kif stalks were wrapped carefully before being thrown away.

The bell of the Spanish church clinked twelve times: it was midnight. Boujma was bedding down, and the hound had come out of its hole and was stretching itself in anticipation of the all-night vigil, when Cabell came in.

"Ah, Boujma. Has anyone been looking for me?"

"No, nobody. Here, take this; it's ready."

He handed Cabell the stuffed bladder.

"Good." Cabell squeezed the little sack and bounced it in his hand. "I've just seen a film about the Algerian revolution," he said.

"That's nothing. The war in the Rif, against the Spanish and the French, now that was something different." Boujma put his hand on Cabell's arm. "Did I ever tell you about that engagement I took part in near Targuist?"

"I don't think so," said Cabell, rolling his eyes.

"We'd cut off one of their outposts, and the Spanish soldiers were without water or supplies. Every day an airplane would fly over and drop food and cakes of ice."

"Why ice?"

"They would melt it down for water. Sometimes the ice would fall inside the outpost, but mostly outside. Meanwhile, we waited."

"How many days?"

"Many days. We built our cook-fires to windward of the fort, so the Spaniards could smell the odor of roasting lambs. As we ate our meals we heard them screaming and cursing. Then one night at dinnertime we left our smoking fires and crept around to leeward of the post."

"The Spaniards were thinking about their stomachs."

"They didn't have much time to think about anything else before we were over the walls."

"What happened?"

"We killed them, chopped them to bits, every one of them."

"Moroccans know how to fight."

"Yusef, if you Americans didn't have all your tanks and airplanes, we Moroccans could defeat you, too."

"Boujma, your conception of war is hiding behind trees, sneaking up behind someone with a knife, and staging ambushes with rifles and pistols."

"The modern wars are too big. The old battles were exciting and fun."

"With the action always terminating in rape and pillage."

"Why not? When you win, you get a reward, have some fun. Isn't that fair?"

When Cabell went up to his room, Boujma spread out his sheepskins and settled down for the night. Except for the sound of the Sultan of Dogs licking and scratching itself and snuffling after fleas, the courtyard receded into silence.

The clock in the Spanish church had just clinked twice when a figure appeared in the doorway of the hotel. Entering uncertainly, it staggered up against the wall. It was Hamid. She was dressed in her white Moroccan clothes, with a brown leather envelope hanging from her shoulder by a braided cord. The dog growled as she passed through the courtyard, but she paid no attention and went upstairs. At Cabell's door she hesitated, then entered quietly and sat down on the chair in the center of the room. The sound of regular breathing came from the bed; then the breathing changed and the bed springs moved.

"Is that you, Hamid?"

"Yes."

"I didn't know whether you were coming or not, and I was so sleepy I couldn't keep my eyes open any longer. Have you been there long?"

"Just a few minutes. Go on sleeping; I'll wait."

"I'm awake now."

Cabell left the bed, crossed the floor barefoot, and slipped on his trousers. Then he turned on the light and stood before her. She was looking at him. His chest and shoulders were brown from the sun. Bringing out a brandy bottle and glasses, he poured out two drinks.

"Yusef, what shall I do with all this money?"

"What money?"

"The money I won in the lottery."

"Keep it, it's yours."

"Did you know the ticket would be a winner?"

"Yes."

"But how?"

"The ticket's a gift from a friend who always knows."

"How can he?"

"He doesn't want any questions asked."

"Oh, I'd like to meet this friend."

Hamid took out a package of cigarettes and lit one. Cabell altered the direction of the table lamp so that most of the light fell on her, and the tiny blue tattoos on the backs of her hands stood out precisely. She brought a tattooed hand to her face and touched one of the prominent cheekbones. The extreme pallor of the face, with the black eyes and the short crop of reddish hair, gave her the appearance of a half-caste Oriental; the impression of addiction was suggested by the intense manner with which she inhaled her cigarette. The hand passed from the cheekbone to the eyes; the light was too bright for her.

"Yusef, I can't see you."

Cabell changed the position of the light so it shone on the wall above the bed.

"What's your news from France?"

"My husband, Ali, has written that he expects to return to Morocco in the fall."

"And so you'll be going south with him."

"If I can wait that long."

In a neighboring house a woman was shouting and a child cried. The angry voice of a man answered, a door slammed, and the sounds became muffled.

"And what news from the Sahara?"

"I have word from Ali's brother Abdelmalik. Did I tell you about him?"

"I don't think so."

"He lives in the village of Icht and owns a truck. He claims he has found the perfect location for our café and grocery store —a mud dwelling at the edge of the village."

Cabell was pouring more brandy into the glasses. "Sounds good."

"He wishes to become a partner in the café; we can grow vegetables on his plot of land in the oasis."

"That sounds even better."

"He wants me to come to Icht, to see for myself if this house will be suitable for the café."

"When?"

"Now."

"Are you going?"

"I don't know. I told Ali I'd look after the house in Agla."

"You have some money to travel on."

"Yes, thanks to you."

"Nothing's going to happen to the house."

"Ali might be disappointed that I didn't wait for him."

"You'll be coming back."

"You know me, Yusef, I put things off from day to day, and nothing happens. I've become lazier than the laziest Arab. What's your advice?"

Cabell switched off the lamp, went to the window, and opened the shutters. "Go," he said.

"When?"

"Now, tomorrow. Can you?"

"Yes, I can leave right away."

"Then do it. I'll put you on the bus to Casablanca in the morning."

"May I spend the night here?"

"Of course."

On a rooftop across the street a group of Moroccans was seated around a charcoal brazier. They had been talking and smoking, and now one of them began to play on a lute. A tambourine took up the accompaniment, and someone began to dance, slowly, as the others sang:

"*There's a slave woman sitting in the cabin . . . She's got a big fat ass . . .*"

The end of Hamid's cigarette glowed as she drew on it, and the brandy bottle clicked against the glasses as Cabell refilled them.

"Hamid, do you remember our conversation at Merkala?"

"The mission. Oh, God, where do you want me to go?"

"Imjijt."

"Imjijt? Oh, Yusef, that's in Rio de Oro. I can't go there."

"Have you ever been?"

"Once—I passed through on the way to Smara."

"So you know where it is."

"Right inside the frontier. Who do you know in Imjijt?"

"A man called Atkinson. He's a geologist who's been wandering around the desert for a couple of years, but I've known him long before that. I brought him to Rio de Oro with me. He's kind of eccentric and talks so big that he impressed the Spanish with tales of fantastic mineral deposits he's discovered around the world."

"Has he?"

"He found a lot of copper in the Andes. Anyhow, the Spanish let him poke around on his own, which is what he likes to do. They used to keep a close check on his activities, but they don't take him so seriously any more—I bet they don't even know he's in Imjijt. He's been there several months, the longest he's ever stuck anywhere, and he may be on to something. The letter's for him."

"What does he have to do with watering the desert?"

"He might be able to show me how it could be done."

"Why would he know and not you?"

"I'm not sure that he does. I just want to find out if he has any new ideas."

"Don't you want to deliver the letter yourself, Yusef?"

"If the Spanish heard I'd been in Imjijt, I might have trouble explaining myself."

"What about me? They've already put me in jail once."

"Actually, there shouldn't be a Spaniard in Imjijt, but in case there is, you're the only person who can slip across the border and back without being noticed. Will you go? You'd be doing me a great favor."

"It's dangerous, Yusef. What if there are soldiers about?"

"You know how to avoid them."

"What if I do get into trouble?"

"I'll get you out."

"How?"

"Don't worry, I'll hear about it."

"If there is trouble, will you promise to come yourself?"

"I promise."

"All right, Yusef, I'll go to Imjijt for you."

Hamid had allowed her hand to move across the table; her fingers were playing with the hair on Cabell's arm. As her chin rested heavily in the palm of the other hand, her elbow kept slipping off the edge of the table.

"I'm drunk, Yusef."

"I know."

"Am I doing the right thing?"

"I think so."

"I'm exercising the greatest restraint in order to remain calm. I feel I'm on the edge, and I don't want to slip off."

"On the edge of what?"

"On the edge of many things—on the edge of my patience, on the edge of the Sahara, on the edge of this chair . . ."

As she spoke, the chair slipped away, and she fell to the floor underneath the table, where she sat and began to laugh. Cabell pushed his chair back to look at her.

"Are you all right?"

"I'm all right. Leave me here, Yusef; don't touch me."

"Are you going to stay there?"

"Yes, I want to stay right where I am, here on your floor."

"Go ahead."

"It's where I belong, and besides, I want to look at your feet."

"Good. Can you see them in the dark? Shall I turn the light on?"

"You have such beautiful feet, Yusef. You don't mind if I touch them, do you?" She was stroking his feet and running her fingers between the toes. "Such nice feet."

"Thank you, but the doctor disagrees."

"Oh? What does the doctor say?"

"He says they have a structural defect."

"What does that mean, Yusef?"

"It means that they're not very well put together. If I walk over a long distance, they begin to hurt."

"Do they hurt now, Yusef?"

She gave one of them a kiss.

"They feel fine when you do that."

"Good."

She was resting her head against his ankle.

"Do you want another drink, Hamid?"

"Yes, please."

He poured out another glass of brandy and handed it down to her.

"You don't mind if I stay here, do you?" she asked.

"Not at all."

She pulled herself up into a sitting position with her head resting against Cabell's legs; one of her hands had slid up his calf and gripped him behind the knees. There was a long silence. Suddenly she fell over backward and lay stretched out on the floor.

"What's the matter?"

"Oh! God!" she moaned and began to roll about on the floor, knocking her legs against the table, nearly upsetting the bottle of brandy. Then she lay still for a moment and looked up at Cabell.

"Are you all right, Hamid?"

She rolled away from the table and disappeared under Cabell's bed.

"Oh, my God, where am I?"

"You're under my bed."

There was a minute in which neither spoke.

"I like it here."

"Good." Cabell was pouring himself the last of the brandy.

"Are you sure you don't mind if I stay here for a while?"

"Of course not."

"I'm nervous about this trip."

"Why?"

"Part of me wants to go, part of me wants to stay here with you. Won't you come?"

"I'll be here when you get back."

"We must travel together some day, Yusef."

"We will."

Another minute of silence followed.

"Yusef."

"What?"

"I'd like to come out now."

"Come on."

"I think I'm stuck."

Cabell went over to the bed, took hold of one of her legs, and pulled her out. Then he sat down on the bed. Hamid remained on the floor and wrapped her arms tightly around his legs and rested her head against his knees. Gradually she slid her arms up over his thighs.

"You don't have syphilis, do you, Yusef?"

"God, I don't know, I hope not."

"You mean you're not sure?"

Cabell lay back on the bed and began to laugh.

"What's so funny?"

"Do you always ask a man if he has syphilis before you make love?"

"Not always, sometimes."

"Why didn't you ask before?"

"I don't know. I forgot."

"What about yourself, do you have syphilis?"

"No, but I had it once, and I don't want to catch it again."

"Well, you won't catch it from me."

Still on her knees, she unbuttoned Cabell's pants and was kissing him gently up and down his thighs, as he arched to meet her. Her hands were behind his buttocks, and he locked his fingers around her head to guide her movements. Gradually the movements subsided, then ceased altogether. Her grip around Cabell relaxed.

"Hey, don't stop now."

When there was no answer, he sat up and looked at her. She was breathing deeply and regularly; she had fallen sound asleep.

Gradually the darkness faded, and gray light entered the room where Cabell lay naked on top of the bed and Hamid, covered by his shirt and trousers, was curled up on the floor. Outside, the swallows had risen from their nests, and through the open window they could be seen wheeling and soaring above the city. Cabell stirred and looked at the clock on the bureau: four forty-five. Hamid was still asleep, with her knees drawn up close to her chest. Cabell leaned over and shook her gently.

"Hamid, we better get up."

"Already?"

"You want to make that bus, don't you?"

"I want to sleep, too."

"This is a big day; the desert is waiting."

While Hamid splashed water on her face, Cabell placed an envelope on the table. Then he called her over.

"This is the letter for Atkinson. You must bring his reply back with you."

"All right."

"No letters through the post. You must insist on this, do you understand?"

Hamid put the letter into her leather envelope.

"Are you ready, Hamid?"

"Yes."

They left the room and went quietly down the stairs, across the patio, and out into the street. As they walked through the Place de la Kasbah, the call to prayer sounded from the mosques of the city. It was a Friday, and a black flag flew from the tower of the Kasbah Mosque. Passing through the Kasbah gate, they had a view of the Medina, with smoke rising from the early-morning cook fires. Beyond, the wide arc of beach before the city lay deserted; the placid surface of the bay was broken only by the wake of a fishing boat making its way into port from the open sea. The sun was rising through the mists over Cape Malabata; already it was so bright that they had to look away. The lighthouse blinked three times and went out.

They went down the long stairway into the Medina, past the Arab shops and tailor stalls all shut up with the long metal bars padlocked diagonally across the doors. Cabell strode along while Hamid bounced along behind, attempting to retie her turban and at the same time keep the bulging leather envelope in its place at her side. The alley leveled and came out into the Socco Chico: here the street cleaners were at their work, plying the homemade brush brooms and talking, or taking time out for a pipe of kif. A handful of insomniacs and other night people regarded Cabell as he went by, with Hamid following like a Moroccan servant.

The air was full of swallows swooping and rushing before the yellow Spanish façades. In front of the bus station there was the usual collection of shoeshine boys, candy vendors, kif salesmen, Spanish ladies on their way to Tetouan, and Moroccan ladies with their chickens and bundles and children. Sleepy baggage loaders and ticket punchers wandered around, only the drivers seemed wide awake.

Cabell went inside and bought a ticket; then he and Hamid crossed the street to a café.

"Yusef," Hamid said as she stirred her coffee, "you'd already written that letter to your friend Atkinson before I arrived last night, hadn't you?"

"Yes, that's true."

"Did you know that I'd be delivering it?"

"I figured that if that lottery ticket paid off, you might want to use the money to leave town."

"But what if I hadn't come to your hotel last night?"

"In your note you said you were anxious to talk to me."

"So you already knew I would be departing for the Sahara."

"I was hoping. Hamid, where's Blanco?"

"Some friends are taking care of him for me."

"So you had an idea you might be going away, too?"

"Yes, I'd made my own preparations."

The Pullman Sud Express was ready to go; the passengers were saying goodbye to their friends and climbing aboard. Cabell and Hamid drank the coffee and recrossed the street.

"Oh, I nearly forgot. Here, Hamid, take this." Cabell took out the goat bladder.

"Is it what I think it is?"

"Yes, Boujma's finest."

Hamid got on the bus and took a seat next to the window where Cabell was standing.

"Thank you for everything, Yusef, especially for this."

She patted the goat bladder.

"You're welcome."

"I'm sorry if I was too drunk last night."

"Nothing to be sorry about."

"This morning I feel ready. I've been preparing myself for a long time."

"I know."

The bus roared.

"Can I bring you something from the Sahara?" she shouted.

"Yes!"

"What?"

"A camel-udder box!"

"What?"

"A camel-udder box!"

"All right! I'll do my best! They're hard to find!"

"I know! Don't forget about Atkinson!"

"I won't!"

The bus roared again and began to move.

"Yusef!"

"What?"

"Am I traveling light?"

"Looks that way!"

Hamid laughed and kissed the bladder.

"Goodbye, Hamid! Good luck!"

"Goodbye, Yusef! Thank you!"

"Goodbye."

The bus went off in a cloud of blue smoke. Hamid put her arm out the window and waved. Cabell waved back and dropped his arm as the bus disappeared down Avenida de España.

It was going to be a hot day. The power of the sun, which had not risen very much in the sky, could already be felt; the sky itself had assumed that opaque quality which means heat. Along the avenue the heavy palm fronds drooped in silence; there was no breeze of any kind this morning. When Cabell came to the Hotel Nicaragua, he stopped and looked up at Maxwell's window. The window was wide open, and there, framed in the center, was Maxwell's head; unmoving, he was looking out at the sea. Cabell raised his arm and made a signal, but he did not notice. Cabell took a few steps backward; from this position Maxwell's neck and shoulders were visible. He had no shirt on. Cabell signaled once more and whistled, but Maxwell didn't seem to hear. His vision seemed to be fixed upon some distant point on the horizon. Cabell called his name, but there was no response, so he walked off down the avenue. Arriving at the stairs that led to the beach, he went out onto the sand. Near the water a European woman in a bathing suit was walking with her dog; she and Cabell were the only people on that wide beach before the city.

August 2 This morning Hamid left for the south. Her going reminds me that this is the great act, the act of departure, perhaps the greatest of all. To make the final decision, to disengage oneself from encircling bonds, and to set off on an adventure of lonely freedom may be the ultimate gesture one can make. Take that first step out into the desert; imagine oneself as a solitary figure on a horizon, or as having arrived in some isolated place, whence all paths lead off into dust.

Hamid: her spirit and independence make her desirable. She has assumed the dress of a man without losing her femininity. And the courtesy of the Moroccans allows that, if she wishes to pass for a man, she ought to be treated as one. Her hermaphroditic quality makes her desirable, too. This is what a man should want in a woman: that she be all things, both a man and a woman, who can live with him in a sort of amorous comradery.

Shall I say it? She leads my thoughts away from Driss. Perhaps she knows this; it might even be her intention. How strange, in some ways she resembles him; in others she exceeds him. She's a woman, but an incredibly mobile one.

# *Palmeta*

LATE THAT AFTERNOON Cabell was making his way down Calle Libertad in the direction of the Medina. He wore the same clothes he had put on at five o'clock in the morning—light-blue shirt, tan trousers, and sandals. At the same moment Palmeta Gordillo was coming up the street; she caught sight of him and stopped in her tracks as he went right by her. Hesitating for a second, she changed direction and began to follow him. Cabell was walking swiftly along the crowded street, and the woman had difficulty keeping up. He turned a corner and stopped in front of a Moroccan bazaar to examine the Berber jewelry in the window. Palmeta Gordillo, hurrying along, rounded the corner and nearly bumped into him as he bent over before the window, partially blocking the sidewalk. Quickly she crossed to the other side of the street and waited in the shadows. Dressed all in black, she carried herself very erect and looked like any respectable Spanish lady, except for her unusually dark complexion.

Cabell had entered the bazaar. The shopkeeper's hand went into the window display and picked out an olive-green chrysolite pendant in the shape of a pomegranate. Cabell took it and turned it over in his hand; from across the street Palmeta watched the bargaining commence. Cabell spoke, the shopkeeper shook his head; the shopkeeper said something, Cabell threw up his hands. The shopkeeper, a wizened gentleman in a peaked gray tarboosh, began a long monologue. Cabell tried to interrupt, but the old man waved him off and continued with his speech. Cabell handed over the pendant; the man shrugged his shoulders and pretended to put it back in the window. Cabell edged toward the door, pretending to leave, but the man called him back and they bargained some more. Finally Cabell just shook his head and went out, but the man ran after him, and after another flurry of words, handed him the pendant. Cabell took out his wallet, paid, and they shook hands.

Across the street Palmeta was moving along a course parallel to Cabell, then had to stop once more when he entered the Café Cinco Minutos, a Spanish football bar. A blackboard in the window announced the evening game: 1815 H REAL MADRID VS MANCHESTER UNITED EUROPEAN CUP (TEAMS) QUARTER FINAL. Inside, tables and chairs had been arranged like a theater, all facing the television set, and every chair was occupied. Cabell went to the bar, ordered a Heineken, and glanced at the set. Real Madrid was moving the ball well, and murmurs of approval escaped the audience. The ball went into the corner, and the Spaniards began to chatter in expectation; now they were shouting as the ball was lofted perfectly in front of the Manchester goal. A Madrid forward attempted to head the ball into the net, but the tall English goalkeeper leaped up and snared it; there was a groan of disappointment as he kicked the ball far downfield.

"Are you Dutch?"

Cabell turned to face a short Spaniard in blue working clothes who stood next to him at the bar. "No, I'm not Dutch."

"Ah, I thought you might be Dutch."

The barman placed a plate of hot sausages and another of mayonnaise salad before Cabell.

"Just passing through Tangier, are you?" the Spaniard was asking.

"You might say that, yes."

"You better keep on moving until you find a town where they don't have television."

"Why?"

"Look at this café—it's been ruined. We used to play cards in here and dominoes and the like; one came here to have a drink and to talk with one's friends. The box does all the talking now. You know what I think?"

"What's that?"

"I think the box has a woman inside. Look, you go to your home, open the door, and your woman starts talking. Turn on the box and the same thing happens. Am I right?"

"I see what you mean."

"Don't get me wrong: I like football. I follow the teams like everyone else, but when I want to see a match, I go to the stadium on Sunday. That's enough football for me. But café life has declined because of the box. Even the quality of tapas has gone down."

"How's that?"

"The cook is watching the game when he should be in the kitchen with his squids and eels."

Real Madrid scored, causing the man's voice to be drowned out by shouting and applause. The players were leaping about and embracing each other, and the spectators in the stadium chanted and waved their flags. Even the unhappy Spaniard seemed satisfied. Cabell finished his beer, waded through the audience, and went out.

Palmeta Gordillo, who had been waiting patiently in the Jewish Arcade, saw him coming and hurried across the street to confront him.

"Señor Cabell?"

"Yes."

"Ah, good. Señor Cabell, you don't know me, and I certainly do not know you. As a matter of fact, I've only set eyes on you once before, and that was from a taxi."

"Oh?"

"My name is Palmeta Gordillo. I'm a friend of Jorge Maxwell's."

"Ah, yes, he spoke of you."

"Excuse me for approaching you on the street like this. My dark complexion may make me appear like a bold woman, but I am not. Quite the contrary. But I have something very important to talk to you about."

"What is it?"

"I was afraid to enter the café, which isn't a place for ladies, for people would have had the wrong impression. You see, I've been following you. Does that sound strange to you, Señor Cabell?"

"I admit I'm surprised."

"I've been waiting here in the street for you to come out of that café. I wish to talk to you about our mutual friend, Jorge Maxwell."

"I saw him early this morning."

"You did? Why how is that possible? Oh, dear, I should have never followed you here and waited for you. Perhaps this is just another one of his games."

"I saw him staring out of his hotel window. He looked as if he were naked."

"That's it! It's not a joke after all, Señor Cabell."

"What's the matter with him?"

"Our friend Jorgito has taken to sitting in his room without a stitch of clothes on."

"Good Lord."

"He refuses to move, refuses to talk, refuses to eat or to dress himself, and, what I find even more alarming, he has stopped smoking and drinking."

Cabell struck a match to a cigarette.

"If I give him a shirt or a blanket and say, Jorgito, please cover yourself, he just casts it away and goes on looking out the window."

"I couldn't get his attention even though I shouted at him."

"Now, I'm too old and have seen too much of the world, especially during our terrible Civil War, to be shocked by a man's nakedness."

"Does he want to shock you?"

"I don't know, Señor Cabell. I just want him to cover up for fear of catching pneumonia, sitting as he does all day and all night before that open window. You know how quickly the temperature changes in Tangier."

"How long has he been like this?"

"Two days now, as a matter of fact, ever since we caught sight of you and that black man who plays football."

"Basketball."

"Whatever it is. I've been so worried, Jorgito pays no attention to me, and I don't know what to do."

"I'll go see him."

"Will you? Oh, thank you, Señor Cabell. Talk to him, and perhaps he'll listen to you. Perhaps you can convince him to cover himself, or shut the window at least."

"I'll do what I can."

"Good. I'm sure he'll listen; he speaks so highly of you. Normally he's a very critical man, and I've never heard him talk in such a way about anyone."

"Thank you."

"He admires the way you can travel around and feel at home wherever you are. Poor Jorgito, he dreams of traveling and being free like you, but I'm afraid he never will. When will you visit him, Señor Cabell? Tonight?"

"Yes, tonight."

"Good. I'll be on my way now. I hope you didn't mind my stopping you on the street, but I didn't know anybody else I could turn to."

"I'm glad you did."

"You see, Jorgito has very few friends, at least that I know of."

Cabell nodded.

"So goodbye, Señor Cabell, and I hope we shall meet again under more pleasant circumstances."

"Goodbye, Señora."

Cabell watched her go, then went down into the Socco Grande. The big market place was unusually full for this hour: the fruit and vegetable stands were doing a busy trade, taxis were arriving and departing, and beggars roved about soliciting alms. Moving with the flow of Moslems returning from the European quarter to the Medina, he picked his way among the soap and glass vendors along rue des Siaghines and turned off on Calle Tuajin, the street of the Jewish gold merchants. This is a quiet street; people do not hurry but linger before the glittering window displays. Mostly Moroccan ladies in haiks and djellabas and veils were chattering and pointing at the gold bracelets and earrings and rings. Still others were in the shops having the gold weighed, and bargaining with the Jews. Cabell chose a shop with no women and went in. A young man in a skullcap who was working in the rear with a blowtorch came forward and listened as he explained how he wanted a gold loop passed through the peak of the chrysolite pendant and a fine gold chain attached. The young goldsmith examined the green stone and nodded, and they quickly reached a price.

Re-emerging onto rue des Siaghines, Cabell walked down past the Indian bazaars and tourist shops to the Socco Chico. The scene was loud and busy; cafés on all four sides of the square were packed with Moroccans watching the game. Tables outside were occupied mostly by young travelers smoking kif, drinking mint tea, and contacting Moroccans. In spite of the numerous lights a sort of semidarkness pervaded the square, and smoky side streets led off to all parts of the Medina. A diversity of people paraded in front of these cafés—old Moroccan gentlemen in elegant summer djellabas, bent-over Spanish ladies supported by their daughters and granddaughters, all dressed in black, half-wits mumbling to themselves and pointing, exhibitionists with their rags falling off, hustlers in tee shirts, little boys chasing each other, little girls with towels draped around them carrying bottles, albinos and freaks, one man in a blue robe peddling a powder guaranteed to enlarge the male sexual organ, rabbis in black robes, beards, and skullcaps. Heads poked out of the windows of cheap hotels and watched as beggars and shoeshine boys circulated among the foreigners, asking favors, receiving tips, making appointments.

Cabell found Shahid and Omar on the terrace of the Café Tingis, and sat down with them. A bearded tramp came up and tried to show them something under his tattered overcoat, but Shahid shooed him away as great shouts and applause erupted from the cafés. Real Madrid had scored again. A good-looking boy in a green satin jacket came by; on the back of the jacket were the words POPE PIUS XII. A pack of Jewish boys, all with long noses, huge eyes alert and intense, went trotting past.

After a while the three friends left the Socco and went to the Dancing Boy Café. The large square room was filled with stone-top tables and chairs; there was a glowing samovar, where mint tea is brewed, and a raised platform covered with mats and sheepskins, where the musicians play. The green walls were hung with musical instruments, photographs of the favorite football teams and local boxers, lanterns, plates, a ladder, crab shells and conch shells, hundreds of tiny flags, mirrors with paper fringes, and pictures of the Sultan and the Sultan's father. Hardly a chair in the room was unoccupied, and the musicians were resting and smoking kif because a bingo game was in progress. A man was shaking a wooden box and calling out numbers in Arabic as the clients peered intently at their cards and covered numbers with bottle caps.

The waiter led Cabell and his friends to a table next to a window where fresh air entered, somewhat dispersing the kif and tobacco smoke, and the window overlooked the Jewish cemetery. The waiter brought tea and bingo cards.

When the bingo game came to an end, conversation filled the large room; the musicians tuned up their violins and lutes and patted clay drums, the dancing boy got to his feet, and the music began. The musicians were singing as the dancing boy halfheartedly twirled and wiggled. Before long the music ended, and the bingo recommenced. Omar was following the game carefully and covering numbers with bits of paper torn from Cabell's notebook. After several games he won, and the prize, passed from hand to hand across many tables and customers, was a live rooster.

Later that night Cabell knocked on Maxwell's door. No one answered, so he just pushed it open and entered the room. Some light entered through the window from the street; next to the window was the figure of a naked man.

"George, is that you?"

The figure grunted.

"It's me, Cabell. I've come to pay you a visit."

Cabell shut the door, drew up a chair in the center of the room, and took out a package of cigarettes.

"Do you want a smoke, George?"

"No."

Cabell lit a cigarette, and the two men sat in silence.

"I ran into your friend Palmeta this evening."

"I thought so."

"She told me you had taken to sitting naked in this room and refused to speak to anyone."

"So you've come to see for yourself."

"I think she's a good woman, George."

"Full of Spanish nonsense."

"Apparently she'd been following me around, uncertain whether she ought to approach me or not. She was afraid she might be mistaken for a whore."

"She is one."

"A whore?"

"They're all whores."

"Manchester United defeated Real Madrid."

"Is that so? What score?"

"Three to two."

"Well done. That's my team, Manchester United."
"Did you see me in the street this morning, George?"
"Yes."
"Why did you pretend you didn't?"
"To see what you would do."
"And what did I do?"
"You walked away."
It was a typical North African summer evening, with the warm air barely moving the palm trees outside the window.
"You probably think I'm crazy, don't you? Sitting like this in front of the window."
"No, not crazy."
"Palmeta must be shocked by my nakedness."
"She says she's not."
"I admit I'm not much to look at any more, but do you know something, Cabell?"
"What?"
"I like being without any clothes."
Maxwell shifted his position, and bands of neon light off the street moved over his body.
"I feel liberated from my clothes," he went on, "like the young people who run on the beach."
"Then take them off on the beach."
"My body is ugly."
"Find a deserted beach, then run and jump in the water."
"Ah, Cabell, I'm bordering on the great depression."
Cabell lit up another cigarette.
"I'll take one now," Maxwell said.
"Good."
For a few minutes they smoked in silence. A procession of taxis passed in front of the hotel. Flutes and drums sounded; people were singing and shouting and pounding on the sides of the cars.
"What a lot of noise."
"It's the season for weddings now."

"I was walking past Bubana Cemetery the other day. Do you know the one, Cabell?"

"I know it."

"It's where anybody can be buried. Transients found dead in their hotel rooms, tourists who have been asphyxiated in bathtubs by leaking Butagaz, poor people with no money for a proper burial—they all wind up in there."

"And that's where you figure you'll end up."

"Bubana Cemetery is for foreigners like me, leading a marginal, isolated life in this city, with no real friends or ties."

"Do you want to know something, George?"

"You think I'm feeling sorry for myself."

"Not that. I'm going on a trip soon."

"A trip? What trip?"

"And I want you to come with me."

"Where to?"

"Melilla."

"Melilla? I've never been there! When are you leaving?"

"In a few days. Are you coming along?"

"To Melilla? Yes, with pleasure."

The taxis were coming back, and the drums and flutes sounded louder than before as the women warbled and shrieked with excitement. As the procession passed in front of the hotel a firecracker exploded, and all the taxis began to honk their horns at once.

*Dear Friend,*

Here in Tiznit there is unbroken flatness beyond the ramparts. The wind is blowing; dust is swirling and entering everywhere. We have a Chergui over the Souss, and the temperature hovers around 100° during the day and does not seem to decrease by night. Through clouds of heat and dust the shadowy outlines of the Anti-Atlas are visible in the distance. At four o'clock in the afternoon, with the heat at its greatest, dust sucked from the earth by the wind envelops whole groves of palms, then moves on, an opaque wall blanking out even the mountains. The palm trees bend away, and unripe dates rattle to earth.

The ride from Tangier seemed terribly long and hot, and my feet were burning. In Casablanca I extravagantly purchased a sheep's head for 4 DH—you know how I love them, and when I spied it roasting over the coals, I could not resist. I ate it with cumin and salt. Then my conscience began to bother me, so I spent the night in a café rather than pay for a hotel. Do you approve of my economy? The following day was the fifteen-hour bus ride from Casa to here—fifteen hours of continuous theater—I would say that at least two hundred passengers got on and off with their goats and chickens and children. And all the time the land was becoming drier. It was after dark when we finally arrived in Tiznit; as I alighted in the wide red square of this town, I could not help reflecting on the strangeness of my life.

For the past two days I have been confined to these low mud houses and streets, but this morning I walked through the palm groves to the edge of the desert. All was silent except for the sound of the wind in the trees. I am again becoming accustomed to the harsh rustle of palm fronds.

I came upon some men building a mud wall. Pounding in unison, they sang the song of completion as they took the supporting boards down from a finished section. (The wall-builders' song.) The old man on the wall was joking about the boy who carries the earth in baskets on his head. He's a "little crazy" from "too much weight on the brains" and is often in jail. Otherwise . . . earth, stones, and hard work in the sun. They make sixteen meters a day, and the result is beautiful, as you know, like smooth red cement. Watching them, I thought of you and your two friends the masons.

It is nearing sunset now, and the sun is a dull red ball suspended in the dusty sky. I lie on this rooftop as the croaking ravens fly by in pairs from the plains to roost in the palmery; below me men in blue robes move with such grace through these red streets. I have been to the hammam, where I was scrubbed down by an enormous Negro woman who sells fish in the market. Now I'm eating an orange and feeling clean and relaxed and grateful. Tomorrow I hope to catch a bus which will take me close to the frontier, although there seems to be a disagreement among the bus drivers whether it will depart or not.

*Hamid*

August 9 Shahid's skin is so smooth . . . I must be careful. And he has so many fans! When we are out on the street together, they catch sight of him and shout: "Congo! Long Congo! Big Congo!" They gather around him and shake his hand and feel his muscles and stroke the Senegalese shirts which have become so famous. I stand aside while they talk basketball. After a while Shahid will extricate himself from his admirers, and we walk on together.

August 11 This morning the sun overheated. It was too hot to go outside, too hot to do anything, so I ended up in this room fighting a constant battle against the flies. These were not of the gentle buzzless variety, my old friends, but the persistent kind which stick to you. While I dozed through the afternoon, there was a shower. This was the first rain since the great storm, and when I awoke I went out into the city, very sober this time. The rain had taken the dust and dryness out of the air; it was cool now and soft. I was still glazed with sleepiness from the nap, and as I walked through the streets, I felt a gentleness come over me, as the air had been made gentle by the rain. I saw a beggar asleep, knees drawn up, his face resting on the enamel bowl he held in his lap. Passers-by were slipping coins into the bowl, and when he awoke, he would find them beneath his chin. There were puddles where the earth, hardened by so many weeks of sun, would not allow the water to sink in. The light had changed, and the Spanish coast and Gibraltar were very clear. The inhabitants of Tangier City were experiencing a sense of relief from the long dry spell and had come out of their houses to talk about the unexpected shower.

I crossed town to see Amigo Maxwell. He was still by the window, but had put on his underwear against the change in temperature. "Do you think I'm making progress?" he asked me. "Is this the beginning of a comeback? But don't worry," he added, "I'm going to stay naked until we set off on this trip together." I told him to put his clothes back on, because we're leaving tomorrow.

August 13 On board *Las Palmas*, a steamer that serves the Spanish outposts along the northern Moroccan coast—principally Ceuta and Melilla, but Peñon de Velez de la Gomera and Peñon de Alhucemas as well. These are no more than rocky islets off the shore, where Spain still keeps military detachments. I have a feeling they're penal colonies.

Yesterday afternoon Amigo Maxwell and I took the bus from Tangier to Ceuta. Maxwell was so excited he could hardly stay in his seat.

"When do we arrive in Ceuta?" he asked the driver.

"Only God up in the sky knows that," the man replied. As boss of a Moslem bus, there were many time games he could play with an eager Christian.

"Certainly within an hour, no?"

"We can only make a rough calculation."

We sailed from Ceuta at midnight, the man on the pier casting off the last of the hawsers and shouting, "Free! Free!" With a slight rain descending, we slid through the harbor, past the breakwater with the red light on the right, green on the left, and out to sea.

This is a clean little ship, built about fifty years ago—it runs slowly and silently over a glassy smooth sea. My cabin is small but comfortable. Maxwell and I stayed up most of the night drinking brandy. We are the only passengers on the ship, so it's like being aboard one's own yacht; today Maxwell has been roaming the decks with binoculars, getting into long discussions with the captain and crew, and rushing back to me with new information about nautical miles, depth charts, horsepower, and the like.

This Riffian coast is extremely precipitous and rocky. At Alhucemas the people standing along the dock looked to me more like American Indians than Moroccans. There were goats up on the rocky hillsides and wooden fishing boats under construction in the port. Spanish fishermen lounged about—how compact and tough they seem with their bright eyes and leathery faces.

This evening we arrive in Melilla. Escobar has arranged for me to meet with Colonel Rivera, who's up here on vacation from the Sahara. Of all the Spanish officers I've known in the desert, I'm on the best terms with him, and he alone has the authority to change the terms of my contract. I really don't think there's much chance of this, but I'm keeping my fingers crossed. And I admit I'm nervous.

# *Melilla*

"TELL ME ABOUT Melilla, Jorgito. Why did you and Señor Cabell take this trip?"

"It was his idea."

"It used to be such a charming place, full of Spanish people who came over from Oran, I recall."

"We took a boat from Ceuta, which was pleasant enough."

"But why did you go?"

"I just went along for the ride. Cabell thought it would do me some good—he had an appointment to meet with a Colonel Rivera, who's boss of the Spanish Sahara. They were going to talk about his work in the desert."

"Is Señor Cabell going back to Rio de Oro?"

"I don't know what that man is going to do with himself."

"What do you mean?"

"If you'll be quiet, I'll tell you."

"Oh, Jorgito."

"We disembarked at dusk. Melilla's an ugly place."

"Do you really think so?"

"Within a few minutes we were asking ourselves how we were going to get out of there."

"What about Colonel Rivera?"

"A Spanish officer met us at the boat saying that Rivera had gone off to Madrid."

"Señor Cabell must have been disappointed."

"Disappointed? He started raving like a madman."

"Goodness, Señor Cabell? I thought . . ."

"All of a sudden he insisted that we return to Tangier right away."

"Why?"

"I don't know why. Planes were leaving, boats were leaving, buses were leaving—we were running around, but we couldn't find a place on any of them."

"You could have gone over to Spain."

"I suggested this, but the man on the boat didn't know if there would be places for us or not. Communications between the boat and the ticket office were poor."

"What did you do?"

"We were told to wait until a half hour before departure. Meanwhile, night had fallen. We were wandering around. Suddenly Cabell grabbed my arm and said: 'Maxwell, look at these people!' "

"What people?"

"The monsters had come out. Old women with horribly deformed purple faces clung to the lampposts; limbless individuals scuttled about like crabs; abnormal children tugged at our trouser legs."

"How awful! Melilla certainly isn't the town I used to know."

"The boat was due to depart at eleven, so we consigned our luggage at the bus station. But when we returned, the man with the key had disappeared."

"Oh, dear."

"Perhaps he's at his café, perhaps at home, perhaps he's gone off on vacation, we were told."

"Did anybody realize that you were leaving?"

"All the hotels in town suddenly filled up, as six football teams had arrived for a tournament."

"So you had no choice but go away."

"The monsters had disappeared. Young girls and boys in leather clothes had come out to see the football players."

"I think there used to be a midnight bus to Tetouan."

"The waiter sweeping napkins and shrimp shells out of the tapa bar knew nothing. Another bus was supposed to leave at seven in the morning, but we found out that it had been canceled."

"What about the man with the baggage key?"

"The waiter said he saw the fellow around there a few minutes before, but he couldn't be sure, it was so dark."

"It's true that the street lights of Melilla have never functioned properly."

"In the semidarkness thieves and rough ladies had taken over the pavement."

"Did they bother you?"

"We discovered that the airplane to Malaga was booked solid for the next nine days."

"What about Señor Cabell?"

"Cabell? I think the man's gone mad."

"Oh, dear, he seemed like such a nice fellow."

"In the bus station we were accosted by this midget with no legs. Ugliest critter I ever laid eyes on. Fuad was his name. Well, it turns out that he and Cabell knew each other from somewhere, and they started jabbering together in some idiot language I'd never heard before. Hassania, it's called. They speak it down in the desert."

"Señor Cabell must be quite a linguist."

"And that was only the beginning. Cabell picks this cripple up and carries it around under his arm, as if it were a doll, all the while babbling away like a ventriloquist with his dummy—

and pours brandy down its throat every bar we go into. Turns out the poor devil lost its legs sleeping on the railroad tracks. Train ran over it."

"Poor Señor Cabell. I suppose anyone who has spent a long time in the desert might become anxious in such a city."

"He was asking everybody in the street how to get out. Fuad was giving insane orders but finally directed us to an ex-seaman who had tattoos and wore wooden shoes. He suggested that we hire a taxi."

"That sounds sensible."

"So we looked for taxis. Only someone called Jaime took long trips, but he was nowhere around; he was already on a trip."

"How did you escape?"

"Jaime finally showed up, but he wanted too much money. Cabell beat him down, practically with his fists. Fuad was screaming at him. Poor man was scared to death of Fuad, thought he was some evil spirit."

"There was no choice but to leave, was there?"

"The idiot with the baggage key reappeared, and we jumped into the back of Jaime's black Mercedes. Cabell wanted to take Fuad along, but I said it was either Fuad or me, and Jaime refused to go anywhere with that monster in his car, so we dropped him back at the bus station, with a brandy bottle to suck on."

"Melilla used to be a pleasant little town. Nobody ever thought of escaping."

"We crossed the border into Morocco, and Cabell was shouting out the window: 'Never again!' "

"I hope not."

"We hadn't gone more than a few kilometers when we were stopped by the Moroccan police. Jaime had no license to drive in Morocco, and for a moment it looked as if they might send us back to Melilla. I had visions of the three of us sleeping on the floor of the bus station."

"Three?"

"Fuad."

"Oh, dear."

"But Cabell pulled himself together and spoke Arabic to them, and they let us through."

"Thank goodness."

"So we raced over the mountains, driving all night, Cabell jabbering the whole time to keep Jaime from falling asleep at the wheel. It all reminded me of the first night I met him, the way he carried on."

"Jaime must have thought he had a couple of lunatics on his hands."

"Jaime drove like a madman himself. It's a miracle we ever got back here alive."

"Is Señor Cabell better now?"

"I don't think so."

"Why? What's the matter?"

"On the boat he told me that the only reason he stays on in Tangier is because he doesn't know where else to go."

"But we all feel that way."

"I think he wants to return to Rio de Oro."

"Is that not possible? Won't they have him back?"

"The person he loved there is dead."

"I've always suspected Señor Cabell to be a widower."

"It was a young Moroccan who was with him in the Sahara."

"A young lady?"

"A man."

"Oh, I see. Is there anything we can do for Señor Cabell?"

"I don't know. He's not in very good shape now."

"It was lucky that you were along to look after him, Jorgito; otherwise something terrible might have happened."

"He thought that the trip to Melilla would bring me to my senses, and he was right. I was the one who had to lead him out of there."

"Good, Jorgito. I'm glad Señor Cabell has a friend like you."

"I was glad to help him out; that was good for me, too. But I'm still worried about him."

"Why, Jorgito?"

"I went looking for him in his hotel this evening, but he wasn't there—gone off again, nobody knows where."

# *The Recovery*

THE GROUNDS of the Spanish Consulate General are immaculately kept. Early every morning Spanish workmen arrive, clad in blue work suits, close-fitting black berets, and canvas shoes. With brush brooms they sweep the long sandy paths between the residence and chancellery, and climb ladders to clip dead fronds from the bulbous palms, which grow along the paths. The lawns are in perfect condition and require a great amount of water during the dry summer months. Then there are hedges to be trimmed, gardens to be cultivated, walls to be mended, and other things that gardeners know how to do. At noon these men go off and lie in the shade with their bread and fried fish and bottles of red wine; after the long siesta they appear once more for a final watering or clipping.

It was just about noon when the Spanish Consul General, followed by Cabell, came out of his office. As they passed down the long corridor of the chancellery, there was a sound of chairs being pushed back and quick footsteps on the wooden floors. Old men—some thin and pale in shiny gray suits with black arm bands, as if all their mothers had recently died; others fat, with brown faces, looking like Peruvian Indians—appeared in the doorways along the corridor. They all bowed ceremoniously, and Escobar had a word for each of them. As the two men descended the marble stairs, the Moroccan cleaning woman greeted them cheerily, and the doorman stood solemnly aside as they went out.

Cabell had on his beige suit and carried a wide-brimmed Panama hat; the Consul wore a gray pin-striped suit of a heavier material. They began to walk along the sandy path toward the residence. The sun was directly overhead in a white sky, palm fronds drooped, and the yellow and white surfaces of the chancellery glared and threw back the heat. It was one of the hottest days of the year.

Striding along, Cabell was speaking rapidly, even waving the hat in the Consul's face. Every so often the Consul would halt and give his reply. They disappeared behind the residence, came out on the other side, and strolled back and forth along the shady paths. Escobar was doing the talking now, and Cabell was shaking his head. As they approached the residence once more, Señora Escobar came out and greeted them. She was a small lady with fair skin and dark hair drawn back from her forehead; she wore English shoes and clothes and addressed Cabell in English. The subject of conversation changed, and after a few minutes Cabell excused himself and walked off down the path.

Later that afternoon he got down from the farmers' bus and set off along the dirt track that led to Sidi Kacem. He had changed his clothes and carried a small leather bag. There was no shade anywhere, and the big hawks rode the hot air currents high overhead—sweeping and soaring, they watched the unprotected land for any sign of life, but the only moving thing was Cabell. Up ahead the long blue line of ocean was visible, broken only by the dark area of the olive grove. Out on the shimmering plain before Sidi Kacem, another man was making his way among the prickles and thistles. There were several dogs with him, and when they caught sight of Cabell they barked and ran on ahead.

"Joseph," the man called, "what are you doing out here?"

"I've come to visit you and Lydia."

"Lydia's in Tangier, but she'll be back this evening. You haven't walked all this way in the sun, have you?"

"I took the bus as far as the airport."

"Will you spend the night with us this time?"

"You wouldn't mind if I stayed out here a few days, would you?"

"Of course not. You're welcome to stay as long as you like. Is something the matter?"

"I just need to get away from Tangier for a while."

"I know what you mean. I may complain about life in the country, but it's the best place for me. Come on, let's get out of the sun."

"Grigory, why are you wandering around in this heat?"

"I've been down to the beach, Joseph. Two boys are lost in the sea."

"Who?"

"Two Moroccan boys. One came from the village of Mediouna. They say he was a schoolteacher. I don't know about the other."

"How did they drown?"

"They were fishing off the Caves of Hercules, eating and sleeping out there, too. One night they went fishing and never came back. The body of the schoolteacher was found yesterday morning, but the sea still has the other."

"Do you think they'll find it?"

"You never can tell; sometimes they float all the way to Spain."

"Is the sea dangerous here?"

"I don't know, I never swim, but every year it seems to take five or six people, with such regularity that the Moroccans have come to regard the drownings almost as a sacrifice to the sea."

They walked through the olive grove to the house, where Grigory showed Cabell his room. Later Cabell went down to the ocean for a swim. As he strolled along the beach, he began to pass Moroccans, mostly old men, sitting on the high dunes. Shading their eyes from the sun, they were all gazing intently out to sea. Cabell turned his head to look, but there was nothing but the glittering vastness of blue. Two men were now approaching; as they drew near Cabell raised his hand in greeting.

"M'siksif!" he called.

"Ah, Yusef!"

Cabell shook hands with M'siksif, and with the other old man, who was wearing only a makeshift bathing suit and a torn shirt.

"Two boys have drowned in the sea, Yusef."

"I just heard about it."

"One body was found yesterday, and we are still searching for the second. This man is the father."

"My son went fishing and was drowned," the old man stated.

"His son went fishing at night," M'siksif repeated. "And he drowned because he was drunk from wine," he added in Spanish.

The old man looked down at his spindly legs, then away toward the sea.

"We are waiting for the sea to give up his son," M'siksif went on. "Sometimes it will keep a body for a long time."

"How do the currents flow, north or south?"

"We don't know. There are many currents."

"This spring a man came down to this beach to wash himself before prayer," the old man put in. "The sea took him and cast his body in Arcila."

"We expect the sea will give up the body tomorrow or the next day. It never keeps dead people for more than three or four days."

"All is written," the old man mumbled and went off to look

at a net which had been staked out in the surf. M'siksif and Cabell sat down on a sand bank.

"The drowned boy came from Agla, Yusef. You knew him; he used to play the flute in my café."

"Ah. He's the one that drowned?"

"Yes, a real musician, and now he's gone. I told him—a thousand times—smoke kif but don't drink wine: you're a musician, and wine is no good for musicians. Wine! Look what it does."

Down the beach a long-tailed cormorant was stretching its wings to dry in the sun; the old man coming out of the sea frightened it, and the bird took flight and flew away low over the waves.

"All these people on the dunes, are they looking for the body?"

"These are all that are left now, Yusef. The first day there were more, but many went away, especially the young men. They doubted that the bodies would be recovered."

"How long are you going to keep up the search?"

"Until the body is found. Now it rolls with the current, a meal for the fish."

"Do you expect to see the body floating?"

"We don't know. It might still be caught under the rocks at the Caves of Hercules; it might have been carried off into the Straits. But this cannot continue; the body must have a resting place in the earth."

"Where are you sleeping, M'siksif?"

"At the Caves. We are all there, watching and waiting."

The sun was going down into the sea now; as soon as it dropped below the horizon all color left the sky, and darkness came on quickly. M'siksif and the old man set off for the Caves of Hercules; one after another the other old men left their places on the dunes and followed them. Cabell returned to the farm.

Early the next morning the tide changed, and currents brought the body near the shore, where the waves caught it and rolled it about and finally washed it to the beach and deposited it there. Yellow-shirted, bare-footed, the body lay, still licked by the ends of the waves. The water receded, and the white rubbery skin dried in the early morning sun. Far down the beach from the Caves of Hercules the body lay, half buried in the sand, with one arm outstretched in a direction parallel to the sea. There were no loud noises at this hour, none louder than the cry of a gull above the muffled rush of the sea. Around the body were the tracks of birds. Otherwise, the beach was totally deserted until Cabell came into view, casually strolling down to the sea for an early-morning swim.

Up at the Caves the old men were having their breakfast. There was sadness among them and nobody spoke except M'siksif, who greeted each of them in turn as he distributed glasses of coffee. It was a clear, bright day, and the sea and sky were everywhere. Suddenly the silence was broken by a cry; someone was running along the beach waving a shirt. Immediately everyone was on his feet, and the father recognized the shirt of his son. A shout went up from the men, a shout of relief and excitement as they scrambled down the rocks to the beach. With Cabell in the lead, they were hurrying as fast as they could along the hard-packed sand. But it was a long way to run, and the men were old. One by one they became winded and slowed to a walk; one by one they came to the body and stopped and circled. It was lying on its back, face to the sky. Cabell had turned it over to remove the shirt, and now only the pants remained. The skin was wrinkled and white, like the skin of anyone who has been too long in the water. The fish had eaten away most of the hair; the eyes had gone out of the sockets.

The father arrived and broke through the circle. As he kneeled down to examine the body, a coffin was brought. The father did not like the half-naked body of his son to be seen by the others and directed that it be placed in the coffin straightaway. The men hoisted the coffin to their shoulders, and the funeral dirge commenced as they carried it from the beach.

*Dear Comrade,*

I am in Icht now and happy. The trip from Tiznit was broken by the detour to Imjijt, where I met your friend Mr. Atkinson. However, I didn't think I'd make it that far. Some spiny-tailed lizards were running back and forth across the road south of Bou-Izakarn. I happened to be riding up next to the driver and mentioned to him that I'd seen some of these lizards on sale in Casablanca. Well, this fool slammed on the brakes, jumped out of the bus, and began to chase lizards. Of course, they immediately disappeared into their holes, and, like any animals that live in the ground, they have many entrances to their homes. The driver began to dig away with a stick and then ran back to the bus for a shovel. Naturally, the passengers thought he had gone mad and were shouting at him to get back into the bus. He shouted back that these lizards were worth a fortune in Casablanca and that they could wait while he caught a few. At this piece of information there was a moment of silence inside the bus; then all the passengers piled out and went after the lizards. With sticks and iron bars and shovels they tore the earth apart—they even set fires and tried to smoke them out—but they failed to capture even one. This was all under the hot desert sun. You would have laughed.

Crept into Imjijt the next day and went immediately to call on "Crazy-man" Atkinson. (This is how the local people refer to him.) He received me very cordially, although he didn't seem to know quite what to make of me. He was very anxious to have news of you, and I told him everything I knew, which I soon realized was not very much. As I talked, Mr. Atkinson prepared me a very good meal in his pressure cooker, which he says is the only means to make the local meat tender, which indeed it was. He himself claims to have discovered pure magnesium in Imjijt—by some freak of nature it has refined itself; there are eight million tons of it and worth $32,000 a ton. I don't know whether to believe this or not. I gave him your letter, and he read it several times—I was tired out from the trip and dozed off. When he finished he shook my shoulder and handed me a reply to bring to you by hand. I have it with me.

That night I spent in Imjijt's only café. I still have a fear of dark and of snakes, and left a candle burning all night, lest a serpent come in and take me by surprise. Imjijt is full of vipers and cobras, according to Mr. Atkinson. The next day he showed me the mine shafts he had dug. They are beautifully sculpted things, with steps carved into the rock; there is no doubt that he is a professional miner. And as soon as I entered the mine, I realized that Mr. Atkinson may not be so crazy after all. Just below the surface the rock turns a bright blue color, and as you go deeper everything begins to shimmer. It was like diving into a deep, clear pool of water. Mr. Atkinson claims that the whole mountain is the same.

Imjijt comes close to being paradise. In the middle of a landscape consisting of solid rock (Mr. Atkinson insists that the town lies at the center of an ancient volcano, and it is true that uniform black ridges ring the valley), one comes upon this oasis with its numberless palms, all loaded with dates. Beneath the palms grass grows in cultivated plots, and little canals run everywhere, with paths and dikes. Tiny black birds with orange beaks flit through the trees. The air is warm, with cool patches in the shade. There aren't many people about (and not a single Spaniard—*gracias a Dios*) and hardly any houses are to be seen, as the palms hide all. Occasionally one spies a woman in black, passing through the trees carrying a clay water jug on her shoulder. Or you come upon a man singing as he works with a hoe on his little plot of land. Or you overhear the laughter of children from behind crumbling mud walls. And always there is the sound of water running in the little ditches. Time has stopped in Imjijt. One could live there for a century without being aware that a moment has passed. But the snake might have already entered this paradise: Mr. Atkinson boasts that soon a big American company will move in to exploit the magnesium deposits. Is this the way the world will end—exploited and industrialized?

Presently I am living in the mud house which I hope one day will be my café and grocery store. I'll describe it briefly: it's built around a large courtyard; on two opposite sides are large rooms, one for the store, and the other will be the café; along the other two sides are smaller compartments where travelers can sleep. Two large palms are already growing in the courtyard, and we must install a fountain and make a garden. I have discovered a wonderful flat roof, perfect for sleeping outside during the summer. Actually I hardly sleep at all, but lie awake all night, hypnotized by the stars just overhead, listening to the dogs barking everywhere, and thinking of what this life might bring. I have hopes that this will be a "famous café," to which people such as yourself will travel long distances to reach. Yes? Abdelmalik has already made the first payment on the house. He is confident—he considers Ali's job in France as a guarantee. He has been very kind to me, and all the people here are very gentle. They are mostly of Haratine stock—black, with high cheekbones, broad cheeks, narrow nose bridges, and nostrils flaring out like funnels.

So all has gone well for me, and I thank you once more. Just one bad experience, which was my fault: last night I left my roof for a walk through the oasis, and soon I found myself in a dry river bed that divides the palmery. On either side the palms reared like enormous dark flowers of another planet, and the moonlight could have been the sunlight of that distant planet. Silence must be universal. Then I had a feeling I was not alone in the ravine, and suddenly realized there were jackals everywhere. A whole pack of them were following me like shadows—not barking, but their claws grated on the rock. I knew they came out of the hills every night into the outskirts of the village, where they do battle with the pariah dogs, whom they invariably defeat. Lately they have become so intrepid that I'd seen them myself in broad daylight, fighting with ravens on refuse heaps outside the village. But now it seemed they wanted to eat me. Still, I did not cry out for help because I wasn't sure how serious the situation was. I found a stick and threw it at one of them; it growled but didn't go away. Then I began to shout and look for a way out of that gully. A voice answered and I made for it. A man appeared and threw a cudgel at one of the jackals, hitting it on the back, and dispersed the others with stones. He must have broken the poor animal's spine, for it just lay there and howled, unable to move. He killed it with another blow (his club had a big knob on the end; mine was just a piece of cane) and then turned on me. He was furious: he even gave me a couple of cuffs (he thought I was a boy from the village) and sent me home feeling like a fool.

Now it is midafternoon, and there is great sun and heat and silence in the courtyard. Day after tomorrow Abdelmalik will take me in his truck as far as Ouarzazate, where I will find my own transport to Marrakech and Tangier. Do you miss me?

*Hamid*

P.S. I have all my scouts out looking for a camel-udder box.

August 20 Don't know what came over me in Melilla, but it was like going berserk in an elevator . . . and that Fuad, how did he get from Port Etienne to Melilla? Did he appear like another succubus just to aggravate the nightmare? I was glad Maxwell was there—I really needed him then and felt grateful for his English fussiness and concern. But since Escobar has no explanation why Rivera couldn't meet me as planned, I have to admit that I don't understand anything. Was Rivera putting me off, or did he really have to rush to Madrid on important business?

Then I had to stumble upon that body, which so startled me that at first I thought it must be Driss, that somehow the currents had carried his remains all the way from Tarfaya. Then the corpse became a vision of myself: this was my own body, come to an end on a deserted shore. These fantasies vanished in a second, and the great thing was to rip the shirt off and run along that hard flat beach, shouting and waving my flag of discovery. I felt that a great weight had been lifted from me, as if I had been dragging that corpse around with me all this time.

Three days at Sidi Kacem were good therapy for me, especially the long walks and long talks with Lydia. She's a wise Russian lady; her words are soothing, like the hands of an old Negress, who instinctively knows where to touch and where not to touch as she massages away at the edges of pain.

Now this morning comes a telegram from Hamid. She's in Marrakech alone, broke, and down with fever. So I must set off once more—tonight on the midnight express into the southern country.

August 23 *Marrakech* I found Hamid in a squalid Moroccan hotel—it wasn't even a hotel, but a fondak, where itinerant merchants and country folk keep their donkeys and spend the night. She was lying in the corner of an empty cubicle, knees drawn up beneath her. There was dung on the floor and flies swarmed over her. She knew it was me but wouldn't open her eyes. I got her out of there and into a hotel; the doctor came and diagnosed the sickness as tick fever. High temperature and terrible headaches. No wonder she couldn't look at me—when there's agony in sight, the world smothers the mind. The doctor prescribed chloramphenicol and today she seems better.

Marrakech is a good place to get well again, I think. Each new day opens with extraordinary clarity of sun and air. The Atlas Mountains form an abrupt gray wall against the desert sky. It's dry here; no rain in two years. The goats eat stones, I am told, and the dogs will eat anything. Chickens run to a rock you have thrown to drive them away. By day the heat can be oppressive, but the people come out of their houses at dusk, which is the hour I choose to wander through the city. There is such a softness to the air; the shapes of palms are etched against the redness that still lingers in the western sky; the people in their robes seem to flow through the streets, conversing with each other in whispers. From somewhere comes the sound of drumming. This is an African city; there are many dark faces and dark eyes.

August 27 *Mogador* We've come out here to the coast, the two of us, to escape the heat of the interior. We're staying in an old hotel built into the ramparts which has large airy rooms with windows looking out to sea. Hamid rests during the day while I wander through the arcaded markets of the Medina, examining ancient coats of arms carved in stone lintels and wondering about the Jews who used to live here. This morning I passed an old slave woman sitting on the sidewalk with her feet in an irrigation basin. It's hot here, too, and I spend a lot of time in the water.

In the evenings we walk the Portuguese ramparts as the light vanishes down the long arm of the sea. We dine in the fish restaurant on the beach and afterward play cards back in the hotel. The card game is a joke, for by that time we've smoked a lot. Under hashish, Hamid's sensitivity and vulnerability are even more evident. She's like a little boy in a state of excitement —wide-eyed, eager, and afraid before the world. When she's like that, I find her irresistible. It's so easy to throw my arms around her. She's affectionate and grateful that I came for her. I, too, am grateful, perhaps more than she realizes.

In bed she's extraordinary and knows it. She's almost impossible to hang on to, she wriggles around so much, squealing with laughter. With her, fun and passion are mingled. Afterward, she insists upon cuddling in my arms, and falls asleep instantly, like a child.

August 29 Back in Marrakech. Hamid has quite recovered now, and tomorrow we set off for the north. Meanwhile, we are enjoying these delicious Marrakech melons. You buy them early in the morning, fresh off trucks from the country, and keep them in a cool place, preferably on ice, as the day stokes up. Then, when you feel you can't resist the temptation any longer, you cut one open. "Women for duty, boys for pleasure, melons for sheer delight." Isn't that how the old Persian saying goes? When I quoted this to Hamid, she gave me a funny look, as if to say, "Is that so?" Then she carefully sliced off a long thin piece of melon and forced it into my mouth. "Women for duty," she says.

August 30 *Casablanca* The train ride from Marrakech to Casablanca: how can I describe the charm of the Marrakech railroad station, with its trees and fountain and the reddish walls? Or the sense of mingled sadness and freedom at waving goodbye to Marrakech? All the windows of the train were open, and a German seated across from us in the compartment was speechless and nearly fainting from the heat. Then we rode out into a hot blast of desert air. Why did that heat, that arid landscape, and the charming little African railroad stations we passed make me feel I was somewhere, that without doubt I was existing at a very definite time and place? I think the heat did it —heat made that landscape and that train ride seem terribly important. An alert was passed from car to car to close the windows, for a sandstorm was approaching. The sky turned rose, and grit hissed against the glass. I thought the German was going to suffocate. Then the air cleared, and we could open the windows once more. The sun was poised on the horizon like a molten plum. We were leaving the plain of the Houz, and the air suddenly became much cooler, the first real coolness that I have felt in days. How can I explain what that change of air made me feel? Not relief particularly—in Mogador there was the sea and Marrakech evenings are comfortable—but I was grateful for change and for the possibility of movement. I shall always be.

And the streets of Casablanca—cool, spacious, already quiet at the time of our arrival. I left Hamid at the hotel and, walking alone to the restaurant, once more felt that freedom—of passing through half-deserted streets where prostitutes beckon from doorways, of being alone, of sensing who I am and what I respond to and what means nothing.

Today I have seen those mud dwellings on the hot plains, with the stacks of threshed wheat, the animals, the children waving and running after the train; I was moved by the unspoken openness and glory of that plain. I don't have to look into their houses or examine their lives: I know that that landscape and the Moroccans in it represent something totally human, something harmonious to which I give my full allegiance. The heat did it, and the gratitude for coolness as the sun slipped behind the mounting horizon. That old wooden train, trundling along with the windows wide open, simply filled my heart with joy.

# *Boujma's Garden*

THE SULTAN OF DOGS growled as Mohamed I entered the garden, and Boujma looked up from his work.

"Good morning, sidi," Mohamed said.

"Good morning."

"I'm looking for Yusef."

"He's not here."

"Where is he?"

"Gone to Marrakech."

"Marrakech? Ah."

Boujma was leaning on his hoe; beneath the palm tree the Sultan of Dogs was rolling in the freshly cultivated soil, wagging his tail and groaning.

"When will Yusef come back?"

"With him you never know. Are you a friend of his?"

"We met in the Sahara, and we came to Tangier together."

"In the Sahara? It seems that all of Yusef's friends are connected with the Sahara."

Somewhere in the hotel a woman was singing in Arabic.

"This is a good garden you have here, sidi."

"A small one, but I think it's a good garden, too. Thank you."

"Did you plant all these flowers yourself?"

"Flowers, trees—everything."

"Even these big trees? Trees take a long time to grow. Are you so old, sidi?"

"Do you see that big palm tree over there?"

"Yes."

"That palm and I are the same age to the day."

"So you crawled out from between your mother's legs and planted your own seed."

"My father was gardener here before me, long ago, when this hotel belonged to Jews. To celebrate my birth he killed two sheep and planted the tree."

"So at one time you were taller than this palm."

"Can you believe it?"

"I'd say it got out ahead of you."

"Long ago."

"So you had a friend to grow up with."

"Still growing, still a friend."

They looked up the long shaft of the palm trunk, to which ivy vines clung; above the tile roof of the hotel the fronds were rattling in the wind. The railing along the balcony was a mass of climbing geraniums, and a passion-flower vine had somehow traversed the space between the wall and the palm, and was using the tree to support itself. In the garden all the plants were green and well watered; the ground was moist and the air was cool. Beneath the palm were a small grove of banana trees, a flowering belladonna, a prickly mimosa tree, and a hibiscus bush. A few assorted cacti had been planted around, and there was a stand of cane off to one side. Little paths ran in between.

"You have to be faithful to plants," Boujma observed. "They need to be looked after, just like animals and people."

"Yusef must like to sit in this garden."

"At first he hardly ever left his room."

"I know."

"He just lay in his bed all day listening to the radio."

"That's changed now, hasn't it?"

"In the mornings he comes out on the balcony to do his exercises; afterward he squirts himself with the garden hose."

"And then?"

"He goes up on the roof while Fatomah is cleaning his room. Some days he stays up there all morning, looking at the sea and writing in the notebook."

"He's thinking a lot."

"If he leaves the hotel, he might stay away for two or three days at a time. I don't know where he goes. People come looking for him, but I have nothing to tell them."

"For a while he was sleeping in the café at Merkala."

"Yes, but every day he came by here after taking food to a friend of his in the jail."

"That was me."

"Ah! It was you! So you're free now."

"Free and working, thanks to God."

Behind them the Sultan of Dogs was digging a hole for himself and snuffling in the soft earth.

"There's not much more I can tell you about your friend Yusef," Boujma said. "You probably know more about him than I do."

"I'll come back another day."

"Christians are strange people. There's no explaining them."

"Why did he go to Marrakech?" Mohamed asked.

"To fetch the one they call El Hassani. You know who I mean?"

"El Hassani from Agla."

"The one who wishes to be one of us."

"She wishes to be a Moslem."

"And a man."

"Is she?"

"Is she what?"

"Is she either?"

"I don't know what she is. I don't think she does, either."

There was a shout from inside the hotel; a man and a woman were arguing.

"That's Shahid and Fatomah," Boujma commented. "He makes her clean Yusef's room every day, even when he's away, and she doesn't like to do it."

"Better to stay down here."

"No shouting in a garden."

"Yusef must enjoy this garden."

"I told him that if he didn't want to spend the whole day in that hot room, he could pass the time down here, sitting in the shade, reading or writing, doing whatever he likes."

"So he does?"

"Yes, he spends many days with me now."

"It's a good place to relax in."

"There's peace here."

"I think Yusef needs peace."

Boujma nodded. "Who doesn't? That's what gardens are for."

"When Yusef returns, say that his friend Mohamed was here. Mohamed the mason."

"I'll do that. Any other messages?"

"Tell him I'm sleeping in Tangier now. I've found a place of my own. In a day or two I'll come around again."

"Come any time you like. You're always welcome in the garden."

"Thank you, sidi."

Mohamed went out, and Boujma returned to his work, filling in the holes that the Sultan of Dogs had dug in the garden. From upstairs in the hotel the arguments had turned to laughter.

September 4 Back in Tangier City. I realize now more than ever before that I am in need of both desert and sea (or is it just space?), Moroccans and Europeans, aridity and lushness. There are times when I want to smoke kif, others when only whiskey can satisfy me. I can trudge over treeless hills, feeling that the correct way to travel is on foot; but it's good to know there's an airport nearby, too. Long ago I learned to cherish my solitude; yet I have found people in Tangier who care for me, and I am in need of them. Some evenings I prowl the alleys of the Medina, ready for any adventure; others, I prefer to stroll the wide boulevard, quietly read a newspaper in a French restaurant, or strike up a conversation with an acquaintance at a sidewalk café. I love to get into bed with Shahid and Hamid. I enjoy speaking English, Spanish, French, and Arabic. I've discovered that needs for ascetic withdrawal, and for release in sensuous delight do not necessarily conflict, but actually encourage and define each other.

September 6 There has been an abrupt change in the weather, as the first rains have come early this year. For the past few days, mornings have been overcast, with the sun breaking through about midday and shining brightly all afternoon. Yesterday I was aware of a bright orange light as the sun rose over Malabata. Then there was a great explosion of thunder, the rain began to fall, and it hasn't stopped since. The landscape around Tangier has suddenly become sodden, and there has been some flooding. Summer has come to an end, and autumn is upon us, reminding me that before long I must move on.

September 10 Driss's birthday. Exactly one year ago it was, when he accompanied me into the desert for the first time. We were based in the southeastern corner of Rio de Oro. There wasn't much to do, so we took a Jeep and made a tour of the surrounding area. Gazelle were everywhere, and I shot one. When it became dark, we found a sheltered place in the lee of a sandy embankment and set up camp for the night. There was no question of being lost, because I knew exactly where we were, or at least I thought I did, and the Jeep was loaded with plenty of gasoline and supplies. We'd come away to be alone in the desert anyhow. A haunch of the gazelle was roasting over the fire and we were sprawled out on the sand, smoking and talking. It was one of those exceptional desert nights—so quiet and clear—we knew that there wasn't another soul for miles around.

Then something very strange began to happen. The earth was making a noise. At first I thought I was hearing things, but when I put my ear to the ground, the noise was still there, a kind of buzz. Driss heard it and asked me what it was. I said I didn't know. It became louder and louder until the earth was actually vibrating. Driss jumped up and tripped and fell in the fire and scorched himself. Suddenly a light appeared far away, flashed once or twice, and came on stronger. In a second I realized what it was—the train!

We ran up the bank, and on the other side there they were—two gleaming strips of metal in the sand. By mistake we had crossed over into Mauritania, and these were the railroad tracks from the iron mines of Zouerate to Port Etienne. The ground had been shaking because the great ore train was just coming out of the long Choum Tunnel, and we sat down on a bank to watch it pass. It's impossible to describe the racket it made—after the total silence of the desert it was deafening—first the great double engine rolled by, and we could see the native engineers and the firemen with turbans wrapped around their heads and faces against the dust and their eyes protected by goggles. Then the ore cars rattled past, and we counted more than two hundred—they say these are the longest trains in the world. When it had gone by the noise continued for some time.

After that, neither of us felt like sleeping, so we stayed up most of the night talking and throwing brush on the fire. Although we laughed about it, the train had really frightened us. Driss said that if I hadn't been there he might have just started running. He could have become lost in the desert. As it was, he had only burned his foot, and I made him keep it in a bucket of water.

That incident struck up a strange knowledge between us. For I had just observed Driss—who naturally felt more at home in the desert than I did, even though I knew it better—far more terrified than I. In fact, it was his fear that had really frightened me. As we discussed it later, we both came to realize that it was I (and others like me), who was introducing the clamor of trains and oil wells, which could only destroy forever the tranquillity of the desert, and terrorize anybody accustomed to tranquillity. And there was Driss, with his foot in a bucket of water; and there was I, in full possession of the means to terrorize him.

And so, later that year, when the water came gushing out of the ground, we looked at each other and knew that if there was any way I could be useful in the desert without disturbing its peace, this was the answer.

# *Night Fires*

"LOOK, HAMID, they're setting fire to the cafés at Merkala."

One after another the flimsy structures burst into flames, sending clouds of smoke and sparks spiraling up into the night. At both ends of the beach at Merkala and on the hill behind, night fires were burning. First a spark of light would flash in the darkness; then a small flame became visible; in another minute the stick and grass construction was ablaze. Already the first ones to be set afire were collapsing in explosions of sparks—pieces of the fiery debris rolled away down the hill, spilled over the cliff, and were extinguished in the sea. The flames illuminated the beach, where the arsonists could be seen running back and forth in wild excitement, dancing and wrestling on the sand. It seemed to be a band of Moroccan boys that was setting the fires. The flames were reflected on the surface of the water; moving across the bay in wide arcs, the waves turned red as they broke against the beach. Then, on the far side of the cove a large fire suddenly ignited, and the leaping flames exposed the whole face of the cliff.

"That must be M'siksif's café," Cabell said.

"How do you know?"

"It's the only one located under the cliffs."

"Look at it burn."

"His was the biggest café of all, and the best constructed."

"M'siksif is going to be furious."

"Oh, no. He abandoned it last week, when the rains began."

"What about all the equipment?"

"He took it back to his place in town."

"Does the same thing happen every year?"

"At the end of the season the proprietors leave the cafés, and within a few days the boys come from the town and set fire to them."

Hamid and Cabell had been walking down through the trees from the Marshan when the fires broke out; now they were seated on the rocky bluffs overlooking the beach at Merkala, watching the spectacle below them. Cabell was carrying a long-handled net, and Hamid had a bucket; both wore flashlights strapped to their waists.

"I think it's a good idea," Hamid remarked.

"What is?"

"Burning houses when you have no more use for them."

"Do you?"

"I'd like to set fire to my own."

"Then why don't you?"

"Burn my house?"

"Yes, burn it or sell it."

"I told you I can't sell it. Nobody will buy."

"Then burn it if you don't want to live there," Cabell said. "Just stop talking about it."

"Do you really think I ought to?"

"You don't want to live in it, do you?"

"Nobody can because it's falling to pieces."

"Are the smugglers still there?"

"They shit in the corners and piss against the walls."

"If the police ever discover they hideout there, Hamid, you'll be in trouble."

"So what's the use of having such a house?"

"I'll buy some gasoline, and one night we'll set fire to the place."

"Are you joking, Yusef?"

"I'll bring along something to drink as well. You like aguardiente, don't you?"

"You know that."

"We'll celebrate while the house burns."

"Are you serious?"

"The house is constructed of wood, isn't it?"

"Wood and plaster, mostly wood."

"Then we better do it soon, before the rains soak into it."

"What about my husband, Ali?"

"What about him?"

"The house belongs to him. He'll be angry if he learns I've burned it down."

"Just write him that you were tired of looking after a house that had no value and which might get you both into trouble with the police because smugglers were using it as a headquarters, and as a woman you had no power to throw them out."

"And so I decided to burn it to the ground."

"And you'll meet him in Icht, where you'll have the café and grocery store."

"All right, we'll do it."

"Good."

"Yusef?"

"What?"

"I become a little frightened sometimes."

"Of what?"

"Of you."

"Of me? Why?"

"Because sometimes I think you could talk me into anything."

"Like burning your house down? We haven't done it yet."

"Yes, that, but other things as well."

"What other things?"

"You came and got me in Marrakech."

"You were sick."

"Oh, I've been sick many other times—sicker, and in worse places."

"Wasn't there anybody to take care of you?"

"Oh, yes, the Moroccans looked after me. I had malaria in Rio de Oro and lay delirious in a tent for weeks it seemed, until the women brought me around with their own medicines, but you're the first person who ever made the effort to travel in order to look after me."

"Well, if you're ever in trouble, just send word."

"When I sent off that cable from Marrakech, I knew you'd come, and that gave me a peculiar sensation."

"What sensation?"

"Of absolute certainty that as soon as you received it, you would be on your way south."

"Nothing unusual about that."

"But I've never experienced that before—that instant knowledge that someone is going to arrive."

"Hamid, you know the time's coming when you'll be off to Icht with Ali, and I return to the Sahara."

"But we'll meet again. I mean, we'll have our rendezvous in the desert, won't we?"

"Did you ever consider it another way?"

"You mean, break my promise and travel with you?"

"Yes."

"I have, but I think meetings in the desert will be more exciting. More our style."

"I insist we pick exotic places."

"How about Timbuctoo?"

"Or Agades."

"Tamenrasset."

"Taghit."

"Where's Taghit, Yusef?"

"On the edge of the western erg, Algeria. Huge orange dunes all around, oasis full of fruit trees—there are bathing pools. Village is a labyrinth of covered streets, like tunnels, and crumbling mud walls."

"Yes, that sounds right."

The cafés had been reduced to glowing mounds of coals, against which the boys were silhouetted as they raced about.

"Yusef, I don't feel like going frog hunting again tonight."

"Why not?"

"I've had enough wading around in those swamps, and besides, I don't think elephant toads really exist."

"The people of Agla swear they've seen them."

"But we've never seen one."

"We've seen thousands of little frogs, so there must be big ones somewhere."

"We've also seen snakes and rats and leeches and spiders."

"They say those toads are worth a hundred dollars apiece in any zoo."

"But is it worth it? Haven't you had enough of that mud? I'm so cold when we come back in the morning, I'm afraid we'll come down with pneumonia."

"All right, we'll forget about the frogs."

"Thank you, Yusef."

"You talked me out of that one without too much trouble, didn't you?"

The boys had gone away, and the beach at Merkala was deserted.

"Yusef?"

"What?"

"When are we going to set fire to my house?"

"The sooner the better."

September 14 Mornings colder now. Today I went for a walk and a swim—perhaps the last swim of the year. It was a clear day, and these fine September days we are having now are the clearest of all. On the deserted beach at Merkala a Moroccan as dark as mahogany was doing somersaults and handstands on the sand. He was wearing his bathing suit, and all the muscles in that long dark body were visible. He was watched by his wife, as black as himself, who was dressed in a white haik and was sitting on the sand with two ebony children. Farther along the shore I came upon a student perched on a boulder, chanting passages from the Koran. And across the Straits, Spain appeared as precise and as false as a painting on the horizon.

I took off my clothes and plunged in. The water was so transparent you could have dropped in a penny and followed it all the way to the bottom. The tide was low, so I could stand on submerged boulders—these mossy rocks feel like moist rugs beneath one's feet. When I climbed out of the water, my skin burned and tingled, and I had a sensation of my own strength and good health.

As I made my way back along the shore, the student walked beside me and began a conversation in French. "I have often seen you swimming here with your two friends—the tall black fellow and the young boy with the fishing pole," he said. "Where are they now? Do you swim all year round? There is nothing better than to be alone by the sea on a day like this, no?" Back at Merkala the tumbler had put on a beige djellaba and was lying on the sand next to his wife, with the hood of the djellaba drawn over his head. One of the children was trying to pull the hood away so he could see his father.

For many years I have been fortunate enough to find myself almost constantly in environments of natural beauty—I mean extremes of beauty. Now I cannot live without. Yet when one is confronted, as I was today, with such a precision in nature, one's own purposes and definitions seem fuzzy by comparison.

I have seen such a clear demarcation of the limits of things, where the fine line has been drawn, separating earth from sea and sky; one is tempted to gaze out, to seek answers written by the undulating sea kelp, or described in symbolic cloud formations. But there are decisions to be made, and conclusions must be reached within the confines of one's reason. I have to make up my mind how much longer I'm going to stay in this town. Should I continue to roam about Tangier with comparative freedom, as do these buzzless flies which circulate in the middle of the room, apparently never needing to rest? Or do I accept this new contract which Escobar daily urges me to sign, which is not really a contract at all, but only a preliminary endorsement to another contract to be negotiated by a certain date in El Aaiun?

So I am still undecided; and kif is no good for making decisions. Tonight I go out to Agla in order to burn Hamid's old house down to the ground.

# *The House Burning*

HE WAS WALKING DOWN a path through the pine trees, whistling to himself. It was a clear autumn night, with silence in the forest, and lights were twinkling along the Spanish coast across the Straits. A shadow moved among the trees, and a figure appeared on the path before him.

"Is that you, Yusef?"

"Yes."

"Have you brought the gasoline?"

"Yes."

"Have you brought the aguardiente?"

"Yes, but I had a hard time finding it."

"Why?"

"Another Cuban ship is in the port with a load of sugar, and the sailors have drunk up all the cheap whiskey in town. I had to search all over before I found a fisherman who sold me two bottles."

"Where is it?"

Cabell handed her a paper bag in which the bottles clinked together.

"I think I'll take a little right now," she said.

"Go ahead."

Hamid uncorked one of the bottles and drank.

"Ah."

"How is it?"

"Good."

She took another swig and handed the bottle to Cabell.

"Hamid, are you sure you want to do this thing?"

"Yes."

"Is everything ready?"

"I opened the doors and windows, like you said."

"What about the furniture?"

"Whatever I could find I dragged into the center of the room and made a pile with the mattresses next to the stairs."

"Good."

"Yusef, have you ever burned a house down before?"

"No."

"Then how do you know what to do?"

"I just imagine how it might be done."

"I discovered some kerosene, so we can use that, too."

"Let's go then."

Cabell picked up the can of gasoline he had been carrying and followed Hamid down the path. For a while neither spoke; the two bottles of aguardiente clinked together in the bag.

"The smugglers have been back in the house, Yusef. They've made a terrible mess of everything."

"They're not there now, are they?"

"No, not now."

"Do you know these men, Hamid?"

"I used to know some of them—I felt sorry for them. I allowed them to use the house from time to time when the weather was bad and they had no other place to sleep. They used to give me whiskey and cigarettes, but they hated my dogs."

"So they killed them?"
"I'm sure it must have been them."
"Where's Blanco tonight?"
"With friends in Tangier."
"So you still see these smugglers?"
"Sometimes. But I'm afraid of them now."
"Why?"
"One night they found me alone in the house. They were drunk and tried to rape me."
"When was this?"
"Oh, a long time ago."
A great ocean liner came around the cape, only a few hundred yards from the shore; she was glowing with light and moving very swiftly through the dark water; a breeze carried the faint sound of dance music to the shore.
"Did they succeed?"
"Yes, they did."
"How many were they?"
"Three men."
"What happened?"
"Just what you would expect."
"What's that?"
"Do you want to hear?"
"Yes."
"Two of them held me down while the third got on top. At first I screamed and kicked, but it was useless, and they were threatening to cut my throat. So I calmed myself and let them have their way."
"All three of them?"
"When the first was finished, they changed places. They were so drunk they could hardly function."
"Which made it last longer."
"I think they had a better time beating me up."
"How was it?"
"Being beaten up?"
"No, being raped."

"You mean, did I like it? Is that what you mean?"

"Yes."

"No, I didn't like it. I hated it."

They came beneath the massive eucalyptus trees and passed through the gate to the property; the old house loomed up ahead. Cabell set the can on the front porch. Hamid sat down, tugged the cork out of the bottle and handed it to Cabell; and for the next few minutes they smoked cigarettes and drank quietly, passing the bottle back and forth.

"I've never set fire to a house before, Yusef. Do you think it will burn right down to the ground?"

"I don't know. It depends on how much of the house is made of wood."

"I looked today. I think there is a great deal of wood."

"Then the house will burn."

"What about the chimney? And the roof is made of tiles."

"The roof ought to collapse into the flames, and the tiles will break. But if the chimney is well constructed, it might stand."

"I hope it doesn't."

"We can always knock it down with sledgehammers afterward."

"I wish nothing to remain. I hope the grass will grow up around the ruins and cover all. By next spring, it will be as if the house never existed."

"And you shall be in Icht."

"Yes, Icht, God willing. And where will you be next spring, Yusef?"

"Most likely in the Spanish Sahara. Spring is a good time to be in the desert, especially early spring."

Again they drank in silence. A breeze moved the eucalyptus boughs above their heads, and the boughs rubbed against the side of the house: somewhere inside itself the old house creaked.

"Hamid, are you quite sure you want to go through with this?"

"Yes. How are we going to do it?"

"Shall we begin now?"

"Yes, before I lose my nerve."

Cabell got to his feet and carried the can of gasoline into the house. Once inside he took out a flashlight; the thin beam leaped about the room and stopped at the boxes, broken chairs, and mattresses piled at the foot of the stairs.

"Is this all there is, Hamid?"

There was no answer. Cabell turned around and flashed the light on the doorway.

"Hamid, where are you?"

He went onto the porch and called out in a loud whisper.

"Hamid! Hamid! Where are you?"

A voice responded from the darkness, and in another minute she was beside him.

"Where did you go?"

"I was just putting the aguardiente in a safe place where we can have some later."

"For a second I thought the smugglers had returned and carried you off."

"I've prepared a little nest for us."

"A nest?"

"A place where we can watch the fire from."

"But I want some more aguardiente."

"Right now?"

"Yes, now."

"Shall I go and get it?"

"Yes, get it."

She went off again and returned with the half-empty bottle. Between them they quickly finished it off.

"We'll save the other bottle for later."

"All right."

They re-entered the house, and again Cabell shined his light on the heap of broken furniture and boxes.

"Is this all there is?"

"Yes."

"Where's the kerosene you were talking about?" They were speaking in whispers.

Hamid brought the kerosene; Cabell mounted the stairs, then

descended backwards, pouring the kerosene on the stairs. What was left he poured on the mattresses. Next he opened the can of gasoline.

"Move away."

Hamid stepped back, holding the light as he spilled the gasoline onto the boxes and chairs and all over the foot of the stairs. When the gasoline was nearly finished, he began retreating toward the door, still pouring and leaving a trail of fuel behind until the can was empty. At the door he recapped it and handed it to Hamid.

"Take this and go outside. You say you have a safe place for us to hide and watch the fire?"

"Yes, I have."

"Go on, then. Get away from the house."

After Hamid went out, Cabell shined his light around for the last time. The light switched off, and he went down on one knee and struck a match. For an instant he held it above the dark stain on the floor before him; then he dropped it. Immediately, a weak yellow flame sprang up and widened to the perimeter of the stain; it began to spread, quite slowly, along the avenue of gasoline which led from the door to the stairs. When it reached the piled mattresses and furniture, it seemed to hesitate for a second, almost to disappear. Then there was a loud thump as the rest of the gasoline and kerosene ignited and a tinkling of glass as the windows burst. A great flame shot up, completely engulfing the stairs. The house was afire.

Cabell and Hamid were running through the trees; the light from the fire cast their shadows before them and illuminated the way over the rough ground. Hamid led him to a little shed built into a bank of earth, where vines and bushes concealed the doorway. She ducked her head and went inside; Cabell followed her.

"Is this it?" he asked.

"No one will find us here."

In the rear of the shed was a bale of hay. Hamid began to pull it apart and throw the hay on the floor.

"What are you doing, Hamid?"

"Don't you want to lie on the floor?"

"I hadn't thought about it."

"If we spread this hay around, we can make ourselves comfortable and have a good view of the fire through the door."

"All right. Where does the hay come from?"

"I brought it here."

"To lie on?"

"Yes. You want to, don't you?"

"Yes, of course. When did you do that?"

"The day after the fires at Merkala, I met a man on his way to market with two bales of hay. I traded a basket of apples for one bale and dragged it back here."

While Hamid spread the hay around, Cabell stepped outside and peered down through the trees toward the house. The fire was still contained inside the house, but the doorway looked like a hatch to a roaring furnace. As he watched, tongues of flame curled out from the windows and began to lick the sides of the house. Fire spewed out the front door, and the porch began to burn. A great rumbling noise was heard. Hamid came and stood by him.

"Shall we go inside now, Yusef? The hay is ready."

"Wait a minute. There's no one to see us yet."

"Is the house burning properly?"

"You can see for youself."

The porch was blazing fiercely now: flames spiraled around the supports for the roof, and the wooden railing looked like a great row of fiery teeth. Red light could be seen through the windows on the second floor, and sparks poured out of the chimney. The rumbling noise was becoming louder. Suddenly a figure in a djellaba appeared at the edge of light.

"All right, Hamid, here they come. Let's go inside now."

They crept into the shed and lay down together in the hay—from this position they had a perfect view of the house down an alley through the eucalyptus trees. Several people had gathered to watch the fire; some carried buckets, but because of the intense heat they were unable to approach the house. One side of the porch roof collapsed in an explosion of sparks, the flames shot up to an even greater height, and the spectators had to retreat farther away. These flames ignited the eucalyptus branches overhanging the house, and sheets of fire raced through the leaves with a crackling noise audible above the rumble of the inferno.

"My trees! Yusef, my trees are burning!"

"Just leaves and branches, nothing more."

There was a loud explosion, and a great ring of fire shot up from the house and disappeared into the night.

"What was that?"

"Oh, my God, the Butagaz bottle! I'd forgotten all about it. How stupid of me! Now I won't be able to get my deposit back."

"Where's the aguardiente?"

Hamid produced the bottle, and together they began to drink it down.

"Look at that!"

The remainder of the porch gave way, and with it a section of the front wall of the house suddenly disintegrated. The blazing inferno inside was exposed; huge flames swept out through this new opening and leaped up into the darkness.

"My poor house."

"Are you sorry now that we did it?"

"I didn't realize it would burn so fiercely."

"The house must be made entirely of wood."

By now a group of Moroccans had been attracted by the fire; although they stood some distance from it, they were still forced to shield their faces from the heat with their hands.

"Do you recognize them?"

"Of course I do. They're my neighbors."

"I wonder what they're thinking."

"I suppose they're happy to see my house burn. Now they know the smugglers won't be coming back."

"Let's hope they think it was the smugglers who set fire to it."

Large portions of the roof began falling in, causing great

swirls of sparks to rise into the air. Next the walls gave way with fiery explosions; and the house lost its form. Some of the eucalyptus branches were still burning, and red embers and flaming twigs rained to earth.

"Look at my trees, Yusef! I didn't mean to destroy them as well."

"They're too green to go on burning. As soon as the heat from the house diminishes, the flames will go out."

"I hope so."

She moved closer to him in the hay.

"Yusef, I'm happy we did this."

Cabell continued to drink and watch the fire.

"Do you like this nest I prepared for us, Yusef?"

"An arsonist's paradise."

Hamid began to laugh to herself.

"What's so funny?"

"I wonder what my neighbors would think if they knew I'd set fire to my own house?"

"And what would they think if they knew you were here in the shed having a good time watching the blaze?"

"If they knew I was lying on straw brought especially for the occasion, they'd really think I was crazy."

They both laughed out loud.

"We better be quiet," Cabell whispered.

"Am I crazy, Yusef?"

"We both must be a little crazy to set fire to houses."

Hamid moved closer until their bodies touched, Cabell put the bottle to one side, and in a few minutes they were making love in the hay. Meanwhile, the flames gradually subsided, and one by one the Moroccans drifted off into the darkness.

At dawn they crept out of the shed and went quietly down through the eucalyptus trees, whose massive trunks still retained the heat which had been radiated into them from the fire; among them the morning air was warm. A fog had rolled in from the sea, and out in the Straits the ships were using their horns. The fog combined with the gray smoke rising from the ruins of the house. Very little of the house remained—just a heap of ashes and embers, with little flames still flickering here and there among the wreckage. In the center of the heap the chimney stood like a great stone pole; the smell of smoke and wet ashes permeated the forest.

Cabell squatted on his heels at the edge of the ruins and rubbed his hands together over the warm ashes, as if this were an early morning campfire in the desert. Hamid was down on her knees beside him, blowing the ashes away from a smoldering branch. From time to time she cast her eyes upward at the tall chimney which dominated the mound. Neither of them spoke a word, nobody else seemed to be around.

Grasping the branch by its unburned end, Hamid withdrew it from the ashes and waved it above her, making a circle of smoke over her head. She got to her feet and pointed the branch at the chimney. Cabell rocked back on his heels and regarded her sleepily. Then Hamid began to dance: it began as a halting skip, in which she brought one knee high up, until it almost touched her chin, and ducked her head forward in the same motion. After two or three skips, she leaped high into the air and landed with her feet wide apart, the djellaba billowing around her. Pointing her smoking stick at the chimney and shaking it violently, she mumbled curses in Arabic. After pausing for a moment, as if she were expecting some reply, she continued this irregular skipping dance. Following each great leap, she would again brandish the stick toward the chimney, and the curses became shouts of anger. As she followed the perimeter of ashes, which always kept her equidistant from the chimney, the smoking branch reignited from being waved about in the air. Then she picked up a pebble and hurled it; the pebble glanced off the chimney with a sharp click, which was followed by Hamid's ringing laughter.

"Yusef!" she called out. "Everything is destroyed except this damn chimney!"

"Sometimes it happens that way," came the reply out of the smoke and mist.

"But you didn't tell me it was going to be like this—this giant thing presiding over a mound of ashes."

"We'll come back later and knock it down with sledgehammers if you like. Too hot to do it now."

"No, leave it. I want to see it."

"A reminder of the time you were attacked by the smugglers?"

"Yes, let this thing stand."

Hamid went on with her dance, singing to herself as she performed the high skips, grunting when she landed with her feet wide apart, and shouting as she pelted the tall chimney with stones. Three times she circled the smoking ruins, and each time she passed by Cabell she made a sign over his head with the flaming brand. All the time he remained seated on his haunches, rubbing his hands together and staring into the ruins. Suddenly some children appeared under the eucalyptus trees; Cabell signaled to them to come closer, but they did not move. He called to them to come forward and warm themselves, and one by one they came and crouched down by the warm ashes on the opposite side of the ruin. There were four boys.

"Do you know them?" Cabell whispered to Hamid.

"No."

"Are they from the village?"

"I don't think so. I think they're shepherd boys."

"Are you shepherd boys?" Cabell called out.

The boys looked at each other.

"Why are you here?"

The boys looked uncertain.

"Did you set fire to this house?"

They shook their heads; they were frightened now.

"Do you know who did?"

They shook their heads again.

"We did," Cabell said.

"Oh, Yusef, don't say that. They might tell somebody."

The boys looked at Cabell, not knowing whether to believe him or not.

"Do you know why we did?"

The boys didn't know.

"We did it so we could warm our hands over the ashes in the morning."

They still didn't believe him, but they giggled among themselves over this piece of information—they were a miserable-looking lot, barefoot, clad only in ragged djellabas.

From among the trees there came the sound of voices, adult voices. Cabell and Hamid looked at each other, jumped to their feet, and dashed off into the woods. The shepherd boys, frightened by this sudden action, ran off in another direction.

When they came out on the road, Hamid sat down on a rock.

"Yusef," she said, "I'm hungry."

"What's there to eat around here?"

"Nothing."

"We'll go into town, then."

"Yes, please."

They caught a ride into Tangier on the back of a truck. A restaurant on the main boulevard was just opening its doors as they arrived, and they went in and ordered coffee, a whole bottle of white wine, liver pâté, fried fish fresh from the market, eggs, more coffee, and several glasses of brandy. A drunken man came in and sat down at the bar and watched them eat. "Life is beautiful," he mumbled to himself. "Just a little money . . . Confound the weather. . . . The rest is good, good, good."

September 18 The house is down, reduced to ashes and rubble, with only the stone column to mark where it once stood. Hamid seems like a different person: no more complaints about Tangier, now that the only restraining link has been severed, utterly. Through destruction of the thing which controlled her, she has been released and projected, irrevocably, toward the desert; all that concerns her now is the future.

As we rolled in the hay while the house burned, thoughts were exploding in my head; my mind was lit by alternating visions of absolute clarity and total madness. (The line separating the two must be very thin.) Invariably, when I hold her in my arms, I think desert.

Would I be insane (or just plain stupid) to implement this scheme, which may bring unknown and possibly ugly consequences? Am I simply being selfish, devising a way of keeping myself usefully occupied in the Sahara? Would it be safer and cleaner and wiser to keep my hand out of the desert altogether?

I'm no longer interested in progress; the word and practically everything connected with it fills me with revulsion. But . . . if what H. A. brags about is for real, somebody's going to find out about it very soon, if they haven't already. Then it'll be out of his hands and I won't be able to touch it. Too big for either of us to handle.

But that big stone column . . . Am I going to rape her Sahara?

# *Rain*

"YOU MAY TELL THEM to expect me in El Aaiun December the first."

Wearing a dark-blue suit, with a gold watch chain dangling between the vest pockets, Cabell was sitting in a big leather chair, smoking a cigar. On the wall behind him hung a full-length oil portrait of General Franco, painted in 1941. Before him the Spanish Consul sat at his mahogany desk; he was smiling. A fire crackled in the fireplace at one end of the old-fashioned office; outside the window the rain poured down. The Consul folded his hands together.

"Not before, Señor Cabell?"

"No, not before. They can wait."

"They have already been waiting five months. I think they're becoming somewhat impatient."

"They should know better: one cannot be impatient in the desert—it always leads to trouble."

Escobar pressed a button, the secretary came in, and he dictated a telegram. Cabell listened and looked out the window; his cigar held the long ash. When the secretary had gone out and shut the door behind her, Escobar got to his feet and walked over to the fire.

"I suppose I'm happier about this than you are," he said.

"No, I'm glad the date has been set. I'm ready now."

Escobar nodded. "But it won't be the same as before, will it?"

"No."

"Apparently you and your Moroccan friend made quite a name for yourselves down there."

"He was the lighthouse keeper, and I knew where to find water in the desert."

"Those are solitary occupations."

"We had the whole desert to ourselves."

"Ah, yes. Space. I'm sure it will be a relief for you to leave Tangier. There are indications that the population explosion here is getting out of hand."

"All those thousands of children loose in the streets. I won't miss them. It's as if there had been an invasion of tiny people from another planet."

"There have been rumors that packs of wild boys are attacking tourists on the beach," Escobar said.

"Did you know that children have taken over Calle Larache altogether? It's difficult and even dangerous to pass by there for they grow angry if their games are interrupted."

"Is there nobody to control them?"

"They'll retreat before a Moroccan adult who knows how to talk to them, but the moment he turns his back, they surge forward again."

"We had to shoo them away from the area where they play football next to the Consulate here because their shouting disturbed our work. The following day five or six hundred of them poured out of Ain Hayani and stood around the chancellery, just looking in the windows. I'm sure it was meant to be a threat."

"I have a young Moroccan friend, a student, who says the schools are like cinemas—the first group of students arrives at eight in the morning and leaves at twelve; another comes at twelve and is out at four; and the last bunch begins at four and ends at eight in the evening."

"And when they finish school only a few of them are able to find work."

"The rest go into the streets. Even the police are afraid; they are attempting to infiltrate with child informers."

Cabell got to his feet, and the two men went out of the office. As they passed down the corridor, there was the usual scuffling noise as the old men got hastily to their feet, putting away newspapers, lottery sheets, and football score cards to stand at attention in their cubicles. At the entrance to the chancellery the consular car was waiting, the long black Mercedes. The chauffeur stood by, and the doorman had the umbrella ready. Rain was being driven along in horizontal sheets by the wind, and the palms whipped about. Many fronds had fallen to the ground. Cabell and the Consul shook hands.

"Look at this rain," Cabell said. "It's one of the reasons I want to leave Tangier."

The Consul nodded. "I've never seen anything like it."

"The walls of my hotel room are actually turning green."

"My wife suffers from asthma. She's having a hard time breathing."

"You should see the mildew on my shoes. I have to wipe them off with a cloth soaked in vinegar."

"I suppose I ought to take her out to the Canary Islands."

"Yes, the weather in the Canaries is perfect all year round."

"Anything would be better than this rain."

"The Sahara is clean and dry."

"The air must be good for breathing."

"That's why I'm going back."

"By the way, Señor Cabell, whatever happened to the boy who was put in jail?"

"Mohamed? He's been free for some time now."

"I know, but what is he doing with himself? Is he working?"

"He has a good job out at Villa Harris."

"Glad to hear it."

"How did you know he was free?"

"Well, since he was a friend of yours, I put in a good word for him, and I heard later that he'd been released."

"So that's why they let him go so easily. Well, thank you, from him and from me."

"No need to say anything to the boy about it."

"No, I won't, but thank you again."

Protected by the doorman's umbrella, Cabell got into the automobile, and the Mercedes moved off. Settling back into the deep leather seat, he looked at his cigar, opened the window a crack, and threw it out into the street. Through the steamy window he was watching the gray, wind-swept city slide by. The schools had just recessed at midday, and Moroccan children in slickers and miniature djellabas huddled in doorways out of the rain. Beneath the arched gateway to the Kasbah a crowd of these young people was seeking refuge. The Mercedes moved slowly up the ramp, blowing its horn, and to allow it to pass the children were forced to step out into the rain, which they did not like to do. Cabell was peering at the multitude of young faces through the window when suddenly he tapped on the glass partition behind the chauffeur and ordered him to stop. Opening the door, he called out Omar's name. The boy extricated himself from the crowd, and, to the amazement of his friends, leaped into the large black automobile. He threw his arms around Cabell, gave him a kiss, then immediately rolled down the window and proceeded to wave at his stupefied schoolmates as the Mercedes pulled away.

Back in his hotel room, Cabell lit the gas heater and hung Omar's wet djellaba over the back of the chair. The two of them were walking around in circles, rubbing their hands together, as the rain pelted against the windowpanes. Water was leaking in along the window sill and dripping down the wall. Cabell called in Fatomah and had her mop it up, and by the time she had finished the windows were steamed up with condensation. The room had become warm at last.

"Omar, I'll be leaving soon."

"Yes?"

"I have to go back to work. I don't have any more money."

"When?"

"I told Señor Escobar I'd be there December first. Señor Escobar is happy. He sent off a telegram immediately."

"But Señor Escobar doesn't know anything."

"He knows everything."

Water vapor was rising from the damp djellaba, and a puddle was forming beneath it. The odor of wet wool permeated the room.

"You're taking me with you, Yusef, aren't you?"

"You may come part of the way, but then I'll have to send you back."

"I want to go to Tarfaya."

"I know you do, but it's so far. How will you return?"

"On the airplane."

"I don't know if the planes are flying out of Tarfaya now."

"You said there were airplanes."

"They might have dug out the runway, but I doubt it."

"Then I can come back by truck."

"That's a long journey."

"I like trucks."

"I know you do."

There was a knock on the door and Shahid entered. He was wearing a long wool djellaba.

"Congratulations, Shahid. I read in the newspaper that you won your match in Casablanca."

Shahid was still half asleep; when he shut the door he gave a great yawn and stretched himself, and his fingertips brushed against the ceiling.

"Yes, we won, but we had to drive all the way back afterward in the rain."

"No good?"

"I hate those long trips. I hate to stay up late."

"I don't blame you."

"I prefer to go to bed early and to get up early, like we used to do in the army."

"So how's Casablanca?"

"In Casablanca they asked me if I would play on the national team."

"Oh, that's good."

"You know what that means, don't you?"

"What?"

"Long airplane trips. I know; when I played on the Senegalese team we traveled all the time in airplanes."

"You don't fit very well into an airplane?"

"Like a grasshopper with nowhere to jump."

"Shahid," Omar said. "Yusef is leaving."

"What?"

"I'm going with him."

"There's time yet," Cabell said.

"Where are you going?"

"South, into the desert."

"When? Now?"

Cabell was pacing back and forth with his hands in his pockets. "No, not for another month or so. Omar is going to accompany me part of the way; then he'll return to Tangier and I'll cross the border into the Spanish Zone."

Shahid sat down on the bed and cracked his knuckles. Cabell went to the window, and rubbed the moisture off the glass and looked out. The slanting rain continued to beat down with great force as it was carried along by the wind. The Place de la Kasbah was empty; the guard with the submachine gun had left the prison roof. In the narrow street directly below the window men in red fezzes stood under the dripping eaves chatting with shopkeepers. Veiled ladies with their djellabas hiked up to their knees circumvented the puddles. Little girls carried buckets from the pump.

Shahid yawned once more and stretched out the long black arms until it seemed as if they extended from one end of the bed to the other.

"I think I'll go and sleep some more."

He got up, slipped his feet into the yellow babouches, and shuffled to the door. Before going out he turned and looked at Cabell.

"I wish you weren't going."

"Perhaps I've stayed on too long already."

"Stay here with us through the winter, and we'll all travel south together in the spring."

"I'll be coming back."

"Yes, and we'll be waiting for you, all of us."

After Shahid went out, Cabell changed out of his suit into a sweater and an old pair of blue trousers. Omar was drawing pictures with his fingers on the steamy windowpanes.

"Come on, Omar, let's get some lunch."

They both drew the wool djellabas over them and went out into the rain. Not far down the steps from the Kasbah gate is a café known simply as Mohamed's, which is famous for its bysar, a thick pea soup made with olive oil, red pepper, cumin, and lemon. It's a winter soup and must be served hot. Cabell and Omar entered the café and took seats on wooden benches, and two bowls of the steaming soup were brought immediately to them, with half a loaf of bread. As they blew on the soup and warmed their hands on the sides of the bowls, a man sitting on a platform at the rear of the café began to pluck a lute and sing. After a while Mohamed himself came over. He was a big man with a thick mustache and always wore a red fez. People referred to him as "The Turk."

"Everything all right, Yusef?"

"Everything's fine, thank you."

"How's the soup?"

"Too hot to taste, but it looks good."

"Do you want some more sudani?"
"I don't think so. Everything is fine."
"Would you like some pinchitos?"
"How about some pinchitos, Omar?"
Omar shook his head. His mouth was full of bread.
"This is all we want, Mohamed. What we have is fine."
Mohamed went off, and Cabell and Omar concentrated on the bysar as the lute player continued to pluck his instrument. Outside the open door the rain kept on falling; gray water sluiced down gutters and drains; the stairway leading down into the Medina had become a series of miniature waterfalls. A pall of mist and smoke had spread through the streets.
"Omar, don't eat so much bread."
"I like this bread. At home we only have brown bread."
"Brown bread's better for you, but eat your soup instead."
"I'm waiting for it to cool off."
"Too much bread will make you fat. You don't want to become a fat boy."
The two ate in silence, blowing on the bysar and carrying it to their mouths in the wooden spoons. The lute music came to an end, someone switched on a radio, and the voice of a taleb came on, reading from the Koran.
"I think I'll be glad to go back to the Sahara, Omar."
"Why? Just because it's dry and warm?"
"No, there are other things I miss."
"Like what?"
"Well, there's a good cinema."
"Do they have a cinema in the desert?"
"On Saturday nights your brother and I used to cross the border into Mauritania and go to the open air theater in Port Etienne. The theater consisted of nothing more than a brick wall around a level sandy area, but it was always crowded, and on a hot night it was a good place to be comfortable in. The place used to be packed with Spanish sailors and fishermen from Japan and Russia and Korea; none of them understood the words because only French films were shown; so the theater

used to become so noisy with these foreigners speculating out loud among themselves about what was being said that finally the management did away with the loudspeakers altogether and showed only the old silent films which you don't see very often these days. Everybody understood these films, and it didn't matter that the theater was full of laughter, because there was no sound to compete with."

"I don't know what a silent film is, Yusef."

"The kind they used to make before they knew how to put the voices in."

"How do you know what the stars say to each other?"

"You don't, or you try to guess from what they're doing."

"But if you don't know what the stars are saying, how can you tell what they're really doing?"

"You just watch; it's all quite clear."

"That's like saying, you know what a man thinks from what he says."

"I didn't say that."

"I don't think I'd like silent films."

"Why not?"

"Too many tricks."

"Anyway, afterward we used to take long walks among the sand dunes. That's when I first heard your name."

"What did Driss say about me?"

"He said he hoped you would do something else than work in lighthouses. One brother in the family is enough."

"I don't mind, I like lighthouses."

"I know you do."

"I want to do exactly what my brother did."

"Well, you've got a big head start on him."

"Yusef, will that cinema still be there when you go back?"

"I don't know why not."

"What else did you and Driss do?"

"Well, I've already told you about how I used to visit him at the lighthouse."

"Yes."

"And about the times we spent together in the desert."

"Yes."

"Guera's a pretty small place. Not much going on in the town. We used to play a lot of volleyball."

"With the Spaniards?"

"No, just the two of us."

"But volleyball's a team sport. Many must play at once."

"Out at the lighthouse, there just wasn't anybody else around. We strung a rope between two poles on the beach and batted the ball back and forth. When it got too hot, we ran and jumped in the sea."

"I never heard of just two people playing volleyball."

"Same with soccer."

"Just you and Driss? No other players?"

"Your brother used to bring a ball with him into the desert, and when work was done, we used to go off somewhere, find a flat sandy place with no bushes or rocks, and kick the ball around until the sun went down. Kicked that ball all over the desert."

"You and Driss."

"Nobody else. To tell the truth, we didn't want anybody. We liked playing together, alone, out in those empty spaces. Only problem was the wind."

"The wind?"

"Often the wind would be blowing so hard that if one of us made a bad kick, with the wind behind it, the other had to chase it across the desert. Sometimes we had to go after the ball in the Jeep."

Cabell paid up. They pulled the hoods of their djellabas over their heads and went out into the rain. They walked a little ways together, then Omar went off to school and Cabell returned to his room. On the floor was the puddle from Omar's wet djellaba; he called in Fatomah and had her mop it up.

September 21 The Berlin Zirkus has come to town, but a storm blew down the big top—will this wind and rain never stop?—all Tangier is sad because the citizens are fond of this excellent one-ring circus which visits their city every year. Passing by the fairgrounds last night, I noticed that the mobile lion cages were lit up and a small crowd had gathered, so I wandered over to have a look at the lions. The first person I spotted was Mohamed I. It's extraordinary the transformation that comes over a young man who has a steady income for the first time in his life: he was very well dressed in a pink shirt and necktie and overcoat and new black shoes. He offered me a cigarette, and I immediately noticed that he had switched from Casa Sports to Marlboros. He works twelve hours a day, but doesn't mind because the pay is good, and he has received several raises because he is such a skilled mason. I was really impressed by his serenity. One forgets that poverty such as he experienced is a state of psychic shock, in which all other disciplines are set aside in the scramble for some kind of security.

He had made friends with the lion tamer, a thin, very fair young Dutch fellow. He and his burly Spanish assistant were preparing horsemeat for the animals. There were two mobile cages, one full of Dutch lions, which the Dutchman used in his act, and the other with Spanish lions, which belonged to a Spanish lion tamer who was now recuperating from a mauling. They were all good-looking beasts.

The Dutchman informed us that he had worked with elephants, tigers, bears, and buffalos as well, and had traveled all over the world with various circuses. As he talked he put his hand through the bars and scratched the lions' heads; I sensed an air of quiet detachment about him, and patience, which seemed to say—the world may be going one way, but I go my own, and here are my traveling companions, the lions. He said he had been working with animals for eight years now; soon he would leave this circus for another headed for Israel; in fact he had only joined the Berlin Zirkus to fill in for the injured Spaniard. As soon as the Spaniard was on his feet and had retrained his lions, the young Dutchman would be on his way. In between the cages and piles of hay truncated sections of limestone columns lay about—the fairground is the site of an ancient Roman basilica, of which only these broken stones remain. The Dutchman complained that Moroccan children threw pebbles at his animals.

After a while we left the lion tamer and went into the Medina, as Mohamed wanted to show me where he was living, so I followed him to an old Arab hotel, several stories high and built around a narrow interior courtyard. Everything made entirely of wood. He had taken a room on one of the middle balconies, and here he kept his possessions—a radio, work clothes hung up on the wall, and cooking equipment; there was an old woman who prepares the evening meal for him, and we found her sitting on the bed cleaning out his sebsi with a wire. "Kif will make you sick if you smoke it in a dirty sebsi," she said. Mohamed sent her off to fix tea, and I stepped out onto the wooden balcony. Above and below me Moroccan ladies were leaning over the railings and chatting with their friends across the open space; their voices drifted up and down as they conversed from one balcony to the next, while the rain kept falling and spattering on the courtyard below.

Mohamed called me inside, and we drank the tea, and talked about the lion tamer and Mohamed II and about Driss. For some reason that talk made me very sad, as if we were all condemned to eventual separation, and there was no force on earth that could prevent it.

Left a note at the Nicaragua, inviting Maxwell to the circus. He's not very happy with me now, since he knows I'm leaving soon.

# *The Zirkus*

THE BIG TOP was full, an iron cage had been set up in the ring, and the audience waited in its seats; on a raised platform, the circus orchestra struck up the music. A woman wearing a spangled bikini began to shriek into the microphone as the slender young Dutchman, clad in a brilliant blue uniform, strode into the ring, snapping two white whips.

"Is that your friend, Cabell?" Maxwell asked.

"That's him. Here come the lions."

The burly Spanish assistant opened the chute, and nine snarling lions entered the ring, where they were expertly guided to their stools. The trainer twirled and snapped the whips and the lions all stood up on their hind legs; another flourish and snap and down they came. As the spectators clapped, a big male lion turned on his stool and sprayed a thick stream of urine into the audience behind him. Maxwell got to his feet shaking his fist at the trainer.

"I won't stand for this, you hear? This is a new coat!"

Meanwhile the Dutchman was going around to each of his beasts, fondling and hugging some females, deftly avoiding the bared claws of others, and purposely baiting the males with the whips. When he dropped the whips, all tension went out of the lions. They relaxed. There was a stool in the center of the ring, and the trainer lay down in the sawdust and rested his head on it. One by one, in perfect order, the lions left their stools and lay down beside him, around him, on top of him, until the blue uniform had completely disappeared beneath the pile of lions. At last a hand emerged from among the tawny skins, tapped one of the beasts, and in reverse order the lions returned to their stools. The trainer got to his feet and brushed himself off. When he picked up the whips, the animals became tense once more. Next, he was provoking snarls and bared teeth with the twirling whip motions and singled out one lioness to come to the center stool. Once more he dropped the whips and immediately all the lions relaxed. Climbing on top of the lioness, he pried the massive jaws apart and as the drums rolled, slowly inserted his head between the yellow teeth. When he extricated himself and allowed the lioness to return to her perch, the audience applauded.

The act was nearing its end. Cracking the whips and gesticulating, he had the lions running in a circle and allowed them to depart one after another into the chute, which they seemed very anxious to do. Now only one male lion, the most dangerous and the one which he had been continually taunting with the whips, remained with him in the ring. The Dutchman went to one side, received a strip of raw meat from the burly Spaniard, lay down in the center of the ring with his back arched across the low stool, and placed the raw meat across his bared neck. The big lion approached, circled, quickly snatched up the raw meat in its jaws, and trotted out of the ring. The lion tamer stood up, picked up his whips, bowed and smiled in all directions, and strode out.

"Those lions adore that boy," Maxwell said.

"He's trained them well."

"Ought to have them house trained."

The lion cage was quickly dismantled and a tarpaulin was spread over the ring. The music started up again, and four athletic-looking men in gold-lamé jump suits strutted into the arena.

"What's this?" Maxwell asked.

"THE BASQUE BALANCING TEAM!" the girl shrieked into the mike.

The Basques stood on their hands and made pyramids; after each act they would trot about with smiles frozen on their faces.

"I don't think I like this group," Maxwell commented.

"Too stuffy."

"Cocksure of themselves."

"No juice."

After a while they went away, and the attendants set up a tightrope. A little man in a cape and mask bounced into the ring.

"PABLO THE TIGHTROPE WALKER!"

Pablo did a dance with a cardboard triton; then he rather unceremoniously doffed this costume and, clad only in tights and displaying a hairy chest, climbed the ladder and walked out onto the rope. An elderly gentleman in a raincoat and Alpine hat was adjusting the tension of the rope with a lever.

"I think that chap must be the director," Maxwell whispered.

The young man was bouncing up and down and did a few flips on the rope, sometimes landing on his feet, sometimes sidesaddle, sometimes on his crotch.

"I say, that must hurt, landing that way," Maxwell said.

"Doesn't seem to."

"Must be wearing something to protect himself."

Now the big moment had come, and Pablo directed the old man to increase tension. Two big bounces on the elastic rope, a flip forward, another backward, and a double flip as the music raced with him. He landed unsteadily on his feet, however, and had to leap to earth. The crowd sighed. The young man had a pleasant round face. Unperturbed, in another second he was out on the rope again, bouncing and directing the old man on the lever. Once more he attempted the difficult double flip and failed, leaping to earth.

"I don't think he's concentrating," Maxwell remarked.

A third time he mounted the ladder and skipped out onto the rope as the musicians played frantically. There was an expression of determination on his face.

"PABLO WILL ATTEMPT THIS DIFFICULT FEAT ONE MORE TIME!"

The crowd hushed as Pablo bounced, flipped, and landed squarely on his crotch.

"There, do you see what I mean, Cabell? That boy must have hurt himself."

Grimacing with pain, Pablo let himself down, bowed perfunctorily, and ran out of the ring.

"It looked like a difficult trick for anyone to do."

"That boy must have bruised his gonads."

"He didn't look very serious."

"He better get serious if he wants to keep his balls."

"I prefer the lions."

"Speaking of lions, Cabell, I'm hungry. I missed my breakfast."

"Breakfast at ten o'clock in the evening?"

"But I just got out of bed."

"I keep forgetting."

"Usually I have a cheese omelet after leaving the hotel."

"I doubt they have cheese omelets here."

"Perhaps they sell popcorn or peanuts."

A new group rushed into the ring and was setting up jumping platforms and catapults.

"I say, this circus is well organized," Maxwell remarked.

"They don't waste any time in between acts."

"There, Cabell, you see how all the performers help each other? That boy with sore gonads is helping with the catapults."

"THE SPANISH CATAPULT TEAM!"

Two acrobats jumped down from the tower and catapulted a smaller fellow somersaulting up into the air, who landed on his feet on the shoulders of the strongman with the handlebar mustache.

"I say, this is an old-fashioned circus, Cabell."

Then two were catapulted together, one landing on the shoulders of the strongman, the other on a stocky woman, who appeared to be an anchorman as well.

"Take note of those thick legs and muscular arms, Cabell. A regular Amazon."

The building of the human tower commenced. The strongman set himself and took an acrobat of medium size on his shoulders; a third member of the team was flipped high up on the shoulders of the second. Drums rolled as the husky woman climbed the tower, then jumped down, catapulting the littlest of all, just a boy, it seemed, but with long gray hair, who landed cleanly on the third man, completing the human tower of four.

"CHEER THEM, LADIES AND GENTLEMEN! THE SPANISH CATAPULT TEAM!"

The attendants rushed in and were setting up a large round table with a ramp leading up to it, while a wiry, grim-faced young man wearing roller skates was checking the surface of the table with a carpenter's level and adjusting thumbscrews on the metal legs. Then he ran off behind the curtains, the band began to play some fast Russian-sounding music, and two big girls dressed in artificial fox skins and wearing roller skates dashed up the ramp, followed by the young man.

"NIKOLAY, SONYA, AND MAROUSSIA! THE RUSSIAN ROLLER-SKATE TEAM!"

All three carried swords, and they skated in a circle on the table, holding hands and clashing their swords together in time to the clashing music. The long braids of the girls flew out, and the girls displayed wide toothy smiles.

"Look at those teeth!"

The Russians threw away the swords, and the young man leaped into the girls' arms. As they whirled him about, he was looking down at the table and frowning. Something was still not quite right with the level; then one of the girls stumbled and almost fell; an element of uncertainty had been introduced into the act. Meanwhile the roller-skate wheels continued to roar. One girl jumped down and began to clap her hands and shout, Russian-style, as the young man hoisted the other onto his shoulders and spun about. The audience clapped rhythmically with them, and the girls' grins became even larger.

"Looks like a shark, Cabell. A man-eater."

The great moment was approaching. Still spinning, the couple on the table were linking their necks together with a leather loop. Around and around they went; the girl lifted one foot off the boards, then the other, and she was suspended by her own centrifugal force, while the young man arched his back.

"Do you think they're Russian, George?"

"Certainly not. I know a Russian when I see one. Lived with one for years."

"Is that so?"

"After I came down from Cambridge I went to Paris and met a Russian lady. She was twelve years my senior, but we lived together until the war broke out."

"Then what happened?"

"The British Consulate said I wasn't needed at home owing to my sinus troubles. So I stayed on in Paris."

"And the Russian lady?"

"She was sent off to a concentration camp. After the war we were reunited, but it wasn't the same."

"What happened?"

"She went to Switzerland as a governess with an American family, then to Rio de Janeiro, where she is right now."

"You've never seen her since?"

"We still write each other. She wants me to join her in Rio."

There was a musical interlude while the trapeze artists came out to see that a safety net was properly erected. Their blue capes only partially concealed bare torsos and bright-orange tights. The roller skater, the strongman, and the tightrope walker helped them set up poles and attach pulleys, and in a few minutes the net was tautly stretched above the ring.

"FOR THE LAST ACT OF THE EVENING, LADIES AND GENTLEMEN, THE BERLIN ZIRKUS PRESENTS THE FAMOUS GERMAN TRAPEZE TEAM—HANS, LOLA, AND TONI!"

In pranced the three Germans—a tall, lanky bald fellow with bandages on his hands, a stocky blond girl, and a muscular young man with sideburns and a lantern jaw. This last exuded such confidence and expertise—it was he who had most actively supervised the setting up of the net—that the audience sensed immediately that this would be the man to watch, the star. Quickly and expertly they climbed the rope ladders, the young lady and the star to a little platform high above the audience, and the lanky bald fellow to a trapeze at the far end of the tent. The star was rubbing his hands on a resin bag. The musicians played faster as he took the trapeze and timed the swing of the lanky fellow, who was now hanging upside down from his trapeze.

"NOW TONI WILL LEAP!"

The star completed a somersault in mid-air and with a smack of flesh locked hands with the bald fellow.

"AH! BRAVO! BRAVO!" The girl at the mike could not restrain her enthusiasm.

The star returned to his own platform; now it was the girl's turn. She completed the same maneuver as the star but remained swinging in the bald man's hands as the trapeze returned to the star. Without hesitation he swung out, again somersaulting in mid-air, and locked hands with Hans, while at the same instant the girl regained his trapeze. Another swing and the star was grasping the bar beside the girl, and they returned together to the little platform.

Meanwhile the anchor man continued to swing back and forth upside down. The music changed tempo, and the audience, sensing that the great moment was approaching, grew silent. The star had been at the resin bag again; now he mounted a ladder above the platform and began to swing out with great force, until at the peak of the arc he nearly touched the tent.

"TONI WILL NOW ATTEMPT THE DANGEROUS DOUBLE SOMERSAULT!"

Maxwell nudged Cabell with his elbow, "Sounds like the announcer has a crush on that fellow, eh?"

Next came the double somersault and the smack of hands as he made contact with his partner, but the star tumbled into the net. A huge gasp sounded through the public address system.

He bounced immediately up, however, landed on his feet, and in another second was up the rope ladder again. He took the trapeze from the blond girl, and swung out.

"TONI WILL ONCE MORE ATTEMPT THIS DIFFICULT AND DANGEROUS FEAT!" The woman was breathing heavily into the mike.

This time he successfully completed the flip. The act was over. The anchorman slipped from his perch, plummeted into the net, and bounced to the ground as the audience applauded. Next the blond girl swung out, released the trapeze, and dropped into the net. The star did a final somersault, dove headlong into the elastic net, sprung up, flipped again, and leaped to the ground. Grinning broadly, the trio bowed and waved.

Off they went, and as the music continued to play, the Dutch lion tamer in his beautiful uniform appeared, followed by the Basque Brothers, the tightrope walker, and the Spanish catapult team. Next came the grim-faced roller skater and his two enormous female assistants, who blew kisses to the crowd.

It was late, past midnight, when Cabell and Maxwell arrived at Café Marco Polo. The place was brightly illuminated as usual and contained the regular collection of Spaniards and Moroccans. Inside, it was warm, and the big espresso machine gurgled and gave off its own heat. The waiter recognized Maxwell and took his order for whiskeys. Cabell sat down with his back to the wall, Maxwell across the table; the whiskeys were brought immediately. Cabell raised his glass.

"Cheers."

Maxwell said nothing but clicked glasses, and the two men

drank. Outside the rain began to fall once more, and there was a scraping of chairs on the pavement as the customers moved farther back under the awning.

Cabell drank off his whiskey and asked the waiter to bring two more. "I wanted to tell you my plans, but perhaps you don't want to hear," he said.

Maxwell slammed the empty glass down on the table. "I've heard enough of your plans," he shouted.

The other customers looked up from their newspapers as the waiter arrived with the whiskeys. Amigo Maxwell took his directly from the tray and swallowed it in one large gulp.

"Is that all you have to tell me—that you're leaving? Do you have nothing else to say?"

Cabell looked at him blankly.

"You, with all your damned mobility, which we all envy, leave a lot of people behind in your travels, isn't it true?"

"What are you talking about?"

"Why do I wait here while you do all the traveling and have all the adventures?"

The waiter had backed off a step and was listening to Maxwell's outburst. Maxwell slammed his glass down on the waiter's tin tray.

"Bring me another! And food, I want food!"

"What will it be, sir?"

"You know what I like—cheese omelet and toast! Don't overcook the omelet; I like it to be soft inside."

The waiter went off. Behind the counter a fellow in a white jacket was craning his neck to get a better look.

"I have only Tangier, Cabell. Don't think Tangier fulfills all my needs because it doesn't! Tangier wins by default, but it allows me to live in a decent manner."

"I know."

"You don't need Tangier like I do."

"I've needed Tangier these past months."

"Tangier has been good to you, Cabell. Don't deny it."

"I've never denied it."

"But now you abandon us."

The waiter came back with a whole bottle of whiskey, a metal ice bucket, soda water, and Maxwell's omelet; the whole lot he set down on the table.

"That's more like it," Maxwell said.

As Cabell watched, Maxwell ravenously devoured the omelet and toast, taking swallows of whiskey in between mouthfuls.

"George, do I need to explain my actions?"

"I don't want any explanations."

"What do you want, then?"

"I don't want you to leave."

"I have to."

"I know you do."

As Maxwell lowered his voice, the other customers returned to their own conversations and newspapers. In the corner an emaciated Moroccan who had been asleep gaped uncomprehendingly.

"How's Palmeta these days?"

"Never see her."

"Why not?"

"You know why—I can't put up with that Spanish nonsense."

"But she cares about you."

"I know." All of a sudden Maxwell banged his fist down on the table top. "Cabell!" he cried. "Take me out of here! I have money. I can pay my own way!"

"What?"

"I won't be a burden to you!"

"George, you're the only one who wants to go somewhere. I'd rather stay here in Tangier."

"That's not true! You told me you're fed up with this rainy weather!"

Maxwell was banging his fist on the table with every word now. The waiters stood around and watched, the customers had turned around in their chairs, and the people outside were pressing their faces up against the window.

"My books!" Maxwell shouted. "Bring me my books!"

One of the waiters went away and came back with a leather satchel. Maxwell snatched it from him.

"I'm leaving," he said.

"Finish your whiskey."

"I'm going."

"If you want to come with me to the desert, come on, then. That'll make three of us."

"Who else is coming along?"

"Omar."

"That boy? Why're you taking him?"

"He wants to visit his brother's grave in Tarfaya."

Amigo Maxwell, who was about to say something, shut his mouth. Everyone in the café was watching and listening. The emaciated Moroccan had left his table and was standing at Maxwell's elbow, his mouth gaping. Maxwell glared at him, and the man moved back a few steps.

"Where shall we go?" Maxwell said at last.

Cabell shrugged. "To the Sahara."

"What shall I do down there?"

"I don't know."

"I have my books."

"Yes."

"I'm a scholar of sorts; scholars always travel with books."

"You can do a few translations."

"I'll keep a journal to record my observations of the land and people. A traveler's journal."

"All right."

"How's the light?"

"Plenty of light in the desert."

"I don't mean sunlight. Sunlight's no good to read and write by."

"Most of the towns have their own generators, but they shut down at midnight. I do a lot of work by candlelight."

"Candlelight?"

"Or with a flashlight."

"Oh, it's hopeless!" Maxwell said, raising his voice once more. "I can't go with you!"

"You must be prepared for some hard traveling."

"You don't really want me to come with you!"

"You'll have to expect some discomfort."

Maxwell brought the flat of his hand down on the table and knocked the whiskey bottle to the floor. The shattered bottle lay in a spreading pool; immediately everything smelled of whiskey. Maxwell looked at what he had done, then got to his feet, gathered up his book satchel, and walked toward the door.

"Where are you going?"

"I won't pay for that!" he shouted without turning around.

"Where are you going, George?"

"I can go to Rio anytime, you know!" Maxwell yelled as he went out the door. There was a scraping of metal on pavement as the customers outside swiveled in their chairs to watch him pass. Cabell jumped to his feet and ran out after him, but a waiter caught up with him and placed a hand on his arm.

"You must pay, sir."

"I'm looking for my friend. Did you see which way he went?"

"A bottle of whiskey has been broken, sir. You must pay."

Cabell returned to the café—the place was in an uproar, but the loud voices reduced to whispers while he stood at the bar and paid up. Then he went outside again, hailed a passing taxi, and jumped in. The rain was coming down hard, distorting vision through the windshield, and the side windows were so fogged up that it was nearly impossible to see out. The taxi reached the Place de France, but no one was in sight. It cruised slowly down the Boulevard Pasteur, which was empty of all pedestrians, as the water came sluicing down the side streets to form deep puddles at the intersections. It stopped in front of the Café Commedia, where Spaniards play backgammon and checkers all day and Moroccans play dominoes and cards all night; Cabell got out and went inside while the taxi idled at the curb, the smoky exhaust rising into the rain. Through the steamy bay windows of the café the waiters could be seen shaking their heads. Cabell reappeared, running and ducking his head from the rain, and got back into the taxi, which moved off once more, the tires leaving parallel strips on the flooding pavement. Returning to the Boulevard, the taxi descended to the Socco Grande; Cabell and the driver got out. No sooner had they vanished into the Medina than a figure ambled out of the darkness and tried to open the doors of the taxi. They were locked. Next he unsuccessfully attempted to pry open the trunk and the hood. He felt along the tops of the windows and pressed against the vents. Several times he circled the vehicle, pulling here and tugging there with much grunting and curses, but nothing would come loose. Exasperated, he returned to the doorway where he had been waiting and squatted down out of sight. When Cabell and the driver reappeared, the man came over and stated that he was the night watchman and had been keeping a close watch on this vehicle. Thieves were about, he said. The man in fact had some sort of badge on his arm. Cabell handed him a coin and got into the cab.

Yellow headlights were sweeping down steep alleys on the slopes of the city—rue Cook, rue Magellan—past aging façades of cheap hotels for transients. There was no sign of Maxwell, and the rain kept coming down, flooding the streets, turning public stairways into cascades, washing the city clean. The taxi came out on Avenida de España and pulled up opposite the Hotel Nicaragua; the motor was turned off, the lights went out; a long silence followed.

Except for a dim bulb in the lobby, the hotel was totally dark. Down the street the sign of an all-night filling station was swinging violently back and forth in the wind, sending great shadows sweeping across the glistening pavement.

The door of the taxi opened; Cabell dashed across the street and into the hotel. A few seconds later Maxwell himself came around the corner, hugging the walls for protection against the rain. He wore no hat, and his clothes had been soaked through; he looked miserable. When he saw the taxi, he took a step backward and stood behind a palm tree; from this position he observed Cabell re-emerge from the hotel and get back into the taxi, and the taxi drive off.

A few minutes later, Cabell was mounting the stairs of the Hotel Splendid; as he approached his room along the rain-soaked balcony, a line of light became visible under his door. After a moment of hesitation, he pushed it open. At the table in the center of the room a man was seated. His head was completely bald and shiny on top, but hair grew thick and bushy along the sides. He had been dozing with his head in his hands; when he realized that someone had entered the room, he jumped to his feet, knocking the chair to the floor behind him. He was a big man, with skin deeply tanned by the sun.

Cabell shut the door and leaned against it.

"Harry, you finally got here. How did you get in?"

"Ju-just walked in. Did I surprise you?"

"Yes, you did, even though I've been waiting weeks for you to turn up."

"Were you expecting to find someone e-else?"

"As a matter of fact, I was."

"Where've you b-been?" He bent over and picked up the chair.

"At the circus."

"Circus? It's t-two o'clock in the mor-morning."

Cabell took off his coat and wiped his face with it. "Been waiting long?"

"C-couple of hours. C-came in at midnight, you weren't in, s-so I-I took a walk in the Medina and got so-soaking w-wet."

"Horrible night."

"W-went to a café, ca-came back here, cou-couldn't stand the rain. T-told Boujma I-I'd wait in your room. My feet are wet, I may c-catch c-cold."

"It took you a hell of a long time to get to Tangier."

"I'm on my way to A-A-America."

"What for?"

"Go-going to t-talk to some people. This time, Cabell, I'm on something b-big."

"Magnesium ore worth $32,000 a ton? Sun's been roasting your brains."

"I may have exaggerated a b-bit, you know me, but it's pure, Cabell, p-pure."

"I don't believe it."

"No-nobody will believe me, a-as usual. Sp-Spanish geologists picked over the area, they found nothing; I-I doubt if anybody will believe they could have overlooked a whole m-mountain of m-magnesium. That's why I'm going to A-America."

Cabell took a bottle of Fundador out of the drawer and set it on the table with two glasses. "Who else have you told besides Hamid?"

"Nobody."

"Who's nobody?"

"Nobody is no-nobody."

"The way you blurted it out to her, probably every Spaniard in the desert has wind of it by now."

"O-only if she's been talking. She h-hasn't, has sh-she?"

"She's the last person who would want such a thing to be known."

"Th-then it's just the thr-three of us."

"Let's hope you're right."

"By-by the way, Cabell, how's the lady wrestler?"

Cabell poured out two drinks, which they drank off in one swallow. "What lady wrestler?" He poured another round, and they tossed it back in the same manner. The glasses were filled a third time; these they sipped.

"Th-thanks, Cabell."

"What lady wrestler you talking about?"

"She didn't f-f-fool me, I knew who she was right away, but she f-f-fooled the boys in the café."

"Boys? What boys?"

"B-beardless young men, she b-bam-bamboozled them all right."

"Who are you talking about?"

"El Hassani, the lady wrestler. The one you sent me."

"El Hassani? You mean Hamid?"

He finished his third Fundador and poured himself another. "L-looks like I'm drinking up all your br-brandy, Cabell."

"Drink all you want, I've got plenty."

"When this El Hassani left me, I followed her to the café where sh-she s-said sh-she was sl-sleeping. Didn't have anything else to do. I was a little concerned, too."

"Why?"

"She had a big supply of k-k-kif with her, a whole sa-sack of it, and sh-she was plenty high at the time."

"I gave that kif to her."

"F-figured you did. Anyway, out on the dark road under the palm trees, heard sh-shouting from the café. H-hurried on a little faster. F-figured she was being r-r-raped."

He refilled his glass with the last of the brandy. Cabell pulled out another bottle.

"Feeling better now, Harry?"

"Th-think so. Th-thanks, Cabell." He took another sip. "Looked in through the w-window, and there she was on the fl-floor, all right, not being r-raped, but wr-wrestling."

"Hamid?"

"And sh-she was getting the better of it, too. Sh-she had this boy down and was pushing his face into the floor. Pr-pretty soon he gave in. Sh-she let him up and immediately took on another."

"How many of them were there?"

"Three or four, about fifteen or sixteen years old. Si-simple country boys. As I watched sh-she wrestled with all of them."

"She's strong and wiry, that girl."

"S-sounds like you're sp-speaking from experience, Cabell; well, she beat them all except the last, which ended in a dr-draw, sh-she being tired by then."

"Then what happened?"

"They sat down and she bought them all Coca-Colas, and I-I overheard her telling them all sorts of f-fan-fantastic tales about herself."

"What tales?"

"Oh, that she had tra-traveled th-three t-times around the wor-world, rode elephants, sw-swam under water, fought against the Ch-Chinese. Th-things like that. All in perfect Arabic."

"Did you believe it?"

"I-I didn't know whether to believe all th-that or not, but those c-country b-boys' mou-mouths were hang-hanging open."

"They didn't realize what had come to town."

"I don't know wh-what happened afterward. M-maybe they all g-ganged up on her, but I doubt it. N-next day she turned up at my place again, and I showed her around the mines. Sh-she left town the same day, s-said sh-she was on her way to Icht."

"She wants to open a grocery store there."

"That's what sh-she told me. S-sounds crazy to me."

"She's quite serious about it."

"Her husband is away in France working in the mines and saving money for the project—sh-she even suggested that he work for me when he returns to Morocco. Is th-this tr-true, Cabell?"

"All true."

"Where is she now?"

"She's in Tangier. As a matter of fact, I haven't seen her since last week. We burned her house to the ground."

"Burned h-her h-house to the ground, did you s-say?"

"She had this old house out in the country that she wanted to dispose of."

"Yeah."

"She couldn't sell it, it was in such bad shape, and smugglers were using it as a kind of staging area and hideout, which could have gotten her in trouble with the police, since she knew about it."

"So-so you decided to get r-rid of the house, eh?"

"It was a beautiful fire. Everything went up but the chimney."

"I see."

"I suppose that must sound a little crazy."

"Yeah, it sounds a little cr-crazy."

The wind was rattling the windowpanes as the rain continued to beat down, and water entered under the door from the balcony.

"Where are you sleeping tonight, Harry?"

"I have a room in the Hotel Cuba."

"Where's that?"

"Near the Dancing Boy. N-not much of a hotel, but there's a view of the po-port from my window. When I'm in a po-port town, I like to be reminded of it as soon as I g-get up in the m-morning."

"Why's that?"

"J-just makes me feel easier—know I-I can get the hell out, if I want."

Above the sounds the wind and rain were making, a dog could be heard barking somewhere.

"Sounds like the Sultan of Dogs," Cabell said.

"The S-Sultan of Dogs?"

"Boujma's dog—there must be someone trying to get into the hotel."

"I believe I had a confrontation with the Su-Sul-Sultan of Do-Dogs myself. Is a-a-another visitor on the way?"

A great commotion broke out downstairs, with barking and shouting audible above the rain and rattling shutters; heavy footsteps were coming up the wooden stairs as the barking became much louder.

"Wha-whatever it is, Cabell, it's coming our w-way."

Suddenly the door was flung open, and there stood Maxwell, with the Sultan of Dogs yapping at him. Boujma was out there, too, brandishing a club and babbling in Arabic. Wind was entering the room, and rain, and Cabell's papers were fluttering from the bureau. The overhead light swung back and forth on its cord.

"It's all right, Boujma," Cabell called. "You know him, he's a friend."

Maxwell stepped into the room, the wind blew the door shut, and the barking and shouting abruptly ceased. Maxwell was absolutely soaking wet: the long wet hair was plastered down over his face; the suède jacket was black with saturation; water dripped from the bottom edge to the floor. He was still clutching the book satchel under his arm; this, too, had become waterlogged and shapeless. And what with the combined weight of the books and the water, the satchel must have been as heavy as lead to carry. A puddle was forming where he stood, but still he did not move. Then, without a word, he began to pace around the table while Cabell and Harry watched. He was leaving a trail of water on the floor, his shoes oozed and sloshed, the folds of the leather jacket glistened with water. After a few turns, he abruptly opened his mouth and began to speak.

"Cabell, what were you doing in my room?"

"I was looking for you."

"How did you get in?"

"Just walked in; you must have left the door open."

"Impossible."

"How did you know I was in your room—were you hiding there all the time?"

"I was out in the street watching. I saw the taxi parked in front of the hotel, I saw the light go on in my room."

"Why didn't you come up?"

"I didn't want to see you."

"Do-do you mean to say, Cabell," Harry put in, "th-that wh-while I was w-waiting here in this hotel room for you, you were wa-waiting in another hotel room, be-belonging to this gentleman?"

"That's right. Well, George, if you didn't want to see me in your hotel room, what are you doing here in this one?"

"G-good question."

"I came here to lodge a protest."

"What protest?"

"I don't like people to enter my room while I'm away, I don't care even if the door is open."

"All right, I'm sorry."

"That room is the only domain of privacy to which I have access. Otherwise I live in the streets, I eat and drink and do my translations in public places."

"I know. I apologize."

"I must have an area of my own, where friends enter only at my invitation."

"I'm sorry, but after you ran out of the Marco Polo like that, I was anxious about you. I looked all over Tangier for you."

"I know."

"You know? You saw me?"

"I saw you driving around."

"Well, sit down and have a drink. This is Harry Atkinson, who has just arrived from the south. Harry, this is my friend George Maxwell."

"So—another man from the desert?" Maxwell asked.

"That's right, a geologist."

"Another geologist from the desert, eh? Sounds like a conspiracy. What are you cooking up down there? Up to no good, I'll wager."

Cabell smiled. "No conspiracy, George, just friends. Have a brandy."

"I think I'll take off this wet jacket first."

"Go ahead."

Maxwell placed the satchel on the table and commenced to struggle out of the jacket. Beneath the jacket the plaid shirt was wet as well.

"George, you're soaked through."

"Do you mind if I take off this shirt?"

"Not at all."

Maxwell unbuttoned the shirt and drew it off. As he did so,

he bumped the satchel off the table. It fell to the floor and split open along the seam, and books slithered out and came to rest in a spreading puddle. Maxwell and Cabell went down on their knees and lifted the soggy bundle from the puddle to the table; Atkinson bent his head sideways in order to read the titles.

"Hm. Th-thucydides."

Amigo Maxwell frowned at Atkinson, then proceeded to stuff the books back into the satchel. However, either the satchel had shrunk or the books had become swollen with water, for not all of them would go in.

"I've had this bag for thirty years, ever since I was a student."

"Perhaps it's just as well," said Atkinson. "It might be b-better if you stopped carrying b-books altogether."

"But I've been carrying books all my life."

"Th-that's exactly wh-what I mean."

Maxwell took up a glass of brandy, drank off the contents at one gulp, and set the glass down on the table. "There's something you don't understand, my friend," he said clearing his throat. "I have to do my translations."

"B-but you w-weren't doing your translations to-tonight, w-were you?"

"No."

"I see."

"I know what you're thinking. You think I tote this book bag around with me all the time, whether I intend to do my work or not."

"Th-that's what I thought."

"Well, you're wrong. I picked the books up at the café. Isn't that true, Cabell?"

"That's right. The waiter brought them."

As Maxwell spoke, he took off his shoes and stockings and placed them under the table.

"Cabell, you don't mind if I take off my pants, do you?"

"Not at all."

Maxwell slipped out of the wet trousers and hung them on the back of the chair.

"I'm going to take off my underwear now."

"Go ahead."

"There's no point of keeping on underwear if it's wet, too, is there?"

"N-no p-point at all."

Maxwell took off his undershirt and drawers and stood naked on the floor.

"Stay near the heater, George, or you'll catch cold. The room is damp."

"I have great resistance to cold."

"Is that so?" Atkinson commented.

"I'm well-padded. Look at these arms, have you ever seen such fleshy arms?"

"N-n-never have," Atkinson remarked.

"And look at these legs, note the size of them. Aren't they well-equipped to ward off the cold?"

"They are indeed. With legs like that you could find a job at the circus."

"Trying to get me to run away with the circus, are you, Cabell? Notice the middle, it's well-padded, too."

"I see that."

"With all this extra flesh I hardly need blankets on my bed. And I sleep naked."

"Th-they say it's th-the healthiest way."

Maxwell was parading around the table and looking at himself in the mirror. "When I'm naked, I feel I've gone as far as I can go."

"It's as f-far as anyone c-can go, I suppose."

"I mean, other people travel and do things. I take off my clothes and dream."

"What are you dreaming about now, George?"

"Nothing. How do I look?"

"You look fine."

"I think I'll put my clothes back on now."

"They're still wet."

"Doesn't matter; my warm body will dry them out."

While Amigo Maxwell dressed, Cabell opened the window and looked out. The sound of water dripping and of water washing along in a culvert could be heard. Clouds rushed by just a few feet overhead.

"I think it's stopped raining."

"Then I'll be on my way." Maxwell gathered up his books and went to the door. "I'm glad I found you here tonight, Cabell. Otherwise I would have wandered through the city all night long, grinding my teeth and mumbling to myself. Good night Mr. Atkinson."

"Good night."

"Cabell, I don't think I'll accompany you into the desert after all. It's better that I stay in Tangier."

"Whatever you say, George."

He went out and shut the door behind him. Atkinson was pouring out the last of the brandy.

"Wh-what is all this, Cabell?"

"What's what?"

"F-first you send me this l-lady wr-wrestler who dresses up as a man."

"How was I supposed to know she likes to tangle with Arab boys?"

"Th-then you tell me you burn down houses just to see the glow."

"What else do you do with a smugglers' nest?"

"N-now there's this idiot who visits you late at night, so-soaking wet and toting a load of books."

"George's no idiot. He needed shelter out of the rain."

"He wanted to take his cl-clothes off in fr-front of someone."

"He's a friend of mine."

"B-better in front of friends than str-strangers, I-I suppose."

Cabell sat down and began to finger the glass of brandy on the table. "I'm exhausted," he said.

"I-I know you are, and I'm going to leave in a minute." Atkinson leaned back in his chair. "But tell me, what are you going to do with yourself?"

"My plan is to return by the first of December."

"The Sahara?"

"They want me, and I'm going back."

Atkinson lifted his glass to his lips and looked at Cabell. Then he looked at his own hands. They were large hands, and the backs were covered with thick brown hair.

"You m-must be out of your m-mind."

"I've already told them; the thing's done. They'll be waiting for me."

"Going back alone?"

"Probably."

"Going back to Guera?"

"I don't know where they'll send me; I have to sign a new contract in El Aaiun. But I wouldn't be surprised if they want me to go back to Guera."

"What are you going to do with yourself once you're back there?"

"Same as before."

"Scratch around for oil? There isn't any, ev-everybody knows that."

"Everyone except the Spanish."

"So? Wh-what are you going back for?"

"I have to work; I'm running low on money."

"B-but why th-there? You'll just be wasting your t-time."

"What other choice do I have?"

"Go b-back to South America. You-you can find work anywhere you want."

"I'd sort of like to stay close to Tangier."

"Then stick ri-right here."

"There's no work for me in Tangier."

"And there isn't any oil in Rio de Oro."

"I don't care if I never find another drop in my life."

"Yet you're going to scratch around a-anyhow. L-like some cr-crazy prospector."

"Like you."

"Yeah, like me. But I got m-m-magnesium."

"I've got something, too."

"What? Oh, God, are you s-still trying to promote th-that water scheme?"

"Yes."

Atkinson shook his head. "I thought the desert would make a realist out of you. B-but it h-hasn't. You-you're still a d-dreamer."

"Do you trust people who never dream?"

Atkinson shrugged.

"Besides, it's not just a dream. The water's under the desert, and you know it."

"And under the desert it'll st-stay."

"Unless we can persuade the Spanish to pump and irrigate."

"What do you mean 'we'? Forget about water, man, Spain dreams of r-r-riches—oil, gold."

"And goes on dreaming, too, as long as wild-eyed geologists keep filling their heads with tales of El Dorado in the desert."

"This time it's the r-real th-thing, I tell you."

"Look, if it weren't for me, you wouldn't even be in Rio de Oro."

"S-so you got me in, now wh-what do you mean by that?"

"All right, I'll put it to you straight—I want to make a deal."

"What deal?"

"I want to wrap your magnesium, if it really exists . . ."

"It does exist, I keep t-telling you!"

"Your magnesium and my water in a package and present it to Rivera, tell him where the magnesium is only if he pledges to use part of the revenues to raise water."

"Jesus! You really are a dreamer!"

"I'm dead serious."

"Wha-what in the w-world makes you think he would honor such a pl-pledge?"

"No guarantee, but he just might."

Atkinson took a sip of brandy and carefully put the glass back on the table. "Yeah, he might. And what's in it for me?"

"What do you want?"

"L-look, if you think I plan to wan-wander around that desert for the rest of m-my l-life, y-you're out of your m-mind! I'm going to make some m-money out of this."

"What are you going to do with it?"

"Wh-what do you th-think? Sp-spend it, goddammit!"

"On what?"

"On me! I've worked, goddammit; now I want to re-relax for a while. S-so, what do I get out of it, Cabell?"

"You know what the Spanish pay."

"You're d-damned right I do. That's why I'm not telling them. Go-going to A-America instead, get the b-big b-boys in on it, get my c-cut from them."

"If they listen."

"They will. I've got p-pl-plenty to show them."

"So the answer is no."

Atkinson stood up and was putting on his raincoat. "That's right, Cabell, no, definitely n-no."

"No way you'll change your mind?"

"No way. Waloo."

September 27 A crystal day. The sky so blue, with only a few white houses and the sea beneath it. Fishing boats in the port rest on perfect images of themselves in the water. What shall I do on such a day? I could walk down to the beach for a quick swim before the city—or I may drive out into the country with Harry—or perhaps I'll just stay by the window. The sun enters this window and covers the bed; I've taken off my shoes and socks and lie here, either reading or napping, and rubbing my bare feet together in the warmth. A luxury. VIVA TANGIER is what the citizens like to scribble on the walls of their city in their moments of enthusiasm.

I see the Kasbah has been invaded by a boatload of blazered, capped, stripe-tied, knee-socked English school children on a holiday. I never saw such beautiful kids. Red-headed, tow-headed, some with thick glasses, all peering, gaping, agog at everything, from mules to Arabs. But sitting atop a high stone wall, a Moroccan girl, one half of her face mutilated by congenital syphilis, watches the procession of healthy youngsters pass beneath her, and is in turn watched by me. Today is Friday, and the black flag flies from the Kasbah mosque. It inspires a kind of dread in me, as if it were the pirates' Jolly Roger and some new terror were approaching. It also reminds me of how quickly the weeks are passing.

But now I feel I have a city.

# *Stuck in the Mud*

THE GEARS WERE in low-range and four-wheel drive, but no matter if the vehicle lurched forward or rocked in reverse, the big tires spun around and around, the ruts grew deeper, and the Land Rover became ever more hopelessly mired in the mud. Cabell and Atkinson got down to survey the situation. The wheels were in up to their centers, and even as the motor idled, they seemed to sink more deeply. The shiny surface of paint was spattered with mud; great clods of the stuff hung dripping from the fenders.

"This isn't supposed to happen to a Land Rover," Cabell commented.

He had taken off his shoes and socks, rolled his pants up to the knees, and was standing there with his hands on his hips. Atkinson came up and stood beside him; he had removed his trousers and wore only his underpants and shirt.

"This mu-mud feels g-g-good between my t-toes."

"Are you getting ready to take a bath in it?"

"They say those radioactive mud baths w-work w-wonders for you."

"What wonders?"

"Loosens the joints."

"Then what?"

"They hose you down like a mo-motorcar."

They had progressed about a hundred yards off the paved road: the double row of wheel marks came on quite evenly at first; then they began to weave and at one point almost went off the track altogether. Over the last twenty yards the ground was all torn up where Atkinson had first attempted to back out, then turn around; finally he had gunned the vehicle forward in a vain effort to reach a sandy stretch of road up ahead. This still lay some yards off, and now the Land Rover could not move in any direction.

"Wh-what do you think w-we ought to do?"

"We need help."

"I th-think I s-see it coming."

A red tractor came bouncing slowly across the meadow, followed by a flock of white egrets. The Moroccan at the wheel seemed to be having no difficulty in navigating the mud, as the fat tires stayed right on top of the ground. The tractor drew up beside the Land Rover, and the driver turned off the motor. He was an extremely white-skinned fellow, with deep creases running all through the face, and he wore a brown djellaba and high gum boots.

"We're stuck," Cabell said to the farmer after having greeted him formally in Arabic. "Can you drag us out of here?"

The farmer surveyed the stalled vehicle from his high seat and squinted into the sun with his pale eyes.

"Have you got a rope?" Cabell asked.

The man lifted up his djellaba and brought out a large ball of string. Cabell looked at it and shook his head.

"Not strong enough."

Without uttering a word the farmer got down from the

tractor and went off a little ways to a grassy knoll, where he put down the ball of string and took off his djellaba. Underneath he was wearing a blue shirt and baggy trousers; his bare legs and arms were milk-white. Spreading the djellaba on the ground, he sat on it, and proceeded to unravel the string. Atkinson switched off the Land Rover's engine, and he and Cabell wandered over and squatted down on the grass. The farmer had thrust a stick upright into the soft earth and, drawing several lengths of the string around it, began to twist the strings tightly around each other.

"He's weaving a rope."

"L-look how white he is, Cabell."

"Must be an albino. I think I saw him dancing with the Jilala at Sidi Kacem this summer."

Cabell took out a package of cigarettes and offered one to the man; he accepted it, placed it behind a pink ear, and went on with his work. While Cabell smoked, Atkinson stretched out on the grass with his hands behind his head. The day was clear and warm, and the sun shone brightly. Fresh green grass was coming up, and wild flowers of many different colors grew in large patches like natural rugs of the earth. Birds seemed to be everywhere, or at least their songs were clear. Not far off a long-legged black-and-white stork was wading sedately in a pond—this was the springlike season which follows the early autumn rains in North Africa.

Cabell was sprawled out beside Atkinson, smoking and looking straight up into the sky. Meanwhile the farmer went on with his work. The white freckled hands had woven a length of rope as thick as two fingers. This was put to one side, more of the thread was unraveled, and work on another commenced. Cabell rolled over and watched him.

"Is this your land?" he asked in Arabic.

The farmer pointed to his own mouth and shook his head.

"What?"

"N-not much of a talker, is he."

Cabell pointed to his own mouth; the man shook his head.

Cabell put a finger to his ear; the man shook his head again.

"Harry, I think this man's a deaf-mute; he can't hear and he doesn't know how to speak."

Harry sat up. "Can't speak?"

"He can't hear or speak."

Harry clapped his hands loudly together, and the farmer made a noise indicating that he had heard something.

"He's not totally deaf."

"Harry, do you know any sign language? Find out if this land belongs to him."

Harry patted the ground, then pointed at the farmer. The farmer nodded.

"The land's his."

"How much does he own?"

Harry patted the ground again and drew a circle with his finger. The man did not understand until Harry began counting on his fingers; then a happy look of comprehension came over his face, and he raised six fingers.

"He owns six hectares."

"Or he has six sons."

"I wonder what he grows here."

Once more Harry rubbed the ground and pointed to the fresh grass that was springing up everywhere, but the man did not understand. Harry made motions with his hands as if he were eating bread, the man shook his head and dug his hand deep into the pocket of his baggy trousers, bringing out a handful of sunflower seeds.

"Ah. He grows sunflowers."

The man grinned and handed Cabell the seeds. As Cabell cracked them beneath his teeth, Harry lay down on the grassy earth once more, and the albino farmer went back to his work. Another thick strand of rope had been woven, which he laid beside the first, and began on a third. In the pond the stork had caught a frog: it dangled at the end of the long orange bill until the bird tilted its head back and flipped it into its gullet.

A boy in a djellaba came running across the fields toward the three men, arriving out of breath, and the farmer had them understand that this was his son. And indeed the boy bore the same albino complexion, with the white curly hair and pale eyes; although he communicated with his father in sign language, he himself could speak and hear, and in response to Cabell's question explained that the tractor belonged jointly to his father and to his father's brothers, all of whom raised sunflowers in the area.

The cords completed, the farmer rapidly plaited them together into a rope as thick as his wrist, took up his djellaba and walked over to his tractor. This he maneuvered in front of the Land Rover and attached the rope as Atkinson got in and started up the motor. The farmer put the tractor in gear, the homemade rope stretched but held, and the tandem vehicles began to move. Once the Land Rover was free of the ruts, progress became easier; in another minute they were moving out of the mud toward the sandy soil as Cabell and the boy ran along behind. The farmer stopped on dry ground, climbed down from the tractor, and untied the rope. Atkinson got out and thanked him; the man smiled but refused to accept anything for his services. Nevertheless, Cabell slipped a silver coin to his son.

"Why do birds follow the tractor?" Cabell asked him.

"The plow finds the worms."

The farmer climbed back on his tractor, pulled the boy up beside him, and they went bouncing away over the meadows.

"Omar should have been here to see that," Cabell said.

"Why?"

"It would have been his first silent film."

"Do these things h-happen to you all the t-time, Cabell?"

"What things?"

"Oh, like when you get st-stuck in the m-mud, a fellow just ha-happens to come along, w-weaves a r-rope out of a ball of thread."

Cabell laughed. "People have helped a lot. You're going to meet two more now."

"H-how have they helped?"
"Just by being themselves. You'll see."

Lydia was walking with Cassandra through the olive grove; keeping to the path that wound among the tangled roots, they moved from shadow into light beneath the gray branches. Cassandra did not tug at the leash, but was content to trot at Lydia's side. Lydia wore her usual farm outfit—black trousers torn at both pockets, so that a patch of skin was visible, canvas shoes, a faded blue shirt—and carried an ebony walking stick. The gray hair which she wore in braids was mostly hidden beneath a scarf bound around her head in the manner of a turban. They were followed at a little distance by two other dogs from the farm. When Cassandra paused to sniff at something along the path, Lydia would wait for her, and the two other dogs would stop and wait, too. At the edge of the olive grove, a rabbit bolted in front of them, and the two free dogs went after it.

"Leave it alone!" Lydia shouted after them in Russian. "You stop it, too," she said to Cassandra, who was straining on the lead. She threatened the dog with the free end of the leash; the dog calmed down and received a lecture about animals. All animals could live on Lydia's farm, even rabbits; no animals were to be killed on her land, not even sheep on Moroccan feast days. The dog seemed to listen and to understand. Meanwhile the rabbit had hidden itself in the scrub and the dogs had overrun it; after a few moments of frantic searching, they returned and were scolded by Lydia. They, too, listened humbly and seemed to comprehend the Russian language.

The slope of the hill from which Lydia and her dogs looked out ran down to the sea, with the line of beach and fringe of white water extending to the north as far as the Caves of Hercules; southward, it simply stretched away out of sight. Rainstorms of the past days, combined with high flooding seas, had caused large lakes to be formed on the sand, so that not much of the beach remained above water. Even the plain before Sidi Kacem had been partially inundated, and cows were wading around, feeding on the fresh green plants, while bunches of dirty sheep kept to higher ground, where they were watched over by shepherds in turquoise rain burnooses. The big storks and cattle egrets were numerous, wading and feeding along the edge of the pond.

Atkinson's Land Rover came over a small rise and made its way along the edge of the flooded plain, scattering cows and sheep from its path. At the base of the hill it stopped; Cabell swung his legs out, picked up a twig from the ground, and proceeded to clean his feet.

"This North African mud is the w-worst I've seen anywhere in the w-world," came Atkinson's voice from inside the Land Rover, where he was scraping his toes with the blade of a hunting knife.

Somewhere dogs began to bark; far away someone was calling. Under the olive trees on the hillside a figure was standing. The dogs were racing around.

"Is that Lydia?"

"Yes." Cabell was waving. Lydia was coming down the hill, with Cassandra barking furiously and dragging on the lead. The shepherds' dogs began to be excited, and the shepherds were shouting and throwing rocks as the sheep moved uneasily about.

"You told me she was old. She's not so o-old."

Lydia crossed the track and kissed Cabell. Cassandra growled and sniffed at his feet.

"Stop it, Cassandra!" She scolded the dog in Russian.

"Lydia, this is Harry Atkinson."

"How do you do, Mr. Atkinson?"

Atkinson stuck out his hand. "Pleased to meet you, Madame."

"He just arrived from the desert."

"How nice. You've come all this way just to see Joseph?"

Cabell glanced at Atkinson. "He's just passing through on his way to America."

"Oh, I see."

"How are you, Lydia? Where's Grigory?"

"We've been having a terrible time—stranded for three days. The mud is so bad we've been unable to get out, so Grigory walked to the main road this morning to catch the farmers' bus to town. We have no meat, and the weather's been so bad that the fishermen have brought us nothing from the sea. And on top of everything the pump isn't working; Grigory's going to consult a mechanic in Tangier. He'll be back this evening, I hope. Poor brother!"

"What's the matter?"

"Because of the mud he had to set out in his rubber boots, which he doesn't like to walk far in. His toes are crooked, and the boots make them sore."

"We got stuck ourselves, even in Harry's Land Rover. An albino farmer pulled us out with his tractor."

"Yes, I know who you mean. They are the seven Jilali brothers, and they're all like that—milk-white."

"That's it—brothers. We thought he had six sons or six hectares."

"This f-fellow was a d-deaf-mute."

"Yes, some are deaf and dumb, some normal."

"They grow sunflowers."

"That's right. They've formed a collective among themselves and purchased the tractor, which they rent out to their neighbors. At harvest time they come with their wives and children to pick my olives—the men beat the branches with long poles, ladies pick the fruit off the ground."

"Lydia, shall we leave the Land Rover here?"

"Yes, part of our little road has been washed away. It'll be safe here. Come now, and I'll prepare some lunch."

When Harry and Cabell finished cleaning their feet, Lydia led them up the path as the dogs ran on ahead. At the house she had them sit down in wicker chairs on the veranda, with the wide view of the Atlantic before them, and placed a bottle of rosé and a pitcher of orange juice on the table for them to mix together or to drink separately as they pleased. Then she disappeared into the kitchen. The two men sipped the drinks and closed their eyes, with the warm sun on their faces, as the dogs lay quietly on the grass. When Lydia returned with the first course, they sat down at the table and hungrily ate potato salad seasoned with fresh dillweed and sardines out of a tin. The dogs edged closer on their bellies, wagging their tails even in the presence of these strangers, until they were under the table, where they were fed bits of bread dipped in olive oil from the plate which contained the sardines. The main course was a mass of fresh carrots, steaming and buttered, with brown rice. Harry wondered if they had been done in a pressure cooker; Lydia said they had been steamed and apologized for having no meat to serve them. The men said they didn't want any meat and devoured everything. Next she brought on a fresh sheep's cheese, which soon disappeared. Lydia regretted that she didn't make very good coffee, that Grigory always made it, so Atkinson jumped up and made coffee, and afterward they sat around and smoked. Sparrows picked up crumbs from the table; the dogs had fallen asleep on the grass. As the sun lowered to the west a slight chill came into the air. Cabell stretched and declared he would like to take a look at the pump.

Lydia led him down a path through a citrus grove to the pump house. Oil drums lay about; inside was a diesel engine, blackened by soot and grease.

"Lydia, did Grigory say what was the matter with this motor?"

"I think it's just old and tired."

Cabell detached the belt connecting the diesel and the pump, opened the fuel line, and cranked the fly wheel. The motor sputtered.

"Do you enjoy repairing motors, Joseph?"

"It's good therapy. What do you think of my friend Harry?"

"Such a strange man; is he all alone?"

"He's always been alone as long as I've known him. I don't think he has any friends."

"Except you."

"I must be about the only one." Cabell was rummaging in

the tool box. "If you get a chance to talk with him, get him going about the desert. He could help me with the water, if he wanted to."

"Won't he? Why not?"

Cabell shook his head. "Just stubbornness, I suppose. But don't let him think you're trying to talk him into something. He's terribly claustrophobic, can't even wear a wristwatch."

When Lydia returned to the house, Atkinson was pacing back and forth on the lawn.

"Would you like to go for a walk, Mr. Atkinson?"

"I was just thinking the s-same thing—always try to take a th-thousand st-steps after a meal."

Lydia took up her walking stick and they set off through the olive trees. Coming out on the sandy track where the Land Rover was parked, they found a goatherd curled up in his djellaba, using one of the tires as a headrest, while he took a siesta as his animals wandered aimlessly about, sniffing at the wheels and scratching their backs against the fenders. The track skirted the flooded plain and entered the wiry brush that grows along the coast; then they had to make their way through the sand dunes. All of a sudden the whole expanse of the Atlantic was before them.

"Mr. Atkinson, how do you find Joseph? Do you think he should return to the desert?"

"I tried to talk him out of it, b-but no use. Says he has a j-job to do."

"But he doesn't believe in it."

"He has his w-water dr-dreams."

"Does the water really exist?"

"Yes, it d-does, plenty of it."

"Will Joseph ever see it brought out of the ground?"

"If he t-talks the Sp-Spanish into it."

"How can he do that?"

"By showing them it's economically f-feasible."

"Is it?"

"I su-suppose s-so."

"It sounds like a big project for one man. Is there no one to help him?"

"Nope. It's his dr-dream."

"You sound pessimistic."

"Just not my st-style. Cabell, he gets mixed up in all kinds of things—people, situations, ideas. Not me, if I find something of v-value, I take my cut and move on. I don't like to get involved."

"Is that the pattern of your life?"

"Wh-why do you ask th-that?"

"If you don't mind me saying so, Mr. Atkinson, perhaps I'm just old-fashioned, but it seems selfish always to take and never give in return."

"Are you t-talking about pl-places or p-people?"

"Everything."

Down the beach some gulls were resting on the sand, all facing into the wind; the birds took flight at their approach and flew off in a great circle over the waves. One bird stayed behind, however; it had been somewhat apart from the others.

"Looks like it's sitting on some e-eggs."

When they came to within a few feet of it, the bird got up and fluttered away.

"Something's the matter with it."

As they drew near once more, the bird took to the air and glided with the wind for a short distance, again landing in their path.

"D-doesn't s-seem to have much str-strength."

This time it struggled into the air and flew out over the water, to land in the foamy shallows near the beach. The big swells were breaking farther offshore, but smaller waves buffeted the helpless bird. Then the main flock of gulls, which had been circling farther out, returned to the solitary gull and hovered over it. Their cries split the muffled roar of the surf.

"I-I think they're tr-trying to protect it," Atkinson said. "It's sick, and they're encouraging it to get out of the w-water."

Suddenly the gulls began to make passes at the sick bird.

With driving swoops they were slashing at it with their bills.

"Hey, what are they doing?" Atkinson exclaimed. He kicked off his shoes and ran out into the water. Dispersing the gulls, he picked up the bird and returned to the beach. It had been disemboweled. As Atkinson held it up to Lydia, the body went limp and the wings drooped.

"It's dead."

"Yes, it's out of it's misery now."

"Wh-why did they do that?"

"Out of self-protection."

"B-but they killed it."

"They knew it was sick, so they put an end to its suffering. And to protect themselves. It might have a disease that could kill them all."

"What'll I do with it?"

"Put it back in the water."

Atkinson waded out once more and placed the bird on the water. The head went down and the wings spread out as the current took it. In the meantime, the gulls were gathering in large numbers; in a great spiral they rose into the air, all the while chattering to each other in notes resembling laughter. Mounting and mingling together to an immense height, they all moved off in a direct line toward the south.

"I've never seen so many together," Lydia said. "Perhaps they're migrating."

"Is th-that another reason for killing that gull? It w-would have slowed down their pr-progress?"

They had walked a long way down the beach now, and the sun was dropping toward the horizon.

"All animals know when the time to die has come."

"Wh-when they sense they cannot survive any longer."

"Or when their survival becomes a burden to the others."

"Th-that's called preservation of the species."

"Moroccans live close to the earth; they also know when death is near. Instead of fighting against it, they choose to sit quietly."

"If they don't struggle, they're already d-dead."

"They don't fear death like we do; they're preparing themselves. We can watch them and learn."

"Wh-what can we learn?"

"How to wait."

"Do you wait, too, Lydia?"

"All my life I've been waiting."

"Waiting for what?"

"Just waiting. I had an uncle who was a famous composer—he used to spend many hours alone, sitting quietly in a chair or lying on a couch with his hands behind his head, staring up at the ceiling. Once I asked him, 'What are you doing, Uncle?' 'Waiting, Lydia,' was his reply. 'Waiting for what, Uncle?' 'Just waiting.' "

"W-waiting for inspiration, I s-suppose."

"Mr. Atkinson, haven't you ever waited for something?"

"Hey! Why do I call you Lydia and you call me Mr. Atkinson?"

Lydia laughed. "I'm an old Russian lady and you're an American."

"C-call me H-Harry, it's better. You know, I've been w-waiting, too."

"For what?"

"Don't think I've ever known. How do you know if what you've been w-waiting for has arrived?"

"If you've been waiting, you'll know. Whatever must be done seems very close, like a person standing next to you in the dark."

"Like the b-birds. They always know."

"The birds were waiting for the gull to die; now they depart—every act has its moment."

The incoming tide was running up over the sand, spilling into the brackish lakes on the other side and obliterating their tracks. The beach seemed to extend without limits in either direction, and not one other person was visible upon it. As the sun touched the horizon, shadows of denser atmosphere passed across it; egg-shaped, it seemed to rest on the sea; then it contracted into what looked like a yellow balloon; as it sank more deeply it took on the form of a red dome. The wet sand took on all the colors, like mother-of-pearl.

Meanwhile, the last of the red light was entering through the open door of the pump house, where Cabell was down on his knees—he had rolled back his shirt sleeves, his arms and hands were black with grease and dirt. The diesel was partially dismantled, pieces lay about on the floor, and one by one he was bolting them back into their places. When the machine was reassembled, he cranked the flywheel; the motor began to turn over, while he quickly made further adjustments. Then he shut it off and was attaching the leather belt. There were voices outside; Grigory was calling for his sister. In another minute he entered the shed.

"Ah, here you are, dear Joseph. Did I hear the motor running?"

"I got her going."

"I'm afraid I'm not much of a mechanic. What I learn one day I forget the next."

Grigory sat down on an oil drum and took out his pipe. Without filling or lighting it he kept it in his mouth and made little sucking noises through it.

"How was your day in town, Grigory? Lydia was worried about your toes."

"I spent the day with the Sicilians."

"Sicilians?"

Just then there was an uproar of barking in the yard. "Grigory!" Lydia called.

"Lydia! Lydia!" Grigory shouted back, mimicking his sister's voice.

Several dogs entered the shed, followed by Lydia and Atkinson.

"Grigory, this is Harry Atkinson."

"How do you do, Mr. Atkinson."

"Pl-pleased to meet you. You can call me H-Harry."

"Grigory was about to tell me about the Sicilians."

"The Sicilians?"

"Go ahead, Grigory."

Grigory had taken out a pocketknife and was cleaning his pipe. "Well, I had to wait a long time for the bus. When I decided it wasn't coming at all, I began to walk. I hadn't taken more than a few steps when there was a noise and the bus appeared from nowhere. I ran back to the bus stop; just as I arrived some men I'd never seen before came out of the fields, and we all jumped on together."

"Wh-what's this all about?" Atkinson whispered to Cabell. "When these R-Russians speak, I-I'm always one step behind."

"First thing I noticed that although they were all very dark-skinned, they weren't Moroccans. The ticket collector asked one of them, the one with the thick black mustache, how many they were, and the man replied in a very peculiar-sounding Arabic: 'Seven.' Whereupon the ticket collector proceeded to count heads and, counting me, since I got on the bus with them, said: 'No, eight.' I explained that I wasn't with this group, so the man with the bushy mustache bought seven tickets, and I bought my own."

Cassandra yawned and lay down on the floor.

"The bus was deserted except for ourselves, and we all sat down together in the front, these seven men and myself. I began to look at them. They were very dark-complexioned, as I said, a sort of deep chocolate-brown, but without negroid features, so I took them to be Indians. There was one old man with white hair and a white mustache, three plump middle-aged ones, two boys, and the young man who had bought the tickets, who seemed to be their leader."

Grigory took out tobacco and began to fill his pipe.

"The bus started up, they were chattering among themselves, and I noticed they were speaking a very bad French, a kind of pigeon Spanish, and a halting Arabic. I said to myself: 'Who can these people be?' "

Taking out a box of kitchen matches, he struck one and lit his pipe.

"Then one of the boys leaned over and addressed me in such bad French that I could hardly comprehend what he was saying. It seemed that he wanted to know what time the cinemas opened in Tangier—they were on their way to Tangier to go the cinema. I finally got it across to him that as far as I knew the cinemas didn't open until the afternoon."

"They had g-got an awfully early st-start," Atkinson commented. "Is there some m-message to all this?" he whispered in Cabell's ear.

"This information was communicated among them in various languages and was received with sighs of disappointment. Then I said in French to the leader, who was sitting near me: 'What nationality are you all, anyway?' He looked at me and replied: 'What nation you dink?' The others had stopped talking and were listening closely. 'Indian?' I guessed. 'Indian? He dink we Indian!' he shouted to the others. They all had a good laugh over that. 'If you're not Indian, then what are you?' I persisted. 'Pakistanis?' 'Pakistanis!' he shouted, and the laughter continued. Then his manner changed. 'No,' he said quite seriously. 'We Sicily.' 'If you are Sicilians,' I asked, 'why don't you speak the Sicilian language among yourselves?' 'Because we laka do practiz du udder lenguas,' he said."

Grigory's pipe had gone out, he had been talking so much; he brought out another kitchen match and struck it on the wall.

"There was a moment of silence when they all looked at me. 'What national you?' the leader asked me. 'Russian,' I said. 'Russian? If you Russian man, why no spik Russian lenguas?' I spoke a few words for them, and the leader announced to his friends while pointing at me with his thumb, 'He Russian man.' The others nodded respectfully. 'Russian,' they said among themselves. 'Russian man.' "

It had become quite dark now; Grigory's pipe glowed when he drew on it.

"We rode into the city and got down at the Socco Grande, where I said goodbye to my Sicilian friends. I bought some meat at the butcher's, left it in his refrigerator, and walked to the Café de Paris. Just as I was drinking a cup of coffee, the Sicilians came along. 'Where Teatro Cervantes?' they wanted to know. I led them there, but the theater is closed in the mornings. There was an Indian film on in the afternoon, and I realized that they had been directed there by someone who thought they were Indians, looking for an Indian film."

"They must be fed up being t-taken for a bunch of Indians," Atkinson said, laughing.

"They seemed somewhat dejected. Armando—that was the name of the leader—was admiring my rubber boots, so I let him try them on, right there in front of the Cervantes Theater. And he bought them from me."

"Oh, Brother, your new rubber boots."

"You see, Armando's foot is one size larger than my own, so the boots fit perfectly."

"What did you have on your feet, Brother?"

"Nothing, I went barefoot."

"Barefoot through the streets of Tangier?"

"With that all the Sicilians wanted new rubber boots, so we went down the Cuesta de la Playa, where a man with a cartload of them came along. The Sicilians sat down on the curb trying on boots until they found the right sizes, and I bought these sneakers from the same mobile salesman."

"At least they look comfortable."

"Meanwhile Armando was telling me of their travels."

"Who are these people?"

"They're roamers, travelers, Mediterranean men."

"What are they doing here?"

"Armando and his father, three cousins from his mother's family, and their two sons set out from Sicily a few years ago. Their plan was to travel the whole way around the Mediterranean."

"Sounds l-like a good plan," Atkinson said approvingly.

"How do they live, Brother?"

"I don't know, but they had some good luck while traveling

through Spain. They happened to arrive in that town—Palomares—where the Americans had let the atom bomb fall by mistake, on the very day the Americans began paying the Spanish farmers for damages done to their land. Armando said that an American soldier was seated at a table in the main square of town, with piles of pesetas before him. As soon as Armando realized what was going on, he went right up to the soldier and said: 'Looka here, we tomato farmers in dis lan. Here my fader an cousin an sons. Look, we poor people, we work wid da han. Your bomba fell our lan, now lan no good. Nobody want buy tomato. How you expect us live?' 'All right, mister, how much is your claim?' was all the soldier asked. 'You pay me 50,000 pesetas,' Armando demanded. The soldier nodded, made Armando sign a piece of paper, and gave him the money. They left town the same afternoon and lived for over a year in southern Spain on that money."

"Oh, Grigory, he told you that story because he thought it would amuse you."

"Why?"

"Because he knew you were Russian."

Atkinson laughed out loud. "Never thought of that!"

"But it's true. He carries the receipt around with him in his wallet. I saw it."

"Wh-where do they live, Grigory? H-how do they support th-themselves?"

"They've found work at the airport—construction work on the new terminal. So they don't get a chance to go into Tangier very often."

"They d-don't go to the cinema very often, th-that's for sure." Atkinson was shaking his head and chuckling.

"They have a tent at the airport."

"L-live in a tent, do they?"

"That's what Armando said—they've been living in a tent ever since they left home."

"M-must b-be gypsies."

"Sort of gypsies, I suppose." Grigory was stroking his beard and sucking on the pipe. "Except for the old man, they all like the life. Armando confided in me that his father is worried because he doesn't know where he's going to die."

"Sure! The old man's afraid he'll never get back to Sicily! That's natural!" Atkinson was nearly shouting.

"Going to see them again?"

"They invited me to visit their tent."

All color had left the sky; it was quite dark in the shed. Lydia went to the door. "I must feed the dogs."

They all left the shed. A few minutes later there was the sound of a generator starting up, and the lights in the house came on.

After dinner Atkinson walked to the bottom of the hill where the Land Rover was parked. The night was clear and starlight reflected in the semi-inundated plain before Sidi Kacem; somewhere out beyond the lake a big fire was burning. Atkinson saw that the Land Rover was locked, then leaned against the fender and lit up a cigarette. A breeze out of the west bore the faint sound of surf; over the sea some flat-bottomed cumulus clouds were moving up the coast.

Later he made his way back up the hill through the olive grove. The dogs began to bark as he neared the high mud wall of the courtyard; as he stepped through the gate and was pulling it shut a figure moved out of the shadows.

"Who's that?"

"Who do you think?"

"Oh, Cabell, you sc-scared me for a second."

"I've been waiting for you."

"Took a little w-walk, made sure the Land Rover was locked up. Such a beautiful night, I stopped and smoked a couple of cigarettes."

"Something I want to talk to you about."

"Somebody's got a big f-fire on the other side of the lake. You don't su-suppose it could be Grigory's friends the gy-gypsies, do you?"

"I don't know."

"He can really tell a story, can't he? Should have a-asked him why those gypsies d-decided to leave Sicily in the first place, must have been a re-reason. And I w-wonder if they'll ever go back home again. Story sort of reminded me of my own life."

"How?"

"I'm like the old man."

"What old man?"

"Didn't you listen to the story? Armando's father. It's not the f-fear of dying so much as wh-where. The life I lead, m-moving from one wild place to another, wh-who knows where I'll end up. Is that abnormal, Cabell?—to worry about wh-where you're going to d-die? Look at the old man, Armando's father."

"Seems natural to me."

"Right, just w-wanted to hear you say that."

"After America, Harry, then what? Are you finished with Rio de Oro?"

"God, I'll probably k-keel over in the desert and won't be found for days—w-weeks, if ever."

"Harry, do you think they'd take me on as a ground-water geologist?"

"The Spanish? I d-doubt it."

"I could make a complete survey of their water reserves, then leave."

"Good pro-project, but the Spanish won't be interested. You know th-that."

"They should have an accurate idea of how much water they actually have, in case they change their minds."

"Mighty gen-generous of you, Cabell, but you've got to learn how to wait."

"Christ, everybody keeps telling me that."

"Well, it's tr-true."

"What do you know about waiting?"

"I just realized that I've been w-waiting."

"Waiting for what?"

"To st-stop, and I think the moment has come."

There was a rattling of a chain and stamping of hooves; the donkey stuck its head out of the stall and began to bray. The dogs howled.

"Wh-what's the matter with these animals, has Lydia got them sp-spooked?"

"What are you talking about, Harry?"

"Cabell, I guess you've been w-waiting, too, haven't you?"

Cabell nodded.

"Cabell, I want to come back here and stay! I've had enough moving around."

"You do? To Morocco? Tangier?"

The dogs quieted down. The donkey kept its head outside the stall and seemed to be listening to the conversation with its big ears as hot breath steamed from the nostrils.

"It's a nice place, n-no? I mean, I-I could l-live here—there are a lot of p-people I could get to kn-know, n-no? L-lydia and Grigory, even old M-maxwell, the l-lady wr-wrestler—I-I bet there are plenty of interesting p-people."

"There are."

"A base—isn't that what you were t-talking about?—all North Africa would be my t-ter-territory—d-dig up the d-desert. Wh-what do you think?"

"That was my plan."

"M-mine too!"

"Since when?"

"Listen, wh-when you get to Aaiun, s-sound out Rivera on your idea."

"What?"

"Without m-m-mentioning anything, of course. I'll do the same in A-America. F-figure whoever takes out the m-magnesium can go in on the water, too."

"Are you serious?"

"Of course I'm serious. Is it a deal? Hey, get your paws off me!"

Cabell tried to throw his arms around him, but Atkinson fended him off.

"So it's a d-deal. Let's go inside now. I'm c-cold."

Just as the two men were walking to the house, the cumulus clouds began to pass overhead; raindrops spattered inside the mud enclosure.

"Are you going to tell me why you changed your mind?"

"It's the R-Russians, they sp-spooked me, too."

Cabell laughed.

"A-all this talk about tr-travels and t-timing and d-death. M-made me n-nervous, thought they were talking about me. Made me r-realize one thing th-though."

"What's that?"

"We have a good thing going, don't we?—we ought to s-settle into it and s-see it through."

"Did you remember to fill in those mines in Imjijt, Harry?"

"Wh-what do you take me for, an idiot?"

October 8 Another miserable day of rain. This is the beginning of the cold wet North African winter, and I am just another European itinerant, trying to keep warm in an unheated Arab hotel. I am anxious to travel southward with the sun now; yet I am reluctant to depart. The company of friends holds me back, and Tangier has its power over me. I long for an unblemished sea of yellow sand, but fear I will find no completeness in it.

There was a time, before I met Driss, when I could look out over the desert and feel that I lacked nothing. Then he and I began our travels together; sometimes it was hard traveling. I remember one evening we arrived in Smara—the wind was whipping dust around, you could hardly see your hand in front of your face—in all directions lay the Sahara—a hard, rocky lunar landscape. I remember the wailing calls to prayer from a distant mosque; it was during Ramadan, and there was nobody around and no food to be had. As we were wandering through the empty streets, someone hailed us from a doorway, and we went over and joined a trio of truck drivers. Together we shared a tajine prepared by an old man with one arm. I distinctly remember the taste of that tajine. Squatting beside Driss on the floor of the tiny room, I couldn't help wondering at the impulse to invite strangers to share a meal, at the happiness and fatalism of these desert people, and about my place among them. They seemed wise and happy, they take life as it comes and—God willing—make the best of it. Being around them, I felt I was learning something.

I'm prepared to take life as it comes, too, but it's difficult to live with tragedies. I suppose it's because I've been trained to look at life in terms of possibilities. I tend to reflect on future moments, while Saharans inhabit the present. Even in that mud room in Smara, watching Driss laugh and converse with the truck drivers, I was thrown into a thoughtful mood—happy and appreciative of them, but vaguely asking myself how it was all going to work out. That wasn't so long ago.

October 14 Dead flies on the white ledge beneath the window. Morning light and morning shadows. Boujma has a headache and declares this means a good stretch of weather is coming on. Yesterday a note from Hamid: her husband has arrived unexpectedly from France; today they depart for Icht. So sudden; I can hardly believe it. Not even time for a goodbye.

A weird dream last night: I was in Tangier trying to get down to Casablanca in order to meet Driss before he went off on a trip. To obtain permission to ride on the bus to Casablanca I went to see Escobar, who had become the headmaster of a school, the Spanish Consulate being the school. Escobar said I must kill a male goat, cut off the testicles, and take them to a certain wall. This I did. A small black-and-white goat. I cut his throat in the biology lab, where the professor showed me an extensive collection of large, rather greenish human testicles. Balls of Aztec sacrificial victims, he said, collected by the priests (only the largest examples) and somehow preserved down through the years. I took my goat testicles and placed them on top of a mud wall among hundreds of others (some of flesh, others made of clay, metal, wood). Then I went to an enormous library to obtain written permission from the librarian. All this time the buses were leaving, and I became more apprehensive that I would miss the last one and never see Driss again. In the library I made my way down long wooden stairways past shelves of books bound in green leather to the main floor, where I had to compete with gangs of children clamoring for similar permission to travel. At last I emerged and began to run through the grounds of the Spanish Consulate. All the buses had departed, and even if I could find some other way to get to Casablanca, Driss would already have left. I passed Mi Amigo Maxwell playing basketball. With me I had binoculars and a camera, which at the last moment I decided to leave behind. I couldn't find the key to my room, then found it at last, and locked the camera and binoculars away with my hat. Next I decided to take my hat along after all, but once more I had difficulty locating the key. The last bus had long since departed, and I was still frantically searching for the key, hoping that some means of transport might still be available.

# *The Woods at Sidi Amar*

ATKINSON, OMAR, AND CABELL were crouching behind the trunk of an umbrella pine tree, where a cluster of ferns and fallen branches hid them from sight. Below them lay a path indented into the forest floor; the path was smooth and covered with pine needles and led diagonally across the side of the hill and lost itself among the trees. Farther down the steep slope mist clotted around the uniform trunks; moisture dripped from the high branches; it was early morning and cold. When the men breathed, it was as if they had smoke in their lungs.

"H-how much longer do we have to w-wait?" Atkinson whispered.

"Until we find him," Cabell replied in a low voice.

"I had the feeling we n-n-never should have come out here in the first place. N-now I'm soaked through."

"You said you wanted to come."

"I'm going to smoke a cigarette."

"Go ahead," Cabell said, parting the ferns and peering through. "Just keep your voice down, or he'll hear us."

"This is r-r-ridiculous."

Cabell shrugged.

"You-you don't know wh-where he is, Cabell. For all you-you know, he m-may have gone back into town."

"If he has, then there's nothing to worry about."

"Then w-wh-what are w-we doing here?"

"If he's still wandering around in these woods like a wild man, we ought to catch him and at least talk to him."

"He's pro-probably back in his hotel room right this minute, r-r-rolling around in his bed, and laughing h-his h-head off."

"Maybe you're right."

"But so wh-what if he isn't? Let him r-run w-wild for a-a while, pr-pro-probably do him some good. F-forget ab-bout those b-books at least. Wh-what do you w-want to talk to him about, anyway?"

"I'm partly responsible for him being out here."

"Wh-what have you-you got to do w-with it?"

"I just do, and I want to see him, that's all."

"He'll c-come b-back eventually."

"I don't know. I just hope he's all right."

"Well, if he's out in these w-woods, he must be half fr-fr-frozen by now. Look at you, Cabell. You're sh-sh-shivering."

"I know, I can't help myself."

"God, I can h-hardly h-hold this match to this cigarette."

Cabell's teeth began to chatter.

"Cabell, how long has he been gone?"

"It's been over a week since anyone's seen him in town. Omar heard he was around here about five days ago, isn't that right, Omar?"

"Where is that boy?"

"He must have crawled off into the bushes."

"H-hope he doesn't get lost."

"Anyway, Maxwell's been sighted by shepherds and fishermen, not doing anything in particular, just sitting on rocks or wandering in these woods."

"Do you think he's gone off h-his h-head?"

Cabell shrugged. "Maxwell has a wild streak in him."

"Whenever he feels the urge, he j-just takes off for the w-w-woods, d-does he?"

"Looks that way, doesn't it."

A few yards off, Omar stuck his head up from the ferns and whistled softly, motioning with his hand for Cabell and Harry to come forward, and the two men crawled over to the boy. In his brown djellaba Omar was practically invisible in the foliage.

"What is it, Omar? Do you see him?"

With one arm the boy drew aside the bushes, and the two men looked through the opening. About a hundred yards off the figure of a man could be seen moving among the formations of scaly tree trunks, then went out of sight altogether in a pocket of mist.

"I-is that him?"

Cabell nodded.

"Let's go get him!"

"Hold on. I think he's coming this way."

At that moment Maxwell came into view on the forest path: he was wearing a plaid shirt and gray flannel trousers, now dirty and torn; his beard had grown considerably and covered the lower half of his face; he still had on the rimless spectacles. Barefoot, he was ambling noiselessly down the forest path. As he drew closer, one could make out that he was terribly grimy: with hair in disarray, the bottoms of the trousers ragged, and there was a large sore at the corner of his mouth. Passing just below where the three men were in hiding, he stopped and sniffed the air.

"He smells your cigarette!" Cabell whispered.

"L-look at him, he's turned into a w-wild b-beast! Let's leave him alone!"

Suddenly Cabell stood up from behind the bushes. "George, look here. It's me, Cabell."

Maxwell opened his mouth and took a step backward, half staggering from surprise. Then Omar and Harry rose into sight behind Cabell.

"George, here are Harry and Omar. We've been looking all over for you, George."

Without uttering a word, Maxwell turned and bolted off through the trees.

"George, it's me, Cabell! Don't run away!"

"God, look at him go! We'll never catch him!"

"We better try. Come on!"

Cabell leaped down the embankment and took off after Maxwell. For a man of his age and build, Maxwell was moving over the rough ground with amazing speed; plunging down the steep slope in great bounds, he had almost disappeared from his pursuers' view when he tripped over a root and went sprawling.

"We've got him now!" Atkinson shouted.

Before Cabell could catch up with him, however, Maxwell was up and off again, climbing on his hands and feet up an outcropping of gray, lichen-covered rock. In a few seconds he was over the top and out of sight. Cabell halted and called after him.

"George! Where are you going? We only want to talk to you!"

Above the gray rock formation the umbrella pines grew densely together; no sound came from them. Atkinson ran up, panting and out of breath.

"He's like a mou-mountain goat, that man! Where did he go now?"

"Up those rocks."

"L-let him go. It's obvious that he's at h-home out h-here."

"I still think we ought to bring him, or at least talk to him."

"H-how are you going to t-talk to him if you can't even get cl-clo-close to him?"

"Where's Omar?"

"Don't know. I thought he w-was following m-m-me."

"Well, let's climb these rocks and find the trail again."

They scrambled up over the large gray boulders and wandered uphill through the dripping forest; except for the sounds of the birds in the trees, all was silent.

"W-wonder wh-where he sleeps at night?"

"I don't know."

"Probably m-makes a n-nest for himself somewhere, l-like the animals do."

"God knows."

"Wh-what does he l-live on? Wh-what do you su-suppose he eats?"

"He might have a friend in these woods."

"Berries? Roots? Wh-what do go-goats eat?"

"Leaves."

"Where do you suppose Omar has gone to?"

Suddenly Omar appeared on the slope above them, signaling for them to come forward. When they reached him, he was crouching behind a rock, pointing at two shacks among the trees at the bottom of a ravine.

"I saw him go down there."

"So th-that's wh-where he hides out."

As they went down the hill a big mansion became visible through the trees.

"That's the old Perdicaris house," Cabell pointed out. "Deserted now. These shacks where George has taken up residence must be the outbuildings."

"God, wh-what a smell! Wh-what is it?"

They looked through the broken-down structures with the doors hanging open and the moss-covered roofs sagging and caving in. A brook could be heard nearby. The shacks exuded a pungent odor of decay and fermentation. Maxwell was nowhere around.

"I don't see him anywhere. This must be where he sleeps, though."

"Look at the b-bed he's made th-there in the corner—just r-rags and l-leaves and a piece of old ma-mattress torn in two."

"It must be cold up here during the night. I wonder how he keeps himself warm?"

"Cabell, come here and look at this!"

Beneath the crumbling foundations of one of the shacks hundreds of bottles had been deposited. Most were empty, but some still contained liquid.

"This is what's making that terrible smell."

"Wh-where do you suppose these b-b-bottles came from, Cabell?"

"They say that during the Algerian revolution the Perdicaris mansion was used as a home for the Algerian wounded. Apparently they wrecked the place; this must be what they left behind."

"Pain-killers, all right."

"What a mess."

"Looks as if your fr-friend M-Maxwell has been in here, too."

"Some of these bottles have their necks broken off."

"Th-this is h-how h-he keeps warm at night."

"Poor man."

"L-lives on al-alcohol and b-berries and wha-whatever else he can f-find in the f-forest."

"Place really stinks, doesn't it?"

"How can he drink this stuff?"

Atkinson kicked at the pile of bottles, and some of them rolled away down the hill, clicking together as they slithered among the wet grass and ferns.

"Well, where has he gone to now?"

"We b-better find him soon, or he'll ki-kill himself on this al-alcohol al-alone."

"What do you think, Omar?"

"I think he's watching us from somewhere."

"You're probably right."

"Maxwell! Maxwell!" Atkinson barked. "Come down here! We're your friends! What're you hiding for?"

His voice rolled away through the forest and echoed off the cliffs and gray rock formations.

For the rest of the morning they wandered through the woods without catching sight of Maxwell. As the sun came out and burned off the mist, the whole panorama of the Straits of Gibraltar and the Spanish coastline came into view. From these African hills the water appears so blue and clear that one can discern the contours of the sea bottom and make out underwater rocks and shoals, dangerous for ships, and the white sandy places. As usual, a great many vessels of all kinds were passing through the Straits—freighters and tankers, passenger ships, fishing boats, and an occasional ship under sail. Down on the shore fishermen were perched among boulders, casting with their long cane poles; the sea was calm, with only a fringe of white along the coast to indicate where the water rolled against the rocks.

Around noon Cabell and his friends were seated on the cliffs. From the forest behind them the gloom had lifted, and birds were singing loudly. Cabell and Harry were smoking cigarettes and looking across to Spain; Omar lolled on the grass beside them. Suddenly Harry moved and whispered to Cabell.

"Don't move! He's behind us!"

"Where?"

"I just saw him out of the c-cor-corner of my eye. He's hiding behind a tree!"

Cabell made a sign to Omar.

"Just act normal, Cabell, a-as if we don't know he's there. Otherwise we'll s-s-scare him away."

"All right. What are you going to do?"

"I have a plan."

"What is it?"

"I'll get up and walk away, s-saying that I'm going b-back to Tangier in the Land Rover to buy f-f-food. When I m-mention f-f-food he won't stray far. Then I'll circle around behind and gr-grab him."

"All right. We'll stay here and wait for a signal. Don't hurt him."

"Cabell!" Atkinson announced in a loud voice. "We're never

going to catch him! He's t-too qu-quick for us! A t-t-tough cus-customer, no doubt about that! I'm going into town to buy some l-lunch! How does roast beef and eggs and cheese and a bottle of cold white wine s-sound to you?"

"Sounds great! Get some cigarettes, too. Players!"

"You and Omar wait here, and I'll b-be b-back in about an hour!"

"Go ahead! We'll stay right where we are," Cabell replied. "Maxwell smokes Players," he whispered.

Atkinson got to his feet and went off into the forest while Cabell and Omar rested on the grass and dry pine needles, commenting on the view that lay before them. Suddenly there was a shout.

"I've got you now, you old billy-goat!"

Atkinson had surprised Maxwell from behind and was gripping him around the middle. With surprising strength and agility, however, Amigo spun out of his grip, so that Atkinson only had him by the shirt.

"Help me, Cabell! He's going to get away again!"

Before Cabell and Omar could run up, Maxwell pushed Atkinson to the ground, the shirt ripped, and the two men were separated. Cabell tried to grab hold of Maxwell, but he dodged to one side. Then Omar caught hold of one of his legs, and the two men approached. They had him trapped against the edge of the cliff.

"We have you n-now, goat-man! Give up! You can't escape this time."

"George," Cabell was pleading, "what's the matter with you? Why don't you speak?"

"Wh-what are you doing up in these w-woods, anyhow?" Atkinson demanded.

"George, don't you want to come back to Tangier with us?"

Maxwell paid no attention to their words, and his eyes darted about looking for a way to escape. His clothes were in tatters: the shirt was ripped and the zipper to his trousers was wide open, exposing the hair and the red penis to the open air.

"Come on, George."

For the first time Maxwell seemed to notice the boy clinging to his foot. With an angry snarl he kicked his leg loose, sending Omar rolling away. Still seeing no easy way out, he lowered his head and ran at Cabell. Cabell took a step backward before the charge, but Amigo butted him in the chest with his head, knocking him to the ground. Before Atkinson could grab him he was away again, crashing through the undergrowth. A long laugh echoed from the trees.

"Go ahead and laugh, goat-man! Butt your friend in the belly!" Atkinson shouted after him, shaking his fist.

Cabell was rolling on the ground, moaning; the wind had been knocked out of him. When he had recovered, Atkinson helped him to his feet, and they looked off in the direction Maxwell had taken through the forest. Omar's nose was bleeding.

"We better let him go," Cabell said. "When he becomes tired of these woods, he'll return to the city."

"Now you're t-talking sense. In a few days he'll t-turn up at the Marco Polo, drinking coffee and doing his tr-translations."

"All right, I've had enough. Let's go back."

They had not made their way very far through the forest when they came upon Maxwell sprawled on the ground. His head lay beside a lichen-covered rock; blood flowed from his forehead.

"Here he is!" Harry cried.

"He fell down and knocked his head against this rock."

"He's unconscious!"

Cabell knelt beside the body and turned the head to one side. Maxwell groaned; there was dirt in his mouth.

"He's given himself a good cut on the head."

"He smells bad," Harry said.

"Must be that alcohol seeping out through the pores."

"Living in these woods like a-an a-animal, he smells like one. L-looks like one, too."

"He's beginning to come to."

"Look out! We better hold him down, in c-case he tries to run away again."

They rolled Maxwell over onto his back. Harry pressed one arm to the earth and Cabell the other; Omar sat on the legs. Maxwell opened his eyes, blinked a few times, and looked up at his captors.

"How are you feeling, George? You hit your head on this rock."

"Let me up," Maxwell replied, spitting the dirt out of his mouth.

"Oh, n-no we're n-not. W-we're n-not going to let you run away this time."

"Let me up! I can't bear your weight! What's on my legs?"

"That's Omar."

"Get him off! I can't stand to be held down!"

He began to thrash around. Cabell and Harry tightened their grip on the arms, and Omar tried to control the legs.

"Up! I must get up!"

"Calm down, George!"

Maxwell continued to writhe and kick about until Cabell slapped him across the face with his open hand. The blow landed on the sore at the corner of the mouth, and Maxwell cried out with pain. There were tears in his eyes.

"Do you promise not to run away, George?"

"Yes, anything," he blubbered. "Just let me up!"

"No more fights?"

"No! Just set me free!"

Cabell and Harry released the arms, and Omar climbed off his legs. Maxwell sat up. The sore on his mouth was bleeding along with the cut on the forehead.

"Why are you doing this, Cabell? Why don't you leave me alone?"

"You've got a nice cut on your head, George. And that sore on your mouth ought to be tended to."

"That was a mean blow."

"I'm sorry."

"You're a mess, g-goat-man."

"Don't look at me! I know I look terrible." He covered his face with his hands. "Take your eyes off!"

"We're not looking."

"Have a cigarette."

Amigo took his hands away from his face and accepted a cigarette from Atkinson.

"Feeling better now?"

"Yes."

With the cigarette in his hand, Maxwell seemed to relax.

"What are you doing in these woods?"

"Living."

"How did you get up here in the first place?"

"I have an Italian friend who has a house near here. I spent the night with him, and when I was walking back through the forest the following morning, I realized that I didn't want to return to the Hotel Nicaragua."

"Yes, I can understand that."

"I had no desire to go back to my miserable schedule, to the Marco Polo and the damn books. So I said to myself, I'm going to live in these woods for a while."

"How long ago was that?" Harry asked.

"A few days. I'm not quite sure."

"That was almost two weeks ago, George."

"Has it been that long?"

"You l-like l-living l-like a wild man in the forest, do you?"

"The only thing I missed was cigarettes."

"So wh-what did you do for sm-smokes?"

"There's a picnic ground by the road. I go over there in the early morning when nobody's around and pick up cigarette ends."

"We found the shack where you lived."

Maxwell nodded.

"L-looks like you drank up m-most of that Algerian wine."

"I drank myself to sleep every night."

"Planning to stay up here in-indefinitely, w-were you?"

"No."

"You wanted to come back?"

"I became embarrassed over my appearance. I didn't know what to do. I was afraid to show myself."

"You had a mirror, did you?"

"No, but I knew I looked bad. I was thinking of sneaking back into town at night, when nobody would see me."

They smoked several cigarettes together. Cabell got to his feet.

"Do you want to go with us now, George?"

"Yes, I'm ready."

They followed Maxwell along a path made soft by layers of dry pine needles. At one place he stopped and pointed to a glade on the slope below them where the pine trees stood apart with almost symmetrical evenness—their uniform branches roofed the sky, and through the spaces between the erect trunks the sea could be seen shining in the sunlight. Spain lay far away, and the tiny ships plied the band of water dividing the two continents.

"This was my favorite place in the woods."

"It's almost l-like a ca-cathedral, isn't it?"

"I used to come here on the good days, find a sunny spot, and lie on the pine needles."

"If you're wearing l-leather s-soles," Harry remarked, "these pine needles are m-mighty sl-slippery underfoot."

"I used to count the ships out on the Straits until I fell asleep."

"Were you happy, George?"

"In that glade I was."

"Shall we leave you here?"

"No, I've had enough. Take me back to Tangier."

"Back to the old routine?"

"After living in the woods, I feel like drinking whiskey, going to the cinema, and riding around in jet airplanes."

They took Maxwell to a doctor, who treated the sore and sewed up the scalp wound. Next they delivered him to the Hotel Nicaragua, where Palmeta Gordillo was waiting. She had opened the window to give the room a good airing and had spent the morning sweeping and dusting and putting things in order. With the sunlight streaming in through the window, the room seemed pleasant and livable. Maxwell went directly to his easy chair, sat down and looked dejectedly at the floor.

"George," Cabell said after a few minutes, "we're going now."

"All right, goodbye."

"Palmeta is going to stay here with you."

Maxwell grunted.

Cabell exchanged glances with the others. Atkinson tugged at his sleeve, and they left the room. Out on the street, they were about to climb into the Land Rover when Maxwell appeared at the window above them.

"You should have left me in the woods, Cabell!" he shouted.

"Why?"

"You've led me back into the trap!"

"I thought you'd had enough."

"She's trying to seduce me!"

Atkinson laughed as Palmeta appeared at the window, chattering in Spanish and trying to drag Maxwell back into the room.

"If I give in now, I'm finished, I've had it! And it's your fault!"

"Why so?"

"Women always drag me down! Their concerns are as heavy as lead! You know that!"

"Well, come on! I'll drive you back to Sidi Amar," Cabell said, "You can go back to your goat habits."

"No, I guess I'll stay here now."

"Good."

"But this time I won't give in to her, I don't care how much she weighs. I can go to Rio any time, and she knows it!"

Atkinson pushed Cabell into the Land Rover, and they drove off. Maxwell watched them go, then he, too, disappeared from sight.

For a while there was silence in the room. From time to time Palmeta would try to open a conversation, but got no response. She tried to kiss him and ran her hands over him, but he pushed her roughly away. Finally she began to unbutton her blouse.

"I'm going to take my clothes off, Jorgito."

"Go ahead."

Out came the large, pendulous breasts with the dark nipples. In another minute she stood before him entirely naked, and Maxwell lifted his gaze from the floor to survey her. The skin was brown, and there was a mass of black hair between the legs. She bent over so that one of the long breasts brushed against Maxwell's cheek.

"Did you miss me in the woods?"

"No."

"Did you ever think of me?"

"Once or twice."

"Jorgito, aren't you going to shave and take a shower?"

"No."

"Is your head all right?"

"I don't know."

"Oh, look, your trousers have become unbuttoned."

Maxwell watched her hand travel down across his belly, enter the opening in the trousers, and gently take hold of the penis. Maxwell grunted. After squeezing it until it became hard, she began to tug softly on it and so pulled him right out of the chair and so led him across the room to the bed. There she unfastened the remaining buttons, and the trousers fell about his ankles. Stepping back, he kicked them away and with a cry fell upon her, pushing her onto the bed. Flat on her back, she threw her arms around him, but he fended them off and tried to roll her over onto her belly. She resisted.

"I don't want to do it that way!"

Maxwell made no reply but continued to struggle with her.

"I'm not an animal."

Maxwell grunted.

"Jorgito, you smell like an animal!"

"I am an animal; we're all animals."

"But we're not going to make love like animals!"

"Like two goats."

"Jorgito, is this what you learned in the woods?"

She got her heavy legs around his middle and began to squeeze with all her strength, and Maxwell was immobilized. He ceased wrestling with her, and she gathered him into her arms.

In a vacant lot behind the hotel three Spanish boys were playing marbles. Squatting on their haunches, they shot their marbles toward a little pocket that had been dug in the bare earth—softly, if they were aiming for the pocket, or hard, if they were attempting to dislodge an opponent's marble from a position next to it. Crystal balls were flying all over the lot, with the boys scrambling after them. To one side of the playing area a Moroccan boy stood by disconsolately watching the game. He owned no marbles, and the Spanish boys had just refused to lend him any of theirs, so he could not play. Suddenly from up on the hillside there came a screech: the mother of one of the boys had come out on the road and was calling her son to lunch. The game broke up; the boys pocketed their marbles, picked up their book bags, and ran off in different directions. Left by himself in the empty lot, the Moroccan boy took a few steps forward, looked quickly around, unloosened his pants, and defecated into the little pocket. Then he, too, ran off.

Maxwell and Palmeta lay together on the narrow bed. Palmeta held him in her arms as he nuzzled the brown breasts.

"Do you feel better now, Jorgito?"

"Yes."

"In Tangier your poor head will get well quickly."

"I think so."

"No more running around in the woods like a wild animal."

"No, I've had enough of that."

"Making love is good, but there's no need to do it from behind, like horses."

Maxwell nodded; his mouth was full of the nipple.

"Do I ever bore you, Jorgito?"

Maxwell let the nipple go and looked at her, "Sometimes."

"Oh."

"Your laziness, your Spanish nonsense bore me."

"You're so impatient. Oh, let's not fight, Jorgito."

"But you know me better than anyone alive."

"Is it true?"

"You accept more than I. I have challenged you more, much more than you have challenged me."

"I don't know how to challenge a man, and even if I did, I'd never do it."

"Try thinking."

"I've only asked that you be more austere, Jorgito, that you develop more moderate habits."

"I don't want to write poetry or go on trips into the desert."

"Do you mean it?"

"But I must bring flow into my life somehow. When there's no sense of movement, I become frustrated and want to get out."

"How are you going to find flow, Jorgito?"

"I thought Cabell would teach me."

"Won't he?"

"He's a free spirit—he knows how to draw on the forces around him—but now he's preparing to depart. We'll never see him again."

"I hope he comes back from the desert."

Maxwell rolled over on his back and looked up at the ceiling. "I want to give in sometimes."

"Give in to what?"

"To whatever moves me. If I want to run naked in the woods, I'm going to do it."

"Is that what Señor Cabell taught you?"

"Cabell? He's the one who brought me back."

"You've brought him back, too."

"I have? When?"

"From Melilla."

"That's right. I'd forgotten."

"Who knows what he would have done if you hadn't been there? He and that awful Fuad. He needed you then."

"You're right, and he still does."

"Still does what?"

"Needs me. Come to think of it, he's the only one who's ever needed me."

"I need you, too, Jorgito."

"Ah! But you're a woman! I mean a man; Cabell's a man."

*My dear friend,*

We are in Tata now, having crossed the Anti-Atlas in darkness from Taroudannt. The roads were in a terrible state; heavy rains have washed them away in many places; and often we were forced to get down from the truck and clear the way of boulders which had rolled down from the hillside. It was hard work but exciting; you know this is the way I like to travel. We arrived here after midnight but were prevented from entering the town until this morning, as the river was high and flowing very fast, and the driver thought it unsafe to attempt a crossing in darkness. So we spent the night outside, sleeping in the back of the truck. In this oasis on the edge of the desert, nights are cold. A myriad of stars floats seemingly in the void at arm's length, and I was dazzled by their brightness. Before falling to sleep I thought of you.

I have a terrible strep throat that I cannot forget. Yesterday afternoon, I thought that if I had to look at one more glittering rock I would go out of my mind—the sunlight enters the eyes like slivers of shattered glass—and of course we are at the height of the date season, so clouds of flies have settled on the oases. One must live with them, I suppose; one really has no choice. But I cannot understand the reason for their existence. They swarm constantly about, their buzzing irritates me, and my hand passes habitually over my face to keep them away from the corners of my mouth and eyes. I've never been able to get used to them. Under these circumstances I believe that if I were obliged to undergo some further trial, such as the one you experienced, I would be pushed to the very edge of my reason, and perhaps even over that edge. That last sentence makes me consider again your ordeal in Tarfaya. I, too, am still amazed that you want to go back. But you know better than the rest of us why you choose to retravel the same path, rather than take another.

Unless the rains begin again, I expect we shall be leaving Tata in a day or two, bound for Icht. I am in no hurry, and would prefer to remain in this oasis until my throat clears up. We are staying with the village schoolmaster, who gives us too many chickens to eat. Otherwise we are fine. My Ali treats me well. "May I introduce Si Hamid el Hassani," he says to the local officials to whom we are obliged to present ourselves. "That is her pseudonym; in reality she is Madame Bennani, my wife."

I'm always wondering, do you miss me? When shall you be joining us? You have my address in Icht, but if you feel you cannot go so far out of your way, I will come out to meet you where the road divides at Bou-Izakarn. All I need is a few days' notice in order to prepare myself. You will come, won't you? I mean, you won't pass by without informing me in advance, so we can meet. And please ask some doctor there in Tangier what is the best remedy against strep throats. They occur frequently in the Sahara.

*Hamid*

October 23 Dream: Shahid and Hamid and I (and someone else?) are traveling through southern Morocco in an old car. It is rough going over the broken terrain. We arrive at the edge of a precipitous rocky gorge through which an enormous torrent of water is plunging at incredible speed. Where could so much water come from in such a dry landscape? we ask ourselves. Overhead the skies are bright and clear; not a cloud in sight. Looking for a way across, Hamid falls in and disappears. The water rages past with huge spouts and falls. We scramble over the rocks looking for her when Shahid slips and is sucked under by the terrible currents. Both are lost and I stand at the edge of the flood, bewildered by the suddenness with which solitude has been thrust upon me in this barren land. (Is someone else there?)

# *Taking Leave*

MAXWELL AND CABELL stepped out of the Hotel Nicaragua and walked up the Avenida de España. This was Maxwell's neighborhood; he knew all the little Spanish tapa bars in the quarter. Leading Cabell into some of them, he was a little surprised when the proprietors of these bars and the prostitutes they encountered within them, both male and female, came forward to greet Cabell. Maxwell said that he always assumed that Cabell led a moderate life, but now it appeared that he was on familiar terms with every whore and hustler along the Avenida de España.

Next to the bus station they came upon a traveling lottery —an immense stand containing television sets, radios, plastic dolls, glasses, crockery, shiny kitchen machinery of every description—in Maxwell's words, all the brightly polished junk from Europe and America that Moroccans love. Great crackling loudspeakers blared out music, and on a wooden platform before the showcase a Negro danced and mouthed the words of the song. Maxwell wanted to move on, but Cabell insisted they stay for a few minutes. Behind the dancing Negro lottery wheels turned and numbers were barked out by a muscular girl in pirate earrings, red beads, and a long flowing gown. Maxwell detected a beard beneath the make-up, and Cabell recognized her as one of the local wrestlers. Normally she was billed as Abdelkader the Intellectual, Champion of Mexico and South America (aspirant)—Cabell had seen her perform at the Club Neptuno. Then two Spanish boys came on and did the twist, and the crowd was very quiet and serious. Maxwell began to notice familiar faces around him; several people were trying to catch his eye, smiling and nodding in his direction. These were night people—bus station derelicts, insomnious children, and all-night café sitters with nothing to do and nowhere to go. They form a club of sorts: they assemble in the Socco Chico and in the cafés along the Avenida de España; their day begins when the sun sets behind the mosque in the Socco Grande; it comes to an end with dawn over Cape Malabata. They witness all the sunrises; they know the cool hours of the night; and from glances that Cabell was receiving, Maxwell took note that he was no stranger to certain members of this disreputable mob, either.

At last Maxwell succeeded in leading him away; mounting the staircase of the tannery, they went down a narrow alleyway smelling of urine and arrived at the door of the Hotel Cuba. Maxwell didn't know this hotel—it looked undistinguished enough from the outside, what with the yellow paint peeling off the walls, the barely legible sign, and the filthy street teeming with half-starved cats—upon stepping through the door, however, one was pleasantly surprised: the interior had been freshly painted with many bright colors, the place was clean, and the night guardian who let them in seemed to be a pleasant chap. Right away Maxwell started comparing this hotel to his own, the Hotel Nicaragua, where he'd been stationed for nearly a quarter of a century, and reckoned the Nicaragua a poor second: even now they had hung a cardboard sign over the door proclaiming in three languages that the hotel was closed indefinitely for repairs. All service had been cut, so he had to sweep the floor, make his own bed, and was even obliged to search through vacant rooms for clean sheets.

So as they mounted the circular stairway around the interior patio, Maxwell's eyes were taking in all the details of this tidy Arab hotel. On the top floor they heard a radio and the sound of someone rummaging in one of the rooms. Cabell tapped at the door, the rummaging ceased, and someone approached from the other side. There was the sound of heavy breathing a few inches away, as if it were a large animal snuffling around—something was whimpering in the background.

The door opened a crack: Atkinson was in there, down on his hands and knees. When he saw who it was, he jumped to his feet and pulled the door back. The place was in a shambles, with suitcases, packing crates—all turned upside down, the contents spilling out. There was a falcon in a cage, the cage had been knocked over on its side and was rolling about on the floor, with the bird trying to keep its balance. A girl huddled beneath the covers on the bed—she was the one who had been making the whimpering noises.

On the table was a bottle of whiskey. Atkinson took a big swallow, Cabell grabbed it away from him, then Maxwell got hold of it. Finally the whore wandered over from the bed, with a sheet draped casually around her, and demanded her share. When they got her out of the room, Cabell and Maxwell proceeded to pack Atkinson's bags—he was not in a condition to do it himself. The night guardian helped load the Land Rover, and they drove to the port, where a Yugoslav freighter was preparing to depart. The Land Rover was hoisted up onto the deck easily enough, but how they got Atkinson into the cabin was another matter. The sailors helped, then stayed on, opening bottles of contraband whiskey which had burst out of a suitcase. At last they departed, and Atkinson collapsed on the bunk and seemed to pass out. So Cabell and Maxwell left him, with his possessions littered about and the wild bird watching from the cage. When they reached the bottom of the gangway, however, he appeared at the rail, raving, with the sailors pressing about him. "Cabell!" he was shouting, and the voice had a hollow sound, as if it echoed from the bottom of a well. Cabell told Maxwell to wait and remounted the gangway. When he reappeared, just in time to leave the ship as the last of the hawsers was being cast off, he was smiling.

Maxwell regarded him skeptically. "What are you two up to? —scheming, I'll wager—going to make mischief in the desert. Ha! Yes, sir, and don't think it's such a big secret any more, that people don't already know about it. Ha! Ha! Your friend has such a big mouth—if you can wade through the sputterings —why, he'll give any stranger his life's story at a drop of a hat! Ha! Ha! Ha! Spill every secret—so it's silver, is it?—going to get rich quick!—come back to Tangier in a Rolls-Royce—start putting on airs, snub your frinds. Ha! Ha! Ha! Ha! Not with me you won't—silver mines in the desert, ha! I will have high-tailed it to Rio, be cruising the Amazon—no more secondhand experiences for me! You think I'm going to wait around to listen to another one of your stories? You must be out of your mind—no sir! I'm leaving—going—buy my ticket tomorrow. Ha! Ha! Ha! Ha! Ha! What do you think of that? Silver mines in Algeria, and all the time you had me believe you were headed back to Rio de Oro. Ha! No wonder you didn't want me to come along. Silver! Ha! Ha! Ha! Ha! Ha! Ha! You can't fool me!"

November 8 *Tangier* It's late at night, but I'm not sleepy. Once more I'm seated at this table, writing in my notebook, for the last time in Tangier. Tomorrow we'll be on our way south. I've just risen from my bed, but Shahid still lies there, fast asleep, and I've turned the gooseneck lamp away so as not to wake him. He has to draw up his legs so his feet will not stick out from under the covers; one long black arm trails from the bed, with the fingers touching the floor, as if the bed were a barge and the floor the surface of an African lake.

In how many poses have I seen that long black body?—on the basketball court, running along the beach or lounging on the hot sand, diving off rocks into the sea, and in this bed. Having him in my arms is like embracing all of Africa; I think I have a love affair going on with the continent. How much of this is narcissism? I wonder. Here is my own black reflection, my African reflection. He was here waiting for me when I returned from town this afternoon, sitting on my suitcases, which he had carried up from the cellar. He watched me pack and helped me whenever I let him. He wouldn't leave and insisted that I accept one of his fancy shirts as a going-away present.

Today has been a day of farewells. Lydia and Grigory came in from Sidi Kacem. I saw Mohamed I, and M'siksif dropped by, although I had forgotten to tell him what day I was leaving. I couldn't go into the street without someone coming up and shaking my hand. Mohamed, who makes the bysar, the guards in front of the prison, whom I got to know when I used to take Mohamed his breakfast—they all gave me their blessings for a safe trip and a quick return to Tangier. I don't know how they knew I was going away—the Arab telegraph, I suppose. Even Escobar telephoned to wish me a good voyage. How did he know I would be leaving tomorrow? I imagine he has his spies out. He says they're waiting for me down there, whatever that means.

This morning Fatomah kissed me on both cheeks; she was

crying. She is wearing a brassiere now for the first time, which Shahid says her husband bought for her with her mother's egg money. Just before I went to bed Boujma knocked on the door. I had a feeling he'd been up to something; all day long he'd been in his little room. He presented me with two packets of freshly chopped kif, one for me, one a gift for Hamid, whom he refers to as my "Lady Moslem Friend." Now I have enough to last for weeks; I have placed it in an air-tight mason jar to keep it fresh.

So. My stay in Tangier draws to an end. Tomorrow Omar is coming in from Cape Spartel, and we go. I wonder when I'll be returning to Tangier. Here my love for the organic and the natural has been reinforced. It's a great source of confidence when one begins to define oneself against beauty and is able to find self-containment in the balance. In spite of the shoddiness of the town, one senses that the people have remained in contact with the rhythms of the earth.

But I won't miss this winter weather. I'm looking forward to the hot sun and dry air of the desert; my bones are in need of a good baking.

November 9 First night out *Casablanca*

When we left Tangier this afternoon, Mi Amigo Maxwell and Shahid were at the station to see us off. Maxwell stood there with his hands in the pockets of his raincoat, grumpy and apologetic—I think this must have been the first time in years he had left his bed before dark.

From the train Omar and I surveyed the dreary, sodden landscape of Morocco. There has been so much rain this autumn that the country is almost in a state of emergency, what with the flooding rivers, bridges down, and much of the good farm land inundated. Darkness fell early, as if nature were anxious to hide the havoc she had wrought. Hamid told me once that the feeling of melancholy inspired by riding on a train at night and by lying in a hospital ward, also at night, are somehow the same; you are alone among strangers, caught like yourself in an enclosed space surrounded by blackness, for indefinite time or direction. In both situations there is a sense of helplessness or passivity. I know what she means.

We arrived safely and had a good dinner at Chez Milhet; afterward we came to the hotel, and I put Omar to bed. Poor kid, he was so exhausted from excitement—this is the first time he's ever been out of Tangier. Later I went out and walked the streets for a while. Not like last summer, the prostitutes stay in the bars, yet the most brazen of them will come outside and accost you. And the criminals are so obvious in the leather jackets and hats and black pointed shoes—one followed me for a few blocks—I think he expected me to turn my wallet over to him out of fright. When he came too close, I turned around and faced him, and he just smiled and faded away.

November 10 Arrived in Marrakech today. The sun was shining, the air so warm and clear, like some transparent liquid, and the snowy Atlas Mountains gleam in the distance—we could see them 100 kilometers away from the train. I really feel good when I'm on the road; to be at peace with myself I must be excited, and to be excited I have to be moving.

Omar and I checked into a little French hotel and headed for the Jemaa el Fna. There was a huge crowd, and we plunged in. The atmosphere of the place is dominated by the drumming of two competing Gnaoua groups, but we saw everything—the storytellers, Hadaoua with their pigeons, the snake charmers, the bicycle act, all sorts of dancers and musicians, the acrobats, buffoons, freaks, monkey people, etc.—it was an absolute madhouse. Then the sun was going down, the snow on the mountains was turning the color of rose; within a few minutes the temperature had dropped several degrees, but we were warm in our djellabas. Dozens of makeshift restaurants were being set up on the square, and we wandered among them, eating snails, roasted corn, stuffed camel intestines, and kale and hot peppers at the vegetable counters. All delicious. Afterward we went to the hammam.

This must be one of man's greatest inventions. The place was filled to capacity, and beneath a single overhead light bulb, high up on the arched ceiling, hundreds of waxy bodies were writhing in the gloom. I've never seen anything like it—water running everywhere, men and boys scrubbing one another down, pouring buckets of water over each other, talking, shouting, hissing, complaining that the scalding hot water wasn't hot enough, so that the dripping walls of the three great rooms reverberated with their voices. We found a washer who led us to the hottest room, so hot that at first I could hardly stand it. There he pulled me and pushed me, stretched my joints, twisted my limbs, jumped up and down on me, flipped me about like a fish on the slippery floor, levered me up into the air and beat on my back with the soles of his feet, until I was gasping for breath and nearly fainting from the heat. And this was a little old man, about half my size, who knew all the tricks. Next he rubbed me down with a stone until so much dirt came out of my pores that it was embarrassing. The old man kept showing me the dirt and chuckling (couscous, he called it), and Omar had been laughing with my grunts and gasps from the beginning. Following a rubbing came a rinsing, then a soaping and a shampooing, and a final rinsing, in which Omar and the washer poured bucket after bucket of ice-cold water over my head. The feeling was so exquisite that when they had finished I stayed by the cold water tap and kept on filling the wooden buckets and dumping them over myself. I couldn't have enough. It was so refreshing—like standing under a waterfall on the hottest day of summer.

After the hammam, we stopped for a coffee in Gueliz, then came back here to the hotel. The room is warm and comfortable, and I'm about to open the window and let the freezing cold night air in. Omar insists upon sleeping in the same bed with me; he throws his arms around me and falls instantly asleep. He's the ideal traveling companion—wide-eyed and open-mouthed before all the sights we have seen, undemanding but ready for everything. How extraordinary it is to sleep next to the form of a young boy. He could be my own son. Sometimes I feel I'm traveling with a good-luck charm.

November 12 *Marrakech* This afternoon I spent such a long time in a tailor's shop being measured for a new djellaba, that when I finally stepped out into the street, I had the sensation of suddenly having been transported to another city. The crowded streets had emptied out, shops were being shut and boarded up, many of the lights had been turned off, and the temperature had dropped several degrees. I could see my breath and felt cold and uncomfortable from the sense of dislocation.

This is a typical Marrakech phenomenon. You walk into a café you have been frequenting for years and find that the bar has been unaccountably moved from one side of the room to the other and the place has been painted some new, weird color. There has been a total turnover in staff: your friends have departed and nobody recognizes you. You ask for the cook, the Negro with one earring and a limp. "Who? Who?" they demand. "He left a long time ago—went back to Tata." Your other friend the bartender they've never heard of. This is a new group up from the Souss or the Sahara: they've brought their own equipment, paint, friends, and ideas with them.

Or your favorite barbershop has changed locations; the younger brother has returned from Germany with a barber's diploma and has taken over. His modern friends lounge around reading movie magazines, and the shop has been painted an awful pink. Still, for the sake of old times, you let the boy cut your hair, but he wants to curl it and douse you with perfume. In the process you learn that the older brother and his old-fashioned friends have moved to another part of town.

November 14 Yesterday cold and overcast, Omar and I spent most of it wandering around, sitting over glasses of mint tea, trying to keep warm; but this morning when I threw open the shutters, sunlight poured into the room. The air was like crystal—you could feel it all through your lungs after a deep breath. It had been snowing, there was a great deal of snow on the mountains, right down to the level of the hot dusty plain, and the white slopes were streaked with shadow as the sun rose. Plenty cold, too; but within an hour it had become warm enough to walk around with only a shirt on. On days like this Marrakech is like an immersion tank—one cannot feel the air, its temperature and dryness seem to be exactly the same as that of your own skin—there is no resistance, no sensation of air—you want to take off your clothes and expose all the skin. The sun is hot, but I do not sweat; I am neither hot nor cold. I am perfectly at one with the atmosphere.

In Marrakech the weather sets me at ease. It's just the kind of climate I like—clarity, dryness, dependable good weather. As I walked through the olive groves this morning trying to gather my thoughts, my only thought was of unity. This is what I want—affirmation, and harmony with my surroundings, where I see a white egret on a cow's back and say with conviction, yes, this is my style, I feel at home here—and with people, yes, we are in sympathy, with no real cross-purposes—and with myself, yes, I'm attempting to bring order and balance to my days in spite of what has happened and in spite of the unknown. I accept the unknown.

November 16 *Mogador* We came here yesterday, taking this route because the road over the mountains has been blocked by snow. No sooner had we left Marrakech, than we drove through a dust storm, followed immediately by a cloudburst, during the middle of which we had to get out of the bus to inspect a bridge. Right after we had crossed, it was swept away into the red current. So, soaking wet and tired out, we arrived in this town, which was pleasant enough last summer. Now immense waves crash against the Portuguese ramparts, hurling spray into the dark streets. I'm not feeling well; I must have eaten something in Marrakech that disagreed with me.

Then came a rather bad time with majune, which a boy in the hammam gave me. It was so strong and taken stupidly under such bad conditions, in which there was no tea (terrible thirst) and no privacy (terrible paranoia), so that the whole experience became extremely unpleasant. The piece of candy was no larger than my thumbnail, so I took it in the hotel before going out to dinner, thinking that the effect, if any, would come after we had returned to the room. However, we went to one restaurant in the town and then another, but both were closed, so we ended up in the bistro on the beach. Already valuable time had been used up. During soup a bell literally clanged inside my head, and I wasn't sure that I would ever be able to get out of that restaurant. I was screaming with insane laughter, pounding my fist on the table, and all the people turned around in their chairs to stare at me, or so I thought. When I had regained some measure of control over myself, I pushed some money toward Omar and told him to pay up and lead me out. Poor fellow, he must have thought that his traveling companion had turned into a madman. Anyway, we finally left the restaurant. It was raining outside, and I remember rolling around on the grass in agony, for the drops of rain were stinging me like a swarm of bees, or so I thought. Omar got me back to the hotel, where I became terrified that the concierge would see me in such a state and call the police, who would throw us out of the hotel and back into the stinging rain. I just couldn't take any more of that rain. So I crept up the stairs on my hands and knees, moaning and groaning the whole way, and made it into the room unseen, or so I thought.

An overwhelming sense of tragedy engulfed me as I lay on my bed thinking how everything would again be ruined by death or trouble. After I had come so far and striven so earnestly to put the pieces of my life back together, all was about to be shattered anew. My heart was beating so fast, I thought I was dying of a heart attack; I had Omar listen to it and even he grew alarmed. I was going out of control: the police would be brought in, and we would be helpless.

Now it's over, although as I write this the following morning, I still feel somewhat under the influence of the stuff, whatever it was. Last night I became aware of the possibilities of danger in everything—in my scarf, which might strangle me, in the glass, which might break and cut my wrists, in the window I might fall out of, in the food, which might poison me—everything was a threat to my existence.

Then the terrible thirst began. "Sahara!" I was screaming. "Thirst! Thirst!" Omar brought me glass after glass of water, but when I swallowed, the liquid went down my throat in burning hot lumps, as if it were molten lead. All this time I was pleading with Omar to look after me and not to let anything happen. He was begging me not to stand so close to the open window, not to leave the room, and not to grip the glass so tightly, or it might shatter in my hand. After a while I was able to go to sleep, but not without first kicking all the bedcovers off me, for fear they might smother me during the night. There was only Omar to keep me warm.

Perhaps I now understand more fully the dimensions of fear which lie within one and how perilously close I was pushed to insane action. Desperately I wanted to leap out of that window, I felt such claustrophobia in the room; my throat constricted when the water went down, as if I had rabies. I swear I shall never take majune again except under the most ideal conditions

—in a friendly house, surrounded by people who know how to lead me through the fears, who will bring me hot tea when I'm thirsty.

November 19 It's raining in Tiznit now, for the past two days the weather has been wet and cold, but we must wait here until another bridge is repaired before continuing south. Both my shoes have holes in them, so my feet match the weather—wet and cold. The trouble with these small towns is that there's just nothing to do. Last night we went to the hammam, not to wash, but just because it's the warmest place. The night before it was the cinema, where we sat among mysterious men in djellabas. These are the big events of the day. So with the rain coming down and this mud town melting around me, I retire to this hotel room to drink hot coffee spiced with cloves and to write.

At night I embrace Omar as tenderly as if he were my own son—and more. Question: Should a teacher sleep with his students? Should a man sleep with his son? Whatever the answer, we are warm and happy together.

Night before last I did a very foolish thing. I borrowed a charcoal brazier to heat up our room. But Omar and I dozed off. About an hour later I woke up; it was pitch black, Omar was moaning and babbling Arabic in his sleep. At first I couldn't comprehend what was the matter; it was as if I had taken another overdose of majune. The air was thick. Then I realized we were sick—I thought we had been poisoned. I got out of bed and fell down on the floor. I got up and began crashing around in the dark, shouting and waving my arms about; things were falling and breaking. Finally I fell against the door and managed to open it and ran down the stairs and into the street, shouting all the time. Someone came along and realized immediately what the trouble was and opened all the windows in the room. The next day we had terrible headaches.

Every day a new lesson. Now I know what it means to be delirious; I know what it means to feel you are going to die. But I was fighting it, waving my arms about and shouting, I was making a last desperate stand.

# *The Meeting at Bou-Izakarn*

SOUTH FROM TIZNIT the land dries out, as the paved road runs straight over the flat littoral plain. To the east rise hazy red ranges of the Anti-Atlas; the west low sandy hills are visible, marking the Atlantic coastline. Vegetation of any kind is sparse, except along stream beds, where oleanders take root and blossom; there are olive groves and palms, and immaculate mud dwellings which form part of the natural landscape. A few people are about: men tilling the land with wooden plows and women drawing water from wells.

By degrees the mountains draw in, the plain narrows, and the road begins a winding ascent over the last spur of the Anti-Atlas. Here the hillsides are formed of gray, pitted rock, with patches of red earth in between. Even these patches have been laboriously cultivated, with such thoroughness that in some places only one shallow furrow might pass between two rocks. Both rock and soil are gripped by the gnarled roots of the argane tree.

This is goat country: the black, half-wild animals climb with amazing agility right up into the topmost branches, where they devour the argane nuts; the goatherds, barefoot young boys and old men, half-wild themselves, stand half-concealed among the rocks and trees.

The bus passed through the mountains and began the long descent through dry ravines to the flat land below. Vegetation ceased as abruptly as it had begun; thermals bore hawks aloft and snakes flashed across the road and disappeared among the rocks. Ahead lay a broad valley, now shimmering under the heat, with hazy black hills in the distance—the beginnings of the Sahara. Here is the village of Bou-Izakarn, where the road divides—one leg running southeast across the Sahara into Mauritania, the other southwest, keeping to the coast through Rio de Oro. They rejoin at the Senegal River, on the southern boundary of the Great Desert.

A little settlement has grown up around a red-walled military caserne; eucalyptus trees have been planted, which provide shade for two filling stations, a café, a dry-goods store, and other nondescript shacks. Desert men with sparse beards and hawk-like faces, dressed in blue robes and black turbans, squat on their haunches in the dust. Their women, whose dark bodies are swathed in yards of indigo cloth, faces hooded by elaborate coiffures and the blue material, sit apart among their bundles and children. Otherwise, all that can be seen of them is an extended blue arm, the skin having taken on the color of the cloth, or a hand, intricately tattooed, with silver bracelets and rings, or a long dark breast, offered to a naked infant. The local boys go among them, selling hard-boiled eggs, pumpkin seeds, and candy.

Off to one side Hamid was seated in the shade of a tamarisk tree. A loosely-tied black turban covered her head and part of the face, and she wore the indigo robe of the region. As the bus approached along the shimmering road, she got quickly to her feet. The bus came to a stop; Cabell and Omar got down with the other passengers. As they waited for their suitcases to be thrown down, Hamid came over from the tamarisk tree and touched Cabell on the shoulder.

"Ah, Hamid!"

"You've come at last."

"You're wearing another disguise, I see."

"Not a disguise, just comfortable clothes."

"We're happy to see you. Have you been waiting long?"

"Two days."

"We were stranded in Tiznit, waiting for the road to be repaired."

"I thought so."

"I didn't know what to do. I had no way of contacting you".

"That's all right. I don't mind waiting."

"You're in your own country now, aren't you?"

"Yes, I'm where I belong."

"Here's Omar; you know Omar, Hamid."

"Yes, of course."

Omar and Hamid shook hands and greeted each other in Arabic. Meanwhile the bus mechanic was handing the baggage down; Cabell took the bags and set them down on the ground.

"Are you happy to be here, Hamid?" he asked.

"Yes, very happy."

"I am, too—happy to see you. It's hot, isn't it, Omar?"

Omar was watching the Saharans.

"I've missed this heat," Cabell went on. "I want to bake the dampness out of my bones."

He was standing on his toes and stretching his arms into the air as the Saharans regarded him with mingled curiosity and mirth.

"God, I love this heat!" he exclaimed. "I love this dryness, I'm so glad to be back, I like to breathe this dry air. Is it cold at night, Hamid?"

"Freezing cold."

"I'm sure it is. As long as it doesn't rain, I don't care."

Cabell picked up the bags; in a few minutes they were walking among palm trees toward the red walls of Bou-Izakarn. Birds were singing, and men following mixed teams of donkeys and camels directed wooden plows through the red earth. Entering the village by a crumbling archway, they made their way through the narrow streets. Children left off their games to gape at the strangers.

"Christians!" They whispered among themselves. "Spies!"

Some recognized Hamid, and this information was passed around. Women stepped to one side to let them by, at the same time drawing their black robes more closely over their faces.

"I lived in this town for almost a year," Hamid was saying as she led them quickly along.

"When was that?"

"When Ali was a soldier. He was stationed in the army camp."

"Where's Ali now?"

"In Icht, looking after the café."

"Is the café open yet?"

"No, but it will be in a few months."

They went right, then left, making many turnings through the labyrinth of dusty alleys. There were high mud walls on either side: no windows looked out, and one dwelling could be distinguished from another only by the low, recessed doorways, with the wooden doors and heavy metal knockers. With the sun almost directly overhead, heat in the twisting passageways was becoming intense. At last Hamid came to one of the doorways and lifted the knocker.

"Is this it?" Cabell asked. "I'm not sure that I could find my way out if I had to."

"When I first lived here," Hamid said. "I never left the house the first month because I knew I wouldn't be able to get back."

"What did you do with yourself all that time?"

"I talked to the women of the house and perfected my Arabic."

The door was opened by a handsome black boy. "This is Mamou," Hamid said.

They shook Mamou's hand; when Mamou smiled he showed

two rows of beautiful teeth. He led them through a series of low-ceilinged unlit rooms, reeking of goats, into an enclosed courtyard; an interior stairway, made of clay, wound around this central shaft, twisting up into the darkness. Many of the steps had been worn away, so that in some places the stairs had become a steeply inclined plane, slippery and difficult to climb. The house had many levels, and off the stairs were numerous storerooms, exuding the odor of straw, dried rose blossoms, figs, and dates. The living quarters were located on the upper stories: there was a long, immaculately clean room, open along one side, with a view over the flat roofs of the village to the surrounding palm forests, with the dry plain and hills beyond. The floor of the room was covered with rugs and cushions. Cabell threw himself down.

"Whose house is this, Hamid?"

"It belongs to the family of the wife of my brother-in-law, Abdelmalik."

"Suddenly I feel quite tired."

"Rest for a while."

"I haven't had much sleep lately."

"Do whatever you wish; the house is yours."

Cabell leaned against the cushions and closed his eyes. After a few minutes Mamou led Omar away. Hamid was sitting on her heels in the center of the room. The blue robe concealed all but her tattooed hands and wrists, with the silver rings and bracelets; the eyes, lined with antimony, glistened beneath the turban. She was gazing out over the town, from time to time turning her head toward Cabell, who appeared to have fallen asleep. After a while she got to her feet and covered him with a light woolen blanket. There was silence in the room except for the sound of his breathing. A few noises entered from outside: children playing somewhere; a donkey braying out in the oasis. High in the brilliant blue sky a falcon emitted a shriek.

That afternoon they were walking through the oasis; Cabell was wearing his new djellaba. The sun, sinking toward the west, was turning the sky red; surrounding hills took on the light. Strolling from palm grove to olive grove, they came upon men standing up to their knees in the irrigation ditches, diverting the flow of water by means of mud dams. Farmers were meticulously tilling the narrow plots of land; others were driving their cows and sheep home for the night. One old lady was sweeping olive leaves into a sack. Pretty barefoot girls dressed in indigo and black passed by silently, bearing baskets of dates on their heads. Many young men and boys were idle; wandering hand in hand along the paths, they conversed in gentle tones, and greeted their friends who lay about on the grass.

Hamid and Cabell came to the edge of the oasis and continued out over the gravel plain. There was a low hill to climb, where the ground was covered with flat rocks of a reddish-gray color. As the slope became steeper, they helped each other up over the crumbling ledges to the summit which was marked by irregular mounds of stones, with little paths leading between.

"The Bedouins pitch their tents here when they visit the oasis," Hamid explained.

"I see tents out there in the valley."

"They pile these stones to block up the windward side."

They sat down on rocks along the crest of the hill and looked over the oasis. The wind was changing, and noises were rising from the village.

"Do such oases exist where you're going, Yusef?"

"There aren't many oases in the Spanish Sahara. Imjijt is the only one I know."

"What's going to happen to Imjijt? Is the magnesium really there?"

"I think so."

"Then the oasis will never be the same again, I can see that. Isn't there something you can do to prevent it, Yusef?"

"I'll be involved if the revenues are used to raise water."

Hamid sighed. "I don't like to see any of this happen to the desert—not the magnesium, not even your water."

"I know you don't."

"What do they use magnesium for, Yusef?"

"Thousands of things."

"Name one."

"Helicopters."

"Oh, God! How can you get mixed up in such a thing?"

"But the magnesium is there; somebody's going to take it out. Why not use some of the money for the good of the desert?"

"I'm sure you're right, but I wish you'd leave the desert as you found it. May I ask you a personal question, Yusef?"

"Of course."

"Do you belong to an organization?"

Cabell laughed. "Do you mean, am I a spy?"

"Why are you doing these things?"

"Because I see many possibilities, good ones."

"I know, but when you foresee that possibilities might interfere with something pure, something that cannot exist except in a state of purity, why isn't your first instinct to preserve the purity?"

"Perhaps it's the habit of my profession."

"To hell with your profession, it's in your blood."

"Why do you ask if I belong to an organization?"

"Sometimes you sound like one."

"You're a purist, Hamid." Cabell took out a pack of cigarettes.

"You're goddamned right I am, and you're messing with my territory."

"You talk as if it belonged to you."

"Yusef, you know, I admire you in so many ways. I admire your courage and your fairness and your stoicism. I've envied the easy balance and organization you've been able to give to your days. I like your mobility and your style, and I know you love to look out upon the beauty of the world, as I do. You know how to work hard, and that's good, too. And I swear I'd do anything for you. That's why I don't like to say this."

"What?"

"You're a fool."

"Jesus." Cabell broke the cigarette he was about to light and threw it to the ground.

"Is it absolutely necessary that you do this?"

"I'd like to supply some water for the good of the people who live in the desert. All right?"

"Who? What people?"

"The Bedouins."

"How do you know what's good for them?"

"A few oases here and there, they might want to carry on some agriculture."

"Bedouins have never farmed, you'll make them sedentary."

"Drinking water, then; they don't have much of that."

"As much as they've ever had."

"You weren't there when the water came out of the ground; you didn't see them dance."

"Yusef, the Sahara is one of the last great human preserves. Leave it alone."

"Water is sacred in the desert."

"The time is coming when we must deliberately decide to do nothing that is not absolutely necessary, especially nothing excessive or potentially destructive."

"Why?"

"To survive."

"That's what the water will enable them to do—survive."

"The amount of water you have in mind will certainly change them, eventually kill them. You don't know what might happen."

"Look, Hamid, I'm with you all the way, but if I can bring water to the desert I'm going to do it. It'll be the last thing I do."

"Then what?"

"Quit, live, think about the condition of my soul."

"I suggest you get on with that, beginning now."

Cookfires were burning in the village, and a pall of smoke had formed over the rooftops. The sun was going down behind the hills; suddenly the air turned very cold.

"Aren't you in need of this kind of order in your life, Yusef?"

"What order do you mean?"

"The order of what we're looking at—the order of wells and of water flowing in channels and of the narrow plots of land."

"I appreciate it, but I couldn't stay here."

"I need it. Yusef, I want to live like these people. I'm ready to give myself over to God and accept the limitations."

"I know you are."

"Look at the neatness and the extraordinary care they take with everything."

"Nothing is wasted."

"They hold the land in such sympathy and respect."

"This is how man started off, I suppose. Perhaps it's where he ought to have stayed."

"It's where I'm going to stay," Hamid said. "I want to be mobile like yourself, but I need peace and order too."

"You have Ali, he'll take care of you."

"What can you look forward to?"

"In the desert?"

"What can the desert bring now? Besides your work, I mean."

"I don't know, but it's the only choice I have."

"Was there no other choice?"

"For me, all paths eventually lead back to the desert."

"What does that mean?"

"The desert has given me the greatest joy I've ever known."

"The desert or Driss?"

"I think it was the desert."

"But Driss was always there."

"Not all the time, but I always knew where I could find him. When periods of solitude came to an end, he would be waiting for me, and we would meet. You see, I don't have to live with somebody all the time, but I do need someone to travel to, someone who will wait for me, someone who will not grow impatient if I'm a long time coming."

"And Driss was all that?"

"Yes."

"Were you the same for him? I mean, he looked forward to

the meetings as you did? He needed you as you needed him?"

"We discovered a balance between solitude and comradery."

"Which was more important to you—the solitude of the desert, or the companionship with Driss?"

"I never asked myself which was more important."

"Which gave you the most joy?"

"For all its barrenness, the desert has been the source of everything. I've looked out on vistas that were perfect, empty, no one in sight, remote from people; I experienced a passion for everybody who inhabits this planet, whoever he might be. It's also where I've felt my body to be the leanest, my head the most clear."

"But it won't be the same any more."

"Oh, yes. Except that I'm sad now and more alone than ever before. I don't mind the loneliness as much as the sadness—perhaps this just means I'm growing old—Maxwell says the only emotion he knows any more is sadness, which may be the only possible conclusion after making comparisons."

"What comparisons?"

"From balancing the possibilities against the realities. Life against death. But the desert has its own force. It will fill me up again, I'm sure."

"Fill you with what?"

"With love."

"If you really mean that, Yusef, if you love the Sahara, please leave it just as it is."

It was growing dark; they left the hill and re-entered the oasis. Omar and Mamou were wandering among the trees, and they all retraced their steps to the house. Soup had been prepared, with plates of fresh dates and figs. A charcoal brazier glowed in the semidarkness; Hamid poured the hot coffee and milk, filling one by one small glasses set in a row. The room was filled by a faint red glow out of the west.

Later that night, Cabell got to his feet among the pillows and blankets on which he had been sleeping. Pulling the wool djellaba over his head and easing his feet into the Moroccan slippers, he felt his way along the wall, letting himself noiselessly out of the room, and climbed up the twisting stairway to the roof. It was a freezing cold desert night, so clear that all the village and oasis and the surrounding mountains and plains were visible. Great clusters of stars ranged across the sky. There was no sound anywhere; the desert and roofing sky seemed to ring with silence.

A dog on a neighboring rooftop caught sight of him and started to bark. The noise alerted other dogs, and they barked to one another; then dogs in other parts of the village joined in the conversation. As the alarm was passed back and forth, bark answered bark; the whole village was alive with the voices of the animals, asking questions, demanding more information from the dog which had begun the outcry. The circles widened; dogs out in the oasis wanted to know what the uproar was all about—as country dogs, they had their own particular queries and reactions. There was no movement of air; the sound of barking carried a long way. Word was transmitted all the way to the guardians of the black tents, pitched out on the plain. From these desert animals the cry was returned to the village, where the first dog continued to supply a stream of information. Then, together as a chorus, they proclaimed the presence of a stranger in their midst.

*Tan-Tan* Extraordinary barren tableland. Among the sandy bluffs overlooking the town are rookeries of carrion crows, and the wind is blowing all the time. The people here are very polite and gentle; they walk through the white sand streets with their blue robes flowing like cool water. This town once belonged to Spain, so once again I begin to hear Spanish words mingling with the Arabic. The cook at the local hotel, a Mauritanian, speaks American and claims to have lived for five years on Forty-second Street in New York. In a confidential manner he asks me if I want "a piece of ass" and refers to his tajines as "meat and vegetable stews."

November 22  This evening the new moon appeared in the western sky. Ramadan has begun. "You should fast to attain union with Allah . . . to know security from pain . . . so the rich may know the sufferings of the poor and thus be more willing to give alms . . . give up material pleasures and seek the pleasures of Allah . . . allow more time for prayer and for considerations of the spirit . . . shake off old habits and lassitudes . . . know hunger and thirst . . . become hard again."

This evening in Tangier cannons will be booming out over the harbor. The cafés will remain open all night; hammams will not close their doors. At three o'clock in the morning there will be flute music in the Kasbah. Moroccans will turn inward to their religion and will become more difficult to deal with.

"The remembrance of Allah is the greatest . . . love your benefactor . . . through prayer may the human heart be purified . . . the position of the body in prayer be felt by the heart and mind . . . the position of humility."

November 23 I am exhausted from having traveled a long way over the eroded face of the Sahara. After nightfall our convoy descended through cliffs and outcroppings to the edge of Sebkha Tazra, a great salt depression. "The valley of fires," Omar calls it. Night fires were burning everywhere, like great torches in the desert. Another convoy from the south was halted here for the night, and the men had built enormous fires to make tea and to warm themselves. We shared a wonderful meal with them; I'd forgotten what marvelous tricks the Saharans do with fire. They never waste water and are generally clever with their hands. Tomorrow we shall arrive in Tarfaya. I've even heard talk that the Moroccan Government is planning to build a big hotel and turn the town into a tourist center, but I can't believe it. Who would want to go there for pleasure?

# *Tarfaya and Beyond*

IN THE AFTERNOON the convoy reached the sand dunes which ring Tarfaya from the east. As the trucks canted and rocked through the crescentlike formations, I thought it strange that the desert winds should have blockaded the town with these huge deposits of sand, for the adjacent landscape consisted of nothing but bare, scarred rock. Now these restless dunes threatened to choke off a town where practically no one wanted to go or had even heard of.

Nothing had changed—everything was just as I remembered it—the sand-filled streets, the abandoned houses falling into ruin, the crumbling stone jetty with the waves foaming over it, the brightly painted fishing boats drawn up on the beach, and the sturdy castle standing out in the sea. The wind never seems to stop blowing. Blue nylon nets were laid out on the cobblestones, and fishermen sat among them, making repairs. A few soldiers were lounging about; otherwise, nobody was around.

I went directly to the cinema, but the place was shut, with boards nailed across the door. A Moroccan was curled up in his djellaba in the middle of the street, and I woke him up and demanded to know what had happened to the café and where M'barek had gone; he gave me a blank look: there was no café in the cinema and he had never heard of M'barek. I didn't pursue the subject with the man; in place of a nose, he had a gaping hole in his face. Little Omar, who was standing by my side, seemed as bewildered as myself by this news. All the way to Tarfaya I had been telling him about M'barek and how we would sleep in his café; he would prepare us tajines and show us the site of his brother's grave, in case we were unable to find it ourselves. He had seen everything and knew everything; he would be our link with the past; but now he had gone away.

Now that sleeping at the café was definitely out of the question, we had to find some other place. These were the shortest days of the year; soon it would be dark. I couldn't face the prospect of returning to the barracks, so we wandered through the back streets of the town, hoping to find some house that nobody cared about. Coming to a row of shacks near the beach, which looked as if they had been constructed out of driftwood, we were prowling among them when an old man stepped out of one and greeted us. I told him that we were looking for a place to sleep and what about these shacks, were they occupied? The old man scratched his beard and replied that these shacks belonged to Jewish jewelers, who used to make silver jewelry for the Bedouins, who periodically encamped on the edge of town. Since the departure of the Spanish, however, the Bedouins seldom came any more, and all the other jewelers had long since departed, leaving him, the only Jew and the only jeweler, in Tarfaya. The old Jew, Sefardi was his name, rambled on in a mixture of Spanish and Arabic until I got him back to the original subject—was there any place around here where Omar and I could spend the night? Sefardi declared that he had in his possession the keys to the padlocks on the shacks, which his friends had left behind with him for safekeeping, and produced from beneath his robes an enormous bunch of keys. We opened each of the shacks and chose the biggest. I told Omar to clean the place up while I went and reported to the caid with my passport. Sefardi inquired if we wanted anything to eat and offered his services as a cook. I gave him some money and asked him to go and buy a fish from the fishermen.

I knocked on the caid's door, and after a long interval he answered, again clad in the blue pajamas, but it was a different caid. I related to him that I had passed through Tarfaya nearly a year before, on my way from Rio de Oro to Tangier. My traveling companion, a young Moroccan, had died and was buried here; now I was returning to the south and had brought with me a member of the dead boy's family, who wished to visit the grave. The caid nodded and stamped my passport, saying that he had arrived in Tarfaya only a few months before and knew nothing about it. The hour of harira was approaching, he hadn't eaten all day long, and I could see he was hungry and was thinking only of his stomach. He saw me to the door and wished me a safe trip.

As I walked back along the beach, the sun was sinking into the sea behind the stone sea-house, and I recalled the last time I had observed the sunset from this shore. Driss and I had just arrived in Tarfaya from the south. We had set off from La Guera with such great expectations of things to come—glad to be leaving the desert before the heat of summer would make life oppressive. It was exciting to be on the road together, and I was looking forward to spending the summer with him in Tangier. By the time we reached Tarfaya my apprehensions about his leg had mostly subsided, but when I learned that we were to be stranded here for several days, I remember that first tinge of fear, knowing that if anything happened, we would have no way of getting out—then the terror began. All that was seven months ago. It seemed much longer than that.

Omar had swept out the shack, put down a straw mat, and set up our cots and sleeping bags—part of the new camping equipment I had bought in Tangier. Water had been carried in buckets from a well, to be used for washing. My toilet kit was beside the lantern on the portable table, and the lamp was burning. The place now seemed quite comfortable. Sefardi had found the fattest porgy I've ever seen and was busy preparing a tajine—it turned out that his workshop served as a miniature grocery store as well, where we purchased coffee and tinned milk from him. When Omar judged that it was dark enough so you couldn't distinguish a black thread from a white one, we drank our café-au-lait. I was doing Ramadan with Omar. Sefardi said he would prepare harira for us the following day; today there had not been sufficient time. Omar showed him the modern equipment I had brought along for the desert; Sefardi said that if the Moroccan army were as well equipped, he'd join up himself.

While we sat cross-legged on the floor of the shack, eating his delicious porgy tajine with our fingers, I asked Sefardi why he had remained behind in this ghost town when all his friends had departed. He muttered that he didn't even like to cross streets, so how was he going to cross the desert with his friends when they left Tarfaya? It turned out that he was an agoraphobe, with a morbid fear of empty spaces. He had arrived in Tarfaya over thirty years ago, when the town was called Villa Bens under the Spanish, and had been here ever since. He and several other Jews had come in a fishing boat all the way from Mogador. Sefardi liked to talk about the old days in Mogador, when it had been the foremost port in Morocco. I told him we had passed through there on our way south, so he had many questions about the town. Apparently most of the trade had been with England in those days, and English used to be the first European language of the town—Sefardi even knew a few words of English himself—but that was all a long time ago, and most of the large Jewish population had long since departed for Israel or America. When the Spanish had evacuated Tarfaya ten years ago, he hadn't the courage to go out into the great empty desert and so had remained, year after year, still fabricating the Bedouin jewelry and never straying far from the cluster of shacks. He was an old man now, he said. He never did enjoy looking out; now he had become accustomed to looking inwards.

For dessert there were tinned peaches from America and coffee. Sefardi said he had found a crate of these peaches washed up on the beach. He was a kif smoker, and we had a few pipes together. I told him of the circumstances of our arrival in Tarfaya and asked if he recalled the death and funeral procession almost a year ago. He shook his head; he kept to the shacks and didn't go out much into the town. He knew about M'barek's café, however, and understood that M'barek had packed up his café equipment and had slipped across the border into Rio de Oro. I figured that was what had happened.

Later that night I slid out of my sleeping bag, quietly opened the door to the shack so as not to wake Omar, and took a walk out to the edge of the desert, which is my habit in these remote towns. No dogs spotted me, so I could walk in peace. It was another beautiful desert night—clear, with only the distant sound of the sea to disturb the perfect silence. For a moment I considered heading over in the direction of the cemetery, but decided against it—there would be plenty of time for that. In fact, I was trying not to think about those things; I just wanted to enjoy the night. I found the air quite balmy; one could almost strip down and go for a swim.

As I made my way back along the esplanade, I noticed someone following me. Whoever it was was coming closer and closer, so rather than run away, I stopped and lit up a cigarette. A man approached and introduced himself. This was the local postman, sent down from Casablanca, who also took to prowling the streets at night. He seemed a pleasant fellow, and when he invited me back to his house for a glass of tea, I accepted. The house turned out to be no more than one room containing a bed and a table and a chair. The bed was unmade, but the chair was broken, so I had to sit on the bed. All four walls of the room were decorated with an immense collage of naked ladies and musclemen, and from the type of magazines strewn around the floor, it appeared that the postman spent most of his time cutting out nudes and pasting them on the walls. After putting the water on to boil, he started complaining about the heat and in another minute had taken off all his clothes except for his transparent underwear. Then he sat down on the bed, put his arm around me, and we flipped through those worn-out magazines. I was beginning to feel somewhat uneasy. By pointing out the naked parts of men and women, he was trying to discover which I preferred. The naked bodies were closing in on me, and all I could think of was that cool sand and air out in the desert; however, I was thirsty from smoking kif and wanted that tea, so I laughed and fended him off and tried to change the subject. He was anxious to know if I had brought any magazines from Tangier. Not that kind, I said. When he learned that I was on my way to the Spanish Sahara, he begged me to send him some photographs—the legionnaires were sure to have them—he especially desired the ones showing men and boys together and women doing it with donkeys.

At last the tea was ready, and while I gulped down two glasses, pacing back and forth on layers of old magazines, the postman lay on his bed and moaned seductively about the heat. Finally I excused myself and got out of there. Walking back through the town, I breathed in great lungfuls of pure air and swung my arms around in relief to be out in the night once more. How is it possible for anyone to be an agoraphobe?

The time to swim in Tarfaya is early in the morning. Although I had only slept for a few hours during the night, the sun's first rays entered so intensely through the chinks in the shack that I woke up immediately, and to my surprise felt rested. Omar was still asleep, so I went down to the beach by myself. The tide was way out, the damp sand glistened in the sunlight, the sea itself was calm and silent, with only a few ripples splashing on the shore. I contemplated swimming to the castle, which lay only a short distance out, but decided against it; this was a cape formed by tides, and who knows what currents might be flowing beneath the calm surface out there. These were tropical waters as well, and I had seen plenty of sharks along this coast. So I stripped down and waded in up to my depth. Looking back at Tarfaya, I realized for the first time what a pleasant little town this must once have been—I had never viewed it from seawards before—and I imagine that travelers arriving by boat must have been struck by the attractive façade which the town offers the sea. And they must have been grateful for the existence of this habitable spot poised on the edge of the Sahara. Too bad so few people choose to live here any more; too bad nobody cares. Because of what happened to me here, I suppose I feel a special allegiance to the place. But who knows—the Moroccan government might one day follow through with its intentions, and Tarfaya will spring once more to life. One thing's for sure—the weather is warm and the swimming is good in the month of November.

By the time I returned, Omar had straightened up our shack —this was his special job—then he and I set off for the cemetery. On the way he spied a palmetto growing in the sand and stripped off some fronds; he had already filled his pockets with stones. I didn't ask any questions. Taking the route of the funeral procession, we crossed the airstrip, which was still a sea of drifted sand, and entered the big dunes on the other side. I thought I knew where the cemetery was located, but after wandering around for a while, I realized that I had lost all sense of direction. There was no question of becoming lost ourselves—I could have climbed the crest of a dune and seen the town—but I had no idea where the cemetery could be. Out in the sand there are no bearings—in every direction it is the same—a fixed, silent sea of identical sand formations. Yet these dunes are not without motion: they are on the march, grain by grain of sand, in gigantic columns across the face of the desert. Every day in fact their positions change; nothing remains the same except their shape.

I was perplexed, but Omar was frightened—he was convinced we were lost and he kept asking me, why was his brother buried out here? I had no explanation, except that this is where the citizens of Tarfaya chose to bury their dead. Meanwhile the sun was heating up, and shimmering patches of mirage began to appear in the depressions among the dunes.

Then quite unexpectedly a man appeared before us—a bearded soldier—I seemed to recall having seen him somewhere before. Without uttering a word he beckoned us to follow him, and we obediently set off on another course through the dunes. The sun was beating right down through the top of my head, and I think I was becoming somewhat dizzy. I stumbled through the deep sand, as Omar, laden down with sticks and stones, struggled along in the rear.

After walking some way, the soldier abruptly stopped and pointed—at nothing—that is, at nothing more than another dune. I came to my senses right away and realized that this was it—Driss was under there somewhere, buried not in the shallow grave of my memory, but under this gigantic heap of sand some fifty feet high. A regular monument. Behind me Omar gasped at the sight of the great mound which his brother was supporting. The soldier shrugged his shoulders and smiled; I recognized him as the soldier who had stepped forward to shake my hand when I had left Tarfaya the day after Driss died. "One day," he said to me in Spanish, "you might return to find that this hill of sand has moved on. The burial ground will be clear again, and you will be able to sit beside the grave of your friend." I nodded and introduced the man to Omar, saying that this was the brother who had come all the way from Tangier.

So the sand covered all, and I came to realize that, besides this soldier and myself and perhaps the taleb, if he was still around, probably not one person in Tarfaya remembered what had happened. All those whom I had met briefly—M'barek, the Mohameds, and the caid—had departed; the others who had participated in the funeral procession—soldiers and the Mauritanian merchants—had been transferred or had traveled on. Not a trace, not a memory remained. As Omar looked at me in disbelief, as if we were playing a kind of trick on him, all I could do was point lamely at the mountain of sand before us.

But he wasn't at a loss for long. Setting down the bundle of branches, he emptied his pockets of the pebbles he had collected and began to make a pattern of them on the sand. At first the soldier—Moktar was his name—and I stood back and watched, but soon we were down on our hands and knees beside Omar, helping him decorate the sand dune. There were other stones in the area, and as we collected them and laid them out in neat rows, I couldn't help remarking on their beauty. They were all black and perfectly rounded—as if they had once been rolled about by the sea—and smooth except for the windward side as they lay on the ground, where the blowing sand had been eroding them for years, and the surfaces had become grooved and rough, like the skin of a reptile.

Pretty soon we had found dozens of these stones, of all different sizes; Moktar came upon more sticks somewhere, which we arranged in various patterns, according to our whim. I made circles, Omar liked triangles, and Moktar preferred rectangles and parallel lines. We were at it for a long time, but the work was absorbing, and we didn't feel the sun. At last we stepped back and viewed the results. There was no real order or cohesiveness to the designs, but we were pleased. Probably in a few days the moving sand would cover all, but that didn't matter. What was important was that we had come all this way, carrying branches and stones, and had laid them out in patterns.

That night we went to bed early because in Tarfaya there's nothing else to do. For a while I lay outside near the shacks and looked up at the stars and let my mind wander and my thoughts kept returning to that sand dune. Of course, when you are dead and in the ground nothing matters any more, except to those who loved you. It seemed appropriate for the desert to have covered up Driss thus, reminding me of my helplessness before the great powers. The tragedy had exhausted me, I realized, but strangely, in Tarfaya I felt strength flowing back. I'll use my new energy to tame this desert down enough to make it produce in return for what it has taken away.

Later on I crawled into my sleeping bag and lay there, smoking a final cigarette in the darkness. From the next cot came the sound of whimpering, and I asked Omar what the trouble was, and didn't he want to come over and get into bed with me for a minute before going to sleep? Suddenly he was there and threw his arms around me, and I never thought it possible that so many tears could flow out of two eyes or that such sobs could convulse a body for so long. At last he exhausted himself and fell asleep; I cannot ever remember sleeping so deeply myself. It was as if a great weight had slipped away, as heavy as that mountain of sand.

So there we were, the three of us living together in the shacks, and the next day we decided to give a feast. I had Omar go to the market and buy the fattest animal he could find, which turned out to be a young goat. Sefardi and I watched him kill it and skin it and before long it was turning on a spit over a fire. The local oven produced fresh loaves of bread, and Sefardi contributed a concoction of tinned fruits that he had been collecting over the years. I went around to the army camp and told Moktar about it; as a formality I knocked on the caid's door and invited him. They both showed up, and the caid brought along the local schoolteacher, a young man from Fez, who was anxious to meet me. The meal was a great success; afterward the schoolteacher, a young fellow, danced for us.

Whenever a truck convoy arrives in Tarfaya, the whole town gets out—that is, the soldiers who happen to be lounging around the gate of the army camp, the fishermen asleep under their boats on the beach—they all rouse themselves up and wander over to see who has arrived, and with what cargo, and to listen to whatever news there might be from the outside world. Tarfaya is the first checkpoint inside the Moroccan frontier, so a routine search is always made of cargo coming up from the Spanish Sahara. Just as I arrived on the scene, soldiers were taking case after case of contraband whiskey out of one of the trucks, and a driver and his frightened mechanic were being questioned by a fast-talking Moroccan lieutenant. The crowd gathered eagerly around until Moktar dispersed them. Meanwhile I had picked out another driver with a handsome face and was asking him if he had room in the cab for a passenger as far as Tan-Tan. He did, and we worked out a price for the journey. Returning to the shacks, I found Omar sitting on a sand bank talking with Sefardi. Around his neck he wore the chrysolite pendant; beside him was his airline bag, which contained all the clothes he owned, and his djellaba rolled up into a neat bundle at his feet. When he saw me coming he got up, and the three of us went back to the army camp, where the trucks were waiting. After a short delay the motors started up, and Omar climbed up into the cab beside the driver. I handed up the bag and djellaba; the driver took them and placed them behind the seat next to his own djellaba. Above the noise of the motors I repeated my instructions to Omar: from Tan-Tan take the Volkswagen bus to Goulimime. There he could catch the big bus to Agadir, where the midnight special would be waiting. It would carry him over the mountains to Casablanca; from Casa there were several express buses daily to Tangier. In three days he would be home. Omar nodded. The driver put the truck into gear; one by one the big vehicles began to move off. I took a step back and waved. Behind me stood Sefardi, Moktar, the caid and the schoolteacher—all waving. The trucks jolted down the cobble street, turned a corner, and headed out into the desert.

Time passes slowly in Tarfaya. In the remaining days I swam in the early morning and again in the late afternoon. One evening I was invited for dinner at the house of the caid; on another I visited Moktar and his wife. In fact, Moktar has two wives—one from Tangier, who is as white as any European, and a younger, Saharan girl, as dark as mahogany. During dinner Moktar explained that the women take turns: on alternating nights one or the other prepares his food and shares his bed. The system must work, for they were all happy and smiling. The Tangerine woman showed me a little white baby, and the Saharan girl was bouncing a brown one on her knee.

Every morning I walked out into the desert to spend some time by the monument of sand to make sure that our decorations were in order and to place little sticks along the edge of the dune to see if it was moving. It was and after a few measurements I calculated that if I were to return to Tarfaya in about five months' time, I should find that the dune had moved off the grave site. However, for the present I had to content myself with sitting in the sand and thinking about what I would do in Rio de Oro. Bringing water to the surface of the desert, which a year ago seemed an exciting undertaking, now seemed less so. To go ahead with the project, I could not avoid the irony implied by Hamid's warning: *If you love the Sahara, leave it as it is.* Yet did she imagine the barrenness dotted with little oases very much like the one she loves, as I envision? In a way, the idea belonged to Driss, and I felt ready to see it through. In spite of all that Hamid said, it seemed fitting as a final gesture to the memory of him, and to the desert.

Otherwise I mostly lay in the shack and read or listened to the radio and thought about what I was going to do in Rio de Oro. In the evenings Sefardi and I would stroll with a handful of other citizens along the esplanade and watch the sun sink into the ocean. After dinner we would smoke kif.

And so the week passed. One night we were treated to a display of fireworks by an ocean liner bound for the Canary Islands. The first day of December was crystal clear and warm—a good day for traveling—and I took my regular early-morning swim as Sefardi prepared coffee and the last of the peaches. Now he was wearing my sunglasses, which I had given him the night before; a tiny transistor radio, another gift, hung on a nail by his door and never ceased blaring out the music of Spain. I was in no hurry to leave; by the time I had completed my packing, taken a final stroll through the town, and said farewell to my friends, half the morning was gone. Not much later, feeling cool and refreshed, I found myself bouncing across the Sahara in an old truck.

I had hired this truck and its driver, Kacem, to take me to the Spanish frontier. Several days before, when I had first spotted it in Tarfaya, I had thought that it might be the same which had brought Driss and me, but these battered desert trucks all look the same; it's hard to tell one from another.

Tarfaya and its flanks of sand were already far behind; ahead of us broken mesas studded the open horizon. The track was practically nonexistent, but I knew the way by heart, having traveled it many times before, and of course Kacem was familiar with the area. To our left a great salt basin shimmered with eerie whiteness, and I thought I saw a herd of camels out there, appearing and disappearing among the rippling mirages. A layer of heat seemed to be pressing down upon the surface of the land, my eyes were blinking repeatedly into the glare. Owing to the dryness of the air, however, the heat was not uncomfortable, and I whistled above the steady rhythm of the motor. Ahead lay the void: I was resignedly allowing myself to be drawn into it.

A series of parallel ridges presented themselves; we followed the long detours through ravines where solitary palm clumps grew in the sandy soil. Before emerging from behind the final outcropping onto the open desert which I knew lay beyond, I had Kacem stop the truck and turn off the motor. In the silence which followed, when all that could be heard was the wind whistling in through the windows, I got the binoculars out of the leather case, left the truck, and scrambled up a flaking yellow ridge to the summit, where I lay down among the rocks and adjusted the focus of the glasses.

Less than a mile away on the plain were the frontier control points. From one, which was nothing more than a shack, flew the red-and-green flag of Morocco. Although my view through the glasses was heaving with heat distortions, I could make out two soldiers sitting in the shade of the shack. One looked as if he was cooking something; as I watched, the other got to his feet, walked off a little way, and urinated. Then a third soldier emerged from the shack and joined them. This one had binoculars of his own and seemed to be watching something that interested him. The Moroccan soldiers were pointing and talking and passing the glasses back and forth between them. The ground around them seemed to lurch and quiver in the heat.

A few hundred yards beyond was the Spanish frontier post. This low building was made of cinder blocks and had a corrugated metal roof which reflected the light like a mirror. I knew it well. Above it the red-and-yellow flag of Spain was whipping in the wind. Parked nearby were two beige Land Rovers and a camouflaged command car of the Legion; each had its own radio antenna from which smaller flags snapped back and forth. The Moroccans were evidently speculating on the presence of the military vehicles, which are almost never driven so close to this sensitive frontier. Before the vehicles stood three Spanish officers of the Legion, dressed smartly in their beige-and-green open-necked shirts, tasseled caps, riding breeches and black boots. They were too far away for me to recognize, but a fourth officer was striding impatiently back and forth; by the way he walked I could tell that it was Colonel Rivera. Every so often he would stop and put a pair of binoculars to his eyes and look across no man's land at the Moroccans and toward this ridge. Although he could not possibly see me at this distance, I crouched down lower among the rocks. Behind the vehicles tents had been pitched and some legionnaires were milling about. Apparently they had spent the whole night there waiting for me.

So this was it. I had to admit that I was a little puzzled by the imposing welcome committee down there on the plain. Did it mean that they were angry with me for having stayed away from the job so long and planned to interrogate me on the spot? Or were they just very anxious to have me back and meant to impress me with this show of strength? Colonel Rivera was a friend of mine, but I never really knew what was going on in his head. Even though he respected me and was always extremely polite, I think he vaguely disapproved of me. He knew I was useful to them and to the future of their Sahara. But as a civilian I am always somewhat uneasy around military men; they give me the feeling that within their idea for order civilians are expendable.

But the Moroccans were obviously apprehensive over the arrival of these military vehicles; they might have even radioed a report back to Tan-Tan. If they ever suspected that I had anything to do with it, they might not allow me to pass, thinking that I could be an agent carrying secret information to the Spanish. Surely the Spanish would know this, and I was surprised at Rivera for not being more cautious. But I suppose he knew what he was doing. In any case, there was no turning back now; I couldn't very well climb into the truck and go back to Tangier.

The whole plain was shimmering with heat; the horizon was a blur. The rocks among which I had concealed myself were hot to touch, but I sat back and enjoyed a cigarette and the privilege of being able to observe these people and to speculate on their purposes. I noticed a huge dust devil out there—that mysterious vortex, swirling along, sucking dust off the surface of the land and sending it spiraling hundreds of feet into the air—and watched through the binoculars as it leaped along the ground, headed my way.

No doubt Omar would have arrived in Tangier by now; at this very moment he was probably fishing off the rocks near Cape Spartel. I wondered what my other friends were doing. I could see Shahid stretched out on his bed at the Splendid, probably wearing one of his beautiful Senegalese shirts. What about old Atkinson? Probably wishing he were back in the Sahara. If those ore samples he's carrying are as rich as he claims, I hope he's playing his cards right. Knowing Mi Amigo Maxwell's schedule, I'm sure he's still sound asleep at this hour. I wonder if he'll ever move from the Hotel Nicaragua to the Cuba? Lydia always rises early; most likely she's out on the farm with her dogs; if it's not raining, that is. In that case she and Grigory will be stranded in the house. Then again they might be having one of those crystal North African winter days in Tangier, when the Spanish coastline seems only a mile or two away. Those are the days I shall always remember. How about Mohamed I? I should think he and Mohamed II will be having their reunion before too long. I thought a great deal about them in Tarfaya, while I waited for the day of my reunion with the Spanish.

But I shouldn't stay here much longer. A Moroccan patrol might come along at any moment to investigate what the Spaniards were up to, and if they caught me up on this ridge with my binoculars, I would have a difficult time explaining myself.

The dust devil had reached the base of the ridge and was swirling among the boulders that had tumbled out onto the plain. I could hear a hissing voice; the pale yellow dust spiraled up into the air right above my head. Instead of dissipating itself against the rocks, however, it came bounding up the escarpment. I had no chance to escape, and in another second I was engulfed by the whirlwind. Dust and sand were flying everywhere, and I buried my face in my arms. My ears were filled with the sound of a loud sigh, as if the thing were alive, and pebbles rattled over the bare rock. Then it was gone, and I lifted my head to see it flying off across the ravine behind me, eventually vanishing into the translucency of the sky. I got to my feet, shook the dust from my clothes, and started down the ridge. A few minutes later we were driving around the last extremity of high ground. The great plain stretched away indefinitely before us, and heat columns played all over the land. Two parallel tracks led directly toward the frontier control posts.

El Aaiun is a domed town set on a flat yellow desert. At dusk a trumpet blows as the Spanish flag is lowered in the main square; the Legion stands at attention, with the wind whipping in from the desert. When the flag has been caught and carefully folded by the officer of the guard, drums and trumpets begin to play, and the Legion marches smartly away to their camp at the end of a long wide street. This show of strength takes place every night before an assembly of veiled men in blue robes, Spanish laborers and civil servants, and whatever riffraff of the town that might be around. MPs in white German helmets stand in groups of three on street corners, casting suspicious glances at strangers; others cruise the streets in camouflaged Jeeps mounted with machine guns.

The new two-year contract I worked out with Rivera and the other officers and specialists contained roughly the same terms as the previous one. I was to be paid much more than before, of course, most of which would be deposited into my account in New York, some into a Spanish bank in Madrid, the remainder into a local branch in El Aaiun, to be used for my personal expenses. Rivera and the others already knew that I was extremely pessimistic about the possibilities of there being any oil in their desert, so I didn't stress that point as much as I could have, for fear of finding myself out of a job. They were aware of my conversations with the Consul Escobar in Tangier. I did, however, once more call to their attention the existence of immense reserves of water beneath the ground, enough perhaps to alter the ecology of the desert. They acknowledged this, but reiterated that the discovery of oil was their primary objective, and that was what I was being hired to do. If I came upon more water in my explorations, all well and good for the future of the Sahara, but turning the desert into a garden was a long-term proposition that could only be financed by some lucrative new source of income, such as oil. So they reasoned. In the meantime I was to recommence operations in the southern part of the territory near La Guera, and they would supply all necessary assistance. So it was agreed, but I couldn't help feeling somewhat sorry for these men, so enmeshed in dreams of riches and unable to perceive other possibilities. Basically, Spain is in the Sahara for the same reason as every other European power: to take something out, and not to put something in.

Afterward I invited Rivera for a drink. He had been nearly

thirty years in Rio de Oro; the desert meant a great deal to him. I'd watched him deal with Bedouin chieftains, bitter enemies from the old days; they and Rivera respected each other; each knew at first hand the other's fighting ability. Rivera knew how to talk to them in their own language, and he enjoyed this formal comradery. I had heard the young men of the tribes declare themselves to be the "sons of Spain." If Spain were forced to retreat from Africa, Colonel Rivera would regard it as a humiliating defeat for the Legion, especially if not a shot were fired, a tragic conclusion to his country's colonial experience, and a bitter termination of his career as a soldier and man.

So I put it to him straight: if oil or some other mineral were discovered in the desert, would Spain use part of the revenues to raise water? Rivera thought there was a reasonable possibility. But what guarantee, I demanded to know. None. I reminded him that Morocco and Algeria and Mauritania all claim Rio de Oro, and Spain will not be able to hang on in the desert forever, no matter how many legionnaires were prepared to defend it. The history of Spanish presence abroad has been one of exploitation, as the whole world knows; her record as benefactor of mankind is not exactly glowing. If Spain wishes to remain in Rio de Oro, she must show the world she's doing something significant for the territory and its natural inhabitants. The surest, quickest, easiest way to do so would be to bring water to the desert. So I reasoned.

We talked for hours. And why was I telling him all this? he finally asked. If substantial mineral wealth were discovered in Rio de Oro, would he give his support to my plan to raise water? He looked at me as if he suspected I had a trick up my sleeve, and said yes, he would. I believed him; he was a man of his word.

One of the first persons I encountered in El Aaiun was M'barek. He embraced me in the middle of the street, admired my Marrakech djellaba, and we had a long talk in the green park by the church. I told him all about Tangier and the two Mohameds and the return to Tarfaya, and about Omar and the monument of sand. He nodded and nodded. When I had finished my tale, he put his arm around me and looked at me with very sad, bright eyes. His luck had been a little better. He had managed to get himself a safe passage across the frontier and had arrived in El Aaiun with his café equipment. Already he had established a small restaurant called the Nastacha. On evenings when I wasn't invited to the caserne or to the officers' club I would go there for dinner. M'barek has a Spanish cook named Manuel who likes adventure and has seen all of southern Spain. Manuel has a helper, a fourteen-year-old Moroccan, Mohamed from Tan-Tan, who has never been to school but who's one of the brightest boys I've ever met. He and Manuel are always playing games in which Mohamed pretends to be the boss. While I'm eating, Mohamed leans on the doorway to the kitchen, points to Manuel behind him with his thumb and says "Manuel is clean and he works hard, but if he lets up for a minute, into the street with him, I'll kick him out." The two of them are planning to take a long trip together, perhaps to America. M'barek refuses to accept any money from me, and Manuel always prepares special meals whenever I come in. They are served by Pepito, a polite and effeminate waiter from the Canaries.

Heads of chuchos, or sting rays, sand sharks, heads of unknown fish with large teeth litter this beach at La Guera. Offshore, buoys strain on their ropes in the heavy current: a dangerous place to swim. On the point stand the crumbling stone foundations of an ancient fort, now a decrepit fish factory, from which the wind carries the pungent odor of dogfish drying in the sun. The milky green water teems with the gray stinging bottom fish; big sharks are known to lurk farther offshore.

Since my return to La Guera, I have taken to coming down to the shore every day about noon, when the heat is the greatest. Otherwise I have been busy making preparations for a new expedition into the interior. In fact, I try to keep myself occupied as much as possible with the work at hand; I try not to think too much, try not to be sad or to allow memories to engulf me, for it does no good.

La Guera hasn't changed much during the time I've been away. More Senegalese are in evidence—their women parade around in beautiful clothes. Sand dunes as high as the rooftops clog the streets, reminding me of Tarfaya. I still have friends here, and every evening Eusebio the banker, Diego the policeman, Palacio the postman, and I congregate in the Bar Sahara for a drink. It's a crazy place, so much sand has drifted in through the door that they can't close it any more, and the bar is moved farther and farther back into the room to avoid the encroaching dune. Sometimes we are joined by Candido the truckdriver. He's a tough brown man with a black mustache and a lean jutting jaw, and he wears a filmy pink kerchief over his forehead, tied in a knot at the back. Oddly enough, this flimsy piece of material makes him look even tougher, as if it were a battle souvenir. They're always joking, asking when I'm going to make them all rich with oil discoveries. Then there is Mamadou, a slender boy from Mali, who wishes to work for me in any capacity. I may take him on. One night Palacio handed me two letters: one was from Atkinson, enthusiastically confirming the purity of the magnesium and proclaiming the future of a fertile desert. So it looks like we're going to raise the water after all. He's anxious to return to North Africa—the first time in his life, he says, he's wanted to go back somewhere. The other was from Hamid, who describes the virtues of handmade mud walls and urges me to spread word about her café throughout the Sahara.

I have gotten into the habit of taking walks through the town late at night. The police patrols have become used to me by now; we often have a cigarette together and comment upon the weather. When the wind is out of the east, we have brilliant nights here in La Guera; offshore the lights of fishing boats from many nations are visible. I pass beneath the steel skeletons of uncompleted buildings as the town generator throbs across the open sandy spaces. Saharan women in black clothes beckon to me from alleyways. On one such midnight stroll I came upon that jagged fragment of rusted machinery on which Driss cut himself so badly. The next morning I assembled my crew and had them remove it from the sand.

## *John Hopkins*

In 1960, John Hopkins was graduated from Princeton, went to Spain, then to Peru, to buy a coffee plantation; traveled in the Amazon. . . . 1961, Italy, took a trip by motorcycle, Rome to Mombasa. . . . 1962, Paris, taught English and arithmetic to U.S. soldiers, went to Tangier to take a teaching position at the American School of Tangier. . . . 1965, left his teaching post to write. . . . 1967, traveled in Rio de Oro, published *The Attempt*. . . . 1970, traveled in Guatemala. . . . 1971, moved from Tangier to Marrakech. He is presently writing another novel, *Xenophobic Dogs*.